NEW DO

ORPHAN UNDER THE CHRISTMAS TREE

BY

MEREDITH WEBBER

Don't miss this heartwarming new duet by Meredith Webber!

CHRISTMAS IN CRYSTAL COVE

The sun always shines on this close-knit beachside community, and Christmas here is something special!

This year, two Crystal Cove doctors renowned for going the extra mile to help others may finally get everything they've ever dreamed of…

NEW DOC IN TOWN

Jo Harris has given up on love— but gorgeous Cam might just be able to light the sparkle in Jo once more!

ORPHAN UNDER THE CHRISTMAS TREE

An orphan needs a home for Christmas— can Lauren and Tom give him one, and find love beneath the Christmas tree too?

NEW DOC IN TOWN

BY
MEREDITH WEBBER

First published in Great Britain 2011
by Mills & Boon, an imprint of Harlequin (UK) Limited.
Harlequin (UK) Limited, Eton House, 18-24 Paradise Road,
Richmond, Surrey TW9 1SR

ISBN: 978 0 263 88616 0

Harlequin (UK) policy is to use papers that are natural, renewable and recyclable products and made from wood grown in sustainable forests. The logging and manufacturing process conform to the legal environmental regulations of the country of origin.

Printed and bound in Spain
by Blackprint CPI, Barcelona

Meredith Webber says of herself, 'Some ten years ago, I read an article which suggested that Mills and Boon were looking for new Medical™ Romance authors. I had one of those "I can do that" moments, and gave it a try. What began as a challenge has become an obsession—though I do temper the "butt on seat" career of writing with dirty but healthy outdoor pursuits, fossicking through the Australian Outback in search of gold or opals. Having had some success in all of these endeavours, I now consider I've found the perfect lifestyle.'

Praise for
Meredith Webber:

'Medical™ Romance favourite Meredith Webber
has penned a spellbinding and moving tale
set under the hot desert sun!'
—*Cataromance* on
THE DESERT PRINCE'S CONVENIENT BRIDE

'Medical™ Romance favourite Meredith Webber
has written an outstanding romantic tale
that I devoured in a single sitting! Moving,
engrossing, romantic and absolutely unputdownable.
Ms Webber peppers her story with plenty of drama,
emotion and passion, and she will keep her readers
entranced until the final page.'
—*Cataromance* on
A PREGNANT NURSE'S CHRISTMAS WISH

CHAPTER ONE

THE psychedelic camper-van spun through the entry to the parking lot with a squeal of tyres, startling Jo as she inserted the key into the deadlock on the surgery door. She watched, fingers tightening on the key she'd just turned, as a man in tattered board shorts and a bright Hawaiian-print shirt emerged from the van.

A very tall man, thickset.

With very broad shoulders.

Her heart might have skipped a beat but that didn't stop her medical mind checking the man out.

He didn't seem to be bleeding, and he wasn't limping or doubled over in pain, so sending him on to the hospital was definitely the best idea…

Definitely!

But do it politely.

Don't freak him out.

Calm voice, no sudden moves.

'I'm sorry but the clinic is closed,' she called out to him. Took a deep breath and added, 'If you follow the main road down through two roundabouts then turn right at the third you'll find the hospital. It has twenty-four-hour Accident and Emergency cover.'

Jo—Dr Joanna Harris to give her full title—carefully unlocked the door she'd just locked, and prayed that she sounded confident. The man didn't move, standing motionless beside the van, studying her with a slight frown on his face, as if her words hadn't made sense.

Then, like the sun bursting through clouds on a showery day, the frown cleared and the big man smiled.

Against all common sense Jo felt her tension ease, which was ridiculous given that the local pharmacy had been robbed three times in the last six months.

'Shouldn't there be more than one person locking up a medical clinic?' the giant asked, his deep voice rumbling up from somewhere inside a broad chest that was barely hidden by the hula girls, hibiscus flowers and palm trees—a lot of palm trees.

Tension returned despite the fact the voice was warm—teasing almost—and held no hint of threat.

'There are no drugs kept on the premises,' Jo told him, pointing to a large sign posted on the glass door.

'Do people actually believe those signs?' the stranger asked, and though she knew people probably didn't, Jo defended her sign.

'Of course they do! *And* we've got cameras.' She pointed to the camera angled downward from the corner of the building. 'Now, if you'd just move your vehicle, I can put up the chain across the car-park entrance. We're not open at all on Sunday. I was doing some tidying up.'

Stupid thing to say—now he'd *know* there was no one else around—although he'd probably guessed that when he'd seen her locking up. Maybe it was because the man wasn't sending out scary vibes that she'd been prattling on to him.

She still had her fingers on the key and the key was in the lock and she was pretty sure she could get inside before he reached her if he *did* make a move in her direction.

Cam studied the woman who was resolutely—and foolishly—guarding the clinic entrance. She was a midget—five-three at the most, slim built but curvy for all that, and with a wild tangle of pale red hair—yet she was standing her ground.

He'd driven in on a whim, noticing the sign—Crystal Cove Medical Clinic—at the last minute, wanting to see the place, not expecting anyone to be there on a Sunday morning. It hadn't been until he was out of the van that he'd seen the woman. Now he was trying to look as non-threatening as possible, arms hanging loosely at his sides, joints relaxed, although there was no way he could minimise his six-three height.

'I'll be going,' he said, keeping his voice as soft and low as he could. 'I noticed the sign as I was driving past and thought I'd take a look. I'm coming to work here, you see.'

Even across the car park he saw the woman turn so pale he thought she might faint, while her loss of colour made a wash of faint golden freckles stand out on her skin.

'You're coming to *work* here?' she demanded. '*You're* coming to work here?'

'That's right,' Cam told her in his gentlest, most encouraging tone. The one he usually used to calm barking dogs and tearful small children.

And women who maybe weren't the sharpest knife in the drawer. This one had had to repeat his words a couple of times before she got the picture.

'I'm the new doctor,' he added. After all, people were usually reassured by doctors. 'Got the job through Personal Medical Recruitments in Sydney.' He offered another smile. 'Not exactly looking the part at the moment, I'll admit, but I polish up okay.'

'You can't be the new doctor,' the woman wailed, and

shook her head so bits of hair flew everywhere. 'You can't *possibly* be! You're a *man*!'

Well, he could hardly deny the man part, but he was definitely a doctor, so Cam waited for more.

It wasn't long in coming.

'I asked for a mature woman,' she continued, 'preferably over forty, with counselling experience and a motherly manner, not for some overgrown adolescent male with a painted van and three surfboards and probably the counselling skills of an aardvark.'

Cam bit back an urge to ask if aardvarks had any counselling skills and if so how she knew. This wasn't the moment to make light of the situation.

'Maybe I was all they had,' he suggested, although he was well aware he'd conned the woman at the medical recruitment agency into offering him this particular job, using every bit of charm he could dredge up because the surf at Crystal Cove was reputed to be some of the best on the east coast. Geographically, the spot was a perfect stopping-off place on his planned surfing safari. A high, rocky headland reached out into the sea, so if the southerlies were blowing the sheltered north cove would have good surf, while leaving effective swells on the open beach a few days later.

He'd thought he could fill in a few months here quite happily, working and surfing. The working part was important, as he knew there'd be times he couldn't surf—flat sea, bad weather. He didn't want to have long days doing nothing because doing nothing left him too much time for thinking, too much time for remembering the horrors he'd seen. 'And I've not only done extra courses on counselling, but I'm good at it.'

His gut twisted as he said it, and it took all his skill at closing the many doors in his mind to shut away memories of the kind of counselling he'd done. He smiled to cover the momentary lapse.

Jo finally turned to face the man she'd been talking to over her shoulder, although she left the key in the lock. Living in a community where just about everyone rode the waves on one kind of board or another, she was used to seeing men with their over-long hair turned to, mostly temporary, dreadlocks by the salt, so this man's brown, matted, sun-streaked hair wasn't *so* unusual. Neither was his tanned face, which made his pale eyes—he was too far away to see a colour—seem paler, and his teeth, now he smiled, seem whiter.

The smile was good, but he was probably the kind of man who knew that—knew the power of a charming smile.

Charming?

Was it *that* good?

She'd certainly relaxed!

Annoyed by this self-revelation, she stiffened her resolve.

'I'm sorry but I really don't think it will work out. I didn't ask for a woman on a whim, or because I can't work with men—in fact, the former owner of the practice was a man and I worked with him for years. It's just that…'

She couldn't *begin* to list all the reasons this man would be an impossible employee.

'Just that?' he prompted, smiling again but helpfully this time.

'Just that it's impossible!' Jo snapped, but even as she said it, she realised how stupid this was, to be having the conversation across half the parking lot—the man standing where he'd emerged from the van, she on the surgery steps. 'Oh, come up to the house,' she added crossly, then shook her head. 'No, show me some authorisation and identification first—something from the agency, your driver's licence, anything.'

He reached back into the van and brought out a quite respectable-looking briefcase, tan leather, a bit battered, but in not bad condition. He opened it and withdrew a file.

'It's all in here,' he said, walking towards her.

He walked well, very upright, yet with an unconscious grace. She could picture him on a surfboard, cutting across the face of a wave, a conqueror of the ocean, sun glinting off the water droplets on that chest…

Jo gave herself a mental head-slap—a reminder to stay with it, although the longing that had come with the thought of riding the sea remained like a bruise in her chest. The man was still a stranger for all he knew the name of the agency she used to recruit staff, *and* held himself in an unthreatening manner. Reading body language was something she'd had to learn, but he, too, could have learned it.

He stopped a reasonable distance from her and passed her the file, then stepped back. Yep, he'd done the same body language course! Maybe he was the genuine article. but she'd wanted a woman.

She opened the file and stared at the photo it contained. Surely the gorgeous male with the short back and sides hairstyle, the dark arched eyebrows over pale blue-grey eyes, the long straight nose and shapely lips quirked, in the photo, into a slight smile wasn't the surfie type standing right in front of her.

She looked from the photo to the man and saw the eyes, blue-grey, and then the same quirky, half-embarrassed smile, although the beard stubble she could see now he was closer to her hid the shapely lips.

'Fraser Cameron?'

A quick, decisive nod.

'I'm usually called Cam. I'd just got out of the army when they took the photo,' the man explained. 'I had an interview with the agency, put in my résumé, promised to keep in touch by phone and went surfing for a while. Nothing like a few years in the desert to give you a longing for the ocean. Deserts and ocean—well, they have sand in common but that's about all.'

As job interviews went, this wasn't going too well. Cam had realised that from the start. It was becoming increasingly obvious that the young woman in front of him was his boss-to-be, and she didn't seem too happy about any aspect of him, even apart from the fact he wasn't female.

Not that he could blame her. He should have had a shower at the beach and washed the salt out of his hair—at least run a comb through it. But until he'd seen the sign for the surgery and driven in on a whim, he'd been intent on finding a caravan park and having a proper hot shower and shave for the first time in, what—four days? He rubbed his hand across his chin—no, maybe only three. He'd stopped in Port Macquarie and had a shave there…

She was reading through his résumé, glancing up at him from time to time as if trying to fit the printed words to the unshaven man in front of her, and the fact that she was occupied gave Cam the chance to study her in turn.

The wild hair was probably the bane of her life, untamed curls that would refuse to do what she required of them. Today she'd tugged her hair into some kind of clip thing on the top of her head but, like Medusa's snakes, strands were curling out from the containment and glinting a vibrant red-gold in the sun. Her skin went with the red hair—pale and freckled, almost milk white at her temples and so fine he could see the blue line of a blood vessel beneath it. Would he feel the throb of her heartbeat if he kissed that blue thread?

The thought startled him so much he took a step backwards, just as she looked up, clear green eyes fixed on him—still shooting darts of suspicion in his direction.

'I guess you are who you say you are,' she muttered, so obviously put out at having to make the admission he had to smile.

'But still not a woman,' he reminded her, the temptation to tease her too strong to resist.

She shot him a glare that might have affected a lesser man, but he'd grown up with three sisters, all of whom were good glarers, so he met it with a smile, although he knew—also thanks to his siblings—it would make her angrier.

'The house is this way,' she said, leading him across the front of the clinic building then along the side of it to where steep steps climbed towards a house that must look north over the ocean. From the bottom of the steps he could see how the clever architect had cantilevered the building out from the steep slope, and he could imagine the magnificent view of the ocean whoever lived in the house must enjoy.

'Wow!'

He could say no more for the stairway ended on the wide deck of the house he'd admired from below, and the sweep of beach and ocean, the high headland protecting the corner of the bay, and more ocean beyond it simply took his breath away.

'You would have seen the whales migrating north at the beginning of winter, but they're heading south now with their calves, on their long journey home to Antarctica.'

He glanced at the woman who'd offered this titbit of information. She was standing not far away, and he knew from the expression on her face that no matter how often she looked out at this unbelievably beautiful view it would never pall for her. Just seeing it had softened her mood enough for her to share her joy in the annual whale migration.

Softened it enough to accept him as an employee?

'I gather you are Dr Harris?' he said, wishing he'd asked

more about his prospective employer when the woman from the agency had discussed the job. In truth, from the moment she'd mentioned Crystal Cove, he'd been so busy convincing her he would be perfect for the job he'd barely asked a question.

She was smiling now, the petite redhead on the deck with him, smiling and shaking her head.

'Ask that question of anyone in town and they'll say no. Dr Harris was my father, but I am a doctor, Joanna Harris, Dr Jo, or just plain Jo to the locals, most of whom have known me all my life. Some of the older ones are still, though I've been back for five years, a bit dubious about trusting me to diagnose their problems or prescribe medication for their ills. It's because they did that dandling me on their knee thing years ago and can't believe I've grown up.'

'You took over your father's practice?' It was stupid to be asking the obvious but there'd been tension in Joanna Harris's voice and he wondered if it was simply to do with the locals not accepting her entirely, or to do with something else.

'His practice, his house, his life,' she responded, sounding happier now, even smiling. 'My mother died when I was young and Dad brought me and my sister up, then, whammo, two years ago he met a woman who sailed in here on a yacht, and he fell in love. His life is now with her, wandering the world, it's wonderful!'

Faint colour in her cheeks and a shine in her eyes told Cam she was genuinely happy for her father, so why the tension earlier?

And did it matter?

He was coming to work for this woman, he didn't need to know what made her tick.

'But taking over his practice? Was that not so wonderful?'

Okay, so what made people tick fascinated him—he'd *had* to ask!

Jo studied the man who'd erupted into her life. So she'd told him about her dad going off, but did that give him the right to pry further into her life? And why ask that particular question? What had she said to make him think her life back in Crystal Cove was anything but perfect?

It wasn't, of course, and probably never would be, not entirely, and especially not if the refuge closed because without the refuge she'd have time on her hands—time to think—and that meant letting all the mess of grief and guilt from Jilly's death come flooding back. That definitely wasn't his business.

She had no intention of answering his questions, now or ever. Neither was he staying. With school holidays looming and the town due to double or even triple in population for a couple of months, maybe he'd have to stay until the agency found her someone more suitable, but permanently?

No way!

The problem was, given that he was on her front deck, what did she do with him right now? She had to say *something.*

Politeness dictated the answer.

'Would you like a coffee, tea, a cold drink?'

She looked up at him as she asked the question and saw the white lines fanning out from his eyes where he'd smiled, or squinted, in the sun. She saw lines of stress in his face as well. A photo taken when he'd just left the army? An army doctor? In this day and age most army doctors would have been deployed in war zones overseas. He'd mentioned deserts. Of course there'd be lines of stress in his face.

'Water is fine,' he replied, and she guessed he was probably as uncomfortable as she was.

'I'm making coffee,' she persisted, 'so it's no trouble.'

He looked down at her, a slight frown on his face.

'Water's fine,' he repeated, then he crossed to the edge of the deck and looked out over the ocean.

Jo hurried into the house, anxious to read more of the file she held in her hands. It was strange that the agency hadn't contacted her to let her know the man was coming—although maybe it was because he *was* a man they'd neglected to contact her. They *knew* she wanted a woman; they even knew why.

The kitchen faced the deck so she could keep an eye on the stranger as she popped a capsule into her coffee machine. While the milk heated, she flicked through the pages, coming to a highlighted passage about Dr Fraser Cameron's second degree in psychology and his counselling experience. Had the agency highlighted it, or had they told him what she wanted so he'd highlighted it himself?

He'd been counselling young soldiers in a war zone? Doing more than counselling, too, no doubt.

Putting young men and women back together physically as well as mentally.

The very thought made Jo's stomach tighten.

But hard as his job must have been, how would it relate to counselling women in a refuge?

The refuge…

If it closed it wouldn't matter one jot whether the man could counsel women or not.

If it closed she wouldn't need another doctor in the practice…

Jo sighed then stiffened, straightening her shoulders and reinforcing her inner determination.

The refuge was *not* going to close!

What's more, if this man was going to stay, even in the short term, he'd have to help her make sure it didn't.

She poured the milk into her coffee, filled a glass with water from the refrigerator, and headed back to the deck.

'Did the agency explain the type of counselling you'd be required to do?' she asked him as he came towards the table where she'd set down their drinks.

The little frown she'd noticed earlier deepened and he shook his head, then shrugged shoulders that were so broad she wondered how he fitted through a doorway.

Shoulders?

Why was she thinking of shoulders? Worse, when had she last even noticed physical attributes in a man, yet here she was seeing lines in his face, and checking on shoulders…

'They said you wanted someone with counselling experience because although there was a psychologist in Crystal Cove, he, or maybe it was a she, was already overworked. I assumed you probably ran well-men and well-women clinics, sex education at the schools and parenting skills courses. You'd be likely to use counselling as part of these.'

Jo sighed.

'The women's refuge wasn't mentioned?'

His reaction was a blank stare, followed by a disbelieving 'Women's refuge? The town has a population of what, thirty-five hundred and you have a women's refuge?'

'The area has a much larger population—small farms, villages, acreage lots where people have retired or simply moved in. Anyway, just because women live in a small town, does that mean they're not entitled to a safe place to go?'

Had she snapped that he held up his hands in surrender?

'Hey,' he said. 'I'm sorry! No way I meant that, but it came as a shock, the refuge thing. No wonder you took one look at me and saw me as a disaster. My size alone is enough to frighten horses, not to mention vulnerable women, but surely we can work through this. Surely the women who use the refuge come in contact with other men in their lives, men who aren't threatening to them? And wouldn't it be a good thing if they did? If they got to know men who *didn't* threaten them? Men who are just as horrified by what is happening to them, and just as empathetic with them, as a woman counsellor would be?'

He was right, of course! One of the refuge's strongest supporters was Mike Sinclair, the officer in charge of the local police force, while Tom Fletcher, head of the small local hospital, was loved by all the women who used the refuge. But the refuge aside, did she want this man working for her?

The answer that sprang immediately to mind was a firm no, but when she questioned it she didn't like the reasons. They were far too personal. She was judging the man on his appearance, not his ability—judging him on the effect he was having on *her*.

Anyway, did she have a choice but to accept him?

Not right now.

'I suppose you'll have to do,' she said, hoping it hadn't come out as an unwilling mutter. 'But it's a trial, you have to understand that. I'm not promising it will work out, but right now I'm desperate. The town doubles in size in school holidays, which begin officially in a fortnight, but before that we have the wonderful invasion of schoolies.'

'Schoolies? You have schoolies coming here?'

And although she dreaded the annual influx of school-leavers every year, Jo still felt affronted that the man would think her town not good enough for them.

'Not all school leavers want the bright lights of Surfers' Paradise,' she said defensively.

'Ha!' he said, blue eyes twinkling at her in a most disconcerting manner. 'Bet you wish they hadn't discovered Crystal Cove!'

She considered denying his assumption, but knew she couldn't. He'd be working with her so he could hardly avoid seeing how frazzled she became as she worried about drunk, sick and sometimes very unhappy teenagers who were supposedly marking some rite of passage into adulthood.

Adulthood? They had as much sense as fleas, some of them…

'You're right. It's only in recent years that young people have decided the Cove is cool enough for them. Most of those who come are keen surfers and they're not a problem. Anyway, I'll take you on but, as I said, we'll have to see how things work out.'

'I don't mind that,' the stranger—Cam—said calmly. 'After all, I might not like working with you either, and there's still a lot of coastline for me to cover in my surfing odyssey.'

She was about to take affront—again!—but realised he was right.

'Fair call,' she told him, ignoring the smirk that had accompanied his words. 'Now, once the schoolies arrive—that's next week—there'll be no time to show you around so—'

She didn't want to sound desperate but, given the situation at the refuge and the fact that she needed some free time to try to sort out funding problems there, she actually *was* desperate.

'Can you start tomorrow? No, that's stupid. Can you start now so I can show you the clinic, introduce you at the hospital, and give you a quick tour of the town?'

Was she looking dubious that he glanced down at his attire and raised his eyebrows at her, the amused expression on his face sparking an unexpected—and totally inappropriate—flicker of warmth deep inside her body?

This *definitely* wasn't a good idea!

'Like this?' he said, then shook his head. 'Give me an hour

to check in at the caravan park and have a shower and shave. I wouldn't want to give people the wrong first impression.'

The man's amused expression turned into a smile—her stupid flicker graduated to a flutter in her chest that caused another mental head slap.

Reality added a harder slap, this one bringing her down to earth with such a thud her physical reactions to the man paled into insignificance.

'It's no good. You won't find a patch of grass available at the caravan park,' she told him, gloom shadowing the words. 'Well, there might be something for the next few days but after that you'd be out on your ear. Most of the schoolies camp there, then during the school holidays regulars book the same sites from year to year. It's a similar situation with the flats and units in town. Most of them are holiday rentals and, although you wouldn't be looking for something permanent because we don't know if it will work out, there'd be nothing available right now.'

Not put off by the despair in her voice, he was still grinning when he suggested, 'Is there a shower in your medical centre? Will the council evict me or fine you if I camp in the parking area?'

Jo rolled her eyes.

'Great—here comes Dr Cameron, emerging from his van in the parking area. I can just imagine what people would think!' The words came out snappish but she knew she was more annoyed with the offer she'd have to make than with the man himself.

She told herself not to be feeble, straightened her shoulders, and made the offer.

'There's a flat.'

'You make it sound like the castle of doom!' Cam teased, wondering why the woman was looking so unhappy about the revelation. Although she'd hardly been joyous about anything since his arrival. 'Rats? Spiders? Snakes? Cockroaches big as dogs?'

'It's here at the house,' she muttered, sounding even more unhappy, although now he could understand why she was wary. It would be awkward to have a strange man living so close, though if she'd checked out his credentials and read through his references, she shouldn't be too worried. 'Out the back. Dad built it years ago and I used it for a while until he took off on the yacht. It's got a deck, the flat not the yacht, although—'

She stopped, probably aware she was dithering, and she drew a deep, calming breath.

'The deck on the flat—it's not as big as this, but it has the northerly view. In the past, since Dad left, I've hired locums at holiday times and they've used it.'

Temporarily.

She didn't say the word but Cam heard it in her voice. He could understand her reluctance to have a fellow-worker living in such close proximity full time but if locums had done so up till now…

Maybe she had a set against men?

Been hurt by one?

Realising he should be thinking about the job, not the woman who was hiring him, he turned his attention back to the subject.

'I understood that although there'd be a trial period, you were looking for someone for a permanent position this time, not a locum. Has the town grown? Do you want to cut down on your own workload?'

She studied him for a moment, as if debating whether he was worth answering, then gave a deep sigh.

'The town's grown, a second practice opened but no sooner

did that happen than the hospital had staff cuts, then the second practice closed, and with the refuge—well, I decided it was time to expand.'

The explanation rattled from her lips—nice lips, very pale pink, distracting him again—and Cam understood enough to know that the flat, like the job, was only temporary. While she might have been happy having a fortyish woman living permanently in close proximity to her, having a large male surfer was a different story.

'I'll show you over it then you'll have to go back down the steps to the car park and drive along the road towards the highway, taking the first left to bring you up the hill and around to the carport.'

All business now, she led him off the deck, through a sparsely furnished living area. It was functional and uncluttered, decorated in sand colours, but with wide windows giving views of the sea in all directions, the room didn't need decoration.

It was like the woman herself, functional and uncluttered, he decided, following a decidedly shapely bottom in khaki cargo shorts, a khaki singlet top completing her outfit.

A decidedly shapely bottom?

Well, he couldn't help but notice, any more than he could have helped noticing the pink lips earlier. Was noticing such things about his boss unprofessional behaviour?

So many years in the army had left him unprepared for the niceties of civilian life, particularly where women were concerned. He held a mental conversation with his sisters and came to the conclusion that while thinking his boss had a shapely butt was okay, mentioning his opinion of it or of any other part of her anatomy, to her or anyone else, would definitely be unwise.

CHAPTER TWO

A BREEZEWAY divided the house from the little building perched beside it on the steep hillside.

'A double carport so you can keep your van under cover,' his guide said, waving her left hand to indicate the covered parking spaces. She reached above the door for a key, saying, 'I know I shouldn't keep it there,' before inserting it in the lock and opening the door.

The flat was as different from the minimalist-style house as it was possible to be. Roses, not giant cockroaches! The roses dominated the small space. They bloomed from trellises on the wallpaper, glowed on the fabric covering the small lounge suite, while silk ones stood in vases on small tables here and there.

'Ha!' Cam said, unable to stop himself. 'You wanted a fortyish woman to fit in with the furnishings, although…'

He turned towards his new boss and caught a look of such sadness on her face he wished he hadn't opened his mouth. Though now he had, he had to finish what he'd been about to say or look even more foolish than he felt.

'Well, one of my sisters is forty and roses definitely aren't her thing.'

The words came out strained, mumbled almost under his breath, but he doubted Joanna Harris heard them. She'd moved across the small room and opened the sliding glass windows, walking out through them onto the deck.

The way she stood, hugging herself at the railing, told him she wanted—perhaps needed—to be alone, so he explored the neatly organised domain, finding two small bedrooms, a bathroom and a kitchen had been fitted somehow into the tiny flat. The configuration of the bathroom made him wonder. There was a shower above a tiled floor, no cubicle, just a floor waste where most of the water would go. The basin was set low, no cupboard beneath it.

This and a silver bar screwed onto the wall at waist height suggested the room had been built for someone with a disability and now he looked around he realised the doorways were wider than normal—to accommodate a wheelchair?—and hand-grips had been installed in other places.

Jo had spoken of a sister…

A disabled sister?

He looked out at the figure standing on the deck, a hundred questions flashing through his mind, but the way she stood—the way she'd handled his arrival and their conversation since—told him he might never have those questions answered.

A very private person, Jo Harris, or so he suspected, although on an hour's acquaintance how could he be judging her?

She should have redecorated the flat, Jo chided herself. She should have done it as soon as she'd moved into it after Jilly died—yet she'd always felt that changing the roses her sister had loved would have been letting go of her twin for ever.

A betrayal of some kind.

And surely 'should' was the unkindest word in the English language, so filled with regrets of what might have been, or not been. Should have done this, should not have done that. Her own list of shoulds could go on for ever, should have come home from Sydney sooner being right at the top of it!

Jo hugged her body and looked out to sea, waiting for the view to calm her, for her mind to shut away the memories and consign the shoulds to the trash bin she kept tucked away in her head. Coming into the flat usually upset her—not a lot—just brought back memories, but today, seeing the stranger—Cam—there, he'd looked so out of place among the roses Jill had loved, it had hurt more than usual.

'I'll bring my car up.'

He called to her from the doorway and before she could turn he was gone. Good! It would give her time to collect herself. Actually, it would give her time to scurry back to her place and hide from the man for the rest of the day, though that was hardly fair.

She found a little notebook on the kitchen bench and scribbled a note. 'Will meet you in the carport in half an hour, we can get a bite to eat in town and I'll show you around.'

A bite to eat in town.

It sounded so innocuous but within an hour of being seen down the street with him the word would be all over town that Jo Harris had finally found a man!

As if a man who looked like him—like the picture of him anyway—would be interested in a scrawny redhead.

Of course once the locals realised he'd come to work for her, the talk would settle down, then when he left…

She shook her head, unable to believe she'd been thinking that maybe it would be nice to have a man around.

A man or *this* man?

She had a sneaky suspicion the second option was the answer but she wouldn't consider it now. Instant attraction was something for books, not real people—not real people like her, anyway.

The man would be her colleague—temporary colleague—and right now she had to show him around the town. She'd re-clip her hair and smear on a little lightly coloured sunscreen, the only make-up she ever used, but she wouldn't change—no need to really startle the town by appearing in anything other than her usual garb.

Unfortunately as she passed through the kitchen she saw his résumé, still open on the bench—open at the photo…

She added lipstick to the preparations. After all, it, too, had sun protection.

Leaving the house, she drove down to the clinic first, showing him around the consulting and treatment rooms, proud of the set-up and pleased when he praised it. Then back in the car, she took Cam to the top of the rise so he could see the town spread out below them.

'It's fairly easy to get around,' she explained to him. 'As you can see from here, the cove beach faces north and the southern beach—the long one—faces east.'

'With the shopping centre running along the esplanade behind the cove, is that right?'

He pointed to the wide drive along the bay side, Christmas decorations already flapping in the wind.

'There's actually a larger, modern shopping mall down behind this hill,' Jo told him. 'You just drive up here and turn right instead of left. We're going the other way because the best cafés are on the front and the hospital is also down there. Until the surfing craze started, the cove beach was the one everyone used. It's only been in relatively recent years that the open beach has become popular and land along it has been developed for housing.'

Explaining too much?

Telling him stuff he didn't need to know?

Yes to both but Jo felt so uncomfortable with the stranger in her car, she knew the silence would prickle her skin if she didn't fill it with talk.

'Can we eat before we visit the hospital?' her passenger asked, and although there was nothing in his voice to give him away, memories of her own surfing days came rushing back to Jo. When the surf was running, food had been the last thing on her mind, so she'd return home close to lunch-time, *starving*.

'Don't tell me you haven't had breakfast?' she wailed. 'I realised you'd come straight from the beach but…'

She turned so she could see his face.

'You should have said,' she told him, mortified that she'd been proudly pointing out up-to-date equipment while all he wanted was something to eat. 'I could have offered you food at the house—cereal or toast or something. It was just so late in the morning I didn't think of it. Or we could have gone straight to the café instead of doing the clinic tour first.'

She'd turned her attention back to the road but heard the smile in his voice when he replied.

'Hey, don't go beating yourself up about it. I'm a big boy. I can look after myself.'

'Hardly a boy!' Jo snapped, contrarily angry now, although it wasn't her fault the man was starving.

She pulled up opposite her favourite café, a place she and Jill had hung out in during their early high-school days.

'They do an all-day big breakfast I can recommend,' she told Cam, before dropping down out of the car and crossing the road, assuming he would follow. As she heard his door shut, she used the remote lock and heard the ping as the car was secured.

'A big breakfast will hit the spot,' Cam declared as he studied the blackboard menu and realised that the combination of eggs, bacon, sausages, tomato, beans and toast was just what he needed to fill the aching void in his stomach.

If only other voids in other parts of him could be filled as easily…

'I'll have a toasted cheese and—'

'Tomato sandwich and a latte,' the young girl who'd come to take their orders finished.

'One day I'll order something different,' Jo warned her, and the girl laughed as she turned to Cam.

'The sky will turn green the day Jo changes her order,' she said. 'And for you?'

He ordered the big breakfast, absolutely famished now he'd started thinking about food and how long it had been since he'd eaten. He looked out across the road at the people gathered on the beach, and beyond them to where maybe a dozen surfers sat on their boards, waiting for a wave that might never come.

He understood their patience. It wasn't for the waves that he surfed, or not entirely. He surfed to clear his head—to help to banish the sights and sounds of war that disturbed his nights and haunted his days.

He surfed to heal himself, or so he hoped.

'The surf was far better this morning,' he said, turning his mind from things he couldn't control and his attention back to his companion.

'Higher tide and an offshore breeze. Now the wind's stronger from the west and flattening the surf but those kids will sit out there anyway. They don't mind if there are no waves, and now they're all pretty good about wearing sun protection it's a healthy lifestyle for them.'

She spoke in a detached manner, as if her mind was on something else. Intriguing, that's what his new boss was, especially as she'd been frowning as she'd explained surf conditions in Crystal Bay—surely not bothersome information.

'So why the frown?' Yes, he *was* intrigued.

'What frown?'

'You've been frowning since the girl took our order,' he pointed out.

A half-embarrassed smile slid across his new boss's lips, which she twisted slightly before answering.

'If you must know, I was thinking how predictable I've become, or maybe how boring I am that I don't bother thinking of something different to have for lunch. This place does great salads, but do I order a roast pumpkin, feta and pine-nut concoction? No, just boring old toasted cheese and tomato. I've got to get a life!'

Cam chuckled at the despair in her voice.

'I wouldn't think ordering the same thing for lunch every day prohibits you from having a life.'

Fire flashed in her eyes again and he found himself enjoying the fact that he could stir her, not necessarily stir her to anger, but at least fire some spark in the woman who was... different in some way?

No, intriguing was the only word.

'Of course it doesn't, and if my life wasn't so full I wouldn't need to employ another doctor, but the cheese and tomato is a symbol, that's all.'

Small-scale glare—about a four.

'A symbol? Cheese and tomato—toasted—a symbol?'

Now the eyes darkened, narrowed.

'You know very well what I mean. It's not the cheese and tomato, it's the repetition thing. We get stuck in a groove—well, not you obviously or you wouldn't be wandering along the coast in a psychedelic van, but me, I'm stuck in a groove.'

'With a cheese and tomato sandwich, most uncomfortable,' he teased, and saw the anger flare before she cooled it with a reluctant grimace and a head shake.

'It's all very well for you to mock,' she told him sternly. 'You've been off seeing the world with the army. You don't know what it's like to be stuck in a small town.'

She hesitated, frowning again, before adding, 'That came out sounding as if I resented being here, which I don't. I love the Cove, love living here, love working here—so stuck is the wrong word. It's just that I think maybe people in small towns are more likely to slip into grooves than people in big cities.'

He had to laugh.

'Lady, you don't know nothin' about grooves until you've been in the army. *Everyone* in the army has a groove. It's the only way a thing that big can work. Hence the psychedelic van you mentioned—that's my way of getting out of my particular groove.'

And away from the memories…

Jo studied the man who'd made the joking remark and saw the truth behind it in the bruised shadows under his eyes and the lines that strain, not age, had drawn on his cheeks. She had an uncomfortable urge to touch him, to rest her hand on his arm where it lay on the table, just for a moment, a touch to say she understood his need to escape so much reality.

He's not staying!

The reminder echoed around inside her head and she kept her hands to herself, smiling as their meals arrived and she saw Cam's eyes widening when he realised how big a big breakfast was in Crystal Cove.

'Take your time,' she told him, 'I could sit here and look out at the people on the beach all day.'

Which was true enough, but although she watched the people on the beach, her mind was churning with other things.

Common sense dictated that if she was employing another doctor for the practice it should be a man. A lot of her male patients would prefer to see a man, especially about personal problems they might be having. Elderly men in particular were reluctant to discuss some aspects of their health, not so much with a woman but with a woman they'd known since she was a child.

She'd ignored common sense and asked for a woman for a variety of reasons, most to do with the refuge. Not that her practice and the refuge were inextricably entwined, although as the only private practice in town she was called in whenever a woman or child at the refuge needed a doctor.

Mind you, with a man—she cast a sidelong glance at the man in question, wolfing down his bacon, sausages and eggs—she could run more effective anti-abuse programmes at the high school. The two of them could do interactive role plays about appropriate and inappropriate behaviour—something she was sure the kids would enjoy, and if they enjoyed it, they would maybe consider the message.

The man wasn't staying.

And toasted cheese and tomato sandwiches were really, really boring.

'Tell me about the refuge while I eat.'

It *had* been on her mind, well, sort of, so it was easy to talk—easier than thinking right now…

'It began with a death—a young woman who had come to live in the Cove with her boyfriend who was a keen surfer. They hired an on-site van in the caravan park and had been here about three months when the man disappeared and a few days later the woman was found dead inside the van.'

Her voice was so bleak Cam immediately understood that the woman's death had had a devastating effect on Jo Harris.

But doctors were used to death to a certain extent, so this must have been more traumatic than usual?

Why?

'Did you know her?' he asked. 'Had she been a patient?'

Jo nodded.

'No and yes. I'd seen her once—turned out she'd been to the hospital once as well. Perhaps if she'd come twice to me, or gone to the hospital both times…'

He watched as she took a deep breath then lifted her head and met his eyes across the table, her face tight with bad memories.

'She came to me with a strained wrist, broken collarbone and bruises—a fall, she said, and I believed her. As you know, if you're falling, you tend to put out a hand to break the fall, and the collarbone is the weak link so it snaps. Looking back, the story of the fall was probably true but if I'd examined her more closely I'd probably have seen bruising on her back where he'd pushed her before she fell.'

Cam stopped eating. Somehow he'd lost his enjoyment of the huge breakfast. He studied the woman opposite him and knew that in some way she was still beating herself up over the woman's death—blaming herself for not noticing.

'And when she was found in the van? She'd been battered to death?'

Jo nodded.

'I don't think I've ever felt such…' She paused and he saw anguish in her face so wasn't entirely surprised when she used the word.

'Anguish—that's the only way to describe it. Guilt, too, that I hadn't helped her, but just total despair that such things happen.'

He watched as she gathered herself together—literally

straightening her shoulders and tilting her chin—moving onward, explaining.

'After she was dead some of the permanent residents at the park told the police they'd heard raised voices from the van but, like most domestic situations, no one likes to interfere. Her parents came up to the Cove and we found out they'd known he was abusive. In fact, he'd moved up here because she had often sought refuge with her parents and he'd wanted to isolate her even more. They offered a donation—a very generous donation—for someone to set up a refuge here. I…'

She looked out to sea, regret written clearly on her face.

'It was as if I'd been given a reprieve. I might not have been able to help one woman, but surely I could help others. My friend Lauren, a psychologist, had just returned home to work at the Cove and together we got stuck into it, finding out all we could, bringing in people who could help, getting funding for staff.'

She offered him a rueful smile before adding, 'Getting the house turned out to be the easy part.' Then she sighed and the green eyes met his, studying him as if checking him out before telling him any more.

Had he passed some test that she continued, her voice low and slightly husky, as she admitted, 'My sister had just died so, in a way, setting up the refuge helped me, too.'

She smiled but the smile could certainly not be classified as perky, as she admitted, 'It became a passion.'

'And?' he prompted, for he was sure there was more.

One word but it won a real smile—one that lit her eyes with what could only be pride in what she and her friend had achieved, although there were still shadows in them as well. Of course there would be shadows—the memory of the woman who died, then the connection with her sister's death.

A sister who'd loved roses?

He brought his mind back from the roses and shadows in eyes as Jo was talking again.

'Isn't there a saying—build it and they will come? Well, that's what happened with the refuge. It's sad it happened—that places like it are needed—but on the up side, at least now women at risk anywhere within a couple of hundred miles' radius have somewhere to go. I'm connected to it in that I'm on the committee that runs it, and also we, by which I mean the practice, are the medical clinic the women staying there use. Problem is, to keep the refuge open we need ongoing funding from the government to pay the residential workers and that's a bit up in the air at the moment. The powers that be keep changing the rules, requiring more and more measurable 'objectives' in order to attract funding, but…'

She nodded towards his plate. 'This is spoiling your breakfast. Some time soon we'll visit the house and you can talk to Lauren, who runs it, and you can see for yourself.'

Cam returned to his breakfast but his mind was considering all he'd heard. He could understand how personal the refuge must be to Jo, connected to the woman who'd died, as well as to her sister. In a way it was a memorial—almost sacred—so she'd be willing to do anything to keep it going. Even before she'd admitted that the refuge had become a passion he'd heard her passion for it in her voice and seen it in her gleaming eyes as she'd talked about it.

Passion! Hadn't it once been *his* driving force? Where, along the way, had he lost his?

In the battlefields, of course, treating young men so badly damaged many of them wished to die. Dealing with their minds as well as their bodies. No wonder he'd lost his passion.

Except for surfing. *That* passion still burned…

He brought his mind back to the conversation, rerunning

it in his head. He found the thing that puzzled him, intrigued in spite of his determination not to get too involved.

'How would employing a middle-aged female doctor in the practice help save the refuge?'

He won another smile. He liked her smiles and was beginning to classify them. This one was slightly shamefaced.

'It wouldn't do much in measurable objectives,' she admitted, 'but it does bother me, personally, that some of the older women who use the house—women in their forties and fifties—might look at Lauren and me and wonder what on earth we could know about their lives or their problems, or even about life in general. I'm twenty-nine so it's not as if I'm fresh out of uni, but I look younger and sometimes I get the impression that the older women might think that though I've got all the theory—'

'Theory isn't reality?'

He couldn't help it. He reached out and touched her hand where it rested on the table.

'Look, I don't know you at all, but having spent just a couple of hours in your company I'm sure you're empathetic enough to be able to see those women's situations through their eyes. The army's the same—a fifty-year-old colonel having to come and talk to some young whippersnapper straight out of med school about his erection problems.'

He paused, then asked, 'I take it you have staff at the refuge?'

The tantalising green eyes studied him for a moment, puzzling over the question.

'We have a number of trained residential support staff, who work with the women all the time.'

'Then surely at least one of them could be an older woman, maybe more than one. These are the people spending most time there.'

Jo nodded.

'You're right, of course. And a couple of them are older women, it's just that…'

'Just that you want to be all things to all people? No matter how much you do, you always want to do more, give more?'

His new boss stared at him across the table. He could almost see the denial forming on her lips then getting lost on the way out.

'Are you analysing me?' she demanded instead. 'Showing off your psychology skills? Anyway, I don't think that's the case at all.'

He grinned at her.

'You just want the best for everyone,' he offered helpfully, finding pleasure in this gentle teasing—finding an unexpected warmth from it inside his body.

'And what's wrong with that?' she asked, but the words lacked heat and Cam smiled because he knew he'd hit home. She *did* want the best for everyone, she *would* give more and more, but would that be at the expense of her own life? Her own pleasure?

And if so, why?

Intriguing…

Not that he'd ever find out—or needed to. He wasn't looking to stay in Crystal Cove, unexpected warmth or no.

Although…

'Hospital next,' Jo announced, mainly to break the silence that had followed their conversation, though the man mountain had been demolishing the rest of his breakfast so he probably hadn't found the silence as awkward as she had. She replayed the conversation in her head, realising how much of herself she'd revealed to a virtual stranger.

She'd forced herself to sound bright and cheery as she'd made the 'hospital next' suggestion, but the conversation about the refuge had unsettled her so badly that what she really needed was to get away from Fraser Cameron and do some serious thinking.

Did she really think she could be all things to all people? Surely she knew that wasn't possible.

So why…?

She concentrated on sounding positive.

'Tom Fletcher, the doctor in charge, lives in a house beside the hospital so if he's not on the wards, I can show you through then take you across to his place to introduce you.'

'Tom Fletcher? Tall, thin guy, dark hair, has women falling over themselves to go out with him?'

Jo frowned at the man who was pushing his plate away with a sigh of satisfaction. No need to keep worrying about sounding positive when she had a challenge like this to respond to.

'Women falling over themselves to go out with him? What is it with you men that you consider something like that as part of a physical description?'

Her crankiness—and she'd shown plenty—had absolutely no effect on the man who was grinning at her as he replied.

'I knew a bloke of that name at uni—went through medicine with him—and to answer your question, when you're a young, insecure, very single male student you remember the guys who seem able to attract women with effortless ease. I bet you ask another ten fellows out of our year and you'd get the same description.'

Jo shook her head.

'The male mind always was and still remains a total mystery to me,' she said, 'but, yes, Tom is tall and thin—well, he'd probably prefer lean—and has dark hair.'

'Great!'

Cam's enthusiasm was so wholehearted Jo found herself

asking if they'd been good friends. Although if they had, surely Cam would have known his mate was living at the Cove.

'Not close friends, but he was someone I knew well enough. It will be good to catch up with him.'

Would it? Even as he'd spoken, Cam had wondered about 'catching up' with anyone he'd known from his past. Could he play the person he'd been before his war experiences? Could he pretend well enough for people not to see the cracks beneath the surface?

PTSD they called it—post-traumatic stress disorder. He had seen enough of it in patients to be reasonably sure he didn't have it, not the full-blown version of it anyway. All he had was the baggage from his time in the war zone, baggage he was reasonably certain he could rid himself of in time.

Perhaps.

His family had seen the difference in him and understood enough to treat him not like an invalid but with gentleness, letting him know without words that they were all there for him if ever he wanted to talk about the baggage in his head.

Not that he could—not yet—maybe not ever…

Fortunately, before he could let too many of the doors in his head slide open, his boss was talking to him.

'Come on, then,' she said, standing up and heading across the footpath towards the road. 'It's time to do some catching up.'

'We haven't paid,' he reminded her, and she threw him a look over her shoulder. He considered running the look through his mental data base of women's looks then decided it didn't really matter what her look had said. Best he just followed along, took orders like a good soldier, and hoped he'd prove indispensable so he could stay on in Crystal Cove for longer than a couple of months.

The thought startled him so much he found the word *why* forming in his head.

He tried to answer it.

The surf was good, but there was good surf to be had along thousands of miles of coastline.

Surely not because of the feisty boss—a woman he'd barely met and certainly didn't know, and quite possibly wouldn't like if he did know, although those eyes, the creamy skin…

He reached her as she was about to step out to cross the esplanade, just in time to grab her arm and haul her back as a teenager on a moped swerved towards her.

'Idiot!' Jo stormed, glaring full tilt at the departing rider's back. 'They rent those things out to people with no more brains than a—'

'An aardvark?' Cam offered helpfully, trying not to smile at the woman who was so cross she hadn't realised he was still holding her arm.

He wasn't going to think about *why* he was still holding her arm—he'd just enjoy the sensation.

'I was going to say flea,' she muttered as she turned towards him, 'then I thought maybe I'd said that earlier.' She frowned up at him. 'Why would you think I'd say aardvark?'

He had to laugh.

'Don't you remember telling me I probably had the counselling skills of an aardvark earlier today?'

Her frown disappeared and her cheeks turned a delicate pink.

'How *rude* of me! Did I really?'

She was so obviously flustered—again—he had to let her off the hook.

'I didn't mind,' he told her. 'In fact, I was too astonished to take offence. I mean, it's not ever day one's compared to such an unlikely animal.'

Jo knew she had to move.

For a start, she should shake the man's hand off her arm, but she was mesmerised, not so much by the quirky smile and sparkling blue eyes and the tanned skin and the massive chest but by the fact that she was having such a— What kind of conversation was it?

Light-hearted chit-chat?

It seemed so long since she'd done light-hearted chit-chat, if that's what it was, with a man she didn't know, but whatever it was, she'd been enjoying it…

'Are we going to cross the road or will we stay on this side, discussing aardvarks and fleas?'

Far too late, Jo moved her arm so the man's hand fell off it, then she checked both ways—she didn't want him saving her again—and hurried across, beeping open the car as she approached it, so she could escape inside it as quickly as possible.

Except he'd be getting in as well—no escape.

Until they heard the loud crash, and the sounds of splintering glass.

Cam reacted first, pushing her behind him, looking around, apparently finding the scene of the accident before she'd fully comprehended what had happened.

'It's the moped driver,' he said, as he hurried back across the street to where people were already gathering on the footpath.

Jo followed, seeing the splintered glass of the shopfront and the fallen moped, its wheels still turning, the young driver lying motionless beside it.

'Let's all step back,' Cam said, his voice so full of authority the onlookers obeyed automatically, and when he added, 'And anyone without shoes on, walk away carefully. The glass could have spread in all directions.'

That got rid of a few more onlookers and made Jo aware *she* had to tread carefully. Sandals were fine in summer, but as protection against broken glass not sensible at all.

Cam was kneeling by the young man, who wasn't moving or responding to Cam's questions.

'Unconscious?' she asked, as she squatted on the other side of him, their hands touching as they both felt for injuries.

'Yes, but he's wearing a helmet and the bike barely hit the window before he came off.'

Jo lifted the youth's wrist automatically and though she was looking for a pulse she had to push aside a metal bracelet. Remembering the rider's swerve earlier, she checked it.

'He's a diabetic,' she said to Cam. 'Maybe he was feeling light-headed when he nearly ran into me. He might have been pulling over to take in some carbs when he passed out.'

'His pulse is racing, and he's pale and very sweaty—I'd say you've got it in one, Dr Harris,' Cam agreed. 'I don't suppose you have a syringe of glucogen on you?'

'I'd have tablets in my bag in the car, but he should have something on him.' She began to search the patient's pockets, pulling out a sleeve of glucose tablets.

Perhaps because she'd been poking at him, their patient stirred.

'That's a bit of luck! I've seen before how blood glucose can rise back to pre-unconsciousness levels,' Cam said, as he helped the young man into a sitting position and asked him if he was able to take the tablets, but Jo had already sent one of the audience to the closest café for some orange juice.

Their patient nodded, muttering to himself about stupidity and not stopping earlier.

The juice arrived and Cam supported him, holding the bottle for the shaky young patient.

'This will be easier to get into you than the tablets,' he said, 'but even though you're conscious you should take a trip up to the hospital and get checked out.' He nodded towards the ambulance that had just pulled up. 'Here's your lift.'

'But the moped?'

'I'll take care of that,' Jo told him. 'I can put it in the back of my vehicle and take it back to the hire people and explain.'

Cam stood back to let the ambulance attendants ready their patient for transport, and looked at Jo, eyebrows raised.

'*You'll* put it in the car?'

He was smiling as he said it, and all kinds of physical symptoms started up again—ripples, flickers, flutters, her skin feeling as if a million tiny sparks were going off inside it.

'Someone would help!' she retorted, trying really hard not to sound defensive but losing the battle.

His smile broadened and now her reactions were *all* internal—a squeezing in her chest, accelerated heartbeat while her lungs suddenly needed all of her attention to make them work.

How could this be happening to her?

And *why*?

Wasn't she perfectly happy with her life?

Well, she was worried about the refuge, but apart from that…

CHAPTER THREE

Jo watched the patient being loaded into the ambulance, then turned and spoke to the young policeman who'd arrived, introducing him to Cam, who explained what he'd seen of the incident. While some of the onlookers who'd been closer to the scene gave their versions of what had happened and the shopkeeper began cleaning up the glass, Cam had set the moped upright, and was looking at it, obviously checking for damage.

'I'll handle that, mate,' a voice said, and Jo turned to see that the man who hired out the little motor scooters had arrived with his ute, having heard of the accident on whatever grapevine was in operation this Sunday.

'So, hospital?' Cam asked, once again taking Jo's arm, and although she knew full well it was only to guide her across the street—a street she'd crossed without guidance for a couple of decades—the stirrings in her body magnified and all she wanted to do was get away from him for a short time, give her body a good talking to and move on without all this physical disturbance before it drove her mad.

'I guess so,' she muttered, with so much reluctance Cam halted on the kerb to look at her.

'You've changed your mind about visiting the hospital?'

Was her expression such a giveaway that he added a second question?

'Or changed your mind about employing me?'

Cam watched the woman as he spoke. He was teasing her—well, he was almost certain he was teasing her. It was just that for a moment he thought he'd read regret in her expression.

But he hadn't started work so surely she couldn't be regretting hiring him already.

As if he could read the face of a woman he barely knew! Yes, he could guess at his sisters' emotions, but he'd never really been able to tell what his ex-fiancée was thinking just from looking at her face.

'Why would you think that!' the woman he'd questioned demanded, stepping off the kerb so he was forced to move if he wanted to keep hold of her arm. 'I was thinking of the kid—the diabetic. It's one of the worries when the schoolies are here, that any kid who is a diabetic can drink too much, or play too hard, and not take in enough fluids. I haven't had an instance here, but that lad made me think.'

That was a very obvious evasion, Cam guessed, but he didn't say so. Whatever Jo *had* been thinking about was her business, not his, although he did hope she wasn't regretting hiring him before he'd even started work.

And it was probably best not to consider *that* hope too closely—could it be more than the surf that made him want to stay on here?

It *couldn't* be the woman—they'd barely met…

And it *certainly* wasn't the accommodation!

Although thinking about waking in the rose bower did make him smile: waking up in the flat would certainly be a far cry from a desert camouflage tent.

But even as he smiled he wondered if he shouldn't leave

right now, before he got as entangled as the roses in the bower. It wouldn't be fair to any woman to be lumbered with him the way his mind was—the nightmares, the flashbacks, the doubts that racked him.

Jo beeped the car unlocked, then looked at Cam in vague surprise as opened her door and held it.

'Not used to gentlemen in Crystal Cove?' he asked, discovering that teasing her was fun, particularly as a delicate rose colour seeped into her cheeks when he did it.

Jo refused to answer him. Okay, so he was a tease. She could handle that. She just had to get used to it and to take everything he said with the proverbial grain of salt. *And* she had to learn not to react.

Not to react to *anything* to do with the man.

Already she was regretting suggesting she show him around.

She pulled into the hospital car park, enjoying, as she always did, the old building with its wide, sheltered verandas and its view over the beach and the water beyond.

Today must have been 'putting up the decorations' day for the veranda railing was garlanded with greenery while red and green wreaths hung in all the windows.

'Great hospital!' Cam said.

'It's a triumph of local support over bureaucracy,' she told him. 'The government wanted to close it some years ago and the local people fought to keep it. We've even got a maternity ward, if you can call one birthing suite and a couple of other rooms a ward. It's so good for the local women to be able to have their babies here, and although we don't have a specialist obstetrician we've got a wonderful head midwife, and Tom's passionate about his obstetrics work.'

'I vaguely remember him being keen on it during our training,' Cam said, while Jo hurried out of the car before he could open her door and stand near her again.

She really needed to get away—needed some time and space to sort out all the strange stirrings going on in her body, not to mention the fact that her mind kept enjoying conversations with her new employee. It was almost as if it had been starved of stimulation and was now being refreshed.

Impossible.

Was she away with the fairies that she was even thinking this way?

She was saved from further mental muddle by Tom, who was not only at the hospital, checking on the moped driver, but was delighted to meet up with a friend from bygone times.

'I'm sure you've got better things to do than hang around listening to us play "Remember this",' Tom told Jo. 'How about you leave Cam here and I'll drop him back up at your place later?'

Jo's relief was out of all proportion to the offer Tom had made, but she hoped she hid it as she checked that this was okay with her new tenant and made her escape.

He was just a man—Cam, not Tom, although Tom was also a man, though not a man she thought of as a *man*.

This particular dither was so ridiculous it told her just how far out of control her mind had become. She drove home, made herself a cup of tea—very soothing, tea—and sat on the deck to try to sort out what was happening to her.

Was it because it was a long time since she'd been in a relationship that her new employee was causing her problems?

Three years, that's how long it had been.

There'd been the odd date in that time—very odd, some of them—but nothing serious. Nothing serious since Harry had declared that no power on earth would persuade him to live in a one-horse, seaside town for the rest of his life, and if she wanted to leave Sydney and go back home, that was fine by him.

He'd been so underwhelmed by her departure from their relationship she'd wondered if he'd already had a replacement woman lined up.

Not that she'd wondered for long. So much had happened after she'd returned home. Jill's death within a few months, for a start. Jo had been devastated. Fortunately she'd had the distraction of helping Lauren set up the refuge, then her father had fallen in love, then she'd taken over the practice. More recently, she'd started worrying about the refuge closing. A new relationship had been the last thing on her mind.

Not that the town was teeming with men with whom she could have had a relationship if she'd wanted one, and relationships in small towns—well, they had their own set of problems.

She was aware enough to know that the refuge, building it up and working for it, had helped her through the worst of the pain of Jill's death. Perhaps now that there was a possibility of it closing, was she subconsciously looking for a new diversion?

A six-foot-three, broad-chested, blue eyed diversion?

She didn't think so.

Besides, the refuge wasn't going to close, not while she had breath in her body to fight it.

And if she *was* fighting, then she wouldn't—shouldn't—have the time or energy to consider her new tenant, not his chest, or his eyes, or anything else about him…

'Who are those people who arrange marriages in some countries? Wedding planners? Marriage consultants?'

It was a strange conversation to be having with someone she barely knew, but Jo was glad the man—the one with the eyes and chest she was going to ignore, however hard that might be—had brought up a topic of conversation for, when she'd met him in the lunch-room after morning surgery, she'd wondered what on earth they could talk about.

They could talk about patients, of course, but lunch-time was supposed to be a break and unless something was urgent—

She frowned at the man, well, not at him but at not knowing the answer.

'I've no idea,' she said, 'although I do know the kind of people you mean. An old-fashioned form of internet dating, I suppose. I think the family went to the woman and she organised the—matchmakers, that's what they were called. Or are called if they still exist.'

She was intrigued enough by now to actually look at the man who was sitting across the table from her. His face was freshly shaven so quirky lips and pale blue eyes were clearly visible, and his hair, though still long, was shiny clean—brown streaked with gold.

He was more handsome even than his photo, which had made him look formal and a little stern, while this man would have every woman in town booking in for appointments.

Best to stop considering his looks and get back to the conversation.

'Why do you ask?'

He grinned at her, making her forget her decision to stop considering looks just long enough to add super-smile to the catalogue of his appeal.

It also caused just a little tremor in her stomach.

Well, maybe more than a *little* tremor, but it was still small enough to ignore.

'Just that every patient I've seen this morning, the men included, would find it a perfect career choice. Some were more subtle than others, but before I'd written a script, every one of them knew my marital status—single—my career prospects—doubtful at present, although most assured me you'd keep me on—and had asked what I thought about my boss. Didn't I think she was a wonderful woman? I've also been told that you're a good cook, one woman seemed to think you could sew, while several others assured me you were a good financial prospect as you owned the surgery and the house and also had investment properties in the city.'

'Sew?'

Cam smiled again as the word burst from his boss's lips.

'Why the hell would anyone be telling you I can sew? Why would I *want* to sew? Why would you be interested? You've been in the army. I'm sure you're much better at sewing than I am, given the number of buttons you must have had on your uniforms, or are doctors the kind of officers who have people who sew on their buttons?'

Knowing all three of his sisters would have reacted with the same horror, Cam continued to smile.

'I think that particular patient thought it was a nice womanly trait to point out to me, and, no, no button sewers in my army life.'

'You're enjoying this!'

The accusation was accompanied by a fairly good glare, well up on the glare scale he'd set up in his head many years ago. She looked good glaring, too, fiery colour in her cheeks, her eyes seeming greener, a bit like an angry elf.

'Of course,' he said smoothly, teasing her because it was fun. 'Though I do wonder what it is about you that makes everyone think you're incapable of finding yourself a man and that you need help from the whole town to sort out your life.'

A very angry elf!

'Bloody town!' she muttered. 'Honestly, they never let up. I shouldn't have employed you—I knew that right from the start—now we're going to have to put up with every patient casting sideways glances at us, or, as you've found this morning, asking straight out. If I'd had an ounce of sense I'd have come home from Sydney as a widow.'

'Having killed off your husband and got away with it?'

Only with difficulty was Cam holding in a laugh.

'There's no reason I *couldn't* have killed off some mythical husband while I was training in Sydney. Not murdered the poor man, but I could have had him die a painful, lingering death, leaving me grieving for ever. That way they'd have accepted I wasn't interested in a relationship. But coming up here single? Big mistake! I've had patients trailing their sons and nephews and even grandsons through the door—here's Edward in from the farm to meet you, he's got one hundred and forty breeding sows and good teeth. The place is impossible.'

Cam *had* to smile, but just to tease her further he did the maths.

'One hundred and forty breeding sows? What? A couple of litters a year? Twelve to fifteen a litter? Edward would have been a good catch!'

'Edward was not the slightest bit interested in me once he realised I haven't a clue about pork, ham and bacon, and have never known which bit comes from where. What's more, he's happily engaged to a woman who works in the piggery for him, who understands percentage body fat and other things important to pigs.'

Jo hoped she'd spoken coolly enough to put a stop to this absurd conversation, but inside her there was a little glow at the simple pleasure of having someone to talk to, to joke with, while she took a break. Not that she didn't talk and joke to the other staff, two nurses and the receptionist, but talking to Cam was different somehow.

Because he was a man?

Hell's teeth, she did hope not! Her mind went into panic mode at the thought. She didn't know if she was ready for a relationship with a man—well, she was, her body was—but was she ready for the fallout when he moved on? For the talk around the town, for the pain if she was foolish enough to fall in love with him?

Her body's reaction to him could be explained. That was definitely because he was a man, and possibly because her body had been pure and chaste for so darned long she could barely remember what attraction was like.

Until now.

Though surely it hadn't always been this strong—this immediate…

And how could she be thinking of a relationship when the man had shown not the slightest interest in her as anything other than his boss?

'Mrs Youngman.'

He was looking at her, obviously awaiting a response, his eyes looking grey-blue today—the charcoal shirt?

'I'm sorry, miles away,' she muttered, feeling heat rise in her cheeks when she realised just where her thoughts had been. 'You were saying?'

'Mrs Youngman was one of my first patients. The note on the front of her file said, "Query IVF." She's fifty-two. Has she talked to you about this?'

The question brought Jo's focus back to work immediately.

'Helene Youngman? That's who you're talking about?'

Cam nodded, which didn't help at all.

'Query IVF? Who wrote that?'

Now he shrugged, the impossibly wide shoulders lifting

the neat charcoal shirt, moving the material so she saw the V of tanned chest beneath the unbuttoned collar. Nope, her mind might be focussed but her body was still hanging in on the attraction stuff, stirring deep down.

'I've no idea,' he replied. 'I thought maybe you had at her last appointment, or perhaps the receptionist when Mrs Youngman phoned for an appointment.'

'Helene Youngman!' Jo repeated, trying to come to terms with the town's mayor making enquiries about IVF. She had grown-up children and *she* was a widow. Hauling her mind back to work, Jo added, 'She must have asked to see you, to see the new doctor—everyone in town would have known you were here within hours—because she didn't want to talk to me about it, which is a bit of a downer for me as we're quite friendly. Not that it matters who she talks to, of course, but what did you tell her?'

'Only what I knew—specialist clinics in the capital cities, maybe in large regional cities—best to see a gynaecologist first and get checked out before spending too much money. I want to check out information about available programmes so I know for the future, but didn't want to ask one of the nurses because she, Mrs Youngman, gave the impression she was embarrassed enough asking about it, although she must have mentioned it to someone because of the note. I said I'd see what I could find out for her and post it.'

'*Embarrassed?* Poor thing, that's exactly what she would be. Actually, it's hard to believe she came here to enquire, rather than drive down the coast to Port, but she's a busy woman. She's our local mayor and runs two hairdressing salons as well. Although if she goes through with it—and good luck to her if she does—speaking to a doctor about it is going to be the easy part. Facing the local population as it becomes obvious, that's what will be hard for her. We'll need to make sure she gets plenty of support.'

He liked the 'we', as if she'd already accepted him as a colleague, but watching her Cam could practically see Jo's mind working as she tried to puzzle out the request so when she added, 'I didn't even know she was seeing someone, let alone involved enough to want a child with him,' he wasn't surprised to see a blush rise in her cheeks.

She pressed her hands against them.

'What a small-minded thing to say—why *should* I know? That's just what I was talking about earlier. Small-town mentality, you see. We all think we know everything that's going on all the time, and if we don't we're surprised, even a little put out. That's terrible, isn't it?'

The clear green eyes, like the shallow water at the edge of the ocean when the surf was flat, met his with a plea for—understanding? Absolution?

The first he could give.

'It's natural enough, and part of the charm of small towns.' The colour was fading from her cheeks so he went for the second as well. 'And I didn't find it small-minded. To me you simply sounded caring.'

She smiled at him and it was as if the sun had hit the placid green water, sparking golden lights in it.

Golden lights on placid waters? Was his success in getting a job here—even if it was only temporary—turning him fanciful? Had waking up to that spectacular view then the chance for an hour in the surf before breakfast and work altered the chemistry in his brain?

He brought his mind back to work.

'So, what do you know of it? Do you keep information? Is there a specialist clinic in Port Macquarie or would she have to go to Sydney?'

The eyes she fixed on him were serious now, intent, and a little frown was tugging at her eyebrows.

'I've read something recently about some IVF clinics restricting treatment to women over, I think, forty-three. It can't be a totally random age choice but apparently the odds of conception in women older than that are so low they only allow one try.'

'Is that fair?' Cam asked. 'Given the range of ages at which women can reach menopause depending on genetic and other issues, might not a fit fifty-two-year-old woman be as good a recipient of treatment as a younger woman with less healthy reproductive organs?'

Jo smiled at him.

'You'd be wasted surfing along the coast and not working,' she said. 'You're obviously an empathetic doctor and, yes, you're right, it seems strange to pick an age, but funding—it always comes back to money. Check out what you can on the net, ask one of the nurses to dig out the information we have—they won't talk—and we'll take it from there.'

He liked the 'we' part, again, which was foolish given it was his first day at work and the job was temporary. And he'd have liked to talk some more—not necessarily about IVF—but his boss was on her feet, small, neat feet clad in sandals, her toenails painted the palest pink with what looked like little faces or maybe flowers stuck on them.

And since when had he noticed feet? Could he blame the army and its predilection for shiny boots?

Or could he put that down to the view and early morning surf as well?

'Patients await,' she added as she bustled through the door, although it seemed to him she was escaping something rather than hurrying towards something.

Escaping him?

Was it the small compliment he'd paid her—calling her caring was hardly world-shattering, Jo wondered as she fled the lunchroom. Or was it the attraction that was getting harder to ignore whenever she was near him?

He was just a man.

Okay, he was a tall and handsome man with a chest a gorilla would have been proud of, but physical attributes had never been that important to her in a man. Men she'd loved, well, nearly loved, or thought she'd loved at one time or another hadn't been exactly weedy, but given that she was hardly red-carpet material herself, she'd never expected too much in the way of looks in a man. She'd found attraction in common interests, shared jokes and a sense of being at ease with the person.

And, for some unknown reason, she had been at ease almost from the start with Fraser Cameron, even when she'd thought he might be coming to rob the surgery.

She had to get her head straight.

Think about Helene! She was healthy—kept herself fit running and swimming—in fact, Jo often ran with her on the beach in the early mornings.

And she wanted a baby?

A totally unfamiliar sensation coiled in Jo's belly.

No! No way was she going to get clucky now! She *never* got clucky. She handled babies every day of the week and heard not even the faintest tick of the fabled clock.

Because she'd never fancied anyone enough to get involved, enough to consider having children with him?

Even Harry?

That was a scary thought because it prompted the question why now, and she didn't want to consider the answer in case it had something to do with blue eyes and a quirky smile and soft brown hair with gold highlights…

It took some effort, but she turned her mind back to work matters.

She collected the pile of files for her afternoon appointments and headed into her room, promising herself she'd do some research into IVF for older women on the internet later. It would keep her busy after dinner which was good because the previous night, imagining Cam in the flat next door, had been so uncomfortable she'd ended up going back to the beach and running until she was exhausted enough to go home and sleep.

Maybe a bit of IVF research would be good…

And the squirmy feeling in her stomach was probably indigestion.

Fate dictated that her first three patients of the afternoon were babies. Two were in for injections, which one of the nurses would give, and six-month-old Kaylin, a gurgling bundle of delight had decided she didn't need to sleep.

Ever!

'She's okay now because she's been in the car and she always sleeps in the car,' Kaylin's mother, Amy Bennett, explained. 'But we can't drive around all night so she gets some sleep because it means we don't get any. We're getting desperate, Jo, and Todd gets so cranky when he doesn't get his sleep and I know I'll lose my milk if things don't settle down. With the dairy we can't avoid the milking every morning and with a hundred milkers Todd needs my help. In the beginning Kaylin was good, she'd just sleep in the capsule down at the dairy while we worked, but that only lasted about a month. Remember I came in to talk to you before…'

Amy's voice trailed away.

Jo thought about it as she dug through files in the cabinet behind her for information on the sleep programme offered from time to time at the local hospital in conjunction with various government departments.

Any number of babies had problems developing regular sleep patterns, but Kaylin had so far defied all the tried and trusted methods of training babies to sleep and not only was Amy looking stressed and worn out, but the baby, too, was suffering.

Think laterally! Jo reminded herself of her father's words. Running a successful practice in a small coastal town meant understanding the dynamics of her patients' lives. A pregnant woman with complications might refuse to go to the more specialised hospital in the nearest regional city unless someone—usually the family doctor—organised someone to look after her older children.

She'd learnt this from her father even before she studied medicine, hearing him discuss options for patients' welfare that went beyond straight doctoring.

So as far as sorting things out for Amy went, Kaylin's sleeping pattern was only part of the problem.

'I can arrange for you to stay at the hospital while the expert works with you and Kaylin,' Jo explained as Amy leafed through the information, 'but it means Todd will have to get someone in to give him a hand with the milking. You've still got that old house on the property, haven't you? The one you've rented out from time to time?'

Amy nodded.

'Then maybe you could offer it rent free to someone in exchange for help with the milking. That will give you more time to spend with Kaylin. Now she's getting too big for the capsule, you'd have to find an alternative way to keep her safe while you're helping Todd, in any case.'

Amy looked doubtful.

'You know we did it once before,' she murmured. 'I think

it was your dad, just before he left, that arranged for the Scott family to have the house.'

'Oh, dear, not so good a suggestion, then,' Jo replied, remembering the complicated plan she and Lauren had cooked up to get Mrs Scott and the two little Scotts out of the house and into the recently opened refuge when the man Todd Bennett had employed had turned out to be an abusive husband.

Jo shuddered at the memory, thinking of the volunteer who'd driven the wife and children to safety and who had later been targeted by Bob Scott. The volunteer's house had been peppered with eggs and tomatoes.

'But then again, it's hardly likely you'd get another couple like the Scotts.'

Amy shrugged.

'You just don't know, do you?' she said, but after Jo had checked out both her and Kaylin, Amy agreed she'd talk to Todd about it and let Jo know if she wanted to stay in the hospital for the sleep programme.

'Do you know where Mrs Scott and the kids went?' she asked as Jo was walking with her back to the reception area.

'Back to Mr Scott,' Jo told her, remembering how wary she'd been when the woman had made that decision. 'Mr Scott completed a programme they were running in Port to help men like him and I think he joined a support group, so hopefully it all worked out.'

Amy waved goodbye and Jo turned to go back to her room to check who was next. She ran smack bang into a broad chest.

'Men like him?' the owner of the chest repeated. 'Abusive?'

Jo nodded, her mind still full of the uneasiness that thinking about the Scotts had caused.

'And the man went to Port? There's a refuge but no programme for men here?'

Jo had backed away from him, and now his persistence forced her to look up into his face.

'The Scotts were gone two years ago, why the interest?'

Cam beamed at her, his smile so warm she felt it radiate against her skin.

And set alarm bells clanging in her head!

'It's something I can do,' he announced, still beaming with delight at whatever he was thinking. 'Something I can set up. If not a regular programme at least a support-slash-discussion group.'

It was an excellent idea, and something she and Lauren had often discussed, but why was Cam being so helpful?

So he'd have to stay on?

'You're only here for a couple of months,' she reminded him.

'On trial for a couple of months.' His retort was so swift she knew he'd followed her thoughts. 'Anyway, if it doesn't work out here at the clinic, I could always stay on in town and surf for a few more months, maybe pick up some shifts at the hospital. Tom said yesterday that they could probably get funding for a part-time doctor, and after the holidays I can live in my van in the caravan park so I wouldn't be bothering you.'

Bothering her?

Had he guessed how she was reacting to him? Well, not her so much but her body…

Whether it was his proximity—the hall was getting narrower by the minute—or the thought of Cam being around for longer than was absolutely necessary, Jo didn't know. All she knew was that she feeling extremely flustered and she *did* know she didn't do flustered.

Ever.

'We've both got patients to see,' she reminded Cam, and

stomped away, even more put out because the soft-soled sandals she wore didn't make satisfactory stomping noises.

Hmm.

Cam watched her go.

Had he flustered her?

Jo Harris didn't strike him as a woman who flustered easily.

And why was he thinking about her—in particular, why was he thinking about her as a woman? He may not have PTSD, but he certainly wasn't in any state to be getting involved with a woman. He couldn't blame Penny for cutting him out of her life, knowing the man who'd returned to her hadn't been the man she'd loved, but if *she* couldn't love the new him, who would?

Remote, she'd called him. Remote, detached, and morose.

He hadn't liked the morose with its undertones of brooding, but the remote bit had really got to him. It was a word that sounded unpleasant. It could never be used to describe Jo. He'd seen her angry, and snappish, and competently assured as she'd knelt by the injured moped driver. He'd even seen the shadows of sadness in her face, but she was always involved—ready with an opinion, seeking new ideas.

Remote suggested a detachment from the world, and for sure it was one of the symptoms of PTSD that he *had* been able to tick. On leaving the army, he'd felt as if the world he'd returned to was a parallel universe and he was rudderless in it. He'd been on the outside, looking in, aware that none of the people around him could, in their wildest dreams, have imagined what he'd seen and been through.

The strange thing was that he didn't feel that way now. Maybe it was the surf at Crystal Cove clearing his head, but the idea of starting a support group had stirred something akin to excitement in him, *and* he was looking forward to doing some research on IVF treatments for older women.

Looking forward to helping people?

Getting involved?

He wasn't sure what had caused the change, but though he might be on the right track he suspected he had a lot more healing to do before he could think in terms of a relationship with a woman.

Although Jo obviously had her own baggage—her sister's death, for a start.

Could two wounded souls somehow help each other heal?

He remembered how her eyes had looked—clear green pools—and his body stirred in a way that was totally inappropriate as a reaction to one's boss, however temporary his employment might be…

CHAPTER FOUR

'I HADN'T realised how much more quickly we'd get through the day with two doctors.'

Jo had been chatting to the receptionist when Cam showed his final patient out. Now she walked with him back along the hall.

'I phoned Lauren, who runs the refuge, earlier. The two families who are living there at the moment are having a "treat night" tonight, which means there's no one at the house. We could go over later if that suits you. You could see the place and talk to Lauren about how it works and also about the men's programme. Funding is always difficult—sometimes impossible. Originally we got the bequest to set up the refuge, but that's not enough to keep it going these days so poor Lauren gets bits and pieces from different government agencies. One of the local service clubs has it as their main charity, but I can't promise you'd be paid for running a men's programme, although if you start it while you're working for me, but then…'

She stopped and looked up at him, a worried frown knitting her eyebrows.

'Of course you don't have to come with me, you might prefer to go surfing or have other stuff you want to do but—'

'Jo!'

Cam held up his hands as he said her name—a placating gesture, not surrender.

'Calm down. We can't change the entire world right now. Let's take it one step at a time. I'm more than happy to go with you to see the refuge, and seeing it when no one's there is an excellent idea. Do I have time for a quick shower and change of clothes before we go?'

She was staring at him, a bewildered look on her face, then he watched as she gathered herself together, shaking her head just slightly as if to get everything back into place.

'I *never* blather on like that!' she said, her tone so accusing he had to laugh.

'Blathering's okay,' he assured her, but the worried look on her face told him she didn't believe him. He diverted her by repeating his question.

'Shower?'

'Of course,' she said, but he guessed it had been an automatic response, her mind still occupied by the blather business.

Jo was glad he'd left as soon as she'd agreed they had time to freshen up, because now, maybe, she could sort out what was happening to her.

The men's programme was an excellent idea, and she had no doubt Cam, with his training and experience, would be just the man to set it up and run it.

And even if the refuge closed, the programme could still run, so it wasn't that disturbing her…

Was it because he'd talked of staying on that she'd been thrown into a dither?

Had she somehow convinced herself that she could put up with the distraction he was causing her body for a couple of months but once the issue of his staying longer had arisen, her brain had gone into meltdown?

She couldn't answer either of her questions so she locked her office door, said good-bye to Kate who was working Reception today, and hurried up the steps at the back of the surgery.

Maybe a shower would help her brain return to normal, but cold or hot she had no confidence in it doing anything to stop her body reacting to her temporary employee.

It was only a couple of months!

But could she let him live in his van in the caravan park if he stayed on to run a men's programme?

She had the flat…

Best not to think ahead.

But for the second day in a row, she put on just a little lipstick.

Pathetic.

The refuge was behind one of Crystal Cove's still functioning churches. It had been the minister's house—the manse—once, but now the minister lived forty miles up the coast and served a flock spread over a wide area, holding services at the Cove once a fortnight.

'It's fairly obvious, isn't it?' Cam asked as Jo pulled into the driveway.

She looked around at the high wire fence, the security cameras at the corners of the old wooden residence, the playground equipment out the back.

Turned back to Cam.

'In what way?'

'Well, I thought they had to be anonymous places, women's refuges, hidden away—ordinary houses but their use not known even to neighbours.'

Jo smiled at him—he was so darned easy to smile at.

And she'd better think about *that* thought later.

'In bigger towns and cities that might be possible and it's definitely desirable, but in a town this size? As you'd surmised, towns this size don't usually have a refuge. We're lucky because the church not only lets us have the premises rent free, but they pay expenses on it—rates and such. The service clubs did a lot of renovations and they do any maintenance that's required, so immediately you have several groups of people who know where it is and what it's for. And it *is* only two doors from the police station so there's never any trouble here. '

She frowned now as she added, 'Am I blathering again?'

He grinned at her.

'No way. That was a most sensible explanation, very to the point and concise.'

The grin was her undoing. Any good the shower might have done was undone with that grin—a quirky, amused, sharing kind of grin.

Good grief! How could she possibly be thinking this way? Analysing the man's grin?

'Let's go,' she said, opening her door and leaping down from the high seat of the four-wheel drive that had been her Christmas present to herself last year.

Good thing, too, she thought, patting the car when she'd shut the door. Having Cam in the big vehicle had been bad enough, she could only imagine how uncomfortable it would have been if they'd been squashed together in a small sedan.

Lauren Cooper, blonde, beautiful but far too thin and with dark shadows of worry under her eyes, came out of the house to greet them.

'You have to take some time off,' Jo scolded her best friend.

'I'll have plenty of time off if we have to close,' Lauren reminded her quietly, but her dark eyes lit up as she took in the man Jo was introducing to her.

'Well,' she teased after she'd shaken Cam's hand, 'you'll certainly be a great addition to the male talent in this town.'

'All six of them?' Jo countered.

'In our age group,' Lauren agreed, counting on her fingers as she listed the local, older, unattached men. 'Mike at the police station, Tom at the hospital, that new schoolteacher—'

'He's got a partner,' Jo protested, before adding firmly, 'Anyway, that's enough. Cam's already likely to get a swollen head because I've been praising his idea of the men's support programme. We're here to see the refuge and to talk about how we could run a men's programme—not to mention whether men might come.'

'It could be court mandated,' Cam offered, pleased the conversation had shifted from male talent in the town. His body might have reacted to his boss and landlady but after Penny's fairly brutal rejection, he'd accepted that until the mess in his head was sorted out, it would be unfair to get involved with any woman.

Although a woman with killer green eyes…

'Wow!'

His exclamation was involuntary, and his mind right back on the refuge as Lauren led them first into what she called the playroom. Obviously it had been set up with kids in mind, but whoever had conceived and carried through the idea had done an amazing job. Blackboard paint had been used to adult waist height on all the walls so there were chalk drawings everywhere. At one end of the long room—a closed-in veranda, he suspected—was a sitting area with comfy armchairs and bean-bags in front of a television set with a DVD player on top of it. Beside that a cabinet held what must be at least a hundred DVDs.

The other end of the room was obviously for very small people, blocks and jigsaw puzzles neatly put away on shelves, plastic boxes of farm animals, zoo animals, dinosaurs, toy cars and little dolls stacked further along the shelves.

'It's incredibly well stocked,' he said, 'and so tidy.'

'Well-stocked but not always so tidy,' Lauren told him. 'We've instituted star charts. Stars for putting away the toys, stars for cleaning teeth, stars for just about everything you can imagine. Once you get a certain number of stars, you get a treat—like dinner at a fast-food outlet of your choice, which is where everyone is tonight. They left early as they're going on to a movie after their meal. Everyone's been really good this week!'

Lauren showed them through the rest of the house, allowing Cam a glimpse into the three big bedrooms that could accommodate up to five people in each.

'So you can have three women with children—no more?' Cam asked.

'Well, we could arrange to take more if it was necessary, squeeze in a woman on her own, for instance, but the turnover is fairly rapid.'

'So no one is here long term?' Cam asked.

Lauren smiled at him, the smile lifting the tiredness from her face and making him wonder why this beautiful woman—smiling at him—had no effect at all on his body, while the small, pert redhead who was usually frowning, glaring or arguing did.

Not that he needed to give it much thought—he was moving on.

And even if he stayed, he'd be moving out.

And then there was the baggage.

And his lost passion…

'Four weeks.'

He'd missed the beginning of whatever Lauren was saying but assumed she'd told him the time limit on stays as she led him into the communal lounge, the dining area and finally a well-equipped kitchen.

'You're really well set up,' he said, not bothering to keep the admiration out of his voice.

'That's what makes the thought of it closing so hard.'

He heard the pain in Jo's voice, but it was the content, not the pain, he had to think about.

'But as long as you're fighting the closure you've got a chance of keeping it open,' he protested. 'I thought it was because of the refuge you were employing another doctor. The fortyish woman, remember.'

He won a slight smile.

'I was employing her—or you—to ease my load at work so I could put more time into this, time for paperwork mainly, applying for grants, and so on. As I told you yesterday, the refuge began with a bequest and the building itself is available to us free of charge, but ongoing funding for residential staff—the people here every day, including the child-health-care worker—has to come from the government. The government is forever issuing new guidelines and procedures and so-called measurements of success—criteria we have to meet before they'll give us money.'

'Sounds like the army,' Cam said, 'but I thought women being saved from abuse would be counted as successes.'

'You'd think so,' Jo told him, 'but they like "projects".' She used her fingers to put the word in inverted commas. 'That's why a men's programme would be fantastic, *and* we could do more work in schools. It would be such a waste to have to close it now, when we've come so far.'

She smiled, but it was a weak effort.

'The thing is, we've worked so hard for the women who need us to accept us and on top of that we have the most wonderful local support,' Lauren explained. 'People from all walks of life help out in different ways. The local bakery gives us its unsold bread at the end of each day—not to mention buns and bread rolls. We get a discount at the butcher's and the supermarket, and the fruit shop in town also hands over any produce they aren't able to sell.'

'Which is a blessing,' Jo put in, with a far better smile, this time broad enough to gleam in her eyes, 'given that the back yard has a virtual zoo, with rabbits, guinea pigs, chickens and a duck with one leg that someone gave us. At one stage there was a lamb but it turned into a sheep and the neighbours complained about the noise it made.'

Cam looked at the smiling woman who *did* affect his body and regretted mentioning a programme for abusive men. Much better if he moved on at the end of the holidays. He didn't need to get involved in the problems of the refuge, did he? There were other towns with good surf. In fact, he had thousands of miles of coastline to choose from.

But no snappish, elfin-faced, green-eyed doctor…

'If there's a programme up and running in Port, maybe I could go down and speak to whoever runs it,' he heard a voice say.

He was reasonably sure it was *his* voice.

A buzzing sound made him turn towards the woman he'd been considering, and he watched as she pulled her mobile out of her pocket.

She walked through the back door and spoke quietly, but not so quietly he and Lauren didn't hear her end of the conversation.

'I'll come at once,' she said. 'Pack just what you need, and don't forget any medication and the little bundle of papers that were on the list I gave you. We'll be fifteen minutes getting there, but if you feel unsafe leave the house now—go to a neighbour and phone again from there.'

'New tenant?' Lauren asked as Jo came back into the kitchen.

'Jackie Trent, I talked to you about her.'

Lauren nodded and followed Jo, who was hurrying towards the front door.

It was a case of trailing along behind.

Cam trailed, then four of the words Jo had spoken were suddenly clear in his head.

If you feel unsafe, she'd said.

He stopped trailing and hurried ahead, reaching the passenger side as she clambered in behind the wheel, his presence obviously forgotten.

'I'm coming with you,' he said.

'You don't need to,' she replied, her attention on fastening her seat belt. 'You can stay and have a coffee with Lauren and learn more about the house—talk about the men's programme. I'll collect you later.'

'No, I'll come,' Cam told her, fastening his seat belt in turn.

'She's scared,' Jo said, not arguing exactly as she started the engine, put the vehicle into gear and backed out of the drive.

'I won't scare her more,' Cam assured her, not adding that the woman must have reason to be scared and if she did then Jo, also, should be scared. There was no way he was leaving two scared women with no protection.

'She's talked about leaving for the last six months,' Jo told him. What she didn't tell him was that in her heart of hearts she was very pleased to have his support on this rescue mission. 'Apparently he'd always arranged every detail of their lives, but Jackie had seen that as part of his love for her, but then, just last year, he hit her. She was pregnant at the time. She fell, and a few hours later she lost the baby. It wasn't necessarily the fall that caused her to miscarry, it could have happened anyway, but the two things were definitely connected in her mind. She was so upset about it she told me about him hitting her…'

'Did you believe it was the first time?' Cam's barely disguised anger at the thought of a man hitting a woman was so genuine Jo put the memory of Jackie's misery out of mind and found a smile. She was only too aware that there was little to smile about right now, but she was pleased her new employee knew enough about abuse to ask the question. Had he always known or was that why the light had been on in the flat until the wee hours of the morning?

Research?

'It might have been, although while she was in hospital overnight—I did a D and C after it—I met him a couple of times. He straightened everything on the bedside cabinet, ordered her dinner for her, and checked his watch when she went to the bathroom. I realised he was keeping himself under rigid control because I was there, but you could tell he ran her life down to the last detail—a totally controlling man.'

She heard Cam sigh, and saw him shake his head.

'From what I've read,' he said, confirming her guess he'd been studying up on it, 'the first thing to do is persuade the men to accept responsibility for their actions. If they can do that, then they can move on to the next step of learning other ways to resolve problems—other ways to handle anger. The depressing thing from my research seems to be that many will never change, is that right?'

'I think a good percentage do, especially those who have ongoing involvement with a group or a mentor,' Jo replied.

'Even though most men blame the women for their reactions?' Cam said. '"It's her fault—she started it" kind of thing.'

Jo smiled.

'You *have* been reading up on it,' she teased.

'Of course,' he said, sounding slightly put out. 'Wouldn't you have expected me to?'

Jo was pulling into Jackie's street, driving slowly, alert for any parked cars or other vehicles approaching.

'Maybe not quite so soon,' she said. 'This is the house. There's no car here but we won't park in the driveway. That's one of the golden rules of a rescue. Don't make it too easy for someone to block you in. Not that there's any great danger. According to Jackie, her husband's gone to indoor cricket so he shouldn't be home for a couple of hours.'

Jo turned off the engine and although she was sure Jackie was right, she still made sure the interior light was off before she opened the door and slid out. The evening was still and strangely silent, and suddenly she was very glad to have Cam as back-up, right there just a pace behind her as she walked up the path.

Jackie was out the door before Jo reached it, hustling her two children in front of her, both of them wearing pyjamas and backpacks, Jackie towing two suitcases.

Crying.

Cam helped the two boys into the back of the big vehicle, detaching them from their backpacks first. He slid the second one into the middle seat, explaining he'd sit in there with them.

'Mum's crying again,' the older one said.

'She'll be okay,' Cam told him. 'Now, let's introduce ourselves. I'm Cam, and you are?'

'Jared,' the older one replied, then he nudged his brother. 'Tell 'im your name, stupid!'

Cam felt the sigh inside him this time. Okay, so it might be normal childish behaviour but the way the little fellow whispered his name, 'Aaron', Cam had to wonder if the culture of abuse had already been passed from father to son—to the elder son at least.

He'd been helping the kids to keep out of Jo's way as she looked after their mother, but now, before getting into the car with the kids, he glanced around. The two women had disappeared.

Cam lifted the two suitcases they'd left behind into the rear compartment, and had shut the tailgate when they reappeared, Jo hustling Jackie down the path.

'But he gets so angry if I leave a light on after I leave a room,' Jackie was explaining, and Cam realised for the first time the hold abuse could have on a person. Here was a woman literally fleeing for her life and she'd gone back into the house to turn off a light to avoid the anger of the man she feared.

The man she was fleeing.

Cam held the door for Jackie, acknowledging Jo's introduction before climbing in the back with the kids.

'Cam's come to work with me,' Jo said, adding, 'over the holidays,' just late enough to give Cam a little hope that the job might turn into something more permanent.

Although if he continued to feel physical disturbances whenever he was around her, maybe the couple of months' trial period would be more than enough.

And he hadn't wanted anything permanent anyway.

Had he?

A slight disturbance beside him took his mind off his boss. Aaron's body was shaking, the little boy in tears.

'Sook!' his brother said, but under his breath so his mother didn't hear.

Aware it wasn't his place to chastise the older boy, Cam settled his arm around the little fellow and drew him close.

He'd seen too many children cry, and that quivering little body spiked memories into his heart, hurting it so badly he had to take a deep breath and force his mind back to the present.

What he needed was a diversion.

'Can you swim?' he asked Aaron. 'Do you go to the beach? I'm a surfer and I go there most mornings. Maybe one day, if your mum says its okay, I could take you out on my surfboard.'

'Me too?' Jared demanded, and Cam agreed he could take him as well.

'As long as you're a good boy and look after your little brother.'

He had been going to say 'look after your mum' but remembered just in time something else he'd read the previous evening. According to research children were mostly left alone in domestic abuse situations, unless they tried to protect the person suffering abuse—usually the mother.

'I can swim real well,' Jared told him, while young Aaron snuggled closer, warm against Cam's side, and whispered that he, too, could swim.

Cam's arm tightened around him, the feel of the small body pressed to his warming some of the cold places inside his body.

Inside his heart?

It was always the kids who suffered.

They'd reached the refuge, and Cam was pleased that the 'treat' lot were still out. It would give Lauren time to settle Jackie and the two boys into the vacant room.

'Do we hang around?' he asked Jo, aware now the activity had died down that he was starving. He glanced at his watch—nine o'clock—no wonder.

Jo saw the glance and as her own stomach was grumbling she knew what he was thinking.

'We can go,' she told him. 'In fact, it's best we do. Lauren will settle Jackie in before the others come home.'

She was uncertain what to say next—sure Cam wouldn't have had time to do much shopping and not knowing how much food he could keep in his van. Fortunately he broke the silence.

'Well, it's too late to be cooking dinner,' he told her, 'and I'm fairly short of supplies in the van, so, is there somewhere good we can eat?'

His smile caused what were becoming customary disturbances inside her, and she was about to protest that she'd be fine—after all, he could find himself something to eat—when he spoke again.

'Come on, what's the absolute best place to eat in town?'

'Surf club,' she replied automatically, definitely not thinking things through. Things like eating at the surf club looking out at moonlight on the ocean, with a man to whom she didn't want to be attracted.

'Although it could be closed by now,' she finished, but not quickly enough.

'Closed by now?' Cam echoed. 'It's only nine o'clock!'

He sounded so disbelieving Jo had to smile at him.

'Country hours,' she explained, then to escape, or perhaps to hide the smile that didn't want to go away, she added, 'I'll just let Lauren know we're going.'

She slipped away, relieved to be out of Cam's presence, although she'd been pleased to have it earlier. *And* she was stuck with him for another hour or two, depending on how long it took to order, get served and eat a meal.

Stuck with him and the moon and the ocean…

Perhaps clouds had covered the sky while they'd been inside.

That wish wasn't granted. As she pulled into the car

park she had to acknowledge that it was a near perfect late November evening. The moon—yep, almost full—was shining down on the ocean. The clubhouse, tucked away from southerlies behind the headland, looked north across the bay and out to sea.

Unbelievably beautiful.

Picture-postcard perfect.

Romantic.

How could the sudden advent of one man into her life start her thinking of romance?

Was she so needy? Frustrated? Desperate for love?

Love?

Now, where had that word come from?

CHAPTER FIVE

'NOT much surf,' Cam said, obviously checking out the waves while she was muddling around in her head with moonlight on water and other *most* unsuitable thoughts.

The irony of the situation made her smile. Totally unaware of the effect he was having on her, the man who was confusing her so badly was thinking surf.

She could do surf.

And thinking surf was miles better than thinking romance.

'You should get a southerly swell coming up on the open beach south of the headland over the next few days,' Jo told him, having automatically checked the weather report on the internet before she'd left the surgery.

'You surf yourself?' he asked, touching her on the arm as he asked the question, so she had to stop walking towards the clubhouse and turn to answer him.

'Not any more,' she said, then, before sadness could overwhelm her and spoil the magic of the beautiful evening, she added, 'All the local kids surf almost from the time they can stand up on a surfboard, but it's hardly the most sensible sport for someone with my colouring.'

She'd ducked out of the question a bit too neatly, Cam decided as he followed her into the surf club. She led him not into the downstairs part where all the gear would be kept but up some steps to one side and onto an enclosed veranda where the view was even better than it had been downstairs.

The desire to question her further was almost overwhelming, but even on short acquaintance he was beginning to read her 'keep off' signs and there was definitely one in place right now.

A keep-off sign and a look of sadness on her face. Not unlike the look when she'd walked into the little flat.

Some connection?

He didn't like her looking sad.

Not that he should care, but she *was* his boss.

The restaurant was all but empty, another couple sitting close to the windows on the western side, nodding to Jo who crossed to say hello.

Cam let the young man who'd met them at the door show him to a table on the opposite side of the room, a table that gave a spectacular view out to sea. Jo joined him, explaining the other couple were regular visitors to the Cove, coming for a couple of months each year and having their final dinner for this visit at the club.

'Do you come here often?'

He trotted out the trite pick-up phrase with just enough amusement in his voice for her to hear it for what it was, and smile.

'Excellent conversational opening—a little lacking in originality but full marks for sounding sincere.'

She filled their glasses with water from the carafe on the table before speaking again.

'To answer truthfully, I wish I could but I never seem to have time, or when I do have a free evening, I'm usually too tired to be bothered going out,' she said. 'They do the best calamari if you're a calamari eater. Other places manage to make it taste like stethoscope tube but here it's melt-in-the-mouth-perfect.'

She turned to greet the waiter who'd approached their table, introducing Cam to the young man.

'He won't be here for long,' she added, and just as Cam decided he'd had enough of being introduced as a temporary gap-filler he realised she was talking *to* him, not about him. The person who wouldn't be here long was their waiter.

'He's one of the best surfers the Cove has ever produced,' Jo was saying. 'He's off to join the pro tour at the start of next season.'

'I'm not as good as Nat Williams,' the young man said.

'Nat Williams came from Crystal Cove?' Cam demanded, surprised he didn't know that the current legend of world surfing was a local boy.

'Grew up with Jo here,' the young waiter said. 'Everyone said she could have been just as good, but of course…'

He stopped and blushed so the few adolescent spots on his face turned purple.

Had Jo trodden on his foot to stop his revelations?

What revelations?

'And you're having?' the young man asked, startling Cam into the realisation that he hadn't looked at what was on offer, and he wasn't that fussed about calamari, tender or not.

'Perhaps you could get us our drinks while he looks,' Jo suggested in a patently false kindly voice. 'Who knows how long he'll take to choose now he's actually opened the menu?'

Was she taking a swipe at him to divert him from the earlier revelations? He had no idea, and knew it shouldn't matter but why anyone would stop surfing—short of losing a limb to a shark—he couldn't imagine. In his head he'd still be riding the waves when he was eighty.

Ninety?

He *had* to ask.

'You were as good a surfer as Nat Williams? Did you consider the pro circuit? Were you good enough for that?'

She frowned at him, toyed with her glass of water and finally sighed.

'I might have been,' she said, looking away from him, out to the ocean where at some time she must have been totally at home. 'I won junior titles, a few intermediate ones.'

'And you stopped?'

He couldn't keep the incredulity out of his voice, but instead of responding—well, it wasn't really a question—she diverted him by reminding him he was supposed to be studying the menu.

He ordered the fish of the day, feeling it wouldn't be right to be eating steak in a restaurant right on the beach, and sipped the light beer he'd managed to order earlier. And before he could follow up on her surfing past, she diverted him again.

Intentionally?

He had no idea, but it was some diversion.

'You do realise that now you've told those two little boys you'll take them surfing that you'll have to keep your word?' she said.

'I didn't think you'd have heard that conversation,' he replied, to cover his surprise. 'You and Jackie were talking the whole time. But of course I'll keep my word. Poor kids, stuck in a situation like that. It makes me realise just how lucky I was with my childhood. Are they likely to be at the refuge for long?'

Jo shrugged her shoulders, the little movement drawing his attention to her breasts, which lifted at the same time. His mind went haywire—sending him an image of her in a bikini, riding in on a wave, a slight figure but as shapely as a mermaid on the prow of an old sailing vessel.

'It depends on so much,' she was saying. 'She has the option of staying a month, but usually if a woman is serious about not going back to her husband or partner, the organisation has found other accommodation for her before that.'

She studied him for a moment, then asked, 'Would you like me to run through the process?'

Not particularly.

Not right now.

I'd rather know your surfing history…

Those were his answers of choice but his reasoning—he'd rather talk about her—seemed far too, well, invasive at this stage of their involvement, so he nodded.

He also pushed the new door, which was sliding open and revealing totally unnecessary but vividly imagined images of his bikini-clad boss, firmly closed yet again.

'The first thing Lauren will do with Jackie—after they've settled the kids into bed—is sit down with her to make a list of her—Jackie's—priorities. What does *she* want to do? After safety for herself and the children, what's most important for her?'

Totally focussed now, Cam considered this, then asked, 'Will she know?'

Jo smiled. He wasn't stupid, this big hunk of manhood she'd employed—

Temporarily!

'Not immediately but they work on a plan for now—what's most important now. Whenever a woman talks to us about leaving an abusive relationship we give them all the information we can—about keeping as safe as possible within their home until they make the decision to leave, telling someone else the problem, making sure the children know a neighbour they can go to, that kind of thing. We also give them a list of papers to secure somewhere so they can be grabbed in a hurry—all the documents all governments insist we produce in order to prove we are who we say we are.'

'You mean things like birth certificates?'

Jo nodded.

'And marriage certificates, kids' birth certificates as well, driving licence, bank books or bank account numbers, medical scripts, although we can replace those.'

She paused and looked across the table at Cam. He was so darned good looking she couldn't believe she was sitting here discussing work matters with him.

Well, actually she could. He was so darned good looking she doubted he'd ever discuss anything but work matters with a fairly ordinary-looking female like herself.

A twinge of what could only be regret ran through her, then he smiled—an ordinary, encouraging, I'm listening kind of smile—and something very different in the way of twinges rippled down her spine.

It was followed very quickly by a rush of panic.

Attraction was the last thing she needed in her life right now.

Wasn't it?

She had no idea. Perhaps because she hadn't felt it for so long she hadn't given it much thought. She was reasonably sure she hadn't missed having a man in her life.

Well, not enough to worry about it.

'So she has her papers?' he prompted, and Jo blinked and tried really hard to concentrate on the conversation—tried really hard to ignore twinges and ripples and whatever they might mean.

Jackie's papers—that's what they'd been talking about.

'All of them, I hope. If she has no money she can apply

for a crisis payment. Actually, Lauren will ask *her* how she might go about getting money—letting her take control right from the start.'

How much to explain?

'One of the reasons women find it hard to leave their abusers is that they've become dependent on them, so as well as providing a safe place to live, the refuge staff take whatever steps they can to give the women confidence in managing their own affairs. Staff members provide forms and information and can help but the women have to first work out what they want, think about how it might be achieved and then at least begin to get it organised for themselves.'

'With support,' Cam said.

'With whatever level of support they need, and that varies tremendously,' Jo agreed. 'It's all about helping them take control of their lives and mostly they've lost so much control it's very, very difficult for them.'

'Which would make it easier to go back to someone who did all that stuff for them even though he batters them?'

'Exactly!'

She knew she should have let it go at that, but the familiar frustration was building inside her.

'It is *so* exasperating,' she muttered. 'We—well, not me but the support staff at the refuge—can get them so far along the road to independence then suddenly it all becomes too hard and back they go, assuring us all—and themselves—that he, whoever he is, is really, really sorry and he has promised faithfully never to do it again, etcetera, etcetera.'

Her anger was easy to read, sparking in her eyes, colouring her cheeks—the angry elf again but a very attractive angry elf—differently attractive…

Cam knew he should be thinking about the conversation, but he understood only too well what she was saying. He'd scoured the internet for information on battered women the previous evening and everything he'd heard from Jo fitted into what he'd read.

'There are successes, too, of course,' she was saying, pressing her hands to her cheeks as if she knew they'd grown pink. 'And Jackie could be one. I suspect she's made the move now because of the boys. Jared is going on ten, which is an age where he could intervene between his parents and get hurt, or he could begin to ape his father's behaviour and start verbally, or even physically, abusing Aaron.'

'I kind of gathered the second scenario might be happening—and that was just from a fifteen-minute car ride.'

Fine dark eyebrows rose above the green witch eyes.

'Ah!' she said. 'I did wonder. The good thing is, Lauren will get them sorted. There is absolutely no violence allowed in the refuge—no smacking of kids, no kids hitting or punching each other, no verbal abuse or threatening behaviour full stop.'

Cam kind of heard the reply, but his mind had drifted—well, the new door he'd shut was open again and he was wondering what those eyes would look like fired with an emotion other than anger.

Desire perhaps…

He tried to shut the door—this was *not* the time to be fantasising about his boss. Fantasising about any woman, really. He was heading north along the coast, surfing to clear his head, working because that helped as well, trying to come to terms with the fact that the emotional baggage he'd picked up in his army life—the damage from makeshift bombs, the deaths of innocent bystanders, the broken, lost and orphaned children—would probably stay with him for ever, he just had to learn how to deal with it.

As Jackie had to learn to deal with the myriad annoyances of officialdom—

'The fish for you?'

The surfing waiter had returned, sliding a bowl of steaming calamari in front of Jo, then placing Cam's plate on the table in front of him.

'Enjoy!' the young man said, and he bounced away. Cam could feel the excitement the young surfer was trying to keep under control in his body as he looked forward to a future following his dream.

'Was this always your dream?'

Given the way he'd been thinking, it had been a natural question to ask, but from the way Jo was frowning at him, it must have come out wrong.

'Eating calamari in the surf club?' she queried. 'Well, I do enjoy it but it was hardly a lifelong ambition.'

He had to laugh.

'Being a doctor, coming back to work in your home town, working with your father? Was it always your ambition in the way going on the pro tour has been our waiter's ambition? Was it that ambition that kept you off the pro tour?'

She could lie and say yes, kill the conversation once and for all, but his laugh had been so natural, so heartfelt and open and full of fun, she found it difficult to lie to him.

'Not always.' She was going to make do with that when she realised he wasn't going to be satisfied and would ask more questions. 'Any more than surfing your way along the coast was probably yours. Things happen, people change, dreams are reshaped to fit.'

She put down her fork and looked directly at him, although she knew how dangerous that was. The intensity in his eyes, the quirky lips, a faint scar she'd discovered in his left eyebrow—things that combined to start ripples and flickers and twitches and such churning in her stomach she doubted she'd be able to finish her calamari.

'I don't think this is a bad thing. I'm happy with my reshaped life,' she told him, ignoring all the turmoil going on inside her. 'Very happy!'

That should stop him asking any more personal questions, she told herself as she picked up her fork and stirred the remaining strips of pale, translucent seafood.

Cam clamped his teeth together so the questions he wanted to ask wouldn't escape. What *had* her dream been? What had happened for her to change direction—to reshape her life? Her sister's death? More than that?

It was none of his business.

He was moving on.

Okay, so now he'd suggested the men's programme, he could set it up, but someone else could run it.

He looked out at the ocean, black and mysterious, always moving, changing, reshaping itself and the land it slid onto or crashed against, and all at once he knew he didn't want to move on—didn't want to leave this place—and not entirely because of the good surf.

Or the fact that getting a programme set up and running would be a terrific challenge.

She'd argued, as he guessed she would, over the bill, but he'd insisted on paying, so she'd walked out of the restaurant in front of him, slowing on the steps, allowing him to catch up as she reached the ground.

'Is there a good track up onto the headland?' he asked, thinking a walk would be a pleasant way to end the day.

Actually, thinking he'd like to spend more time in this woman's company, and what better than a walk in the moonlight?

'Yes,' she said, and something in the way she said it—hard, abrupt—stopped him making the suggestion. But before he could decide whether he wanted to argue, she sighed and turned towards the dark shape of the headland.

'Come on, let's do it,' she said. 'I've put it off long enough.'

Cam had no idea what she meant, but he was delighted she would walk with him no matter what her reasoning.

She set a brisk pace, but his strides were so much longer than hers, it made it easy for him to keep up. Low scrubby bushes, wind-bent, leaned across the path, the smell of salt and the moonlight, wrapping them in a secret world. The shushing of the surf onto the beach, occasional cries of night-hunting birds and the ever-present crashing of the waves against the rocks reminded Cam of all the reasons it was good to be alive.

Good to be alive with a pretty woman by his side?

'The problem with loving people is…' the pretty woman announced, in a voice that told him her mood might not have been as upbeat as his. They'd paused about halfway up the track at a fenced lookout that gave a fantastic view along the southern beach and were leaning on the railing.

'The problem,' she repeated, 'is that you have to give yourself in love—bits of yourself—diminishing you and making you vulnerable so that when something happens to the person you love, it leaves a hole in your soul. You have to regrow those bits to make yourself whole again, but I don't know whether you can ever refill that hole in your soul.'

He understood she wasn't really talking to him, more giving voice to her thoughts so she could sort them out. Now she'd been silent so long, leaning on the railing, dark against the light of the ocean's reflected moonlight, he wondered if he should prompt her, or maybe simply walk on and let her catch up.

No, he couldn't do that.

He waited, looking at the beach but always with her silhouette at one side of his view, so he saw the moment when she shrugged off whatever melancholy had gripped her and turned towards him, a sad half-smile lingering on her face.

'I'm sorry—I didn't know that stuff was waiting to come out. Talk about needing a counsellor!'

She shrugged again.

'My sister, my twin, was injured off this headland. It had been our playground all our lives, then suddenly I found I couldn't come here. Even now, I don't want to go on up to the top. I thought I could, after all this time, but I can't. She didn't die at once, brain-injured, though, a paraplegic for the ten years that she lived after the accident.'

'Oh, Jo!'

Her name slipped from his lips as his arms folded her against him—a comforting embrace for a woman who was obviously still lost in her grief. He knew from the talk of the patients he'd seen that she would do anything for anyone, had seen her care and concern for Jackie, but who supported Jo? The patients' questioning of him, and their not-so-subtle innuendoes had told him she didn't have a man in her life.

Had she cut herself off from others because love had hurt so much?

Was her passion for the refuge a substitute for love?

He tightened his hold on her, aware that she was relaxing against him now, although when first he'd held her, her body had been stiff and awkward.

'You do know a load is easier to carry when there's someone to help you with it, don't you?' he murmured against her tangle of hair.

She stirred then looked up at him, her face lit by the bright moon, the slightest of smiles playing around her pink lips.

'And just how much of your load are you sharing?' she asked. 'The load you're trying to drown in the surf?'

Had he mentioned his baggage?

Surely not.

So she'd divined it somehow—guessed he'd carry some unresolved mental trauma from his army experience?

Or she *was* a witch!

He'd never kissed a witch.

The thought startled him so much he dropped his arms, and the moonlit face he'd almost kissed disappeared from view.

Jo eased herself out of his arms, bewildered by her reluctance to move. Surely she hadn't mistaken a comforting hug for something more personal?

Although a glint,or maybe a gleam-in his eyes—just then at the end—had made her think he might—

No way! As *if* he'd been about to kiss her…

He must be feeling so uncomfortable, poor man, and wondering if his boss was some kind of lunatic.

Luna—moon—was it moon-madness that she'd blurted out her pain to him?

Made him feel obliged to give her a hug?

The problem was her memories of Jill had come slinking and creeping back into her mind from the moment she'd seen Cam in the flat—the stranger in amongst the roses. Then the talk of surfing and reshaped dreams at dinner, and to top it all off, Cam's suggestion they walk up the headland.

Jo's first instinct had been to say no, but she'd known she had to do it one day. She loved the headland and for one crazy moment she'd thought it might complete her rebuilding—make her whole again—ready to move on…

'To lose a sibling is bad enough, but a twin… No wonder you felt you'd lost pieces of yourself.'

He'd slid an arm around her shoulders and was guiding her back down the path as if the little interlude—the hug and possibly the almost kiss—had never happened. His voice was deep, and gentle, and understanding, and it made her want to cry, which was stupid as she had finished her crying a long time ago.

'Yes,' she finally agreed, hoping he hadn't heard her sniff or swallow the lump that had lodged in her throat, 'but I'm obviously not as back together as I thought I was. I'm sorry to have dumped all that on you. It just came flooding out.'

'Better out than in,' her companion said, and although the remark was beyond trite, Jo knew in this case it was certainly true. She felt a whole lot better—apart from feeling slightly weepy.

They drove home in silence, but as the security lights came on in the carport and Jo knew he'd see the tears she'd been surreptitiously wiping away on the drive, she apologised once again.

'Think nothing of it,' Cam told her. 'Feel free to vent any time. In fact, I should give you fair warning that one day some of my baggage might come tumbling out. You were right in thinking I had stuff to drown during my surf odyssey.'

To Cam's surprise Jo reached over and touched his arm.

'I'm sure that stuff, or baggage as you call it, is far more valid than mine,' she said softly. 'To have seen young men killed and injured in war—to have to mend their bodies and hopefully help heal their minds—I can't imagine the strength it must have taken.'

Cam covered her small hand with his large one, and felt the fragility of her bones beneath the warm skin.

Bird bones.

'I don't think you can rate the baggage we carry around with us,' he told her. 'I think we all have it and we have to deal with it in our own way, day by day, week by week. Then one day it's not as heavy—at least, that's what I'm expecting-hoping—and as I said, maybe sharing it.'

Could he do that? Share the images that flashed before his eyes? Talk about the horror of his nightmares?

The thought startled him so much he gave her fingers a squeeze and climbed out of the vehicle, anxious now to get away, even if his temporary sanctuary was covered in roses and he'd guessed who had used it originally so he felt even more uneasy about staying in the bower.

But what bothered him most was that he'd *mentioned* his baggage. He hadn't talked to anyone about it—not his parents or any of his sisters, not even, really, his ex-fiancée, who had first labelled the mess in his mind.

Yet here he was warning Jo that he might dump some of it on her.

Not that he could.

Could he?

Headlights probed the sky as a vehicle came up the steep hill. Jo was still standing beside the driver's door, and some instinct to protect, perhaps not her specifically but any smaller, weaker person, made Cam pause as the big car topped the rise and turned towards the house.

A police vehicle, not flashing red and blue lights but its markings made it unmistakeable. Cam felt the sinews tighten in his chest—police, ambulance, fire vehicles, as far as he was concerned, none of them boded good.

Jo watched Mike Fletcher climb out of his big, official vehicle and felt her stomach clench with anxiety. She was vaguely aware that Cam had moved closer to her, and her body's reaction was enough to make her straighten up and stride away from him, crossing the carport to meet Mike.

'Trouble?' she asked, looking at the chunky, handsome

man who'd become a good friend in the two years he'd been at the Cove.

'Richard Trent,' he said, and Jo's clench of anxiety tightened.

'Jackie and the kids?' Jo demanded, and Mike put his hand on her shoulder.

'No, they're fine. Sorry to give you a fright, but Richard called in at the station to report them missing.'

'Tonight? Just now?'

Mike nodded, then introduced himself to Cam, who'd closed in on her again.

Protective?

Jo concentrated on what Mike had come to tell her, about Richard Trent and his reaction in calling the police. Why would Richard have acted so swiftly—indoor cricket would have barely finished and surely calling the police would be a last resort?

'Did he check with any friends or family first?' she asked Mike. 'Phone to see if they'd gone there? Not that they have, of course, they're at the refuge—Lauren would have faxed you.'

Mike shook his head.

'I couldn't believe it when I read the fax and I still find it hard to believe. I mean, Richard's the captain of our indoor cricket team and captain of one of the SES crews—that's probably why he came to me, because he knows me—but Richard violent? Had he attacked her tonight?'

'Abuse isn't always violent, and though he might not have hit her before he left he'd waved his cricket bat at her and warned her he'd be home to deal with her later,' Jo told him. 'Something in his tone or maybe in whatever had transpired to anger him convinced Jackie that he meant it. She was terrified when we collected her.'

Realising that this conversation could more easily take place inside her house, she added, 'Come on in,' including Cam in the offer with a glance his way. She offered drinks that no one wanted and they settled down on the deck—the magical sheen of moonlight on the ocean making talk of violence seem unreal.

'So, if he knows they're in the refuge, why are you here, Mike?'

Cam asked the question and Mike frowned as if he was considering not answering—or maybe wondering what right Cam had to be asking it.

Jo stepped in, explaining Cam was coming to work for her and that he'd been with her when she'd driven Jackie to the refuge.

'Staying here, is he?' Mike asked.

'In the flat,' Jo explained, 'but Cam's right, are you worried about Richard's reaction that you came up here? Was it to warn me he was angry about Jackie's leaving? That I might be a target?'

Mike explained that as he'd never suspected Richard might be violent, he'd had no idea what the upset man might do and had thought it best to talk to Jo about it in person.

'Cam's suggested setting up a programme for men with abuse issues,' she said. 'Something that could be ongoing because, as we all know, physical and mental abuse is like substance abuse, it goes in cycles. So although the offender wants desperately to kick the habit, so to speak, it's nearly impossible without strong, ongoing support.'

Cam didn't expect Mike to greet this plan with overwhelming enthusiasm, but a nod of acceptance or a 'Good idea, mate' might have been appropriate. But maybe because he, Cam, was a stranger in town, Mike had a policeman's natural suspicion of him.

Small towns sure were different from the city…

'If you're a friend of Richard's, maybe you could talk to him about it,' Jo continued.

'Hard to do that if he doesn't admit to being abusive,' Mike replied. 'It'd put me in the position of deciding he's guilty whether he is or not, and that would certainly be offensive to him.'

Cam could see Mike's point.

'You don't want to ruin a friendship by stepping in,' Cam told him. 'The man might need help but he needs his friends to stick by him as well. From what I've read, most of the men attending programmes have been ordered to attend by the courts.'

Jo sighed and nodded at him.

'You're right, but less than fifty per cent of our women ever take their partners to court or even get a domestic violence order against them.'

'I can't see that a programme would work if we're expecting men who don't believe they're abusive to attend voluntarily,' Mike told her.

'But we need to get it started. As well as helping men learn to react in non-violent ways, which I accept is the main reason for such a programme, it's just the kind of thing that could add to our worth as far as the funding bodies are concerned. That could help keep the refuge open,' Jo replied. 'It's exactly the kind of thing that they—the relevant government departments—like to see happening. It would fit into their blueprint for long-term solutions for battered women, and it would show we have an integrated service instead of just a safe place for women to stay on a temporary basis.'

'Could we work it through the women's support group that Lauren runs?' Cam suggested, not liking the desperation in Jo's voice and pleased to be able to add something useful to the conversation. 'What if the women concerned could make their partner's attendance in a programme a condition of their returning to the relationship—would that work?'

'It might,' Jo said, offering a rather tired smile—a tired smile that reminded him that it had already been a long day, with more than enough emotion involved, first of all collecting Jackie, then Jo's unhappiness on the walk up the headland.

'It's not the best time to be discussing this,' Cam said firmly. 'We need to get together, maybe get Tom on board as well, and definitely Lauren, and see how we can make a men's programme work.' He turned to Mike. 'Now, do you think Richard Trent represents a danger to Jo? If so, I'm happy to sleep in my camper in the carport. Any vehicle approaching would wake me with its lights.'

Mike looked put out, as if Cam had undermined his official authority somehow.

'I doubt Richard Trent would take his anger out on Jo,' Mike admitted.

'I'll be fine so go home, both of you,' Jo told them. 'We'll talk again tomorrow. Cam's idea of all of us getting together is a good one. I can organise an afternoon with no appointments later in the week—is Friday all right for you, Mike?'

'This week it's okay—next week is schoolies and chaos. But, yes, if you can get Tom and Lauren, we could have it at the community centre in town and brainstorm some ideas.'

Jo led the two men back through the house to the carport, fully expecting Cam to peel off and go into the flat, but, no, he hung around while Mike said goodbye, hung around as Mike drove off, then, as she was beginning to wonder if he'd ever go inside, he touched her lightly on the shoulder.

'Why don't you sleep in the flat—in the second bedroom—just in case?'

They'd been moving enough for the sensor light to have remained on, so she was able to look up into his face, but she could read nothing there but concern and kindness.

'Just in case this man turns up,' he clarified, then, as if aware she could barely fathom the offer, let alone make a decision, he added, 'Go on! You know it's the safest option. I'll wait here while you get your gear and toothbrush, but don't fuss around—I need to get to bed if I'm going to catch a wave before work in the morning.'

Jo went.

It wasn't as if she hadn't spent time in the flat before, she reminded herself. She'd lived there in the rose garden when her father had still been living in the house—when she had been working with him after Jilly's death.

And an angry Richard Trent was an unknown quantity to all of them, so it made sense to sleep in the flat.

In a bedroom right next door to Fraser Cameron?

The same Fraser Cameron who'd held her in his arms, comforted her, and for a moment made her think he might have kissed her?

The same Fraser Cameron who made her stomach drop when she turned and saw him unexpectedly?

Well, she wouldn't be seeing him unexpectedly, would she? She'd be in one bedroom and he'd be in the other and she could stay in bed until he went for a surf then scurry back home to shower and get ready for work.

It would be okay…

And it was.

Right up until she walked into the flat and saw him in the boxer shorts he obviously wore to bed. Not tight enough to be too revealing, they still clung to a butt that could make any woman swoon, while the bare chest, a toasty brown with a scattering of dark hairs, made her knees go weak.

Attraction shouldn't be so strong so quickly. It must be that she was tired and over-emotional that this man's body was tugging at hers, as if invisible threads—finer than spiders' webs—were tangling them together.

'Hot chocolate?'

She heard the words but the picture they conjured up—licking chocolate off that chest, dipping her tongue into a chocolate-filled navel—made her groan out loud.

'You don't like hot chocolate?'

She dragged her eyes upwards to his face and caught an expression of disbelief.

'I thought everyone liked hot chocolate,' he added, with such a warm, open smile she felt doubly ashamed of her thoughts and could feel blood rushing to her cheeks to make her shame obvious.

'Not tonight,' she managed in a garbled voice, and she fled to the second bedroom, so pleased to escape him she had to open the door she'd shut behind her to call out a goodnight.

After which she shut it firmly once again and collapsed onto the bed.

What was happening to her?

Easy to answer that. She was falling in lust with her employee.

And just where would that get her?

Given that he was the epitome of tall, fairly dark and extremely handsome and could obviously have any woman he wanted and wouldn't look twice at a scrawny redhead, absolutely nowhere, that's where.

Not that she wanted this inexplicable attraction to go anywhere. Love led to loss in her experience and she wasn't ready to lose any more bits of herself.

Love? Where had love come into the equation? She'd been thinking lust—nothing more.

CHAPTER SIX

THE flat was curiously empty when she awoke, feeling surprisingly refreshed, the next morning. Her tenant's bedroom door was open, revealing the rose-covered spread drawn tightly across the bed—army training no doubt—but it was in the kitchen, where she went to get a glass of water, that the surprise awaited her. A plate of fruit, but set out like a smiley face, two cherries for the eyes, a slice of pawpaw for a nose, a curved banana for a mouth. Balls of orange rockmelon curled around the face, while her name was spelled out in carefully cut pieces of watermelon—a riot of colour, taste and nutrition.

Assuming he didn't make himself smiley-face fruit breakfasts every morning, it meant he'd done it especially for her.

Wanting to get in good with her so he could stay on permanently?

Or simply because he was a kind and thoughtful man?

A little pang inside her suggested that she'd like to think it was because he liked her, maybe was a little bit attracted to her, but common sense prevailed and she took the plate through to her house, apparently undisturbed overnight, and ate the fruit as she got ready for work.

Work.

She had to contact the Bennetts to find out if they'd

decided what they wanted to do about a sleep programme for Kaylin, talk to Cam about IVF and Helene, contact Tom and Lauren to see if Friday afternoon suited them for a meeting…

She'd walked onto the deck as she was finishing the fruit and considering the day ahead, and now she sighed, thinking of Cam out there on his board, wishing for the first time in years that she was out there too.

Which reminded her of Cam's promise to young Aaron. She was pretty sure the baby boards on which she and Jill had learnt to surf were in the storeroom downstairs. She'd check on her way down to work. They'd be ideal for the two little boys, though Cam couldn't handle both of them safely on his own. Would Jackie join in surfing lessons?

Now it was a squirmy kind of disturbance in Jo's stomach. No, she wouldn't help. Bad enough having to work with a man to whom her body was attracted, but out of office hours?

At the beach?

No way.

Never!

'Can I help?'

The offer startled her as she was hauling the boards out from behind other cast-off rubbish in the storeroom beneath the deck, sorry she hadn't left the task until after work, because her hands were filthy and she was covered with dust.

Her tenant, standing in the doorway, was also ready for work—but clean.

'Thanks, but I've found what I was looking for,' she told him, not that he appeared the slightest bit interested in her reply, for he was lifting her old board—the last board she'd had specially shaped to her own design before she'd stopped surfing—running his hands over its smooth lines, the delight on his face suggesting he'd just discovered hidden treasure.

'It's a Silver Crowne,' he said, in awed tones. 'I've heard of these boards but never seen one up close. Silver Crowne only made pro boards.'

The slight accusation in the final sentence made Jo stiffen, but she refused to answer him, passing him the small boards instead.

'Mind your clothes, these are still dusty,' she said, 'although most of the dust seems to have transferred itself to me. I thought they might do for the Trent boys.'

Cam grinned at her.

'Wow, great idea. Teaching them to surf is a far better idea than taking them for one ride on my board. You'll help?'

No was the obvious answer, but somehow it failed to come out. Jo made a big deal of dusting off her clothes, then gave up.

'I'll just run upstairs, have a quick shower and change into something clean—tell Kate I'll be down in a few minutes.'

He seemed to accept she wasn't going to reply for he asked, 'Will these boards be safe if we leave them out, or should we lock them back in your storeroom but near the front?'

Jo was halfway out the door when she realised he was still holding the boards—*and* she hadn't thanked him for breakfast.

'We'll leave them just inside and if you could shut the door and close the padlock that would be great. And thank you for the breakfast, it made my morning.'

She looked into the blue eyes she'd been avoiding since he'd appeared in the storeroom and read kindness in them, nothing more, she was sure, yet her heart was skipping around like a wayward wallaby, and some stupid sector of her brain was whispering it might be more than lust.

Which was impossible.

Lust at first sight was possible—she had no doubts about that—but anything else?

She wasn't going to give the alternative 'L' word brain space.

Cam watched her dash away. She'd coloured as she'd thanked him for the breakfast that some fit of hitherto undiscovered whimsy had prompted him to make for her. Had he embarrassed her?

He didn't have a clue. For some reason, all the useful information on how women thought, stuff his brain had collected from his sisters and his ex-fiancée, was no help at all in figuring out this particular woman.

Though why he thought it should when he'd only known her, what—less than two days.

And why it mattered…

He pondered these things as he made his way down the steps to the surgery, deciding in the end that it was because his body was attracted to her that his brain was confused.

Well, it would just have to stay confused, because he wasn't going to act on the attraction. Honour was important in the army and how honourable would he be if he did act on the attraction? How could he have an affair with a woman when he was still getting over his experiences in the war, still getting vivid flashes of injured and dying young men, still hearing echoes of their cries in his ears, and not only when he was asleep?

He knew these flashbacks sent him into a kind of shock, making him withdraw, making him appear all the things Penny had said he was—remote, detached, morose—cutting him off from whatever company he was in.

Could he land some other woman with those mood swings?

Make her suffer as Penny must have to have broken off the engagement?

Best to stay unattached.

Jo heaved a sigh of relief when she saw Kate and one of the nurses in the lunch-room. No need for one-on-one again with Dr Cameron, although Cam wasn't present and, no, she wasn't going to wonder where he was. He could have been delayed with a patient, or gone shopping, surfing, anything.

Avoiding her as she would like to be avoiding him?

Her relief was short-lived.

'Heard you and the new doc in town, our delectable Dr Cam, were dining together at the surf club last night,' Kate said brightly, and too late Jo remembered Kate's brother was the apprentice chef at the club.

Small towns.

'We were eating together—late. It had been a long day.' Jo hoped her repressive tone would stop further conversation, but she'd bargained without Kate's persistence.

'Moonlight on the water, was there?'

'Where? When?' Cam *would* choose that moment to come into the room. Not that he seemed interested in the answer, already delving into the refrigerator to check out the sandwiches on offer today.

'Last night,' Kate told him. 'The view from the surf club. Romantic?'

Cam looked up at her and grinned.

'Now I know what your boss means when she talks about small towns.' He put enough emphasis on the 'your' to make Kate look a little uncomfortable. 'For your information, we'd just completed an errand of mercy, it was late, and we were hungry. It was the surf club or fast food.'

He turned to look at Jo.

'Was the moon out? Can you remember?'

Jo was so pleased he'd diverted the conversation she smiled at him.

'Far too interested in my calamari to notice,' she said, then she turned to Ellie, the nurse who did shifts at the surgery and the hospital, to ask about the babies' sleep programme.

But she was aware that the community interest she'd foretold when she'd taken Cam on board was already rife, and with a small twinge of sadness accepted there'd be no more dinners at the surf club with him.

Or was she being silly?

She could handle talk, especially talk that had no basis in fact.

Although given the instant lust thing going on, there was probably a teeny, tiny basis…

'Are you listening?' Ellie demanded.

'Of course,' Jo told her, hoping her mind could rerun Ellie's explanation for her. 'You need at least four nights. If we could get Amy in over a weekend—starting Friday and running through to Tuesday—it might be easier for Todd to get help with the milking.'

'If you left it until the school holidays—another couple of weeks—there might be a high school kid who'd be happy to have the work.'

Obviously Cam had been following the conversation better than she had, that he'd come up with such a sensible suggestion, although—

'If Kaylin's sleep avoidance is as bad as Amy suggested, another couple of weeks might be too long to wait,' Jo told him.

'What about an in-home arrangement?' Coming from Cam, this second suggestion was so surprising Jo had to ask.

'You've been in the army, not general practice, what would you know about in-home arrangements?'

He gave her a smug smile—but even smug it tickled her sensitive bits.

'Three sisters and at last count eight nieces and nephews. One of my sisters had terrible trouble with her second baby and she got someone to come in.'

He turned to Ellie.

'It sounds as if you're involved in the programme at the hospital. What exactly do you do?'

Ellie straightened in her chair and Jo realised she wasn't the only one in the practice who was feeling the effect of the pheromones that had infiltrated the atmosphere with Cam's arrival.

'We put the mum to bed in a separate room and one nurse stays up with the baby, handling it when it wakes. We don't use controlled crying, but use a coaching technique that we've found successful. It's best with babies who've started solids three times a day, and usually it works in three nights, though we say four in case we need the extra night.'

Jo thought about it then nodded.

'Kaylin's six months old and she's on solids. In fact, although she's still being breastfed, I suggested Amy try her on them when she came in about sleep problems earlier.'

She was still thinking about Kaylin when Cam entered the conversation again.

'If you're doing this programme at the hospital, would you be willing to do it at their home?'

Cam realised he'd gone too far—taken the extra step when it was Jo who should be making decisions about her staff deployment.

He turned to her, hands up in the air.

'Sorry, I shouldn't be making suggestions without consulting you, Jo. You're Ellie's employer, not me, but I get carried away.'

Fortunately Jo wasn't put out, flashing him a cheeky smile before saying, 'I was wondering when you'd remember that, but it's an excellent idea. Ellie, if you'd be happy to do it, I'd be happy to pay you for the four nights—and days so you can sleep. What are your hospital shifts like? Could you fit it in some time soon?'

'Next week,' Ellie told her. 'I'd love to give it a go. I don't have hospital shifts next week because I refuse to work schoolies week. Tom gets contract nurses in, and I'm off duty here as well.'

Cam felt a surge of satisfaction out of all proportion to the small contribution he'd made—a surge that made him think maybe general practice in a smallish town would have a lot of rewards, and in this town he'd have the added attraction of fantastic surf.

If he could persuade Jo to let him stay.

Hmm, maybe not such a good idea, given how aware he was of her. Even sitting in a lunch-room with two other women, his body was conscious of every move Jo made, his mind considering changes in the inflections of her voice. Last night, knowing she was sleeping the other side of a fairly flimsy wall, he'd imagined things an employee should never imagine about his boss, no matter how attractive he found her.

Sleep had eluded him for hours, although that was probably just as well, given the aforementioned flimsy wall. He would have hated to have awakened her with his nightmares.

He tuned back into the conversation in time to hear Jo asking Ellie to phone Amy to make the arrangements, then, as Ellie and Kate left the room, he turned to the woman who'd so disturbed *his* sleep.

'Can you afford to be paying Ellie to do the sleep programme? Will you charge the parents of the baby? Are such things covered by government subsidies?'

She turned towards and smiled—second smile in one lunch-break, not that he was counting.

'Worried I won't be able to afford your salary?' she teased, then the smile slid off her face as she added, 'I'm sure there are government subsidies, if I wanted to research them and then do the paperwork, but I can afford to pay Ellie for her time. If this works, we can find out about possible subsidies for the future, but for now, if we can provide four good nights' sleep for Amy and Todd, I'm happy to cop the cost. If it succeeds, well, it's worth more than money to the Bennetts.'

'Four uninterrupted nights' sleep,' Cam said, wondering if he'd ever reach that blissful pinnacle himself. And thinking of that goal, he was less guarded than he usually was. 'Are there sleep programmes for grown-ups as well as kids?'

She looked startled at first, his boss, then he read such compassion in her eyes he knew if he wasn't very careful, he could easily drown in those green depths.

'I wondered that myself after my sister died,' she said softly, then offered him a third smile, and though it lacked the spark of the earlier smiles, it affected him more deeply than either of the earlier ones had.

She rested her hand on his arm.

'For me, it did get easier in time and I'm sure it will for you. Are they nightmares you suffer? Dreams so vivid and horrific you really don't want to sleep?'

She didn't wait for a reply, simply tightening her fingers on his arm as she added, 'That cliché about time being a great healer isn't just a trite expression—we know that in our work.'

Cam looked down at the small hand, pale against his

tanned skin, and felt an urge to hold it for ever—to let it haul him out of where he'd been and into hope and life and…

Love?

Surely not.

They'd finished seeing patients by five in the afternoon, making Jo remember the time when she'd worked with her father, the pair of them taking turns to have free afternoons, he to sail with Molly, his new-found love, while she had worked with Lauren on plans for the refuge.

'So, surfing lessons for the little boys?' Cam suggested as they left the surgery.

Jo considered protesting but with daylight saving they had three full hours before sunset, and the sun still held enough heat to make the thought of hitting the surf very attractive.

Not that she'd surf, just help the boys as they tried the boards in the water—teach them how to balance on the boards.

'I'll phone the refuge and speak to Jackie,' she told Cam as he strode up the steps beside her. 'The key to the storeroom padlock is—'

'Above the door?' he guessed, and she felt her face heat.

'I know it's stupid—I'll stop doing it. It's just that growing up here, no one locked their doors and if you drove down the road for a bottle of milk, you usually left your keys in the car while you popped into the shop. Small towns were safe places.'

'For everyone?'

She knew exactly what he meant. Violence against women in some form or another had probably been around for ever.

'Probably not, although I wonder if the more hectic pace of life that we lead now and the expectations we put on ourselves might not have made abuse within relationships more prevalent.'

'Who knows? But it would be interesting to find if there's documented history of it anywhere.'

Jo smiled, suddenly seeing a different side of the man who'd come to work for her, a side not unlike a side of herself—the bit that always wanted to know more, to delve deeper.

'I think I'll concentrate on the now—on keeping the refuge open—and leave the history for my retirement.'

His reply was one of his quirky smiles, lighting up his face, easing the strain that lined it in repose.

'I'll change and get the boards,' he told her. 'Say half an hour? Will we need to collect the boys or will someone drive them to the beach?'

'I'll get them—well, we'll get them—silly to take two cars. I can put the boards, your board as well, on the top of my car. I think the southern beach will be the best this afternoon. It will be less crowded and there should be some white wash close to the shore. That's best for beginners.'

Cam's smile widened, but this time it wasn't anything to do with their previous conversation—more to do with his passion for riding the waves.

'Great—I haven't surfed there yet.'

'You're going there to teach the boys,' Jo reminded him, although when she'd seen the smile and heard the passion in his voice she'd felt a pang of longing.

'I'll have to show them, too,' he reminded her, before turning to unlock the storeroom and retrieve the small boards.

How had he inveigled her into this? Jo wondered as she drove Cam and two excited little boys down the track onto the southern beach, then along it on the hard sand near the water, looking for a spot that would be good for the lessons?

'Do I need a permit to drive my van along here?' Cam asked. 'I checked out the beach near the headland, where it's accessible, and saw vehicles driving south, but didn't know if anyone could do it.'

'You need a permit but they're easy to get. You can apply at the local council office.'

She pulled up where a lagoon had formed close to the beach, the surf breaking on a sand bank further out. The little boys tumbled out of the vehicle, their faces white with sunscreen, rash shirts covering their chests, arguing over who got what board the moment Cam lifted them down onto the sand.

'We start on the beach,' Jo told them. 'Board on the sand, then lie on it, rise up to kneel on it, then stand and balance on it. The fin will make it a bit wobbly but not nearly as wobbly as it will seem on the water. Left foot in front, right foot behind unless you're goofy footers—'

Both boys laughed, pointing at each other and calling each other goofy footers while Jo explained the term for surfers who put their right foot forward.

'Now, feet in place, knees bent to keep you balanced, arms held out like this.'

'Here,' Cam said, dropping his board in front of her, 'if you're being Teach, you should show them.'

He was so close—his nose, too, white with cream, his chest, at the moment, modestly covered with a tattered T-shirt, but so big, so male!—she felt a shiver of pure, yes, lust run through her. But could lust be classified as pure?

She stood on his board, demonstrating the stance, thinking that if she'd brought her board she could have used it on the sand and Cam could have surfed—well away from her.

But the image of the water droplets on his chest came vividly back into her head.

Just as well he wasn't surfing…

'This is too easy!' Jared's complaint brought her back to earth.

'Okay, we'll try it in the water, and for this first lesson you probably won't be standing up. We'll be in the shallows, showing you how to catch the wave.'

Jared began to argue, silenced only when Jo pointed out that there was no point learning to stand up on a board if you couldn't paddle to catch the wave in the first place.

She bent to lift Aaron's board, but Cam stopped her.

'Nothing doing,' he said. 'Surfers always carry their own boards, don't they, boys?'

He showed them how to tuck the boards under their arms, holding them about midway to balance them, then, a little boy on either side of him, the tall man headed for the water.

Thankfully still with his broad chest decently covered.

Jo slipped off the long T-shirt she'd pulled on over her bikini, hoping she wasn't wiping off all the sunscreen she'd slathered on her pale body.

She was feeling a squirmy kind of embarrassment at appearing so skimpily dressed in front of a virtual stranger, and an employee at that, but it was far too hot to wear a wetsuit, so her bikini had been her only option.

Exactly as he'd pictured her—the curvy body, and pale, pale skin—Cam's heart skipped a beat then Jared butted him with his surfboard, probably accidentally but definitely bringing Cam's attention back to the surfing lesson.

'I'll hold your board, and Dr Jo will hold Aaron's,' he said. 'When you're actually surfing, you don't stand around on your board, you sit on it, waiting for a wave, legs dangling over the side, then you lie on it to paddle onto the wave, so we'll start sitting then lying down paddling to catch a wave. Once you've done that a few times, you can try standing up, but usually that's in your second lesson.'

Jared, of course, wanted to stand immediately and fell off innumerable times before he agreed that maybe paddling to catch waves was fun as well. Jo's pupil was more wary, perhaps a little scared, but he had plenty of determination, working his little arms furiously through the water as he paddled to put his board into the white wash of the waves.

'Enough lessons for one day,' Jo eventually said to the boys as the sun dipped low enough to throw shadows from the dunes across the beach. She turned to Cam. 'Why don't you catch a few waves while I run the boys back to their mother and have a chat to Lauren about the meeting? I'll drive back and collect you in an hour.'

'You don't have to do that. I can go home and get the van.'

'But you can't drive down the beach without a permit,' she reminded him.

Beyond the lagoon, the surf was so tempting Cam gave in, paddling out through the breakers to the calm beyond them, aware that at this time in his life he was more at peace out here on the ocean than anywhere else in the world. Out here the world was forgotten, his only thought which of the set of waves coming towards him would provide the best ride.

Except that today peace, as he'd come to know it, eluded him. He was studying the sets, as usual, picking out the likely waves, but images of Jo kept intruding so he missed the first wave he'd picked out, no amount of paddling enabling him to catch it.

He caught the next one, paddled back out, but after missing another curling green beauty he gave up, sat on his board, legs dangling, and thought about distractions. His psychology studies had taught him that humans are programmed for flight or fight. Adrenalin would pump into the body to help either option. Instinct told us to look out for danger, to predict it and in so doing work out how to avoid it.

Wouldn't that work with emotions as well as physical situations? He knew the attraction he felt towards Jo represented danger—not physical danger but it put at risk his immediate plan, which was to get his head sorted. And having predicted the danger, shouldn't he avoid it—get away from the woman who was distracting him so much?

For her sake more than his!

Yes, he should flee.

And leave her without a second doctor at the busiest time of her year? Very valiant that would be!

CHAPTER SEVEN

WITH an effort, Cam pushed these thoughts behind the new door, the one now labelled 'Jo', and concentrated on the surf, although his concentration was lost again when she returned, pulling up on the beach. She reached into the back of her vehicle, and took out the classic old surfboard he'd admired earlier.

She was buffeted by the waves as she paddled her way out beyond the breakers, and it was obvious that it had been a while since she'd surfed, but when she came alongside him and he saw the sheer joy lighting her face, he stopped worrying about her. Even if the lad at the surf-club restaurant hadn't mentioned she'd been good, he'd have guessed. It was evident in the way she lay on the board, the effortless way she paddled, and now, as she sat, the long-distance focus in her eyes as she stared out to sea made her experience obvious.

'I'm taking the fifth wave in this set and if you drop in on me I'll probably kill you. It's been thirteen years since I've been on a board, and that's *my* wave!'

She paddled sideways towards it, rising into a crouch as the wave caught the board then standing up but still tilted forward so her body mimicked the curve of the wave as she slashed across its face. She bent into the barrel, flying out the other end, her cry one of delight but of triumph as well.

She rode the board towards the beach, standing upright now, as if she owned the ocean, sliding right onto the sandbank. Then, to Cam's surprise, and just a little dismay, she pushed her board into the lagoon, paddled across it, then picked it up and returned it to her vehicle.

He caught the next wave and rode it well enough, but without a thousandth of the grace and skill he'd just witnessed. Assuming she wanted to go home, he, too, paddled across the lagoon, then tucked his board under his arm and strode up the beach to where she waited, wrapped in a towel, still flushed with the excitement she must have felt as she'd ridden a perfect ten.

'Thirteen years?' he queried as he fastened his board next to the small ones on the racks on top of the car.

He regretted the words almost immediately as the excitement died from her eyes and the flush faded from her cheeks.

'Let's go home,' she said, not the words but the way she said them telling him to keep his questions to himself.

And hadn't he just decided that's what he should do?

Predict and avoid emotional danger, remember. In all fairness he had to stay but he had to build a wall between himself and his boss—invisible but no less strong for that—a wall that would keep his emotions at bay, and if it didn't stop the attraction he felt towards her, well, that was too bad.

He climbed into the car beside her.

She shouldn't have done it! The words hammered in Jo's head.

But for those few minutes she'd felt truly alive again. Was that so wrong?

Of course it was, when Jill was dead.

She closed her eyes against the tears welling in them.

Surely she'd shed enough by now. Bad enough it had taken

a year to draw a pain-free breath, but to still be crying for Jilly?

'You okay?'

Cam's voice reminded her that this was the last person to whom she should be showing weakness. He'd probably had natural empathy before he'd studied psychology, so he'd suss out her misery far more quickly than the average person.

She nodded.

'Always drive the beach with your eyes shut, then?' he asked, and the provoking question angered her enough to chase away her maudlin mood.

'I could drive through the whole town with my eyes closed,' she snapped.

'Snippy, eh?' he teased.

'I won't dignify that with an answer,' she said, aiming for snooty but not quite making it, because once again she found a little bit of herself enjoying a bout of verbal sparring with this man.

'But you did,' he pointed out and she sighed, and smiled, steering the big vehicle carefully up over the dune and onto the road.

She put her foot on the brake and turned towards him.

'You win,' she said, then was sorry she'd turned, for he was smiling at her again, not the quirky smile this time but one in which she could read understanding and, yes, the empathy she'd guessed at.

'Your sister?'

He asked the question—well, said the two words—so quietly, she knew she could ignore them if she wanted to, but deep down she knew it might help to talk about it.

Another sigh.

'You'll hear about it soon enough—someone in town will tell you. Yes, my sister was injured in a surfing accident.

When the waves were big we'd get a friend with a powerful jet ski to tow us out beyond the breakers. Jill was being towed out when the rope broke and she was caught by a wave and flung onto the rocks beneath the headland.'

Jo hesitated then found she needed to tell him more.

'What the town doesn't know is that it was my fault. I was the one who wanted to surf that day, although the tail end of the cyclone further north had produced waves far bigger than Jilly liked to tackle. Surfing was *my* passion—the pro tour my ambition.'

The words died on her lips, fading into the silence that filled the vehicle.

'And you gave up your dream? Because you felt guilty?'

The question shocked Jo so much that at first it didn't make sense, then she realised the track his thoughts had taken.

'But I didn't give up my dream—not in a, well, now-I-can't-be-a-pro-surfer kind of way. All I wanted to do was be with her—there was no time for surfing,' she told him. 'Then, because she was so badly injured, because she spent so long in hospitals and rehab centres, and I spent so much time with her, studying medicine seemed a natural thing to do.'

She stared out to sea, replaying her answer in her head then adding, 'I think,' in such a worried, pathetic voice that Cam couldn't help himself.

He reached out and put his arm around her shoulders, shifting so when he drew her closer her head could rest against his chest.

'Sometimes stuff we have shoved into the deep recesses of our minds needs dredging out,' he said quietly, and felt her head nod against his body. Then his other arm snaked around her, and he held her close, dropping a kiss onto the wet red snarls of hair on the top of her head.

'Salty,' he mused then he sniffed, 'and you smell like the sea. It's a good smell, healthy, you should get your hair ocean wet again before too long.'

He was talking to calm her, to reassure her. There was nothing beyond comfort in the hug he was giving her, and if his body didn't agree with that, then too bad.

The warmth of his body crept into Jo's cold one, right into the frozen places that even hot summer weather had failed to warm since Jilly's death. The inner warmth whispered danger, but it whispered—no, shouted—other things as well. Things like desire…

Far harder to handle, desire, than lust. Lust could be put down as a base animal instinct but desire—well, surely that was about softer feelings.

She pushed away from the warmth, and her thoughts.

'Thanks for the hug,' she said, in as matter-of-fact voice as she could summon up. 'I needed it. I didn't realise just how much emotion would come dredging up—to use your words—on the back of one wave. But that's twice I've dredged stuff up to you—now it's your turn.'

He looked startled, but she wasn't relenting.

'Is it just your memories from the army or more than that you're escaping?'

'Escaping?' he echoed, and she had to laugh.

'Of course you're escaping—surfing your way along the coast. Not that it isn't a good way to escape, but can you do it for ever?'

Cam stared at her.

Okay, he was attracted to her, and there was an element of danger in that attraction, but this—this questioning, that was different, disturbing.

'Probably not,' he admitted, and she laughed again.

'That's not nearly enough,' she insisted, touching him on

the arm, something she had done before—something he enjoyed her doing. 'I can understand there are probably things you can't talk about—things people who haven't experienced being a doctor in a war zone could never imagine—but you must have known you'd come out of the army one day and had maybe not a dream but an idea of what you wanted to do. Just as Jilly's death changed my career path, was it just the army experience that changed yours?'

It isn't her business, one part of him insisted.

She's impertinent for asking, it added.

But deep inside a longing to share just a little of his turmoil was growing stronger and stronger, and as he looked into her eyes and saw the depth of compassion and understanding there, he knew that this was a woman he could tell.

'I came home remote, detached, even morose—or so my ex-fiancée told me. The psychologist I saw—they run us all past one of them from time to time—dismissed PTSD but pointed out I was pretty close to suffering it, with flashbacks and nightmares. He suggested drugs but surfing is my drug of choice, hence the coastal odyssey.'

He blurted out the words then heard their echo in his head and realised how ridiculous they sounded.

He shouldn't have mentioned the morose part!

How pathetic.

Heaven help him.

'I'd have been way beyond morose.'

How had she picked up on the one thing he regretted? he thought, then tuned back in to what Jo was saying.

'Though I can't imagine anyone the description fits less than you. As for remote and detached—well, sometimes those are places we all need to be at times.' She squeezed his arm with her slender fingers, sending an electric arc of desire fizzing through his body.

Talk about inappropriate.

He covered her hand with his, hoping, really, to stop the reaction, but touching her while she was touching him seemed to make it worse—far worse.

'And what about this ex-fiancée? Did she dump you because you were remote?'

The zinging in his body was so extreme it took him a moment to compute Jo's words and when he did, and heard the sympathy behind the question, he had to smile.

'Not really,' he told Jo. 'It was more a mutual thing. We'd grown apart even before I went away. Our lives diverged.'

He was about to add that it wasn't a broken heart he was escaping but the gentle tightening of her hand on his arm was so pleasurable he decided to accept a little extra sympathy.

Pathetic, that's what he was…

'Perhaps we should go home,' he finally managed, then immediately regretted it when her hand slid from beneath his and she started the car.

Squinting against the setting sun, Jo turned the car for home, her heart thudding in her chest as she considered how easy it would be to fall if not in love with this man then certainly into bed with him.

No, surely the surge of sympathy she'd felt when he'd mentioned his ex-fiancée was more than lust?

Attraction, would that do?

She should be asking more about the ex-fiancée—or maybe not. Maybe he'd said all he intended saying…

The silence stretched while her mind tossed questions back and forth—how bad had it been in the army? Was the engagement over or did the ex still love the morose man? Cam morose? Not that she, Jo, had seen.

'Have you been on your own since your father left? No

wild affairs, no men passing through your life, no blighted romance?'

Jo found the questions so unexpected—and hadn't it been her turn to be probing?—that she had to stop the car again.

'And you're asking because?' she asked, while just a little twinge of hope twittered in her heart.

He raised his eyebrows as if her demand had surprised him. Then he smiled and she wished she'd just kept driving.

'I just wondered,' he said, oh, so gently, 'whether you might have been punishing yourself for your sister's accident for way too long—not surfing, which you obviously love—and maybe standing back from any kind of close relationship because she can't have one.'

'I suppose I asked for that,' she admitted ruefully, 'telling the story of my life to a psychologist.'

She shifted so she was leaning back against the door, almost out of touching distance—not wanting to touch, although it was so tempting.

Concentrate on the conversation, she told herself. Maybe get *him* talking.

She didn't want to consider why that seemed important right now, so she didn't.

'Do you do it to yourself?' she asked instead. 'Discuss the pros and cons of your surfing escape inside your head? Is it easier to understand grief and loss and horror if you can rationalise it through stuff you've learned from books?'

He smiled again and she *knew* she shouldn't have stopped the car—should have driven straight home and escaped into the house. The problem was, the more she was with this man, the more she wanted to know of him—*and* be with him.

But for all he made noises about maybe staying longer in Crystal Cove, she knew he'd eventually move on.

'I'm not sure it works, doing it to yourself—well, it hasn't so far for me, although every day things look a little brighter and going on gets a little easier,' he said. And this time it was he who touched—reaching out to rest his hand on her arm as she had rested hers on his.

The brush of his fingers on her skin zapped her nerve endings to life and she found herself shivering—not with cold but with a weird mix of excitement and delight.

She definitely shouldn't have stopped the car.

And, no, she wasn't going to cover his hand with hers, as he'd done earlier. Definitely not, although her hand was moving in that direction.

The jangling tones of her mobile stopped the strangeness going on in the car right then and there. She answered it, and listened, her heart sinking in her chest.

'Do you want us to come over?' she asked.

'It's Jackie's choice,' Lauren told her.

Jo closed the phone, not even bothering with a goodbye, then bumped her forehead gently on the steering-wheel as frustration threatened to overwhelm her.

'Jackie going back to Richard?' Cam asked, his voice deep with concern and understanding.

'Apparently he came to see her when the boys were out with us. He took her for a drive so they could talk. He's just collected all three of them.'

'Surely she'll be safe for a while,' Cam said, and Jo shrugged.

'It's so hard to predict. Yes, I'd say in most cases where a woman goes back, the man does try to control his temper for a while, and in Jackie's case the abuse was more emotional than physical, but Richard's such an unknown quantity, and though Jackie is an intelligent woman, she's lived under his domination for so long now, I wonder if she'll ever be able to break free.'

'Are you *his* doctor?'

Jo looked at Cam, wondering where this was going.

'Richard's? No way. He's one of those men who'd drive three hours down the road rather than trust a woman doctor. He used to see Dad but, then, young men like him rarely see a doctor anyway. He was good at all sports so any injuries he had were mostly sport related. He might see Tom at the hospital now, if he has a strain or sprain.'

She hesitated, wondering why Cam had asked, trying to fathom his thinking.

'Why?' she finally asked.

'I was thinking if he did use the clinic, you could have switched him to me. I couldn't have brought up the subject of abuse, not in any way, but he might be harbouring a grudge against you.'

Jo smiled.

'That's a lovely offer, but I'm a big girl. I can handle my-self.'

He shook his head.

'Not so big,' he said, 'and you of all people should know that no one could handle an angry man with a cricket bat.'

The thought of Jackie returning to that situation filled Jo with fear, although the bat, as far as she knew, had been no more than a threat.

'Best we get home,' she said, sliding the vehicle back into gear.

Richard Trent came at ten. Cam couldn't say for certain he'd known the man would come, but his gut feeling—and his knowledge of men from his time in the army—had made him ultra-cautious, so he was sitting not on his deck but in the darkened living room of the flat, music playing softly as he explored the world of programmes for abusive men on his laptop. The backlight of the screen was sufficient for him to read the information offered by the internet.

The vehicle pulled up, a dual-cab, four-wheel-drive ute, a muscle car. At first Cam thought it might be Mike, maybe returning for a private visit to Jo, but as the man came into range of the sensor lights, Cam realised he didn't know him.

Neither did he know Richard Trent, and Jo hadn't answered about having men—or even a man—in her life, so it could be perfectly innocent, but Cam was already out the door, mooching towards his van, the bundle of clean beach towels he'd prepared earlier tucked under his arm.

'Hi!' he said, all innocence. 'Visiting Jo, are you? I'm Fraser Cameron, her new tenant in the flat. Working for her over the holidays.'

The stranger, his face pink but his lips thinned to a white line of anger, stopped about a yard in front of Cam, glaring at him.

'So you're the bastard, are you? Call you Cam, don't they? Cam this, Cam that, my boys haven't stopped, but let me tell you this, Fraser Cameron, *my* name is Richard Trent and you stay away from my kids. If they want to learn to surf, *I'll* teach them, understand?'

Cam held out his free hand in a 'hey, man' gesture, then actually used the words.

'Hey, man, no worries. It was just that Jo found the old boards in her storeroom and, knowing the boys, she thought they might like to try them.'

'Well, they don't and they won't and you can tell that to *Dr* Harris as well. She, of all people, should know how dangerous it is to surf, seeing what it did to her sister.'

It flicked through Cam's mind that Jo had been right—it had taken all of two days for someone to tell him about her sister.

'And tell her to stay away from my wife while you're at it. My family is none of her business, understand?'

Cam nodded, but his mind was whirring. Richard Trent was wound so tightly he was going to unravel totally before too long. Cam had seen it in young soldiers, particularly among those handling new responsibilities, and he knew it was impossible to predict just how the unravelling would happen. It could be an explosive burst, or a crumble into desperation that could often precipitate worse results than the explosion.

Could he help Richard Trent unwind in some way? Offer something to help the man relax? The fact that Richard hadn't walked away when he'd finished his warning suggested he might be looking for help, if only subconsciously.

'Have you surfed yourself?' Cam asked.

'Everyone in the Cove surfs,' the man growled, edging towards his ute. 'I know the boys'll want to do it some time, but they're better off concentrating on their cricket right now.'

'It's years since I played cricket,' Cam told him, hoping to keep a conversation going long enough for Richard to calm down before he got back behind the wheel of his vehicle. 'Though I did quite well at it when I was at school. Is there a local club? I'm probably not staying on at the Cove—two months' trial run over the holidays—but if I stayed I'd be interested.'

In a game that would keep me out of the surf all summer? Cam's head protested, but he could feel a little of the tension easing out of Richard.

'We're always looking for new members and we've an indoor cricket comp as well.'

He turned to Cam now, leaning against his ute, ready to talk a little more, Cam suspected, but rubbing at his left shoulder at the same time.

'You a leftie?' Cam asked. 'A bowler?'

Richard frowned but his voice as he asked, 'How'd you guess?' was less tight.

'Looks like you've got a bit of tendonitis. We've got an ultrasound machine down at the clinic that sometimes helps, and if you wanted to come in some time, I could use it on that shoulder and maybe do a bit of joint manipulation.'

Cam held his breath. He could feel Richard's suspicion coming in waves off his body, yet his shoulder must be very sore for it to be distracting him in this situation.

Was the injury exacerbating the home situation?

Was he in so much pain he was taking it out on Jackie?'

Wishing he had more practical experience at dealing with domestic violence situations, Cam remained silent, then was delighted when Richard said, a little grudgingly, 'Could I get an appointment tomorrow?'

'Of course—in fact, if it suits you to come in early, we could make it eight-thirty. I don't officially start until nine, so I could spend some time with you.'

Richard nodded as if agreeing, but through sheer bad luck Jo emerged from the house, a bag of rubbish in her hand, apparently heading for the bin but probably carrying it as an excuse as he, Cam, had carried the towels.

'You!' Richard yelled at her, swinging towards Jo, his hands forming fists, although they hung on arms held rigidly to his sides.

'Keep away from my wife and my kids!'

He flung himself into his car.

'I almost wish he'd slammed the car door,' Cam said as the ute backed out into the street and Richard drove away. 'If he could let a little of his tension out in normal ways like slamming a door, I wouldn't be so concerned, but his control is so strong it's killing him.'

'Better him than Jackie and the kids,' Jo murmured, then, ashamed she'd even thought that way, let alone said it, she retracted it. 'No, please let's not have anyone dying.'

She looked at Cam, wondering why he was clutching beach towels against his chest.

'Did you bump into him by accident?'

'Not entirely,' Cam told her with a slow smile. 'Hence the beach towels—I wanted an excuse to come out to the van and now I'm here I'd better put them in. They won't work a second time.'

'He won't come back, surely,' Jo said, but she was still puzzled by whatever had been going on in the carport. 'Did you expect him to come?'

'I thought it was a fifty-fifty chance. Helping his wife get away was one thing, but taking his boys to the surf—that was really undermining his control of his family.'

Jo found herself sighing, something she seemed to be doing far too often these days.

'Did he mention it?'

Cam had slid open the campervan door and was putting the towels in a small cupboard under the back seat.

'Told me if they wanted to surf he'd teach them, and suggested I pass the message on to you.'

'But he was here a while, I heard the voices,' Jo said. 'Longer than delivering a message would have taken. That's why I came out. I thought it might be someone who was lost and you were having trouble with directions.'

'I tried to talk to him,' Cam admitted. 'Actually, he's got a bad shoulder and I'd just suggested he come in first thing in the morning to let me look at it.'

'And I came bumbling out and spoiled it all.'

Cam closed the door of the van and turned towards her.

'I doubt that. I don't know if I was getting through—he

hadn't agreed to see me as a doctor. And for a while there, I was panicking, thinking I might have to join his cricket club and it would take up my surfing time.'

He'd have joined if he'd thought it would help Richard. The thought flashed through Jo's head and although she barely knew this man who'd come to work for her, she knew this guess had been correct. He was that kind of man.

Although…

'But would it work?' she asked. 'Even if he comes in for his shoulder, could you talk about other stuff?'

This time his smile was so warm and teasing Jo knew she should sack him right now—this very minute—and somehow muddle through the holidays on her own, or get a locum, or leave town herself. Anything rather than fall in love with Cam.

Fall in love? Where had that come from? What had happened to simple lust?

Or even complicated lust?

'What if the fact he is in pain was adding to his aggro at home?' the smiling man asked. 'And if we could do something for the pain…'

He left the sentence hanging in the air, but the way he'd said 'we' had touched off the zapping sensation along her nerves again, and she muttered a very hasty goodnight and took her bag of rubbish back into the house.

To Cam's astonishment, Richard Trent did turn up at the clinic the next morning, confirming Cam's guess that his shoulder must be extremely painful.

'Have you had ultrasound treatment before?' Cam asked him.

'A couple of years ago—maybe more. Jo's dad did it.'

The way Richard said Jo's name told Cam the man had

calmed down from the anger he'd been feeling the previous evening, but Cam was also very aware he couldn't venture into any matter beyond this particular appointment.

'Then you'll probably remember that I'll put some gel on your shoulder, then rub the head of the machine across it. What it does is send sound waves into your body. They warm the area, which provides some pain relief, but more importantly they increase blood supply to the muscle or tendon to help healing and reduce swelling. Have you had an ultrasound test—same machine, different use—to pinpoint the exact problem?'

Richard was up on the treatment table by now, and Cam applied gel and moved the head of the machine over the skin of the injured shoulder.

'A while back, down in Port,' Richard admitted. 'The doctor bloke there said there was calcification in the tendons around the rotator cuff and I should have an op.'

'Maybe,' Cam told him, 'although sometimes this together with a little manipulation and massage will break the calcification down. Problem is, this treatment is best if you have it for five to ten minutes, two to three times a day. Most people can't fit three medical appointments into their day, although now you can buy small, battery-operated machines that work with the same sound waves. You could check out the local pharmacy or try the internet, maybe get one you could use at home.'

Cam finished and turned off the machine then massaged the shoulder, not talking now, knowing silence was awkward for some people and they would rush to fill it with talk.

Not Richard Trent! He remained stoically still and silent while Cam massaged his shoulder, then sat up, thanked Cam, pulled on his shirt and was preparing to depart when he hesitated.

Was Richard about to open up to him?

Remember whatever he says you have to be non-judgemental. The message rang loud and clear in Cam's head.

'I shouldn't have got upset about you taking the boys surfing—you were probably only doing what you thought was a good turn.'

Cam nodded. He wanted so desperately to help this man, and the wanting reminded him of why he'd gone further than straight medicine and studied psychology as well.

'It was nothing. I'm sorry it upset you,' he said, testing every word before he said it, afraid he could lose whatever slim connection he might have made with Richard. 'I surf every morning, and love it so much I want everyone to know the joy. I suppose it's like you with cricket. Jo was telling me you played schoolboy cricket for the state.'

'Long time ago,' Richard said. 'BM I call it.'

'BM?'

'Before marriage! Jackie was pregnant, we had to get married, I'm not telling you anything the whole town doesn't know.'

But you're telling me you're bitter about it, very bitter, yet you've obviously been married a long time now and the abuse is only recent—what's changed? Cam's mind was racing. He knew many of the cricketers who played for their state or country were married, many with children, so why would it have stopped Richard's career?

Again speaking carefully, Cam asked, 'Would you have liked to play on? Go further?'

'Wouldn't anyone?' Richard muttered, and this time he did leave, but he left behind a man who'd received a precious gift—a reminder for Cam that this was what he enjoyed—helping people and knowing that in his own small way he *could* help people.

Not that he'd done much for Richard yet, but Cam knew he was no longer rudderless—that his career was back on track, his enthusiasm for practising medicine and psychology alive and well again.

Jo must have passed Richard in the hall, for she arrived in Cam's doorway seconds later.

'Any luck?' she asked.

Cam grinned at her.

'His shoulder *might* be less painful,' he replied, 'and I've a feeling of cautious optimism, though that could well be misplaced.'

He grinned at her, wanting to share the new optimism *he* was feeling, but she couldn't have got the vibe because she frowned, and he had a sudden urge to kiss that little frown line away.

Maybe kiss her lips as well—hold her—but not in a comforting way.

Fortunately—well, probably fortunately—she disappeared from his doorway while he was pondering kisses and hugs, leaving him staring at the space where she had been.

Puzzled and a little uneasy about this sudden urge to kiss his boss in a very inappropriate setting, he used getting a beach permit as an excuse to avoid lunch in the communal room. But was she also avoiding him that she was out at lunchtime too, and on Thursday? She actually phoned him in his consulting room on Friday to remind him of the meeting. 'I'll drive you, save taking two cars,' she suggested.

'No, I'll take the van. If we finish in time I might put my new permit to good use and go down the long beach for a surf.'

The surf had flattened out and she probably knew that,

but she didn't mention it, simply reminding him the meeting was at four at the community centre.

'It's the modern-looking building behind the hospital. There's a meeting room on the left as you walk in,' she explained to him. 'See you there.'

It was fairly stupid as he couldn't avoid her for ever, and he did see her at work, passing in the hall, meeting to discuss a patient at the front desk, but in work mode he could forget how she'd looked on a surfboard, body curved, head held high, eyes aglow, at one with the elemental force of the ocean—in control of the curling green wave.

Almost forget.

He was early for the meeting—army training too strong for him to ever arrive anywhere late. But arriving early had its own reward, for he could see these virtual strangers enter the room, and watch the interaction between them.

Mike was an organiser, arriving with a small briefcase that he opened to reveal a laptop and a sheaf of papers, copies of an agenda, Cam discovered when Mike handed him one.

Lauren, now, was different. One look at her face when Tom walked in was enough to tell Cam she was attracted to his old acquaintance, which made the fact that Tom studiously avoided looking at Lauren even more interesting. Lauren was a beautiful woman, and Tom was a man who collected beautiful women. Had he tried and been rebuffed?

The attraction between them seemed apparent to Cam, a newcomer, looking in from the outside, but one was resisting and one was ignoring—interesting!

'Did you come to try the chairs or are you going to get involved?'

Jo's teasing remark brought him out of his analysis of the vibes in the room and he smiled at the people he was finding so intriguing.

'Thinking of something,' he said, then knew he'd made a mistake. Jo wasn't one to let an opening like that slip away.

'So tell,' she demanded, and Cam had to sort some vague thoughts he'd had while out on his board this morning into sensible order. But not before he'd snapped a 'Yes, boss' and a crisp salute at her, and watched the delicious colour rise in her cheeks.

Business! his head reminded him.

'I think long term we—or you lot—need to get the men's programme up and running, and we can start planning it and working on how best to get men to attend. As far as attendance goes, we can contact people who already run these programmes to see if they've any ideas. But…'

He paused, aware he had their attention.

'While outlining what we're doing to get that up and running *might* impress the people who hold the purse-strings, maybe another project, one we could begin right now, would show we're serious about running an integrated programme against domestic violence in the Cove. For a start, get the local council involved. I've noticed as I've travelled north that many towns have big signs on the highway where the town begins, saying domestic violence isn't tolerated in this town, and a toll-free number to call for help.'

'That's a great idea,' Lauren told him. 'I'll get on to the council.'

'Actually, I can do that. I'll talk to the mayor about it,' Cam offered.

Jo was smiling at him—like a teacher pleased with her pupil?—but she wasn't letting him stop there.

'And?' she prompted.

'We should begin awareness programmes in the high schools—right now. This time of year, the final-year students have gone, but the lower years are still there and teachers are at their wits' end, trying to keep their pupils occupied. I know this because army recruitment officers were always welcomed at the end of term time. We could offer to do a school programme focussing on violence.'

Jo caught on first.

'You're right. We need to get kids, especially adolescents, not only aware of DV but thinking seriously about how they handle anger. What do they see of violence? How do they think about it? How does it make them feel? We could do some role playing of appropriate and inappropriate behaviour, get the kids involved, the older ones in doing role plays and the younger ones making posters.'

'We started working on something like that last year,' Lauren said, looking directly at Tom for the first time, and colouring slightly.

Definitely something there, Cam confirmed to himself.

'Just before schoolies,' Tom offered. 'Then all hell broke loose. We had that low off the coast, gale-force winds and rain, and some of the kids' tents were blown away and both the hospital and the refuge became hostels for wet, stranded teenagers.'

'Better weather forecast for this year,' Mike said, but in such gloomy tones Cam *had* to ask.

'Are they so bad, the schoolies? After all, they're legally adults, most of them. They're over eighteen when they leave school. Surely they don't all run wild?'

'Wait and see,' Jo warned him, green eyes pinning him in place—distracting him. 'Explaining schoolies is impossible, although, as an army man, maybe you can imagine it. Picture a couple of hundred new recruits turned loose for a week, alcohol flowing freely—binge drinking is apparently what you do to prove you're an adult—some drugs, although Mike and his crew are very vigilant and we have a great sniffer dog wandering through the gatherings, and then there are hormonal girls and testosterone-laden youths and all the problems of love and lust.'

Cam rather wished she hadn't mentioned testosterone and lust, but he set that distraction aside to concentrate on what he was learning.

'We have a chill-out zone staffed with volunteers where kids feeling sick or lost or just in need of a hug can go. We have bottled water available all over the place, the council provides entertainment on the esplanade, local and imported bands, most nights, and generally speaking we're really well prepared and organised,' Lauren said, and Cam heard the but hanging at the end of the sentence.

'Anyway, let's tackle schoolies when we have to. For now, can we discuss Cam's idea?' Jo said. 'He's right in thinking we'd be welcomed at the high school. Lauren, have you got time to work with him on a rough outline for a programme? And maybe the two of you could do the first run, then whoever is available could do the other classes. I think having a man and a woman running each session makes it easier to do some simulated violence scenes and maybe if there's time, we could talk about control issues as well—equate it to bullying, which is a big issue in schools these days.'

So, Jo's palming me off onto Lauren, and from the look on Tom's face he's no happier about it than I am, Cam realised.

Than I am?

For crying out loud, what was happening to him?

I'm going soft on my boss, that's what, he admitted to himself, and for some bizarre reason the admission sent a rush of heat through his body.

Jo was watching Cam's face and, no, she wasn't going to think about why her gaze had drifted that way, so she saw his reaction to her suggestion about him working with Lauren.

Puzzled? Yes, puzzlement was there, but also present was something that looked like suspicion. She hadn't deliberately suggested they work together, had she?

Of course not, she'd suggested it because they both had psychology training so were the best suited for the job. Of course, Lauren *was* beautiful, and Jo had felt for a long time that Lauren needed a man in her life. No harm in bumping them together.

No harm at all and the squelchy feeling inside her at that thought actually confirmed it was a good idea. She'd had enough internal disturbances over Fraser Cameron.

'We need get the programme organised first,' Lauren suggested, then she smiled at Cam. 'Your boss ever give you time off? If we're going to put our heads together, it would suit me better during the day. With the cutbacks in funding I'm doing the night shift at the refuge. It's not a late night for me, but after it I'm too drained to do any logical thinking.'

Cam turned to Jo and raised his eyebrows.

'Tell me what time suits you, Lauren, and Cam can fit in,' Jo said. 'I didn't know I'd have help this week so I'm palming patients off to him as they come in. We haven't written any appointments up for him so far, so he wouldn't be breaking any.'

Lauren mentioned a time, and Jo ran very efficiently through all the decisions they'd made and the jobs people had to do, listing Cam as the person to get in touch with people running existing men's programmes and telling Lauren that as the chairman of the co-ordinating domestic violence scheme in the Cove she, Jo, would handle the applications for funding.

'I think,' she added, the little frown that creased her brow—one line only—attracting Cam's attention, 'that we have to rename ourselves. Being just a co-ordinating committee for the refuge has been fine up to now, but I think we need to show the funding bodies that we're serious. We need to show we're being proactive in dealing with domestic violence throughout the community, which is what we'll be doing.'

'How about the Domestic Violence Integrated Response Team?' Mike suggested, showing Cam by his use of key words that he was an old hand at filling out forms for government agencies.

'Not sure about the "Response",' Tom said. 'Jo's right, we've got to go beyond responding to situations if we want to prove our worth.'

'Response and Prevention?' Lauren offered. 'After all, we do a lot of work with women to show them how to stay safe in their relationships.'

'Let's think about it,' Jo said. 'We're on the right track and we've enough to go on with for now. But while we're here, can we get back to schoolies? Mike, have you got enough volunteers for the chill-out zone?'

'We've got the usual lot but can always use more.'

He turned to Cam.

'You going to volunteer, mate?' he asked. 'Up to now, Tom and Jo have shared the call-out duties.'

'Happy to do it,' Cam said. 'I imagine Jo can tell me where to be and when. She's good that way, my boss.'

Jo decided to ignore him, although she'd heard the tease behind the words. Had anyone else heard it? Would it start speculation?

Not that there was anything to speculate on.

And why would that depress her?

'Let's all go to the pub for a bite to eat,' she suggested, thinking a relaxing beer and a little light conversation with her friends might restore her equilibrium.

'You'll have to count me out,' Tom said. 'I've a patient coming in from a farm up in the hills, suspected broken collarbone. He'll be arriving any minute.'

'And I'm on duty at the refuge,' Lauren said, 'much as I'd have loved a relaxing evening with friends.'

Whether Mike was going to join them became a moot point when he answered his mobile.

'Road accident,' he said briefly. 'No injuries but both drivers over the limit.'

He left the room as Tom also stood up and closed the file he'd had in front of him. He was watching Lauren as she, too, stood and Jo could see the concern on Tom's face. He was as worried as she, Jo, was, about Lauren's health. Her friend was driving herself to exhaustion.

'I can do some evenings at the refuge,' Jo offered. 'Now I've got another doctor in the practice, I'm not nearly as busy, and Cam could take any late calls that come in if I'm not available.'

'I can manage,' Lauren said.

'Not for much longer,' Jo told her. 'And I'm telling you that as your doctor as well as your friend.'

Lauren sighed. She waited until Tom had followed Mike out of the room, then said quietly, 'You haven't heard, have you?'

'Heard what?' Jo asked.

'Nat Williams is coming home for Christmas. Bringing his American wife and their two kids—they'll be here for a month.'

Jo was so shocked by Lauren's attitude she forgot a stranger—well, almost stranger—was in the room with them.

'You can't possibly still be carrying a torch for that man,' she fumed. 'Lauren, get over it—it was, what, nearly fifteen years ago?'

'I am *not* carrying a torch for him,' Lauren said. 'His dumping me was the best thing he ever did for me. It's not that, it's the family thing, coming here with his wife…'

She shrugged her too-thin shoulders.

'I can't explain it. You know me—practical Lauren—never one to go for vague feelings but the feeling I have isn't vague and I don't even know if it's to do with Nat. Maybe it's the refuge and the trouble we're in there, or—oh, I don't know, Jo, I hate sounding melodramatic and you know that isn't like me, but I have this terrible sense of impending doom.'

CHAPTER EIGHT

'WELL, on that cheerful note,' Cam said brightly, shattering the tension that had wound around them in the room, 'perhaps you and I, Jo, can adjourn to the pub. Best place to prepare for doom, surely. I'll drink squash and do any night calls. Sure you can't join us, just for a meal?'

He was asking Lauren, who'd regained a little of the colour she'd lost as she'd made her strange confession.

She smiled at him—he was a man who could make women smile, Jo realised—and shook her head.

'Not tonight but I'll take a rain-check,' she told him, then she smiled again and in a softer voice said, 'Thanks, Cam.'

Maybe if she pushed a little, the two of them could get together, Jo decided, ignoring the squelchy feeling, smothering it under an unspoken assertion that this was a noble thing she was doing, finding Lauren such a nice man.

'Impending doom?' Cam queried as Jo packed up her bits of paper, shoving them willy-nilly into a file. Considering her house and what he'd seen of her office, he didn't think she was the willy-nilly type, so…

'Don't tell me *you're* picking up on Lauren's foreboding?' he asked her.

Her head snapped up and she frowned at him.

'Why on earth would you think that?'

He grinned at her.

'The way you're shovelling papers into your file. Everything I've seen of you suggests a person who likes things tidy—meticulous—and that's not meticulous behaviour.'

'Well, thanks!' she snapped, then she muttered, 'Meticulous behaviour indeed,' under her breath.

'Well?' he demanded, when they reached the car park where their vehicles stood side by side.

'Well what?' she was frowning again but this time she seemed genuinely puzzled.

'Are you concerned about impending doom?'

She shook her head, then sighed again.

'I *am* concerned about Lauren,' she admitted. 'I have been for some time. She works too hard and she worries too much. We all feel inadequate from time to time, especially when it comes to the women we help, but Lauren takes it more to heart, somehow.'

'As if it's personal? Did she grow up in an abusive home?'

Jo looked up at him, her eyes, silvery-green tonight, widening in surprise.

'Lauren? No way. Her parents were lovely—still are. They run cattle on a property up in the hills behind the town, a farm that's been in the family for generations.'

She paused, then added, 'And I know that a lot of abuse does go on in rural areas and that most of it goes unnoticed so it's unreported, but I stayed with Lauren often enough when I was a kid to know that her father was the gentlest of men. No, there's no hidden violence in her background.'

Jo was very convinced, and reasonably convincing, but Cam had recognised the signs of extreme tension in Lauren and if her experience of abuse hadn't come from her family, that left…

Some boyfriend in her past?

Not Nat Williams, surely!

Not the golden boy of Australian surfing?

Lauren would have been away from the Cove while she was studying—down in Sydney, he guessed. Maybe something had happened there.

But she'd mentioned Nat Williams's return…

'Are you waiting for some sign that you should open your car door? A green flash in the sky? Three crows on a wire? A pelican flying backwards?'

Jo's gentle tease made him realise he was standing by his van, key in the driver's door, fingers on the key, completely lost in contemplation.

'Would Nat Williams have hit her?'

He hadn't meant to ask. It had been nothing more than a continuation of his thoughts, but he'd spoken it aloud.

Jo's 'Nat?' was so disbelieving he knew he'd guessed wrong, until she followed it with a soft 'Oh!' She shook her head and her eyes looked into his with bewilderment and maybe just a little fear.

'Surely not,' Jo added, horrified, pushing away the possibility, but not far enough.

'Surely I'd have known,' she said, watching Cam's face, desperately seeking some kind of answer there. 'Or Lauren would have told me?'

'Would she?' Cam asked gently.

Jo took a deep, steadying breath.

'Given what I now know about domestic violence, probably not,' she admitted. 'When I first got involved with the refuge, I was astounded at how quiet the women kept it, as if they were to blame for it and so were too ashamed to talk about it.'

'Usually the abuser has convinced them they *are* to blame,' Cam reminded her.

'You're right,' Jo told him, despair killing off any last remnants of the upbeat feeling the positive meeting had produced. 'There's also the issue that if they do tell someone close to them, more often than not the person they tell doesn't believe them. Look at Jackie. I know for a fact that her parents think Richard's a fantastic guy. He played schoolboy cricket for the state and Jackie's father is a cricket fanatic so he loves Richard like a son. If she mentioned to them that he hit her, her parents would immediately wonder what she'd done to deserve it.'

She slumped against her car, and bent her head, drawing circles in the sandy car park with the toe of her sandals.

'Sometimes it seems so hopeless,' she said.

'Never!' Cam said firmly. 'All you need is a hug, then you'll pick yourself up and soldier on. I know enough of you by now to understand you're not a quitter. You're just letting Lauren's sense of doom cloud you at the moment.'

And on that note he proceeded to prise her off the car and enfold her in a warm, hard hug. A super-hug if hugs could have ratings, because his body was so firm and well muscled, so warm, his arms so all-enveloping, and she could rest her cheek against his heart and let all the tension of the day flow out of her.

She could also feel his heartbeat, strong, and regular, as vital as the man himself, and given that it was a very comfortable position she indulged herself and stayed a little longer than she probably should have. After all, she was giving him to Lauren and this might be her last opportunity to enjoy a super-hug.

He shouldn't have done it. Cam knew that immediately. He shouldn't have touched her. He should never touch her because it started his libido shouting about the other things he wanted to do to her, like press his lips against that blue vein at her temple, and kiss her just there at the nape of her neck on the bit of pale skin he saw when her hair was up, and eventually he would slide his lips around her neck, and finish on her tempting pink mouth.

And he'd like to run his hands across her back, feeling the bones beneath the skin of this woman who was getting beneath his own skin. There were other bits of her he'd like to touch and kiss as well, but he definitely wasn't going to think of those now, just give her the comforting friend-and-colleague hug he knew she needed and leave it at that.

But she seemed happy in the hug so he held on, pressing her body against his, feeling her warmth, wondering if it was because she'd had so much anguish in her life with her sister's accident that she was attuned to unhappiness in others. If so, it would make her doubly anxious about Lauren.

He tightened his hold on her but only out of sympathy…

'I think perhaps hugging in the community centre car park isn't the best thing to be doing late on a Friday afternoon, seeing that hospital visitors use it and visiting hours are just finishing.'

She eased out of his arms as she spoke, and looked up at him, her face so delicately flushed, her eyes so intriguingly puzzled—what had just happened? they seemed to ask—he wanted to hug her again.

To be perfectly honest, he wanted to hug her again for other reasons, but best he didn't consider them right now.

'Pub?' he asked.

She nodded, then said, 'Come in my car, I can drop you back at the van later.'

Strewth, but she was a bossy woman!

'Not tonight,' he told her. 'I'm the one drinking squash. The van might rattle a bit but it's very comfortable. Before I bought it, the whole thing had been restored by this chap who had a passion for the old original campervans. He'd even re-upholstered the seats.'

Jo didn't seem convinced, climbing into the van and looking dubiously around her.

'A bench seat?' she queried, when Cam got in beside her.

'That's what all the original vans had,' he assured her, not adding that he'd always thought bench seats far better than single seats in vehicles. He wanted to point out that it had a seat belt for a person to sit in the middle, thinking how nice it would be to drive with Jo pressed up against him, but she'd already buckled herself into place beside the door—a million miles away, or so it seemed.

Not that there was any reason for her to be closer. Intellectually he knew that. Physically—well, as far as he was concerned, she could never sit *too* close.

Never?

Was he thinking—?

'If you turn left as you come out of the gates,' the person he wanted sitting closer to him said, her voice so matter-of-fact he knew she wasn't thinking about closeness, 'we'll go to the middle pub. You've probably noticed it, the two-storey one with the iron lace around the top balcony.'

'And the old swing doors downstairs? I've walked past it and wondered that they'd kept them. Most pubs took them out before I was born, I imagine for security reasons as much as for updating their look.'

He glanced towards her and saw a little smile quirking the corners of her mouth.

'I suspect they weren't original to this particular place, but were brought in at some time when the place was undergoing renovation to give it the old-time look it has. There are steel grilles that are lowered to secure the doorways after hours—

spoils the look altogether—but for all that, it does the best meals of the three pubs.'

He drove down to the esplanade and found a parking spot almost opposite the pub, but when he pulled into it, neither of them moved. *He* was watching the way the waves rolled up the beach, seeking out the surfers on the point break closer to the headland, checking out the waves.

Was Jo also watching them? Thinking of the thrill getting back on a board had given her? Would she—?

'The forecast is good for the morning, tide coming in and a good swell, offshore winds later. I usually go out at about five-thirty, just as dawn is breaking. Want to come?'

She turned towards him but the shadows in the van made it impossible to read her face, and he couldn't guess what he was thinking.

'Stupid, isn't it?' she finally declared. 'I'm sure a psychiatrist would say I'm denying myself the joy of surfing as some kind of punishment for Jill's accident, but at the time, well, all I wanted was to be with her whenever I could, and I got out of the habit of surfing every day.'

'I doubt a *good* psychiatrist would tell you that,' he said carefully. 'Sometimes we humans over-analyse things that happen. We look back and try to find meanings in them because we can't accept that often things just happen—there *is* no meaning. But since you've been back living at the Cove, you've not wanted to surf?'

Cam held his breath as he watched her considering the situation.

If she gave in and started surfing again, would she also give in on relationships, something else he was reasonably sure she'd been denying herself?

Then, with a little shake of her head, she said, 'Actually, I run in the mornings these days. It not only keeps me fit but it gives me time to think about the day ahead and plan what needs to be done.'

She slid out of the van, shut the door with care, and walked around to the rear where she waited until he'd locked the doors and joined her. He took her elbow to walk across the street—surely that level of polite touching was permissible in a boss-employee relationship even if his motivations weren't quite as gentlemanly as the act itself.

Damn it all! What was he thinking? He had to get thoughts of Jo as anything *but* his boss right out of his head. As she never tired of reminding him, he wasn't staying, and even on such short acquaintance he was certain she wasn't a woman who would enjoy a brief, no-strings affair. On top of which, he knew he wasn't ready for a relationship himself, although—

The 'although' brought him up short. It had certainly been hours, perhaps even a full day, since he'd had memory flashes of the carnage in the building where the young soldiers had been, certainly days since he'd replayed in his head some of the conversations he'd had with those who'd survived.

And then there was the satisfaction he'd felt this morning, treating Richard—the return of his confidence in himself as a doctor, as someone who could help another human being through tough times.

Maybe…

They entered through the swing doors and Jo led him through another door into a wood-panelled dining room, complete with crisp white linen tablecloths, small silver vases, each holding a single rose, and old-fashioned glass and silver salt and pepper shakers in a silver cruet.

'They certainly carried through with the olden-days feel for the place,' he said, as they slid into chairs at a table for two in the far corner of the room. It was a quiet corner, away from a family group at a larger table and another table where two couples were laughing as they discussed some mishap that had befallen one of their party.

The menus were in a rack and Jo picked one up but didn't open it, looking at him instead, a serious expression on her face.

'What form does your baggage take?' She frowned and shook her head. 'That sounded wrong, but I know about baggage and how we shut it away in dark corners of our minds, but does yours recur in some way so you realise it isn't really shut away at all?'

He found it hard to believe she could ask the question out of the blue when he'd been thinking about it as they'd crossed the road, but he didn't believe people could read each other's minds, so it had to be coincidence.

You don't have to answer her, his head told him, but the anxiety he could read in her face contradicted that.

'I get flashes of images in my head and hear scraps of conversation,' he admitted. 'I hear young soldiers telling me they can't take any more, or crying as they admit to being scared. The voices are worse than the images, although the images are of brutally injured bodies. They bring out all the usual symptoms—cold sweats, racing heart, minor panic attacks—great stuff for a doctor to be experiencing, although I *can* assure you it never happens when I'm with a patient.'

She reached out and touched his hand where it lay on the open menu.

'I wondered because I had images as well, usually at the most—not exactly inappropriate time but at weird times. I'd be really involved in something that bore no relation to the accident, and suddenly I'd see Jill's body picked up by the wave and flung towards the cliff. And although with the crashing of the waves I'm quite sure I didn't hear her cry out, I used to hear this desperate yell…'

Cam watched her chest rise and he knew she was taking a deep breath.

'You must think I'm crazy, coming out with the question—telling you this stuff—but I wanted to say that although you never forget—it's always with you—in time the images fade and the cries become fainter.' She shrugged her shoulders and he saw that delicate flush that fascinated him rise again in her cheeks. 'It probably won't help you, your own experiences must have been so cataclysmic compared to an injured sister, but I thought I'd say it anyway.'

She moved her hand, but he caught it, and squeezed her fingers, feeling his chest grow tight at the same time.

'I'm glad you said it. Thank you, Jo.'

Her fingers moved in his, returning his clasp, and Cam felt he'd like the moment to last for ever—to just sit and hold Jo's hand in his.

For ever…

CHAPTER NINE

ON SATURDAY the schoolies arrived and Cam, wandering down town after the medical centre had closed at midday, was astounded to see the action. Large cars pulling up to disgorge teenagers, luggage and cartons of beer and spirit mixes. Teenagers everywhere, mostly roving in packs, tents springing up like colourful, exotic fungi in the caravan park, high fences up along the esplanade and a stage erected where the bands would perform.

He found the chill-out zone, already staffed by a young policeman who was handing out wristbands to anyone who wanted them.

'Wristbands?' Cam queried after he'd introduced himself.

'All schoolies must be wearing one to gain entry into the fenced areas. We personalise them, using indelible markers that won't wash off in water. We print their best friend's mobile number in blue and a phone number for their family in red. The red is for emergencies should one of them be hurt, but if the person is just lost or a bit under the weather, we call the friend.'

'Great idea,' Cam said, looking around the fenced area with its chairs and rugs and cushions, the stacked boxes of bottle water, a stack of buckets—for people who were sick?—wet paper towels, dry towels and a locked medicine chest.

'Do the kids use this place?' he asked.

The young policeman nodded.

'Just you wait and see. It's not so busy during the day, usually just kids wanting directions or programmes, but at night the volunteers are flat out. Right now the volunteers are out there, giving out pamphlets that explain what's available at the chill-out zone and a list of phone numbers for emergencies.'

'Very organised,' Cam said, but as the mass of young people continued to expand he began to wonder just what lay ahead of him in the week to come.

He didn't have to wonder long. On duty in the zone that evening, the sun had barely set and the bands were thumping out their beats when two young women came in, their friend, agitated and babbling excitedly but not making any sense, held between them.

'She just got all twitchy and hyper,' one of them explained, while Cam helped the woman onto one of the couches in the zone and bent to examine her.

He couldn't smell alcohol on her breath, but she felt hot to the touch and her pulse was erratic. He loosened her clothing, asking at the same time, 'Has she taken anything?'

One of the girls immediately said no, but the other one looked uncomfortable.

'Here,' he said, handing the uncomfortable one a bottle of water. 'I'll sit her up and you give her sips of water.'

He turned to the second friend.

'You can wet one of those small towels and wipe it over her skin to cool her down, *and*—' he looked directly at her as he emphasised the word '—you can tell me what she took.'

'It was only an E,' the friend replied, hurrying to obey Cam, adding, when she returned, 'She's had them before.

She *brought* them for us so they were hers, not bought here off some stranger.'

As if that made it all right, Cam thought wryly.

'Been dancing a lot?' he asked, and the two girls nodded, while their sick friend began to moan and shake. Cam grabbed a bucket, held it while she was sick, then shoved it under a table, thinking he'd have to find out about disposal later. There were three chemical toilet stalls at the back of the zone but he wasn't sure if they were suitable for handling the bucket's contents.

The patient was obviously feeling better, although still pale and shaky.

'Keep drinking water. You're dehydrated and you're very silly to be taking any kind of drug. You've, all three of you, got such a wonderful life in front of you, you don't want to be risking it with something that could kill you and, believe me, badly cut drugs *can* kill people and you've obviously got hold of some Ecstasy that's been badly cut.'

He left them sitting on the couch, looking more scared than penitent, but scared was good. He delved amongst the well-labelled plastic boxes of supplies. Found what he was looking for, some rehydrating salts in tablet form that dissolved to make a palatable drink.

'You drink this,' he told his patient. 'Then rest here for a while. Your friends might like to go back to the concert and come by later to take you back to where you're staying.'

The young woman looked at her friends, who both leant down to give her a hug.

'We'll stick with you,' they said in unison, one adding, 'It's what we promised each other. Anyway, we can hear the bands okay from here—down there on the beach they're far too loud.'

'That's a job well done,' Cam heard a voice say as he left

the girls together on the couch. 'And I've emptied and cleaned out the bucket for you,' Jo added, smiling at him and pointing to where she'd stacked the disinfected bucket. 'In case you were wondering, you *can* empty them into the toilets. Apparently the chemicals they use can cope with anything.'

She moved into the light and he noticed she was wearing a dress for the first time since they'd met. Well, almost wearing a dress for it was a very skimpy mini, all frills and tiny flowers and so unlike Jo's usual uniform of khaki shorts and tank tops Cam was aware he did a classic double-take.

'You look fantastic!'

The words were out before he'd had time to consider them but she didn't seem to mind, giving him a half-wry smile.

'Not my usual style at all, is it?' she said, but she gave a twirl that suggested she was enjoying the difference. 'Actually, it's my schoolies' gear. Look around at what the young women are wearing. In this dress I fit in, and I can wander through the crowds without attracting too much attention.'

'Yes?' Cam said, his eyebrows rising. 'I would think in that gear you'd get all the attention you can handle and probably more. Why the need to wander? Are you the second sniffer dog?'

Jo grinned at him and he felt a spurt of heat in his veins.

'More or less,' she answered. 'I just mooch around and listen so if anything's going on—like a whisper that you can get dope behind the clubhouse kind of thing—we're prepared. A number of the younger lifesavers do it as well, two young couples and another teenager, mingling with the crowds. The problem isn't the schoolies but the lot they call toolies—men usually, a couple of years out of school—who come back each year, some just to hang around but others who could be predators, on the lookout for girls who've had too much to drink and have lost their caution.'

Revulsion now coiled where heat had been.

'Rape?' Cam asked.

'We had one report last year but the young woman couldn't remember what the man looked like, except that he looked older. She left the enclosed area in front of the stage to walk along the beach with him. It was low tide and he took her in behind rocks near the headland. It was two days before her friends persuaded her to tell someone in the chill-out zone and by then it was too late to do anything apart from helping her over the experience. This year we're being more proactive, being more insistent that the young people look out for their buddy or buddies.'

'And you're walking around as shark bait?' Cam suggested, distinctly uneasy at the thought of Jo out there asking for trouble.

Jo shook her head.

'It's fairly obvious to anyone on the lookout for an easy mark that I'm not eighteen, but it doesn't hurt to have people wandering through the crowd.'

She waltzed away, leaving Cam feeling very disturbed, especially as she'd no sooner left the zone than a couple of young men hit on her. He watched as she laughed and joked with them, then moved on, apparently convincing them she wasn't interested in their company.

Was he concerned about her?

The thought brought a tingling sensation crawling up Jo's spine and she probably smiled too warmly at the two young men who approached her as she left the zone. They didn't seem too unhappy when she refused their invitation to the pub, probably realising she was older than she'd looked as they'd approached her.

But if Cam was concerned about her…

Of course, it was probably just in a boss-employee way, so she should forget the tingles, although…

She mooched through the crowd of teenagers, feeling very old among them, aware it was okay to look the part, but she no longer knew the passwords of acceptance—the speech patterns and 'in' words, even what band was hot and what was not.

Two hours later, feeling fairly confident that all was well this first night of the five the schoolies would be in residence, she returned to the zone to find Cam still there, not tending a patient but sitting chatting to a couple of young men. The words *barrelling* and *shore breaks* told her the conversation was about surfing so she didn't intrude, although when the visitors left he waved her over.

'Have a seat,' he suggested. 'You look as if you've been dancing the night away.'

He passed her a bottle of water, their fingers touching, almost lingering together, as he passed it.

It's not happening, she told herself, denying the signals from her body, sending the moon a dirty look—moon-madness.

'How did you go?' Cam asked as she finished a long draught of water and set the bottle down on the grass.

'I'm far too old to do the mingling thing any more,' she told him. 'For a start, it's as if they speak a foreign language and this habit young people have developed of throwing the word *like* into every sentence makes me want to bang my head against a wall.'

She leant down to pick up the water bottle and had another drink while she settled not her thoughts but her feelings.

Surely if she could sit here and carry on a sensible conversation with Cam, her skin would stop sending messages about how close he was.

'It's not that I'm not used to it but on the whole teenagers who come as patients are on their best behaviour, speaking the language their parents speak, not teenage-speak, while as for noise levels—I mean we're, what, five hundred metres away from the stage and even here the ground seems to shake with the thrum of the deep bass notes. Closer to it, inside the fenced area, I needed ear plugs.'

She was giving herself a metaphorical pat on the back for the sensible conversation when Cam moved, just slightly, but enough for his thigh to rest against hers as they sat together on the couch. Just the touch of a thigh, and sensible was destroyed, her mind considering the ridiculous suggestions her body was making.

A brief affair—surely that would be okay? A fling—that's all it would be. He was moving on, so nothing serious, and wasn't it okay to enjoy physical pleasure just for its own sake?

The worst of it was that, as her thigh positively revelled in the closeness of his, her mind didn't seem to be coming up with any answers. It certainly wasn't pouring cold water on the ideas her body was suggesting.

Or even lukewarm water.

Not a murmur from the common sense on which she prided herself.

She moved her thigh—that was commonsense, wasn't it?

Unfortunately, Cam turned at the same time, and his hand fell onto her knee, a casual gesture, no pressure, but she felt the imprint of his fingers searing like a brand into her skin. A momentary regret that she wasn't in her usual cargo shorts was swamped when his fingers *did* exert pressure, and he nodded towards the gate of the chill-out zone where three young men were trying to control their obviously drunk and loudly obnoxious friend.

'Do we take drunks?' Cam asked, standing up and moving in front of Jo in case the young man lurched towards her.

'Mildly drunk, yes,' Jo told him, moving out of his protective shadow, 'but guys like that we give to Mike and his boys. They let them dry out in one of their cells where they can't do any harm to themselves or others.'

She nodded towards the young policeman, in casual dress but still on duty in the zone. He was on his mobile, obviously calling for a car. Once the call was finished, the policeman herded the young men out of the zone to wait by the road, his grip on the drunk man not particularly gentle but definitely effective.

Cam was about to ask if someone kept an eye on the drunks in the cells when a cry from the beach told him there was more trouble.

'Help, please help!'

A woman's voice, high, hysterical.

Jo moved with him but his longer strides ate up the distance across the sand to where a group of young people huddled around a supine form. One of the young men was on his knees, pressing at the unconscious woman's chest, and although his compressions might not have been copybook, Cam congratulated the boy on his fast action as he explained who he was and knelt to take over.

Within seconds Jo was there as well.

'No pulse yet,' she said, her fingers beneath the young woman's chin. 'I'll count and do the breaths,' she told him, and so they worked together. In between breaths, Jo pressed a button on her mobile then handed it to one of the onlookers.

'That will ring through to the ambulance station. Please

tell them we need them on the beach just north of the band area.'

And with that taken care of with her usual efficiency, she told the youth beside her to take over the counting, breathed three times into their patient's mouth, and this time as she looked up she began to ask questions.

'What happened?'

There was a group shuffle in reply, then one of the young women spoke up.

'We were only paddling on the edge, going in up to our knees.'

'Great timing—dusk and dawn are the very best times to get taken by a shark, but as she's still here, that couldn't have happened, so what did?'

'She just dived under a wave and didn't come up.'

The voice was familiar and now Cam looked up, then back down at their patient.

'You're the girl who was at the zone earlier,' he said to the explainer. 'And this is your friend—the one you were supposed to take back to wherever you're staying.'

The young woman hung her head, but the second friend now stepped forward.

'We *did* go back to our motel,' she protested. 'We even got ready for bed, that's why we're in different clothes, then Jodie...' she indicated her friend on the sand '...said she felt better and what she really wanted was a walk on the beach in the moonlight and we didn't know she'd go diving in like that.'

'Pulse,' Jo said, just as two ambos arrived, a folded stretcher held under the arm of the leader.

The paramedics took over, while Jo put her arms around the two friends, asking them to come back to the zone, telling them they needed a hot drink, but probably, Cam guessed, so they could get details about the patient.

'Is it like this every night?' he asked Jo, when a second wave of volunteers arrived at one in the morning to take over from the early shift.

'Most nights,' Jo told him. 'Although by the end of the five days they're here they're getting pretty tired and not as many go raging on the beach.'

She was outside the zone, leaning against the fence, looking as if she was too tired to even make it to her car. The frilly dress was still wet from where she'd held and comforted the young woman who'd pulled her friend from the water, and it clung to her body, provoking thoughts Cam was far too tired to do anything about.

'Come on, I'll drive you home,' he suggested. He put his arm around her shoulders and tucked her close. 'I was here quite early so I found a parking spot right behind the zone. Don't argue. I can run you back down in the morning to get your car, or in the afternoon, or whenever you like.'

Jo melted against him.

He was so solid, so comforting that for a fleeting moment she wondered how it would feel to let go of all the burdens she carried—let Cam carry them. No, that wouldn't be fair as he had burdens of his own—but maybe let him share them.

As if he'd want them.

Want her.

He walked her to the van, unlocked the passenger door, opened it for her then, to her surprise, lifted her as easily as she could lift a child, and deposited her on the seat. She was still getting over her sheer astonishment at this behaviour when he leaned in to do up her seat belt—somehow she was sitting in the middle of the bench—and with that task completed, he dropped a quick kiss on her lips.

Aren't we even going to talk about this? she wondered. He's just going to put me where he wants me, kiss me on the lips and…

And what?

What did it mean?

It wasn't as if it had been a passionate kiss. In fact, if anything, it had been a casual peck, nothing more, which still didn't explain his easing her into the middle seat.

Where her thigh was again, now he was behind the wheel, pressed to his.

It took the drive home—not a long drive but long enough—for her to get this far in her thought processes, but when he stopped, not in the carport but just off the road above the drive where they could look out over the town and the moonstruck ocean, she finally regained enough equilibrium to speak.

'And what was that about?' she asked. Unfortunately, by now he'd looped his arm around her shoulder and drawn her right up against her body.

'What was what about?'

Oh, he was smooth, this man—rich, dark-chocolate images tumbled through her head.

'That kiss!' she muttered crossly, furious with herself for letting him…not exactly manipulate her but make her think things she hadn't ever thought before.

He turned her towards him.

'*That* wasn't a kiss,' he said, and she could hear the smile in his voice, although she was desperately trying to look out to sea—to look anywhere rather than at his face—

'*This* is a kiss.'

His mouth closed on hers, his lips moulding themselves to hers. There was strength in his lips, or maybe not strength but sureness, as if they knew exactly how to kiss her to draw out the response they wanted.

Not that lips could make decisions. This fuzzy thought flitted by as Jo found herself losing any vestige of control she might have had over the kissing situation. Her lips were kissing him back. They were pressing so hard against his she could feel his teeth, and now his tongue traced the outline of her mouth, a subtle manoeuvre that she soon realised was a prelude to invasion.

Warm and sweet! Cam knew she'd taste like this and he revelled in it, thinking nectar, bees—no bees were wrong. The buzzing was in his head—maybe in his body—definitely in his blood…

He deepened the kiss, letting his lips speak without words, drawing a response that added to his excitement because it told him she wanted this as much as he did.

Inexplicable attraction but lack of explanation made it no less real.

Thrumming now, his blood, taking up the beat of the music they'd heard earlier, slow and heavy, his body all but erupting into flames with his need for her.

'We can't do this.'

The whispered words lacked so much conviction he had to laugh.

'No?' he whispered back, his hand finding her breast beneath the frilly dress, cupping it, thumb and forefinger teasing at her nipple.

'No,' she answered, and gave lie to the answer by pressing closer to him, so he could feel the reverberations from the kiss quivering in her body, her nipples pebbling beneath his questing fingers.

Her reactions heightened his need and he shifted in his seat, common sense dictating they go inside to finish off what they—or he—had started, but in moving he might lose her. Besides, he wasn't done with kissing yet, particularly as he'd discovered that kissing Jo banished all the darkness from inside his head, leaving it clear and light and filled with…

Joy?

He didn't know that he'd ever been exactly filled with joy, so perhaps it *was* joy, he just didn't recognise it.

His roaming hand dropped to her waist, feeling the indentation of it, firm muscle beneath the skin on her belly—she was fit, this pint-sized boss of his, but now he wanted to see her naked. Pictured her, firm, and pale, and beautiful.

Her hands were on his face, cupping it, easing it away—easing their lips apart.

'It's not that I'm against kissing in the front seat of a campervan,' she murmured, her voice just breathless enough to tweak Cam's excitement higher, 'but we're out in public—almost—and doctors are supposed to be held in some esteem, particularly in small towns.'

He could see her face in the moonlight, see the scattering of freckles across her nose and cheeks, see lips puffy with his kisses and in her cheeks the rosiness of—what?

Embarrassment?

Desire?

He had no idea, and the realisation that he barely knew this woman struck him with the force of a hammer blow.

How could he be so attracted to a woman he barely knew?

Physical attraction was one thing, but he didn't rush into relationships no matter how strong the pull.

Particularly with vulnerable women, and if there was one thing he *did* know about Jo, it was that she was vulnerable. She had that hole in her soul she'd talked about.

Though wouldn't love fill a hole in someone's soul?

His thoughts jerked to a standstill as abruptly as a car stopping when the brakes were slammed hard.

Love?

Where had that come from?

'Cam?'

Jo's voice was tentative, no, *more* than tentative, for he heard a distinct quiver in it.

'Are we okay?' she added. 'Can we put this down as some kind of minor aberration? Can we go on as we've been going?'

He wanted to give her a hug then decided why not? And he gathered her into his arms and hugged hard.

'Of course we're okay,' he assured her, and felt like Superman when her body lost its tension. 'But I'm not so sure about the minor aberration part. We're attracted to each other. We're both adults. Would taking that attraction further be so wrong?'

Well, yes, probably, his common sense told him, given you're not exactly cured…

'You're not staying,' she reminded him, the words muffled by his shirt as she whispered them against his chest. 'So all it could ever be is a brief affair, and…'

'And?' he prompted, although somewhere deep inside he'd have liked to suggest that he *could* stay on—that he *could* be okay again.

That he'd *like* to stay on!

But should he even be thinking about long-term commitment?

With his mind the way it was…

'And I'd be left behind with the small-town talk, the gossip, the—'

He forgot about his own reasons for not committing and concentrated on her view of things. Got the picture immediately, even finished the sentence for her.

'Whispers and sly looks and snide smiles.'

He reached beneath her chin and tilted her head up so he could look into her eyes.

'I'm sorry, I didn't think,' he said, then he dropped a very quick kiss on her lips. Very quick because anything longer would have led not forward but back to where they'd been. 'I won't do that to you, Jo.'

Well, you brought that on yourself, Jo thought bitterly as she pushed out of the warm security of Cam's arms, eased herself across the seat—when had she, or he, undone her seat belt?—and opened the door.

'I'll walk home,' she said. 'It's only a hundred yards.'

She set off, then heard him start the rattly engine of the van, and saw the lights, dimmed, as he pulled onto the road, driving slowly enough to follow her, a careful, caring man, Fraser Cameron, just not for her.

CHAPTER TEN

AGAINST all expectations, Jo had slept soundly, waking mid-morning to a sunshine-filled day. She made herself a coffee and wandered out onto the deck, her hands cupped around the hot drink, sipping at it, waiting for the caffeine to kick in and wake her fully.

'Morning, neighbour!'

The words startled her, but it was Cam's voice that caused the sudden lurch in her stomach.

'I thought you'd be out surfing,' she grumbled, cranky at being caught in her favourite sleep attire, an ancient T-shirt of her father's worn so thin it was soft and cool and comfortable. Cranky too at the way her body had reacted to his voice, and crankiest of all that he was there, interrupting her morning commune with nature.

'Been there and done that,' he said, so bright and cheerful she wanted to hurl her cup at him—except that it was still near-full and she needed the caffeine.

'Do you always wake up so disgustingly cheerful?' she demanded instead, slumping down into one of the low-slung canvas chairs and glaring at him across the gap between the decks.

'I've been up for hours,' he told her. 'Had a surf and a run on the beach then picked up some freshly baked pastries for breakfast. Want to share?'

He opened the paper bag he'd been holding in his hand and the scent of sweet pastries wafted across from one deck to the next. Now it was Jo's stomach talking to her, telling her how empty it was and how much it would appreciate a pastry.

Too bad! The one thing she'd decided on the short walk home the previous evening was that she should limit opportunities—outside work—for her and Cam to be together and so limit any chance of giving in to temptation as far as touching or kissing was concerned.

Though the kiss had been—spectacular!

'I'll bring them over,' he was saying, completely undaunted by the fact she hadn't answered. 'I'd say come over, but you've got better coffee. I can only do instant and I can smell yours from here.'

He's only coming for the coffee, Jo told herself, and felt a spurt of totally unnecessary disappointment, but out loud she said, very ungraciously, 'Oh, okay, come over. Let yourself in, I'll get changed.'

She hurried into her bedroom and pulled on some clothes—regular clothes, cargo pants and singlet top—pushed her fingers through her hair and clipped it up, washed her face and slathered on some moisturiser, debated lippy and told herself to get over it, then came out of the bedroom straight into the path of a frowning neighbour.

'Can I assume you've been out your front door since you got up? To get the paper, perhaps?'

Her turn to frown.

'I don't get a paper delivered,' she said, mystified by his attitude.

'Put out the cat? Let the cat in?' he persisted.

She threw up her hands in a helpless gesture.

'Have you seen a cat around here? What on earth are you on about?'

'Your front door—it was unlocked.'

He was standing so close she could feel the angry vibes he was giving off—other vibes as well, unfortunately. She stepped back but hit the wall and couldn't finish a decent retreat. Only one thing to do, stand up to him.

'So?'

His anger dissolved as quickly as it had appeared and he shook his head at her.

'Jo, I know you grew up here and to you it is still a small seaside town, little more than a big village, but times have changed. The drug culture changed not only the users but the way we all have to live. An addict in need of a fix will not hesitate to break into his own family's home to steal something to sell, and while you might not have desperate addicts here normally, right now you've got hundreds of strangers in town. You *need* to lock your doors.'

'I know, I know,' she muttered. 'I didn't need the lecture.'

She didn't add that these days she was careful about locking up, she'd just forgotten last night because she didn't want him assuming she'd forgotten because of confusion over his kiss.

Which was why she *had* forgotten, of course, she just wasn't going to admit it.

'Let's eat those pastries,' she said. 'I'll bring coffee onto the deck.'

She'd thought he'd go on out there but, no, he followed her into the kitchen, and began opening cupboard doors, obviously in search of a plate for his offerings, but opening cupboard doors?

Wasn't that intrusive?

Jo knew it was—it was taking liberties. He was a stranger

still and opening cupboard doors in her house was very intrusive.

So why did she feel a surge of pleasure—real pleasure—as if sharing her kitchen with someone was special, and comfortable, and very, very—well, nice?

She muddled her way through producing two cups of coffee, knowing now just how he liked his as she'd watched him make his own with the same machine down at the surgery.

'Tray?' he asked, and she pointed to the refrigerator, where a gap between the fridge and the wall provided a space big enough to take three bright, plastic trays.

He pulled out all three, studying them in turn, finally settling on one that had frangipani flowers all over it. He put the plate of pastries on it, two small plates, two knives—she'd missed him pulling out drawers to get the knives—then the two cups of coffee.

Jo grabbed a couple of paper napkins with the same bright design as the tray, and dropped them on it as he lifted it from the bench. They were close, so it was inevitable their eyes should meet—meet and hold, silently communicating memories of the kiss.

Desire, hot and strong, shimmied through her body.

She turned away, not wanting him to see the signs, read the desire in her face. Determinedly thrusting the reaction aside, she led him out onto the deck, setting the small table down between two chairs in the shade as the sun was heating up.

I don't want to be doing this—

She should say it, not think it.

But saying it, she'd be lying because a lot of her was filled with pleasure over something as simple as sharing Sunday breakfast with this man.

Unfortunately the bit that wasn't filled with pleasure was

shouting warnings at her, warnings only partially soothed by the pleased part telling her he was just a colleague and a neighbour and there was nothing in it.

'It's a very special place, isn't it?' he said, interrupting her internal argument.

She smiled as she agreed.

'Very special!'

She bit into a pastry and tasted the soft creamy cheese and sticky apricot in the filling, and let out a sigh of bliss.

'So is this pastry,' she told him. 'Thank you.'

Aware it sounded far too formal, especially given the heat they'd shared in the early hours of the morning, she fumbled around for some nice neutral conversation.

'Where was home for you?'

After that it was easy, Cam talked of his family, growing up in the southern suburbs of Sydney with his three sisters.

Three sisters explained a lot, Jo thought as Cam was telling her of the games they'd played as children, the camping holidays they'd had. It explained the protective attitude she'd noticed from time to time, and the instinctive rapport he seemed to have with the women at the surgery.

'And speaking of children,' he said, after he'd listed off his nieces and nephews, 'is there a particular O and G specialist you use in Port? Mrs Youngman is coming in tomorrow and I want to refer her to someone for a full examination before she goes too far with her plans for IVF.'

So the conversation slipped into work matters and although the doctor in Jo answered quite sensibly, she hoped, the woman felt again that uneasiness in her belly. It was as if her body, against all rationality, wanted to put itself to the use for which it was designed.

Nonsense, that's all it was.

'Have you talked to Helene about the chances of conception?' she asked, to divert herself from whatever was going on inside her.

'I have,' Cam said. 'Not that I needed to. When I phoned her she knew as much as I did if not more. She'd looked up everything she could find on the internet, and although she knows the odds of conception aren't great, she's still keen.'

'I wonder why?' Jo mused, and Cam straightened in his chair.

'Does there have to be a tangible reason?' he asked. 'Couldn't it be something as simple as a strong desire to have another child? We all have two sides to us and hear two voices, one of reason and one of passion, isn't that true? And couldn't it be passion talking to her?'

Could it?

Jo answered his question with one of her own.

'Passion for someone, or passion to have a child?'

He shrugged and smiled.

'I'm a doctor, so that's not for me to know, but in general do you agree that we have the two voices?'

His eyes scanned her face and she knew he was looking for a reaction. Knew also that the conversation had shifted from Helene Youngman to something far more personal.

Something she didn't want to think about!

'I'm not sure about the passion,' she told him, shifting so she could look out to sea instead of into those probing eyes. 'Emotion certainly, but passion, I'm not so sure.'

'Of course it's passion,' he argued, touching her arm so she had to turn back and face him. 'It might be reason telling you—'

Damn it all, he's going to talk about attraction again. Her mind panicked while her body warmed, but it cooled again when he finished the sentence.

'To keep the refuge open, but it's passion that keeps you working so determinedly for it, isn't that so?'

She stared blankly at him for a moment, still lost on the path she'd thought the conversation would take.

Cam wondered what on earth had prompted him to talk of passion. He'd got a nice medical colleague-to-colleague conversation going and then blown it by bringing emotion into it—passion, in fact.

And the word had re-awoken all the physical symptoms he'd been trying to keep at bay since he'd seen Jo appear on her deck that morning, the sun shining through the fine material of her night shirt, outlining her curves in a golden glow.

He reminded himself of all the cons he'd come up with in his pros-and-cons argument when he'd got inside the flat last night—a brief affair would damage her reputation, maybe even hurt her if her feelings were engaged. And from his side, what did he have to offer? A man whose mind was cluttered with horror he was still having trouble getting over? A man who might never get back to whatever might pass for normal in this modern world?

Although wasn't that changing?

Hadn't he felt the shift?

'I suppose you could call it passion.'

The admission, spoken as if the words were being forced out against her will, caught Cam by surprise so at first he thought she was talking about their attraction—the question he'd asked forgotten as he'd followed his own twisted thoughts.

'The refuge,' she added, in a falsely patient tone, picking up on his confusion.

'Ah, yes, the refuge,' he said, but he had to smile because he suspected her thoughts had flitted to other aspects of passion, so once again they were at a crossroads of some kind.

'I'm having another cup of coffee. You?'

Was she escaping him?

He suspected she was, but now reason was back in control. It was stupid to even consider having an affair with this woman. Maybe in a year he could drift back this way. Maybe in a year he'd have come to terms with the past and be ready to look to the future—he could apply again for a position in Crystal Cove and she might even take him on…

If she hadn't married someone else in the meantime.

Now, where had that thought come from?

And why did it make his gut knot?

'Coffee,' she said again, returning to set down the two cups.

'Have you spoken to the employment agency?' he asked, stirred up now, thinking maybe moving on wasn't such a good idea. 'About getting a woman for the job?'

She shook her head, something he loved watching her do as it always dislodged more tendrils of hair. They coiled down her neck and sprayed out from her temples.

'I haven't given it much thought. Most people who want to work over Christmas are settled into their jobs by now and won't be looking to move so I thought I'd leave it until the new year.'

He wanted to say, Keep me, but doubts tumbled in his head. He knew now he could commit to the job, but if he stayed, given the way he felt about Jo, could he commit to something else?

Like marriage?

He stood up, holding his fresh cup of coffee, and walked to the railing.

What could he offer in a marriage?

Jo had all this and he had, what?

Money in the bank for sure—overseas postings paid well—

a fair amount of superannuation, a refurbished van and, yes, damn it all, still some baggage in his head.

That was what he *couldn't* offer her.

Jo had talked about the bits of self she'd lost to love—love for her sister, her twin. His bits of self had been lost to hate—for wasn't that what war was all about?

She admitted it had taken her years to become whole again—how long would it take him?

The jangling summons of the phone somewhere inside her house broke into his thoughts, and he knew from the moment she reappeared in the doorway to the deck, white faced and anxious, that it was bad news.

'We have to go,' she said. 'An incident on the headland—Richard and Jackie Trent are up there and Richard is insisting on seeing you.'

She offered a rather fearful smile.

'So you must have got through to him the other day!'

Cam crossed the deck in three strides.

'I'm happy to go but you don't have to come, Jo,' he said. 'I know what memories the headland will throw up at you. You can wait here. Mike will keep you posted.'

'And leave Jackie and the boys without support? Leave you up there without…?'

Without what?

What could she offer Cam?

'Support,' she finished, but she knew it was a feeble imitation of what she'd like to offer him.

Which was?

Her mind was whirling.

Surely she wasn't thinking love?

Of course she was.

She was leading the way out of the house, was right inside

the front door, in fact, when he stopped her with a touch on her shoulder and pulled her into his arms, hugging her tightly.

'Remember,' he whispered into her hair, 'that sometimes things just happen, without reason and without anyone being accountable. Sometimes we dig around for reasons when there aren't any.'

Cam tilted her head up so he could look into her eyes.

'You might also want to remember that I think I'm falling in love with you—maybe already fallen. Although I didn't know it until right this minute, and I admit I'm not that good a catch, that I have problems, I want you to know that I'll keep working on them. And one more thing, I am *not* moving on!'

She stared at him in disbelief but warm colour was back in her cheeks and he could feel her body straightening, her resolve stiffening, and now he knew for certain—it *was* love. For who could not love a woman who faced life with such courage—a woman about to return to the place where her sister had been so badly injured in order to help someone else?

CHAPTER ELEVEN

SURFING needed different muscles from running so the race up the path to the top of the headland had Cam puffing and panting. He only kept up with Jo because his strides were longer.

They'd parked in a cluster of police and rescue vehicles in the car park near the clubhouse. The area had been cleared of people, curious onlookers held at bay by police and volunteer rescue personnel. More police would already be on the headland, but what else would they find?

Mike came towards them as they reached the top, both of them breathing deeply to replenish the oxygen they'd used on the run.

'What's happening?' Cam asked.

'Jackie and Richard and the kids came up for a walk—Richard's suggestion—to have breakfast and go up the headland.'

Cam nodded. Jo had talked about her family doing it regularly on a Sunday morning.

'They get to the top and Richard climbs over the barrier.' Mike's voice was strained and Cam remembered he and Richard were friends.

Jo reached out and put her hand on Mike's arm.

'Someone else can tell us,' she said gently, but Mike shook his head.

'No, I'm the one who's been talking to him. He says he's no good to anyone and might as well end it now.'

Cam was thinking clearly—putting all he knew of precarious mental states to use—concentrating on Richard.

'Something happened to him,' he said to Mike. 'A year or so ago—that's when the abuse apparently started—would you know of any change in his circumstances?'

Jo was muttering to herself about the selfishness of suicides, but Cam ignored her, aware Mike was trying to think.

The policeman shook his head.

'He did have a mate—no, that couldn't be it.'

'A mate who died?' Cam guessed, but Mike shook his head.

'I know his mother died, but that was earlier. His good friend from under-nineteen cricket made the Aussie Ashes side last summer but…'

And took the place Richard might have thought was his? Cam wondered. It wasn't much to go on, but maybe it was something.

'Where are Jackie and the boys?' Jo asked, and Mike pointed to the fence, where Richard was clearly visible on the cliff-side while Jackie and the two children huddled against the safe side of the fence.

'That's your job, Jo,' Cam said. 'While I'm talking to him, see if you can ease them back, away from the fence.'

'So if something happens they won't see it?' she whispered, and he knew she was so stressed with memories and her fear for the family he wanted to hug her yet again.

He made do with a smile and hoped she'd read the hug in it.

'With me there chatting to him? Have faith, woman! I just don't want any distractions for him.'

Jo felt the smile go right through her, the heat of it melting her bones so she longed to sag against him and stay there, possibly for ever.

She stiffened her bones and her resolve and smiled back. 'Leave Jackie and the kids to me.'

Cam nodded at her, a special kind of nod that seemed to confirm a lot of things that hadn't yet been said, then he began to question Mike about Richard's request.

'Did he give any reason for wanting me?' Cam asked, as the two men moved towards the fence, Jo following but not too close. She could hear the waves crashing on the rocks, feel the thud of their power beneath her feet, but her fear now wasn't from her memories, but for Cam.

'No, just said he wants to talk to you—asked for you in particular,' Mike was saying as the two men reached the high point of the headland where a safety fence, eight feet high, had been erected.

Jackie and the two boys were crouched in a pathetic heap, crying helplessly.

'Wait until I'm talking to him then ease them slowly away because if he does jump they don't want that memory in their heads for ever,' Cam said quietly to Jo, although he knew the advice was unnecessary. If anyone would know what best to do for the little family, it was Jo, whose mantle of care was like a blanket spread across the whole Cove.

But right now he had to stop thinking about her—stop thinking about anyone but the man who was in such agony of spirits that death seemed the only option.

'Do you want me this side or that, Richard?' he asked.

He spoke quietly but he knew from the gasp behind him that Jo had heard the question—knew too how fearful she must be to see someone else's life in danger on the headland.

'You'd come over?' Richard was asking.

'Of course,' Cam said. 'I might not be able to climb it as

easily as you—I'm not built for climbing—but I think I could make it.'

Richard seemed to consider this for a moment.

'Why would you want to?'

'I thought maybe if I was closer to you I could see what you're seeing more clearly,' Cam told him. 'It's hard to know what people are thinking, but we should be able to see what they're seeing and right now I'd like to know what you're seeing that makes you think life's not worth living.'

'Well, you can see that easy enough,' Richard said. 'I'm no good, that's why!'

'No one's no good,' Cam said.

'I'm no good,' Richard repeated, although the words lacked the conviction the first assertion had.

'Of course you are. We all think that about ourselves from time to time. Look at me—a trained doctor and psychologist yet I'm surfing my way along the coast, looking for a purpose in life. I believed I'd failed the young soldiers I was supposed to help and I let myself forget the good I could do, the help I could give people. I bet you've forgotten the things about you that made Jackie fall in love with you—make her still love you as I'm sure she does.'

'That's different,' Richard muttered, but Cam saw he'd moved a little bit away from the edge.

'Not so very different. I had to learn to live with the guilt and feelings of helplessness. They might never go away but I'm learning to handle them now—learning to accept them, not run away from them. *You* have to learn to live with your temper, how to control it or how to walk away when you can't control it. From the little I know of you, you're not stupid. You can learn to handle the problem, and once you've told your friends about it, they'll help you every step along the way. My problem was I never talked about the horrors that I saw. I tried not to even think about them. Stuff you bottle in just festers but, like an infected wound, once you open it up, it will heal.'

Cam knew he was following good psychological processes using personal admissions so Richard didn't feel he was the only one with a problem, but was it working?

Would Richard think it all a con?

Of all the people gathered on the headland, Jo was the only one who'd know he, Cam, was speaking from his heart. Would she know also that it was because of her he'd changed? Because of her he'd moved on?

He hoped so, just as he hoped he could talk Richard off this cliff, but reason told him he couldn't get through to Richard while they were on opposite sides of an eight foot fence. He sighed inwardly and put a foot into the wire mesh.

'I'm coming over,' he said. 'It's best we sit together if we're going to talk.'

No reply but once again Richard inched further from the edge, giving Cam a spurt of hope. Somehow he clambered over the fence, ungainly as a hippo scaling a wall, then he settled beside Richard on the grassy ledge, trying hard to ignore the waves crashing on the rocks beneath them. Heights had never been his favourite places.

Richard started talking, unprompted, asking him questions about the army, asking him how men who'd seen horrors in their lives could learn to live with them, and it occurred to Cam that Richard's mate getting into the Aussie cricket team was probably not a trigger for his violence but a final straw.

'I went into the army because my family had always had army people in it—my dad and grandfather and a long string before them. What about you? I don't even know what work you do,' Cam said, thinking perhaps something in Richard's job might lie at the root of his problems.

'I'm an accountant but I do volunteer work for the SES.'

Ha! The flat tones as he'd spoken told Cam more than the words themselves, although the SES? The State Emergency Service was made up of volunteers—the members called out to all manner of emergencies, from floods to fires, to searches for missing children, and multi-car pile-ups on the highway.

'That's got its fair share of horror,' Cam said quietly, and Richard nodded, then he began to cry.

'She was only four, younger than Aaron, and I was the one who found her. I should have been happy—well, not happy but relieved her parents had got some kind of closure. But all I felt was anger—anger at a useless waste of life—anger aimed not only at the man who'd abducted her but at myself and all human beings that we allow such things to happen. I didn't know the anger was building inside me. I thought I was okay—I mean, it was six months later. Then the doctor said Jackie—said we—said the baby would be a girl, and something just cracked inside me…'

Cam put his arms around Richard's shoulders and held him while he bled out his pain in stumbling words and shattered sentences, the little girl, his boys, helplessness and anger.

'I knew I must have killed Jackie's love when that happened, and that made me angrier because she kept saying it didn't matter and she loved me and I kept thinking it *had* to be a lie.'

Cam held him tightly, knowing that further along the fence, where it ended near the northern edge of the cliff, the emergency crew was quietly cutting through the wire mesh. He hoped that was all they were doing. Prayed they didn't have some mad rescue plan to suddenly rush at him and Richard with the two of them sitting so close to almost certain death.

Back behind the main stage of the drama, Jo stayed with

Jackie, the two boys having been taken back down the path by Jackie's parents.

Every atom in Jo's body wanted to move forward, to force her hand through the mesh and get a grip on Cam's clothing.

As if that would keep him safe!

She sighed, shaking her head in disbelief at the pain she was feeling—the pain that fear was pumping through her body—fear for a man she'd known only a week.

Could people fall in love in a week?

Cam had said he loved her—or had he said falling in love—either way, love was part of the equation, but could it be real, could it be possible, could it last, something that happened so quickly?

She should have told him how *she* was feeling.

How *was* she feeling?

Afraid! That's what.

And muddled.

And probably in love…

Cam eased himself away from Richard, needing to look into his face as he spoke to him.

'There's so much help available,' he said quietly. 'For a start, there are ways of helping you come to terms with the terrible things you experienced when you found the little girl. And once you can learn to live with those memories, you'll find a lot of the anger has gone and even if it hasn't, you can learn what triggers it, and what other ways you might be able to do to handle those triggers. Right now, you have a wonderful opportunity to begin to change. I'm not saying it will be easy, but isn't it worth giving it a go? You obviously love your family very dearly. Wouldn't it be worth getting help so you can keep on loving them—and they can keep on loving you?'

'They're better off without me!'

Cam felt his gut knot. For the first time Richard had stated his intention, which, given the place, was obviously to jump.

Did that mean he, Cam, was losing the argument?

That he wasn't getting through to him?

He had to try again—try harder.

'Are they?' Cam asked, reaching out to rest his hand on Richard's forearm. 'Look at me, Richard, and tell me honestly, will your boys be better off growing up without a father, without your love—without even knowing how much you love them? Jumping off is the easy way out. You don't have to put any effort into that—believe me, I know it—but is it any way to show you love those boys—to show Jackie that you love her? She loves you very much or she wouldn't have gone back to you, but is leaving her to battle on on her own any way to repay that love? Of course it isn't. You have to fight for love. In your case, you have to fight the things inside you that are hurting the love you have for her. You can do that—you can conquer those ghosts—and your future with your family will be so much stronger and better and brighter because you *have* conquered them.'

Cam saw Richard's eyes widen, almost as if they needed to be bigger, to take in all he was saying. Cam held his gaze, hoping to force his message into Richard's brain while his own brain was questioning the words he'd said, the bits about fighting for love, turning them around to examine them more closely, picking out the bits that could apply to him—to him and Jo.

Conquering ghosts and going on stronger—those bits particularly.

Cam hauled his mind back to the man with him on the ledge.

'Richard?'

'I can't go back now,' he said, and moved his legs.

Despair reverberated through Cam's body, and despair ignited anger, but he held it in check.

'Because you think going back would be cowardly? Because you think if you turn around now and walk away people will think you weren't brave enough to jump?'

Richard turned away from him, but Cam grabbed his shoulder and gave him a little shake.

'Believe me,' he said, 'walking away now will probably be the bravest thing you've ever done because it will mean you've faced up to things that are wrong and you're willing to put them right. Walking away is like a warrior putting on his suit of armour and preparing for war, because what lies ahead is going to be far harder than jumping off a cliff. Except for Jackie, every person behind the fence at the moment is a trained professional and they will understand that by walking back you're making the courageous choice. Then there's Jackie and you know damn well that if you don't walk back through there you'll break her heart.'

Finally Richard nodded. Cam helped the emotionally exhausted man to his feet and Jackie's desperate cry of 'Richard' echoed over their heads. Richard turned and looked towards the cry and Jackie escaped Jo's hold and raced to the fence, taking Richard's hand through the mesh. Like that, holding and releasing fingers through the diamond shaped wires they walked to the cut in the fence, where Jackie fell into his arms.

CHAPTER TWELVE

IT WAS mesmerising, seeing love like that, Jackie and Richard, their fingers looping then parting, all the way along the mesh.

So mesmerising, in fact, that it wasn't until they'd reached the gap that Jo realised Cam wasn't following along behind.

Her heart stopped beating until she traced her way back along the mesh and saw him, sitting down again, leaning back against the fence, still only inches from the edge of the cliff, totally drained of all energy by the tension of the situation.

She sprinted towards the gap, eased past the policeman who was guarding it, and walked carefully along the narrow lip beyond the fence. Reaching Cam, she sat down beside him, resolutely banishing memories of Jilly from her mind.

She tucked her hand into his, and just held on for a while, then, as she felt his tension easing, she spoke.

'Walk you back?'

She said it quietly, not urging him in any way, knowing, for all the hurtful memories the place held, she'd be content to sit—for ever if necessary—until he was ready to leave.

She looked out at the ocean, reasonably calm today, so the waves sloshed rather than crashed against the cliff. The mighty power was leashed, but for how long?

She thought of Jilly, and, looking out at the mighty Pacific, she said goodbye. Oh, her sister, her twin, would live on in her heart, but Cam's arrival in the Cove had shifted Jo's perspective.

Cam's arrival?

Or love's arrival?

Still uncertain, she only knew that things had changed.

'We have to go forward,' she said quietly, 'moving into the sunshine, and letting the shadows fall behind us.'

Cam turned and put his arm around her shoulders, drawing her close.

'That's a thought to hold on to, isn't it?' he said softly, pressing a kiss against her temple.

'Can Richard do it? Will he be all right?' Jo asked.

'I don't know,' Cam answered honestly. 'We can only hope and be there for him and try in every way we can to help him.'

'You're a good man, Fraser Cameron,' Jo said quietly, but her voice was distracted and he could only guess at the thoughts that must be racing through her head. Her mention of going forward had told him so much. Sitting here was helping her not just to say goodbye to her sister but maybe let go of a little of the guilt and grief she'd carried in her heart for far too long.

She snuggled closer and he held her, wanting to prolong this special time together.

Special time?

Why would he think that?

'We should move,' she said, but she didn't make a start and with her warm and shapely body tucked against his, he didn't feel like arguing.

Mike put a stop to this indulgence.

'If you two stay much longer you'll have to climb back over, and I can charge you for being there, you know.'

Jo muttered to herself. Bloody Mike! Just when she was getting herself back together, not to mention revelling being in Cam's arms, so tightly held, so safe and warm, Mike had to go and spoil it.

She waited for Cam to tell Mike they were coming, but he remained silent and she realised, with a rush overwhelming delight, that he was leaving the decision up to her. That he had no intention of moving until she was ready.

Which led to a further revelation that what Cam had said about loving her must be more than words for only someone who really loved her would consider staying here with her and eventually having to climb the fence.

Again!

'We'd better go,' she murmured.

'Okay,' he said, and with that he put his arms around and lifted her to her feet.

'A truly gallant knight would carry you all the way but for all your slight build you're no lightweight and if I staggered and missed my footing we'd both go crashing to the rocks beneath, then Richard would have more guilt to deal with and he'd come and jump and—'

'Okay, I get the picture,' Jo told him, laughing up at him, reading the concern behind the nonsense he was spouting. 'We'll walk together.'

And they did, one step in front of the other, holding the fence with one hand, their other hands linked between them.

'It was a metaphor for life, that walk,' Cam said later, when, all official business done, they sat on the deck, their chairs close but not touching, eating pizza and looking out to sea. 'Taking one step at a time, that's all we can do. Looking to the sun, as you said earlier.'

He put down his crust and turned towards her.

'Could you possibly see your way clear to take those steps with me?' he asked, his blue eyes watching her intently, the tension in his face betraying the worry behind his almost casual words.

Jo was as a loss. She knew for sure she wanted to go forward in her life with this man—to take those steps beside him—but so much remained unspoken—love had come too fast.

'Might it not be love?'

As soon as the words were out there, she realised they'd not spoken of love—not really—so maybe he wasn't offering it.

Although earlier he'd said—

But *she* hadn't.

Now Cam was smiling at her and her heart was melting so maybe it *was* love.

'I can't speak for you,' he said, lifting her hand and raising it to his lips, pressing kisses on her fingers, one by one, then turning her hand to kiss her palm, a sensation that sent tingles up her spine. 'But for me it's love and, yes, we can say it's come too soon, how can we know, and all of that, but my voice of reason tells me it can't be anything else, while my voice of passion—well, it's best we wait until we're in a dimly lit room without our clothes on before I let it talk.'

He paused, tucking her hand tightly into his and holding it.

'I'm not a great catch, I realise that—the baggage, for one thing—but I can promise you my love for ever, Jo, for what it's worth, and should you love me back, I'll treasure your love above all else.'

'Even surfing?' Jo teased, because his words were causing chaos in her body and confusion in her mind and she needed to break the tension sparking in the air around them.

He tightened his hand momentarily on hers, then smiled

as he released it, giving it one last kiss before returning it to her lap.

'Now you're pushing it,' he growled, but his eyes were repeating the messages his lips had given earlier and Jo knew she had to answer.

No more jokes.

She clambered out of her deck chair and moved so she could kneel in front of him, her hands on his knees, looking up into his face.

'What woman could not love a man who makes smiley-face fruit breakfasts for her, who listens to her dredge up all her guilt and anguish, who understands that sometimes there's no need for words, especially when a hug is available?'

'But?' he prompted, no doubt guessing that her cautious self—*her* voice of reason—would be yelling at her.

'What do you think?' It was like a dare—a challenge—to see if he knew her as well as he seemed to think he did.

'You're thinking it's too soon—love can't happen in a week—but, Jo, darling, something has happened, so let's follow the path it's set us on and see where it leads. The steps I want to take with you can be baby steps, not great huge strides. For now, it's enough for me to know you're on the journey with me.'

The pause was probably infinitesimal yet it seemed to Jo to stretch for ever.

Then, 'Well,' he added, and she stood up, hauling on his hands so he, too, had to stand. She moved into his welcoming arms, pressed herself against his chest and whispered her answer.

A simple 'Yes', no qualifications, no doubts or hesitation, just 'Yes' to let him know she wanted to walk into the future with him, whether with baby steps or huge strides—they would be doing it together.

* * *

She wore the ring he gave her for the first time at the raising of the Christmas tree. Crystal Cove had a sister city—although neither town could qualify for city—in Norway, which sent a Christmas tree every year.

The raising of the tree was the biggest public event of the year in the small town, so Jo was aware her action wouldn't go unnoticed.

But two weeks after Cam's proposal she was so in love that not wearing it wasn't an option. Not only did she want everyone to know she was engaged, she wanted everyone to realise just how much she loved the man who'd come, more or less by accident, into her life.

'So, they raise the tree?' They were driving down to the esplanade where the tree would reign supreme until the new year when Cam asked the question. 'Pull it up with ropes while we all watch?'

Jo grinned at him.

'It's more than that! You'll see. In fact, as we're in the official party thanks to Helene Youngman thinking you're the bee's knees, you'll get an excellent view.'

To Cam's surprise the tree wasn't just a tree. Well, it *was*—a huge, weighty pine—but its boughs were already hung with decorations and once it was in place in a specially designed container, someone would flick a switch and it would rise up into position, brilliant in its splendour, a focal point of the Cove's Christmas.

Even with the tree still resting on the ground, Jo's face shone with happiness, and he marvelled that with all the pain she'd had in her life, the open, innocent delight of a child was still there inside her—inside this woman he loved.

And looking at the tree, all ready to be raised, and at the faces of the people all around it, waiting for the yearly ceremony, he realised that the same joy in simple pleasures was inside him as well. Apart from surfing, he'd thought he'd lost all that, but obviously finding love—finding Jo—had given it back to him.

He turned to her and put his arms around her, bending to kiss her on her lips.

'What's that for?' she demanded, being Jo, and he smiled at her.

'For giving me back the power to look at a Christmas tree and smile—to see enjoyment and know I'm sharing it—to feel what other people are feeling—simple pleasure.'

Now she kissed him, standing up on tiptoe.

'*Has* to be love, doesn't it?' she whispered.

'It *has* to be,' he confirmed.

* * * * *

ORPHAN UNDER THE CHRISTMAS TREE

BY

MEREDITH WEBBER

For my sister-in-law Caroline, an inspirational refuge worker

First published in Great Britain 2011
by Mills & Boon, an imprint of Harlequin (UK) Limited.
Harlequin (UK) Limited, Eton House, 18-24 Paradise Road,
Richmond, Surrey TW9 1SR

ISBN: 978 0 263 88616 0

Harlequin (UK) policy is to use papers that are natural, renewable and recyclable products and made from wood grown in sustainable forests. The logging and manufacturing process conform to the legal environmental regulations of the country of origin.

Printed and bound in Spain
by Blackprint CPI, Barcelona

Recent titles by the same author:

MELTING THE ARGENTINE DOCTOR'S HEART
TAMING DR TEMPEST
SHEIKH, CHILDREN'S DOCTOR…HUSBAND

More Praise for
Meredith Webber:

'Meredith Webber does a beautiful job
as she crafts one of the most unique romances I've
read in a while. Reading a tale by Meredith Webber
is always a pleasure, and
THE HEART SURGEON'S BABY SURPRISE
is no exception!'
—*Book Illuminations* on
THE HEART SURGEON'S BABY SURPRISE

CHAPTER ONE

SHE was a psychologist.

She should be able to look at a problem, consider it from all angles, and then solve it.

So why was Crystal Cove's annual bunfight of the raising of the Christmas tree causing Lauren Cooper such grief?

Easy answer!

Nat Williams would be there. Nat Williams, Crystal Cove's very own surfing superstar, current world number one, had been invited to press the button that would engage the ropes and pulleys that would lift the already decorated tree into position in the middle of the park that ran along the esplanade above the Cove's sheltered northern beach.

In her head, Lauren could hear her friend, Jo Harris, saying, 'But you're over him,' and Lauren was.

Totally, and years ago, and relieved to be out from under his spell!

Not even heart-broken, not even then at seventeen, so why now, at twenty-nine, did she feel ill at the thought of meeting him again?

Lauren, Crystal Cove's only practising psychologist, manager of the local women's refuge and general all-round competent person, rested her elbows on her desk, put her head in her hands, and groaned.

'Migraine?'

Wrong time and wrong place to be groaning! She'd completely forgotten she was at her desk at the hospital. The problem was she shared her office space with other therapists, and so it was open to any hospital personnel who happened to be wandering around.

She lifted her head and looked at the person who happened to be wandering around right then.

Dr Tom Fletcher, tall, dark, lean, and so handsome just looking at him sometimes took Lauren's breath away.

'No, I'm fine,' she told him as he pulled a chair over from an adjacent desk and settled down across from her.

'Really fine,' she emphasised, in case he hadn't got the message the first time.

'No, you're not.'

The words jolted Lauren out of her welter of doubt and anxiety and she frowned at him across the table. Eighteen months ago when Tom had first taken up his position as head of the Crystal Cove hospital, he'd asked her out, and she'd been very, very tempted.

But there was something about Tom Fletcher, with his grey eyes, easy smile and over-abundance of charm that had warned her to steer clear. Going out with Tom Fletcher might have meant getting involved. Getting involved might have meant…

She'd steered clear, reminding herself her life was just perfect as it was! She had a good job, a satisfying challenge in running the local women's refuge, great friends, family close by—the life she wanted for herself.

The life she'd *chosen* for herself!

As for Tom, well, her refusal hadn't dented his confidence. Since his arrival in town she'd watched him flirt with every woman in Crystal Cove; watched him squire any number of them around town, although none of the women he'd dated then deserted seemed to bear grudges against him, singing his praises as a companion, their pleasure in the affair, remaining friends with him even after the relationships had ended.

Tom Fletcher, she'd realised very early on, was one of those men all women loved, and apparently he loved being loved by them, but he was of the 'love them and leave them' tribe with no intention of ever settling down.

And to be honest, she wasn't sure about the affairs or even his prowess as a lover because none of the women ever talked.

Which in itself was odd…

'Earth to Lauren?'

She stared at him, unable to remember what he'd said, and unable to believe she'd drifted off into her own thoughts while the man, apparently, had something to say to her.

'Sorry,' she muttered. 'What was it you wanted?'

You, Tom would have liked to say, but he knew he could never say it. Oh, he'd asked her out once, but fortunately she'd said no, because as he'd grown to know Lauren Cooper he'd realised she was a woman who deserved the best of everything the world had to offer and, as far as men went, that wasn't him.

'Nothing,' he said instead. 'Except to know if you're okay. You're pale as milk, you're sitting in an empty room way after working hours, and groaning loudly.'

She looked into his eyes and managed a wry smile.

'Not loudly, surely?' she queried.

'Loudly!' he repeated. 'It brought me racing from my office.'

Her smile improved.

'You? Race? Ice-cool Tom? The one who keeps his head when all around are losing theirs, isn't that the saying?'

'Well, I hurried,' he amended then because it was always

so—well, *nice*—to be sitting talking to Lauren about nothing in particular—something that rarely happened in both their busy lives—he added, 'And you *did* groan, so tell me.'

If only she could! With a supreme effort of will, Lauren refrained from groaning again.

Although…

She studied him for a moment, considering the bizarre idea that had flitted into her head—checking it from all angles.

Tom was a friend, after all, and what were friends for but to help each other out?

Although might it not be tempting fate?

'I *am* a friend.' Tom echoed her thoughts. 'So, rather than doing both sides of the argument in your head, why don't you talk it out with me?'

'Because it would involve you!'

Was it because the answer had come upon her so suddenly that she'd blurted that out?

'Aah!' Tom was grinning at her, laughter dancing in his eyes, mischief gleaming there as well. 'You've killed someone and need help to dig the hole to bury the body!'

She *had* to smile!

'Not quite that bad,' she admitted, 'although there were times today when I could have strangled an obnoxious eight-year-old who thought hosing all the girls who walked past the refuge was a fun way to pass the afternoon.'

'Bobby Sims?' Tom asked, and she smiled again as she nodded in answer to his query. One of the things that made Tom Fletcher so darned appealing—apart from film-star looks—was his empathy. He could sit down with someone and be on his or her wavelength within minutes, or so Lauren had always found.

'But you didn't strangle the terror of the refuge, so what's the problem?'

Lauren shifted her attention away from Tom—too distracting—looking around the room, feeling so ridiculous she wondered if she could make up some story to explain her groan and he'd go away and she'd find an excuse to just not go to the tree raising.

Except she *had* to go!

As her eyes came back to rest on Tom's face, he lifted one eyebrow, a trick she'd tried and failed to master in her youth, and she knew he deserved an honest answer.

'You'll think I'm stupid,' she began, then was furious with herself for being feeble enough to utter such an inanity. 'No, I *am* stupid. And pathetic, and ridiculous, and I've got myself into a tizz over nothing so best you just slope off to wherever you're going and leave me groaning into my hands.'

Lauren didn't do stupid. That was the first thought that came into Tom's head as he listened to her castigate herself. Of all the women he'd ever known, she was the most sensible, practical and level-headed, guided by what had always seemed a boundless store of common sense and a determination that bordered on ruthless—at least, where keeping the women's refuge open was concerned. As far as he knew, in her private life she was just that, private—she lived alone and seemed to like it that way—but stupid? Never!

'I'm not going,' he announced. 'Not until you tell me what's got you frazzled like this. Is it Christmas? Does your family make a big deal of it, so you have relatives who bore you stupid descending on you for weeks at a time, and people arguing about who's doing the cake and the best stuffing for the turkey?'

That won a smile, but it was wan and he realised that, subconsciously perhaps, he'd been worried about Lauren for a while. She was still as beautiful as ever, having good bone structure so tiredness didn't ravage her features as it did some people. But she was pale, and the dark shadows beneath her eyes had deepened so they had a bruised look.

The smile had dried up while he was thinking about her looks, and she was frowning at him now.

Quite ferociously, in fact, so the words, when they came, seemed to have no meaning—certainly nothing to connect them to a ferocious frown.

'I want to ask you out,' she said, her eyes, a golden, greeny-brown and always startling against her golden blonde hair, fixed on his, no doubt so she could gauge his reaction.

Challenging him, in fact!

'Okay,' he managed, though battling to process both the invitation and the fierceness of it, which made the slight start of pleasurable surprise he felt quite ridiculous. 'When?'

'Tonight,' she said. 'In fact, right now—we should be leaving any minute.'

'But it's the great tree raising do tonight,' he reminded her. 'We're both going anyway. The entire hospital staff was invited.'

No reaction beyond another, barely suppressed groan, so he took a wild guess.

'Do you mean after the tree raising? Dinner somewhere perhaps?'

He was speaking lightly, but inside he was a mess of confusion, though why he couldn't say. Perhaps because Lauren looked so unhappy, while her lips, usually full and with a slight natural pout, were pressed together, suggesting the tension *she* was feeling had increased rather than decreased after she'd shot out the invitation.

'I suppose we could eat afterwards,' she mumbled, and Tom had to laugh.

'Now, there's a gracious invitation,' he said, but no glimmer of humour lightened Lauren's face. If anything, she was looking even more grim!

He stood up and walked around the desk, squatting beside her and looking directly into her face, putting his hand on her shoulder—the lightest of touches but showing her without words that he was there for her.

'Tell me,' he said softly, and to his astonishment tears welled in her eyes, overflowed, and slid silently down her cheeks.

She made no attempt to brush them away so he pulled out his handkerchief, checked it was reasonably clean, and dried them for her.

'I *am* being stupid,' she muttered angrily. ' I have to go because of the refuge—it's been the main fundraising focus for the Christmas raffle and I'll be getting the cheque and heaven knows—well, you know too—the refuge needs it, and if Cam and Jo hadn't just become engaged I'd have asked Cam, but it would start too much talk in the town, and then there's Mike but he seems quite interested in that new young probationary policewoman, and the school teachers have all gone home for the holidays, so—'

'So you're stuck with me,' Tom finished for her. 'That's okay, I get the picture. You need a man tonight. That's fine. Do you want anything special? A bit of panting? Lusting? Public displays of affection? Kisses, or just hand-holding?'

She knew Tom was only teasing, but hearing it put like that Lauren wanted nothing more than to shrink to mouse size and crawl into a hole and hide. How embarrassing! How could she have asked him?

And trust Tom to make a joke of it!

But wasn't that for the best? At least he wasn't getting any false ideas. So why did *that* thought make her feel weepy again?

She hauled in a deep, steadying breath, and watched as he straightened up.

'I just need you to be there, that's all,' she said, cross with herself for making such a mess of things.

'But obviously with you!' he said quietly, and she, who hadn't blushed since she was fourteen, felt heat flooding into her cheeks.

Mortified, she pressed her hands to them to cool them, or hide the vivid colour, and nodded.

'No worries!'

But that was Tom! Nothing ever worried him—or seemed to...

He put his arm around her shoulders and looked into her face.

'Now,' he said gently, 'I know you're beautiful enough without it, but all my ladies go for a little make-up when they have to cover the signs of tears. I wouldn't like to think the entire population of Crystal Cove sees you've been crying about having to go out with me. It would do my reputation no manner of harm, so into the washroom with you. We've ten minutes or so before we have to leave.'

He turned her and gave her a little push towards the washrooms, catching up with her to hand over her big tote, which she'd left beside her chair, passing it to her with such a warm smile her stomach turned over.

Was she stupid to be doing this? Stupider than she usually was over men?

Was he stupid to be doing this?

Tom took himself off to the men's washrooms and splashed cold water over his face.

He'd been attracted to Lauren from the first time he'd seen her. Then working with her on the board of the refuge, he'd got to know her as a person and become, *he* thought, a good friend. So her refusal to go out with him had worked out for the best, he'd decided, because Lauren Cooper was a woman who deserved the whole deal as far as love was concerned and he didn't do love.

Oh, he understood it existed. It even worked for a lot of people, but to him it was the most destructive force on earth and he'd decided at an early age that he would avoid it at all cost. The women with whom he'd enjoyed affairs over the years had always understood there'd be no 'happy ever after' scenario ahead of them. He was always honest, explaining right at the beginning that he enjoyed women and their company, enjoyed the physical pleasure of affairs, and hoped the enjoyment was mutual, but that he wasn't looking for anything long term, particularly not marriage.

A few had asked why, and a few more had thought they'd change his mind, but on the whole they'd parted amicably enough and he remained on friendly terms with many of the women.

Lauren, however, was different…

'Are you having second thoughts in there?'

An edge in her voice told him she'd recovered a little of her composure, but he wouldn't have been human if he wasn't wondering what had rattled her so much.

He emerged from the washroom, wanting to ask, but the Lauren who was waiting there was so far from the tense and tearful woman he'd left that any words he might have had dried to ashes on his tongue.

Which, he hoped, wasn't hanging out.

She'd swept her shoulder-length blonde hair into a pleat at the back of her head, making her neck look longer, elegant. Mascara darkened her eyelashes, emphasising her fascinating eyes with their dashes of brown, green and gold, but it was her mouth that drew—and held—his attention.

He tried to remember if he'd ever seen Lauren wearing lipstick and decided, if he had, it must have been a pale, neutral shade, because one thing was for sure, he'd never seen those full, lush, pouting lips covered in a glossy, vibrant, fire-engine red.

A red that yelled danger, and beware, but at the same time tempted and seduced!

'Much better,' he managed to mutter, because wasn't he Mr Cool where all women were concerned?

Inside he wasn't cool at all, not even close.

Inside he was wired—his mind playing tricks on him, showing him flashing images of those lips while his body ached to feel them on his skin—just once—no, more than once—just once would never be enough…

'So, shall we go,' she said, *Ms* Cool definitely, whatever angst she'd been suffering, possibly was still suffering, hidden behind her war paint.

And it *was* war paint!

Those red lips would challenge every man who saw her, distract them from the tree raising, make them think things most of them shouldn't think about a woman they maybe didn't know.

She'd linked her arm through his elbow while his mind was rioting, and now walked him back along the corridor, and out of the hospital, her tote slung across her other shoulder, so her body was pressed to his, all down one side.

At least walking beside her he couldn't see her lips, although he did keep sneaking glances at them—at her…

Tom was obviously regretting saying yes, Lauren decided as they left the hospital building. His usual rattle of cheery conversation had dried up, perhaps because he was trying to think of some way to extricate himself from this situation.

And was the lipstick too bright?

From the day she'd heard Nat Williams was coming back to town she'd searched the internet for red lipsticks, wanting bright and vibrant red, not orangy red or pinkish red, but fire-engine red.

Challenge red!

And it had to last, not disappear the moment she sipped a drink or ate a sandwich…

She knew it was pathetic, still to be hung up over something that had happened to her teenage self, although the psychologist in her accepted that the damage Nat had done to her would probably never go away.

Well, some of it wouldn't—that was for sure…

'You usually chat,' she said to Tom as they crossed the car park, heading for the esplanade.

She'd spoken mainly to divert her thoughts, but also because it was weird, walking in total silence with the usually loquacious Tom.

He *was* regretting it!

'Struck dumb by your red lips,' he said, and something in his voice told her there might be an element of truth in what he'd said.

'*You* struck dumb by lipstick?' she teased, hoping they could reach some comfortably light-hearted plane before they joined the crush by the beach. 'Hardly!'

'You'd be surprised,' he muttered, then he seemed to collect himself, taking her hand in his and drawing her towards the area where the road had been blocked off, and seating erected to one side of where the big tree lay. 'Come on, we're in the good seats,' he said. 'I can see Jo and Cam among the crowd milling near the platform—we can sit with them.'

He pointed out the two doctors. Jo Harris was Lauren's best friend, Fraser Cameron Jo's new fiancé. But he didn't think Lauren was listening to anything he said, and was it because he was holding her hand that he felt her stiffen?

He turned towards her but her attention was on the stands, where a platform marked the place where the guest of honour would press the button to raise the tree. Tom checked out the people on the platform. Helene Youngman, the local mayor, four councillors, the managers of a few local businesses who donated funds towards the Christmas tree decorations, a youngish bloke in casual gear—was he the new dentist? Cam had heard someone had bought the practice but hadn't met the man.

Whoever he was, he had a woman and a couple of kids with him. And everyone seemed to know him so maybe he wasn't the new dentist…

Tom had been so engrossed in checking out the dignitaries on the platform, he hadn't realised that Lauren had dropped his hand. She had also stopped moving, standing there, a yard or so behind him, seemingly frozen on the spot.

She couldn't do it! Seeing Nat there with the woman who must be his wife had made Lauren's stomach turn over—not with remembered love but with remembered fear, *and* apprehension for the woman she didn't know. And most of all regret!

She should have spoken out—told someone—anyone…

Got him the help he must have needed, although at seventeen she'd had no idea help existed for men like Nat…

No idea that there *were* other men like Nat…

Back then she'd blamed herself…

Tom had turned back, taking her hand again, easing her towards the steps, and Jo materialised beside her, grabbing her other hand, the fingers of Jo's left hand squeezing hers, Jo's soft voice telling her she could do this, giving her a quick shoulder-to-shoulder hug, although Lauren was usually the hugger.

They climbed the steps to the platform and before Lauren could catch a strengthening breath, Nat was there in front of her.

'Lauren Cooper,' he cried as he stepped closer, arms out held for a welcoming hug. 'Well, probably not Lauren Cooper any more. Far too beautiful not to have been snapped up by some lucky man!'

Her brain misfired, synapses missing, catching in the wrong places, so she answered far too brightly.

'Hardly snapped up—far too busy playing the field! Wasn't it you who used to quote that tired old saying about why buy a book when you can join a library?'

She flashed a brilliant smile and pulled Tom forward.

'Tom's more a set of encyclopaedia than a single book. Nat Williams, meet Tom Cooper.' And for extra effect she pressed a kiss on Tom's cheek, branding it with a scarlet imprint, then reaching into his pocket, her mind reeling at her own outrageous behaviour, to find his handkerchief to wipe it off.

Fortunately for her peace of mind, because she was too shocked by how far she'd already gone to consider any further conversation, Jo's new fiancé, Cam, was a mad keen surfer and as soon as Jo introduced him to Nat, Cam commandeered the local surfing superstar, edging him away from the little group to talk waves and beaches and barrels and other surfing stuff.

Which left Lauren to face her best friend.

'What is going on?' Jo demanded. 'And don't tell me Tom knew you were going to introduce him like that. An encyclopaedia from the lending library! You made him sound like a hooker—or whatever the male equivalent of a hooker is. I was looking at him when you said it and he was as shocked as I was.'

'Nothing's going on,' Lauren muttered, not able to even glance in Tom's direction, fearful of the disgust she might see.

'No?' Jo persisted.

'Of course not! I panicked a bit, that's all,' she muttered angrily. 'Let's leave it, shall we?'

'Actually, I thought the encyclopaedia bit was great—heftier, more oomph, than an ordinary novel. And I don't know what they call the male equivalent of hookers—hooksters, do you think?'

Tom had materialised beside them, taking Lauren's hand in his and squeezing her fingers in the most comforting way as he joked about Jo's objections.

Still clasping Lauren's hand in his big, warm paw, he turned to Jo.

'Okay, Jo?'

Before Jo could reply—not that there was anything she could say now Tom had taken the wind from her sails—the mayor stepped up to the microphone and was urging everyone to take their seats. Tom tucked his hand beneath Lauren's elbow and steered her after Jo and Cam towards some spare seats in the fourth row of the temporary stands.

'I *am* sorry, Tom,' Lauren whispered to him. 'I don't know what came over me, and Jo was right, I made you sound cheap. The whole scenario was stupid—I can't believe I fell apart the way I did back at the hospital and put you in that position.'

'Hush,' he said. 'No talking. We're here to be an audience to the great and good of Crystal Cove, but do feel free to reach into my pocket for a handkerchief any time!'

For the second time in umpteen years, Lauren felt a blush

creeping into her cheeks, but before she could apologise again, Tom was shushing her, whispering in her ear that they could talk about it later, not, he'd added, that there was anything to talk about.

Although they *would* talk, Tom added to himself. Lauren was his friend and for that reason he was very eager to find out just what the golden boy of Australian surfing had done to Lauren in the past to send the normally calm, cool and collected woman into such a panic. The Lauren he'd seen tonight was so unlike the woman he'd come to know during his time in the Cove that he could barely believe it was the same person.

The mayor finished her speech by introducing 'someone who needs no introduction to most Cove residents, world surfing champion, Nat Williams'.

The crowd gathered in the park and spilling out onto the beach let out a collective roar of approval. It wasn't often the sleepy seaside hamlet had something to celebrate.

Nat Williams acknowledged the applause very graciously, then brought another roar of approval when he said, 'It's great to be home and to see all my old mates again. There's no place in the world like the Cove.'

In fact, Tom decided as the big tree began to rise into position, it was obvious the people in the crowd were more excited about Nat's return than about the tree.

He peered down towards the front row of seats, picking out the blond head of the surfing great. Two small children sat beside him, and next to them a lovely brunette, long, dark locks flowing around her shoulders. She stood out from the crowd not only for her good looks but because of her clothes, a long-sleeved shirt and jeans when most of the women present, if they weren't still in swimming costumes with a sarong wrapped over them, were wearing strappy tops or dresses, minimal clothing as the day had been hot and the nor'easterly hadn't come in to bring relief.

He felt Lauren shift on the bench beside him and turned to see that she, too, was looking towards Nat Williams's wife.

And frowning.

Okay, so putting two and two together was easy enough—they'd had a past relationship, Nat and Lauren—but knowing Lauren as he did, he couldn't understand that she hadn't sorted herself out by now. She was one of the most sensible people he knew and her training as a psychologist must surely have helped her move on, but her reaction to the thought of seeing Nat again had been disturbing.

Could she still fancy herself in love with him that she was frowning at his wife?

Well, that might explain why she hadn't accepted *his* invitation to go out.

Although he doubted anyone as sensible and together as Lauren could still be clinging to some long-gone love.

Not knowing anything of love except that for its destructive powers, he couldn't really judge, but he had always pictured it like a fire—yep, a destructive force—but if a fire wasn't fed it died out—he knew that side of love as well.

So surely Lauren's feelings for Nat, unnurtured for however many years, should have died out.

His ponderings stopped at that point as an ominous creaking from somewhere beneath the temporary stand warned him of imminent danger. The creak was followed by a screech as if metal components were being wrenched apart.

'Get everyone off the stands,' he yelled, as he felt the faintest of movements beneath his feet.

'And everyone away from underneath or near them.' Fraser Cameron shouted his own caution. Cam was already guiding Jo towards the side aisle, telling people who were close to the edge on the lower seats to slide under the railing and jump. It wasn't far, less than two metres, but Cam was obviously thinking of lightening the weight on the straining scaffolding underneath.

Tom urged Lauren to follow Jo, telling her to make sure everyone was clear on that side, then he began ushering the people sitting in front of him off the stands. The important people on the platform, which must have been more stable, were turning around, disbelieving and bewildered by the panic building behind them.

As the noise beneath became more tortured, metal bracing twisting and wrenching from its brackets, the noise above increased, so the aisles were jammed and people were jumping from the top level, way too high, while those on the platform remained in their seats, stunned into immobility by their disbelief that the stands could possibly be collapsing.

Tom thrust through the throng, ignoring yells of protest at his actions, and grabbed Helene, pushing her towards the edge of the platform.

'Jump,' he ordered. 'You've all got to jump. If the stands collapse all those behind you will come down on top of you, burying you and suffocating you.'

He grabbed the two Williams children, one under each arm, and hurtled to the edge of the stage, passing them down into the arms of a couple of helpers who'd appeared from the crowd below.

'Take them as far away as you can and keep people back,' he said, while behind him he could hear Cam telling people to keep calm, they'd all get off in time.

Which might have happened if the temporary seating hadn't suddenly swayed sideways, igniting fresh terror in the crowd. They surged forward, leaping over seats, knocking others down, adrenalin kicking in, urging flight from danger.

Tom kept hustling those on the platform to the edge, telling them to jump then run, but fear could sometimes freeze the body so some people just stood, as if unable to hear the urgent message he was giving, so he had to lift and carry them to the edge where others helped them down.

A sudden howl of protest from the scaffolding and the stand collapsed, metal tubing smashing through the wooden seats and steps, the stands twisting, spilling people everywhere, trapping some while pitching others into the air.

Tom grabbed Nat Williams's wife and leapt, hoping Nat was helping other people, though he suspected the surfing hero had been one of the first to jump, his wife forgotten.

'Thank you. I must find my children.'

She had a soft American accent and dark shadows beneath her eyes.

Maybe being with Nat wasn't all that much fun...

CHAPTER TWO

MIKE SINCLAIR, the head of the local police station, materialised in front of Lauren, as she and Jo were urging people away from the collapsed stands.

'We need to move uninjured people away,' he said, 'and set up an area for those injured.' He indicated an area of the esplanade, already closed to traffic. 'Jo, if we make this space a triage area, can you stay here and treat minor injuries? The ambulances will come through to here, while Lauren, if you can stay with those who were on the stands but aren't injured and those who have friends somewhere in that mess. Keep them calm. The Emergency Services people will be here soon—they'll have bottled water and basic first-aid equipment.'

Lauren understood her role and moved through the crowd, urging the panicking locals back from the stands, helping injured people across to Jo, telling the others to stay clear, comforting tearful women and shocked men, telling children they'd be safe, just to wait over by the tree and their parents would find them soon.

She was doing okay until she found Bobby Sims, rubbing furiously at tears he obviously felt embarrassed about shedding.

Bobby Sims, easily the most disruptive of all the children

who were given temporary shelter at the women's refuge, crying?

'I've lost Mum,' he told Lauren, at first shaking off her comforting arm but eventually accepting it, *and* accepting a hug when she knelt in front of him and folded him in her arms.

He pressed close against her for a moment, then he lifted his head to say, 'She was right there.'

He pointed to where the jumble of metal scaffolding lay heaped with wood and people.

'Right near it. Greg was under there and he called out to her and she went and then it all fell down.'

Would Joan Sims have responded to a call from the man she was in the refuge to escape?

Lauren didn't know. She'd been running the women's refuge for the three years since it opened, and still couldn't tell which women would go back to the partners who abused them, and which wouldn't.

In the meantime, there was Bobby…

'We'll find your mum,' Lauren assured him, 'but while we're looking, will you help me?'

Bobby's startled 'Me?' suggested no one had ever asked him for help before.

'Yes, you. You know most of the kids around here from school. A lot of them will be like you—they'll have become separated from their parents. Go through the crowd and bring any kids who are lost or crying over near the tree. Once you get them there, they can look at the lights and decorations until their parents turn up to find them.'

Bobby seemed to consider objecting to this plan, then he straightened his shoulders and took off, hopefully to do something useful, not set fire to the Christmas tree or try some other devilment.

Lauren continued to herd people away from the stands, but the cries of pain and distress had her turning back towards the scene, checking, seeing Tom there in the thick of it, clambering over twisted metal to tend the injured.

Could the stand collapse further? Tom wondered about it as he lifted people trapped by the metal struts or wooden planks of seating. And had anyone been caught underneath?

Kids often played under scaffolding…

He sent a plea to the fates that this hadn't been the case and knelt to reach a man caught between two metal seats, apparently trapped.

'Can you hear me, mate?' he asked, leaning further in to press his fingers to the man's carotid.

The man didn't respond, but his pulse was strong, and movement of his chest told Tom the trapped man was breathing.

Tom used his hands to search for blood. If it wasn't pulsing out from any part of the man's body, then the best thing to do was to leave him so the paramedics could stabilise his spine before they shifted him.

'Can you give me a hand here?'

Tom glanced around to see Cam higher up in the wreckage, bent over another victim—male again.

'His legs are trapped,' Cam explained as Tom clambered cautiously across the tumbled seating.

Tom took one look and was about to tell Cam to leave it for the rescue crew when he saw the blood on the man's thigh. There was no doubt the man's femur was broken and his femoral artery damaged. They needed to get him out *now*.

While Cam supported the man, Tom began, cautiously, to shift debris from around him, trying to get at whatever was pinning the man's legs and trapping his feet.

A twisted prop lay one way, a wooden seat caught beneath

it, and below both some scaffolding that hadn't moved, holding steadfast to its job, just when they needed it to bend a little.

Tom eased himself into a gap he'd found close by until his feet were on the solid scaffold, then he peered down to see if any unfortunate person had been caught below him and found the area was clear.

'I'm going to jump on this bit and see if I can shake the twisted part free,' he told Cam. 'Hold the bloke in case it all gives way.'

Cam didn't bother with a caution—they both knew if they didn't get the fellow out he could die before the jaws-of-life equipment arrived and the safety crew made the scaffolding secure enough for them to do their work. They were governed by all kinds of workplace safety regulations but Tom wasn't.

He grabbed the twisted bar and held it in his hands, then jumped, both feet rising then thumping back on the solid bar. Nothing happened, although he thought he might have felt a faint give in the bar in his hands.

He jumped again and felt the whole tottering edifice sway to one side then the other—sickeningly!

Maybe this wasn't such a good idea, but looking down he'd seen a lot of the scaffolding still holding in the section directly beneath him so he didn't think bending the piece beneath his feet would do much more damage than had already been done.

'One more go,' he said to Cam, moving so he could stand above the bar he needed to move and jump down onto it. Praying he wouldn't miss as coming down on it could do him a very painful injury.

Putting *that* wince-causing image out of his head, he jumped and felt the scaffold give, felt the bar in his hand tear away, so the seat was released and they could get at the man.

'What the hell do you think you're doing up there? Don't you know there are experts for that kind of thing? Have you got a hero complex, or perhaps a death wish?'

He turned to see Lauren standing far too close to the devastated stands, hands on hips, the fury in her words visible on her face.

'Lovely Lauren, don't tell me you're concerned for my welfare?'

Lauren didn't need to look around to know that plenty of locals had heard the exchange. She was sure Tom had known that too, and had said it as revenge for her demented 'date' ploy and the encyclopaedia reference. She'd kill him! She'd climb up there and do it now if not for the fact that another person up there might endanger him.

Him?

No, she meant the other people still up there. Cam and whoever he and Tom had been tending.

Didn't she?

She didn't have a clue, she just knew that seeing Tom up there jumping on the already damaged scaffolding had sent cold chills through her body and clamped a band of steel around her heart.

'The kids are all gone now.'

The voice, laden with doom although obviously the message was good, made her turn. Bobby Sims was right behind her, fear and apprehension making his usually bright, mischievous face pale and tense.

'And I still can't find Mum.'

The way he said it melted Lauren's heart. For all his exasperating devilry, Bobby was still a little boy who loved his mother and had been with her through her string of abusive boyfriends.

'You stay with me, we'll find her,' she told him. 'If she's not around here, maybe we'll find her at the hospital. I have to go up there to talk to the people waiting to find out about their friends and family. We'll get something to eat and drink up there as well. The canteen will be open.'

To Lauren's surprise, she felt a small hand slip into hers, making her very aware that this wasn't Bobby, the torment of her life, but a little boy who couldn't find his mum.

She gave the little hand a squeeze, then knelt in front of him.

'I'll look after you, whatever happens, Bobby,' she promised, drawing him into her arms to give him a comforting hug, repeating the promise that she'd take care of him, rocking him slightly as she offered comfort beyond words.

To her surprise he not only accepted the hug but he hugged her back, although as soon as she felt he'd had enough, she stood up. She led him up the road towards the hospital, following straggling groups of people who were also missing someone they knew or loved, the night silent with shock so the whispering shush as the waves slid onto the sand sounded loud in the darkness.

Once at the hospital, she realised she needed to start sorting people again—telling anyone not injured to wait on the veranda so the nurses on duty and those who had come in when they'd heard of the emergency listed the others according to the severity of their injuries. Jo, Cam, Tom and the other hospital doctor were all at work, Jo and Cam in the ER, working their way through the patients. Tom, Jo explained as she splinted a sprained wrist, was in Theatre with a man with a broken femur.

After checking with the ER manager that Joan Sims hadn't been brought in, Lauren took Bobby through to the canteen.

'What would you like to eat?'

For the first time since she'd seen him by the devastated stands, Bobby's face lit up.

'I can have any of that stuff?' he asked, looking at the offerings, hastily prepared, Lauren guessed, in the servery.

'Go for it,' Lauren told him. 'Grab a plate at one end and fill it up with whatever you want, but if you eat too much and throw up you have to clean up the mess.'

'Me? I'm only eight!'

'You,' Lauren confirmed. 'You're never too young to learn to do a bit of cleaning.'

She watched as he heaped his plate then put some of his choices back, settled him at a table, told him she'd be on the veranda and to come out there when he finished. She was about to depart when she saw shadows chase across his face and tears well in his eyes.

'No,' she said quickly, 'I should have something to eat as well. Wait here while I get some food and we'll eat together then we can both go onto the veranda.'

She grabbed a sandwich and a cup of coffee and returned to find Bobby had nearly finished his large dinner.

'There was apple pie there and some chocolate stuff and ice cream,' he reminded her.

'Go get some,' she said, 'but, remember, not too much.'

She was surprised to see him pick up his plate and carry it over to the servery, something she knew he refused to do at the refuge, telling whichever woman on duty in the kitchen it was a 'girls' job' in tones of such lofty disdain they knew he must be echoing at least one of the men who'd moved through his mother's life.

Back in the ER things seemed to be more chaotic than

ever, but as Joan Sims hadn't turned up Lauren stopped in her office to phone the police station. She spoke to a civilian helper who'd come in to assist, telling him Bobby Sims was with her if anyone phoned to enquire.

The helper checked his lists.

'No one's called us so far,' he told Lauren, who was beginning to get a really bad feeling about Joan. She looked at Bobby, sitting dejectedly on a couch in the little anteroom where therapy patients waited, and had a brainwave. A lot of the OT and physio patients were kids so there was a TV, DVD player and a stack of DVDs in the small room.

'Can you work a DVD player?' she asked Bobby.

'Course I can,' he scoffed, then his eyes lit up. 'Can I watch one of those DVDs?'

He'd obviously seen the shelves of them.

'They're all yours,' Lauren told him. 'I'll be just outside on the veranda if you need me.'

She was about to walk away when the image of him standing there in front of the shelf made her turn back. She crossed the office and went into the little room where she gave him a big hug, then knelt so they were on eye level with each other.

'Are you okay to stick with me until we sort this out?' she asked him.

He nodded, then for the first time in the turbulent few years that she'd known Bobby he put his arms around her neck and pressed a quick kiss on her cheek.

'Have fun,' she whispered in his ear when she'd kissed him back. 'I'll be back as soon as I can.'

For some weird reason she found she had a lump in her throat and was swallowing it as she came out of the office into the corridor, slap bang into Tom.

'I was looking for you,' he said. 'Are you all right? Do you have to be here? Can't you go home and get some sleep?

Someone should be resting—there'll be a lot of fall-out over this and plenty of traumatised people for you to have to deal with over the next few days.'

He'd put an arm around her as he spoke and was holding her close enough for her to see the concern in his eyes.

For a moment she felt like Bobby—she wanted to return the light hug he was giving her, return it with interest because a hug was what she needed right now—but she'd already embarrassed Tom enough for one night with her encyclopaedia statement so she stepped away.

Practical Lauren returning!

'I'm fine. Have you eaten? Should I be rustling up some food for you and Cam and Jo?'

'We've people feeding us all the time,' Tom assured her, 'but it will be a long night. At last count there are about thirteen with serious enough injuries to be hospitalised, and another seven or so who need bones set, or stitches in wounds, then there are muscle tears, that kind of thing, strains and sprains.'

'No fatal injuries?' Lauren had to ask, although just thinking of it made her cold all over.

Tom closed in on her again, resting his hands on her shoulders.

'You're worried about someone in particular?' he asked, his voice so gentle Lauren had to swallow again.

Unable to speak, she nodded.

He nodded back, his face grave. 'There's talk of someone trapped underneath on the road side of the collapse,' he said. 'And from what I've heard it's unlikely the person would have survived.'

The pulsing siren of an ambulance stopped the conversation.

'They're playing my song,' Tom said, his voice lightening

though his smile was grim, but he didn't hurry off, pausing instead to give Lauren a real hug—like the one she'd wanted to give him earlier. 'I'll catch up with you some time soon,' he said, and the words sounded like a promise…

The woman was so badly injured Tom wondered if there was any bone in her chest that wasn't broken, but he had no time for stupid speculation, he needed all his focus on trying to save her.

Crush injuries to the chest were common from appalling road accidents, and Tom knew the only way to deal with them was bit by bit. She had oxygen pumping into her, the pressure low so they didn't do more damage to her lungs, and her heart was still beating, which in itself was a problem, as it was also pumping blood out of her system through many torn veins and arteries.

'Sometimes it seems as if more's coming out than is going in. I've got the blood group done and we've sent out a call for whole blood but in the meantime the fluids should hold her.'

Tom looked up to see Cam gloved up on the other side of the operating table, ready to assist.

Two hours later they both stepped back, the woman, sadly still anonymous to them, beyond help.

'Should we have been helping with the other injuries instead of trying to save her?' Tom said to Cam as they stripped off their gloves and gowns and were washing together at the tub.

'Jo and your co-worker are handling them all—they were down to minor stuff when I left and I would think they've finished now,' Cam assured him.

They walked together through to the ER where Jo was slumped on a chair beside a couple of nurses, talking to Mike and another policeman. All of them turned towards Cam and Tom, took one look at their faces, and let out a collective sigh.

'We don't even know who she was,' Tom said. He turned to Mike. 'Do you?'

'Joan Sims—Jo and Lauren know her from the refuge. Apparently she's got a little boy.'

'Bobby Sims,' Tom said, remembering with sadness his and Lauren's conversation about the rebel earlier. 'I've met him before but he's always come in with a teacher or someone from the refuge so I hadn't met his mother. Where is Bobby now?'

'He's asleep in the little waiting room off Lauren's office,' Jo told him. 'Now all the other people who came in have been patched and matched and those not hospitalised have gone home, Lauren's in there with him.'

Tom turned and headed for the therapists' office, his mind on the small boy. He must *have* a father, although maybe Joan Sims had been escaping abuse by someone else.

Would the child be safe?

He felt a shudder, as if the floor had moved beneath his feet, and shadows of the past flew by like phantoms in the night.

Of course Bobby Sims would have family…

Lauren was sitting at her desk, her head in her hands, exactly as she had been earlier—however long ago this afternoon had been.

'Bobby?' Tom asked as he came into the room.

Lauren nodded towards the alcove and Tom walked quietly towards it and stood a minute, looking down at the sleeping child. He had sandy-coloured hair rough cut and tousled and a serious over-bite that would need braces before too long, but, like all sleeping children, he looked so innocent Tom had to brace himself against the pain.

'His mother died—we couldn't save her,' he said, returning to slump into the chair he'd left in front of Lauren's desk earlier.

'I was kind of expecting that. Mike came in earlier,' Lauren responded. 'He said she had horrific injuries.'

'Will you take Bobby back to the refuge until someone finds his family?' He wasn't sure why he'd asked, although it probably had a lot to do with the phantoms that had flashed by.

Lauren looked up at him, her eyes dark with concern.

'I couldn't do that to him, Tom,' she said softly. 'I couldn't put him in there with other kids who have their mothers. I promised him I'd look after him. I've all but finished my hospital and private work now until mid-January and when I have to be at the refuge, I can probably take him or get Jo to mind him, but the problem is my flat's so tiny and there's no yard and he's a little boy who needs lots of space. I could take him out to the family farm but my brother and his family and my parents are all away for a couple of weeks—spending Christmas with my sister in Melbourne. I was to go too, but—well, you know how low on funds we are at the refuge, and I've cut the staff and...'

Tom frowned down at her.

'That doesn't mean you should be working yourself to death there,' he muttered. 'But that's not the point, I can understand you taking Bobby home tonight, but surely you don't have to worry about a yard for him to play in—he'll have family somewhere.'

Lauren stared at the man across her desk. Eighteen months she'd known Tom, worked with him, attended various committee meetings with him, thought she knew him as a friend, yet there was a strange note in his voice now—one she couldn't quite put her finger on—not panic, certainly, but some kind of disturbing emotion.

However, whatever was going on in his head, she needed to answer him.

'Joan never named Bobby's father, perhaps she didn't know, and Greg, the most recent of the men she's lived with, is violent,' she reminded him. 'Like a lot of women in abusive relationships, Joan had cut herself off from her family, or they from her. Oh, Mike and his people will try to trace relations, but there's more.'

She took a deep, steadying breath.

'Bobby saw Greg in the stands right before the collapse. He was calling to Joan, and she went—'

'This man was underneath the stands? Did you tell Mike?'

Lauren nodded.

'He wasn't killed or injured there...'

She watched as Tom computed the information she'd just shared.

'Is Mike thinking—?'

'They won't know until the workplace health and safety people inspect the wreckage, but Mike's been to Greg's place—he's not there, or at any of the pubs. They're looking for him.'

A wave of tiredness so strong it was like a blow swept over her, and she shook her head.

'I can't think any more tonight. Best I get Bobby and myself home.'

'Stay at my place,' Tom offered. 'I've three bedrooms, plenty of yard for Bobby to play in, and I can dig out some toiletries and hospital night attire for you both as well. You don't want to be driving when you're as tired as you are, and if Bobby's still asleep you'll never get him up the steps to your flat.'

Lauren stared at the man across the desk from her, wondering just what the offer meant, then realising it was nothing more than the kindness of a friend.

She felt a tiny stab of regret that it wasn't something more, but shook the thought away. As if it could be that…

She even managed a smile as she made a far-too-weak protest.

'You don't have to do that for me,' she said. 'Especially after I was so rude about you earlier.'

He grinned at her and the stab deepened.

'I rather liked the encyclopaedia reference, not to mention putting the surf god in his place.'

'I doubt that,' Lauren told him, but the regret she'd felt earlier was turning to guilt…

'Come on,' Tom added. 'I'll show you where the hospital emergency packs are, or do you know?'

'I know,' Lauren told him, pleased to have something concrete to grasp hold of. 'I often bring in women who have left home with nothing.'

Tom nodded, so much understanding in his eyes she felt like crying, or maybe asking for another hug, but such weakness was definitely exhaustion so she hustled off to get some toiletries and night gear for herself and Bobby. She returned with her haul to find Tom had lifted the sleeping boy and was carrying him along the corridor towards the side door that was closest to his house.

Tom's house was the official hospital residence, built in the same style as the hospital with wide verandas on three sides, all of them providing glimpses of the ocean. As Lauren walked through the door she tried to think if she'd ever been inside the house before. She'd been *to* the house often enough, invited to drinks or a barbecue with other friends, but they'd always sat on the veranda.

The living room was comfortably furnished, very neat and tidy, the only thing out of place a folded newspaper resting on the arm of a leather lounge chair. It was off to the left of the central passageway, doors on the right obviously opening into bedrooms.

Tom pushed the second door with his foot and it opened to show a pristinely neat bedroom, a single bed set in the middle, an old polished timber wardrobe on one side and French doors opening to the veranda on the other.

'Do you want to wake him to do his teeth and change his clothes or should we just let him sleep?'

Lauren considered the question—letting the little boy sleep was obviously the best solution, but he might wake and not know where he was.

'Not that I want to hurry you or anything but my arms might give way any minute,' Tom said, and though there was a smile in the words Lauren knew Bobby must have grown very heavy in his arms.

'I think we'll let him sleep,' she said, and she slipped past Tom and his burden and turned down the bed, then, when Tom put Bobby down on the clean sheet, she slid off his rubber flip-flops and pulled the top sheet over him.

Tom came forward and turned on a bedside light, using a button to dim it.

'All mod cons in this place,' he said, then he touched the little boy on the head and hesitated for a few seconds before following Lauren out of the room.

'Your bedroom is this way,' he said, pushing open the next door. 'There's a bathroom just beyond it, towels in a cabinet behind the door. Do you need anything else? Would you like a drink of some kind?'

Lauren shook her head, then common sense dictated she should ask.

'I don't suppose you'd have a blow-up mattress or a comfortable lounger? I'd like to sleep beside him in case he wakes up in the night and doesn't know where he is.'

Tom smiled at her.

'Great minds,' he said. 'I was intending to do just that, but if you're sure then it would be better for you to do it as he doesn't really know me except as someone who causes him pain when he lands in the ER after one of his wilder pranks. I do have a blow-up mattress from far-off camping days. I'll get it.'

He was about to walk away, but Lauren caught his arm so he turned back to her.

'Why?' she asked, adding, when she saw the puzzled expression on his face, 'Why were you thinking of staying with him?'

Tom's smile was gone, his face now pale and grim, although it would be. It was well after midnight and he must be exhausted.

'I was Bobby once,' he said softly, then he slipped his arm away from her fingers and disappeared back along the passage and into what must be the front bedroom.

His bedroom!

I was Bobby once?

What did he mean?

And why was it suddenly very important to Lauren that she find out? Find out all she could about the enigmatic man she'd thought she knew…

Why had he said that?

Lauren was a psychologist—she'd want an explanation for a statement like that.

But would she ask?

Lauren, his friend, would have, but this Lauren was different.

Because he'd seen vulnerability in her for the first time in the eighteen months he'd known her?

Because he felt, not exactly proud, but somehow pleased that she'd trusted him enough to show that vulnerability?

So he'd shared a bit of his?

Oh, please! Enough with the psychological delving.

He reached up on top of his wardrobe for his old backpack, assuming his blow-up mattress would still be shoved inside or strapped to it. He hoped the rubberised material hadn't rotted. If it had, Lauren was in for an uncomfortable night. Perhaps the reclining lounge chair would be more comfortable for her, although they would probably wake Bobby trying to manoeuvre it into the bedroom, and would it fit?

He tried very hard to concentrate on these nice trivial matters, but in his head the image of a little boy, younger than Bobby by a couple of years, tucked into a strange bed in a strange room—the first of a series of strange beds in strange rooms…

'Tom? Can I help?'

Lauren was in the doorway and it was obvious he'd dithered for so long she'd had time to have a shower for her hair clung in damp tendrils to her neck, and she was wearing what must be one of the ugliest nightdresses ever created. A vague purple colour, faded from much washing, it had something he assumed were bunches of flowers printed all over it, and it hung, shapeless as a deflated balloon, from her shoulders.

'Fetching, isn't it?' she said, smiling at the thoughts she'd obviously guessed he was having. 'Maybe the hospital insists on the design—it'd work better than an old-fashioned chastity belt for randy staffers.'

Though not for him, Tom discovered. Standing there in

his bedroom door, freshly showered, totally exhausted but still so temptingly beautiful, his body would probably have reacted if she'd been wearing a suit of armour.

'You'd look good in a wheat sack,' he told her, hefting the whole backpack down from the top of the wardrobe and turning his attention to finding the mattress, shaking his head in frustration when it failed to materialise.

'Don't worry,' she said. 'I'm so tired I could sleep on a barbed-wire fence. It's a warm night so if you wouldn't mind lending me that puffy-looking duvet you have on your bed I can fold it, probably in three—is that a king-size bed?—and it will be fine.'

Looking at the bed was a mistake. He immediately pictured Lauren in it. And it *was* a king-size bed but right now he didn't want to think about why he used a bed that size, let alone explain it.

'Okay,' he said, realising that the sooner he got Lauren tucked away in Bobby's bedroom the sooner he could sort through the craziness inside his head.

Could he put it all down to seeing Bobby in that neatly made single bed?

Of course he couldn't. It had started back with Lauren's groan, and the strange sensation of…satisfaction?…he'd felt when she'd asked him to stand by her.

Not to mention his determination to find out more about the vulnerability he'd glimpsed in the woman he'd thought was so together.

He'd stalled again, standing in the bedroom, only vaguely aware of Lauren walking past him and hefting the duvet from his bed. He reached out to take it from her, but as he touched her arm she dropped it, and stepped over it so she was close enough to hug.

For him to hug her, although it didn't happen that way.

It was Lauren who moved closer, Lauren who put her arms around him, slipping her hands beneath his shoulders so she could reach around his body, then she hugged him tightly to her, her head pressed against his chest, a whispered 'Thank you for being there for me tonight' rising up into his ears.

Then, just as he was certain she'd feel his body's unacceptable reaction to the embrace, she pulled away, picked up the duvet from the floor, and left the room.

CHAPTER THREE

LAUREN shouldn't have hugged him, she knew. Of course she shouldn't, especially not without asking, but his words had sounded so bleak and there'd been such sadness lingering in his eyes as she'd stood at the bedroom door that she'd been unable to resist.

The problem was that now, lying on his folded duvet, smelling the man that had permeated it, she could still feel the tremors of—what, attraction?—that hugging him had startled into life. Tremors she hadn't felt in years but still recognised for what they were—definitely attraction!

In truth, she had always been attracted to Tom—what woman wouldn't be?—which was why she'd never accepted any of the invitations he'd offered when he'd first arrived in town. Attraction led down pathways she didn't want to follow. Attraction led to trouble…

And disappointment.

Even disgust from one man she'd gone out with—a man who'd called her names that shamed her even now to think about, a man who had been disgusted when she'd tried to explain it was terror that had stopped her, not a desire to tease and walk away, definitely not a wish to anger him in any way…

Go to sleep, she told herself, trying to shut down her mind, knowing she'd need to be ready for anything the following day. Above her on the bed, Bobby stirred, and Lauren reached up to touch his arm, talking quietly to him, telling him she was there and she'd look after him, although she knew he'd probably moved in his sleep and couldn't hear her words.

It was enough of a reminder of her responsibility to Bobby that it enabled her, at last, to stop thinking about tremors of attraction, and Tom, and the past, and drift into a deep sleep.

They were both still sleeping when Tom looked into the bedroom at eight the following morning. The revolting nightdress had ridden up so he could see Lauren's long, slim, tanned legs curled into the folds of his faded navy duvet.

Could he wake up to Lauren underneath that covering? he wondered. Wake up close to her, not practically falling off the edge of his big bed the way he always had when women shared it?

He shook his head at the way his mind was working. It was lack of sleep, and the uncertainty of the outcome of the collapse of the stands, not to mention Bobby's future, that was making him think things he shouldn't think. He should go across to the hospital to see the patients they'd admitted, but he knew someone would have phoned him if he'd been needed and, besides, he was reluctant to leave the house without letting Lauren know where he was.

Somehow the sleeping woman and boy had become his responsibilities, and he, who'd shied away deliberately from any responsibility outside his work, was finding it strange but no less binding for that.

They'd have to stay—

'Good morning? Have you been standing there all night? Scared one of us would wake up and pinch the silver while you slept?'

He looked down to see Lauren smiling up at him, golden hair tousled around her head, looking so unutterably beautiful and desirable his body did its unacceptable reaction thing again.

'Well?' the beautiful desirable woman on the floor prompted.

'I just poked my head around the door to see if anyone was awake. Would you like a cup of tea or coffee?'

He had to move, get away, stop looking at her, so he hoped she'd say yes to liquid refreshment, but instead she shook her head, said a brief, 'No thank you,' then sat up and checked Bobby as she spoke.

'But we do need to talk,' she added quietly, standing so the nightdress hem fell down to cover those long, slim legs most discreetly, and walking quietly towards him.

He led the way into the living room, knowing she'd want to stay within earshot of Bobby.

'So talk,' he said, and smiled when she stared at him, confusion in her beautiful eyes.

'Well,' she finally said, frowning at him now, 'I'm not sure where to start. Bobby first, of course, and probably we don't have to talk about him because Mike might have found some relatives but I'd be—I'd be unhappy about letting him go into care if there are no relatives—not right now anyway. And I know I'm not making much sense but Bobby's had a rough time of things lately, and somehow I'd like to think that even though he's lost his mother, once he's over that initial grief, his life might get better.'

The rush of words stopped abruptly and she looked directly at him, her gaze so deliberate Tom wasn't altogether surprised when she asked, 'What happened to you? Back when you were Bobby? Will you tell me? It's not idle curiosity, I hope you know that, but if you've been where he is now, then maybe your experience will help.'

Lauren guessed immediately that he wasn't going to tell her. It was as if he'd lowered shutters on his face, right there while she was watching him.

The memories must be bad—really bad for him to shut her out like that—and a tremendous sense of guilt that she'd pried swept through her.

Without further thought, she got up from her chair and went to sit on the arm of his, resting her hand on his shoulder.

'You don't *have* to tell me,' she assured him. 'I should have known better than to ask. It was just that Bobby—well, you don't have to say anything and maybe I will have a cup of tea and if you don't mind staying here to listen for him, I can probably find my way around your kitchen and fix it for myself, would you like one?'

The words rattled out, her uneasiness added to by the tension she could feel beneath her fingers, Tom's muscles as tight as steel hawsers. But as she stood, desperate to escape the terrible atmosphere in the room—the atmosphere *she* had caused—he caught her hand and pulled her back and she landed in his lap, her face close enough to see the lines of tiredness in his face and read memories he didn't want to think about in his eyes.

'I'm sorry,' she whispered, touching that ravaged face.

'Don't be,' he said, then he put his head down on her shoulder, slipped his arms around her body, and just rested there, holding her, until she felt his body relax and his lips, surprisingly, move against the skin on her shoulder in what felt like a kiss.

He lifted his head—it couldn't have been a kiss—and looked her in the eye.

'Do you believe in fate?' he asked.

'I don't think so,' she said, 'well, not entirely. I don't think every single thing in our lives happens for a reason, if that's what you mean by fate.'

'Neither do I, but with Bobby coming into our lives right now, I have to wonder.'

Our lives? Lauren thought, but she didn't query it out loud. Tom had something he wanted to say and she didn't want to divert his train of thought, although 'our lives' had brought her tremors back again and, given that she was still sitting on his knee, the tremors were likely to get the wrong idea.

'My parents and my older sister were killed in a car accident when I was six. I survived and was taken in by Children's Services until a relative was found—a grandmother I'd never met because my parents had been cut off from their families. Cue violins for real Romeo and Juliet family feud scenario but they didn't die tragically young, my parents. They lived on to have two children *then* died.'

Lauren rested against him, wanting to hug him as she'd hugged Bobby, wanting to hug the six-year-old orphan Tom had been, but she held back, wary of distracting him from a story that sounded rusty, as if it was a long time since it had been told—if ever…

'It didn't work out with Grandmother, so Children's Services were called in again—and again, and again, and again. I wasn't the kind of kid foster-families liked—not quiet and biddable and appreciative of all they were doing for me. I was rebellious and loud and full of hate and denial. When I was fifteen I finally got lucky with some foster-parents who ignored all the horrible bits of me, and concentrated on some glimmer of good that no one else had found. Perhaps I hadn't had it earlier, I don't know. They were kind people—all of them were kind, in fact—but these two encouraged me to put all my anger and energy into my school work, hence the doctor you see before you.'

Long pause.

Should she break the silence?

But how?

Her mind had gone on strike back when he'd said 'Grandmother' and Lauren had envisaged a stern, upright woman who didn't know how to handle a bereft little boy…

A granny or a nana might have known—would have known for sure—but a grandmother?

Unable to think of a single thing to say, Lauren rested against this man she'd never known existed inside the Tom she did know, and hoped her closeness might ease some of the pain this delving into his past had caused.

He didn't seem to object. In fact, his arms tightened around her and they sat in warm, comfortable silence, and maybe would have sat like that all day had Bobby not let out a yell from the bedroom, which sent her scooting off Tom's knee and hurrying in that direction.

'Hi, Bobby,' she said as she walked into the bedroom, her heart aching as she looked at the sleep-rumpled little boy.

'Where am I? Where's Mum?' he demanded, the Bobby Sims she did know coming to the fore, belligerence written in his face, anger in the taut lines of his slight body.

Lauren crossed the room to sit on the end of the bed.

'We're at Dr Tom's house, near the hospital. You fell asleep watching DVDs and he carried you here.' She pointed to the rumpled duvet on the floor. 'See, I slept beside you.'

She inched closer up the bed, wanting to give him a cuddle but aware he was holding himself aloof from her.

'The bathroom's just along the passageway if you want to use it, then we might all have breakfast.'

He bolted from the room but when he returned he took up his position on the far end of the bed again.

'Where's Mum?' he demanded, and Lauren knew she couldn't put it off.

She edged closer and took hold of his hand, and when he didn't pull it away, she shifted close enough to put her arm around his shoulders. Inside, she felt nauseous. All the psychology training in the world didn't help you tell an eight-year-old his mother was dead.

'Your mum was underneath the stands when they collapsed. The doctors did all they could to save her but she'd been too badly injured and she died.'

The punch surprised her, so his little fist slamming against her cheek sent her reeling backwards.

'She is *not* dead! You're telling lies,' Bobby yelled, pushing at her now, slapping, thumping-hysterical. 'She's not dead, she's not, she's *not*!'

Tom came in and grabbed the flailing child, holding him firmly, talking quietly.

'We're so sorry, Bobby, we really, really are. We know you loved your mum and she loved you, and although we can't replace her, Lauren and I want you to know that you're safe here with us and whatever happens, we'll always be your friends and look out for you.'

The words must have penetrated Bobby's wild surge of grief, for the child went limp in his arms and began to cry, quietly at first but then with huge, wrenching sobs that tore through Lauren's chest like heart pain.

'Give him to me now,' she said to Tom, who settled the boy on her lap so she could rock him in her arms, comforting him with soft words and soothing murmurs.

Eventually he fell asleep, and she tucked him back into bed.

'It's an escape mechanism, sleep,' she said as she joined

Tom in the doorway. 'I wonder if I can take advantage of it and go over to my place to get some clothes. I can call by the refuge and get his things— Oh!'

She put her fingers up to her lips to stop any other ill-thought-out words escaping, and looked directly at her host.

'You might not want us here. I don't know why I was assuming we'd stay. Of course we can't stay—when he wakes I'll take him home. I might go over to the refuge and get his clothes, though.'

Now Tom put *his* fingers to her lips, startling them into silence.

'Do you know that when you're uncertain about something you rush into words? Is it to do with your training, or is it natural? A way of thinking things through by letting it all flow out?'

'I don't do that!' Lauren retorted, not sure if she'd been confused by Tom's words or by the touch of his fingers on her lips.

'Oh, yes, you do,' he said, smiling at her in such a kindly way she thought her knee joints might give out. 'And of course you'll stay here. I've just promised Bobby that we'll *both* look after him and you can't break a promise to a child. So scoot off home and get your gear, but I've already phoned the refuge and someone there will pack up all of Joan and Bobby's stuff and bring it here. Also some bike they know he likes to ride and a few books and toys.'

'You did all that before I woke up?' Lauren was getting the feeling that for all she'd thought them friends, maybe she didn't know this man at all, although as he'd once been in Bobby's position, maybe...

'I knew they'd be anxious for news of what had happened, and I didn't think it would be good for Bobby to go back there and see his mother's things. We can leave them packed away for a while—I've plenty of storage room here.'

Still bemused by Tom's forethought, Lauren hurried into the bedroom she'd been allocated, pulled on yesterday's clothes with some reservations, then came out, finding Tom in the kitchen.

'How long will you be?' he asked. 'Twenty minutes or do you want longer?'

'I'll be as quick as I can,' she said, 'certainly not more than twenty minutes. I don't want Bobby waking up and finding me gone.'

Tom nodded at her, then smiled and said, 'Breakfast in twenty minutes, then.'

They were friends, nothing more, Lauren told herself as she hurried across to the hospital to retrieve her car. And the Bobby-situation had put them together for a while, that was all. Besides, of all the men in the world she shouldn't get involved with, Tom headed the list. Tom was special, a great guy, an empathetic and clever doctor, a man who deserved the best of wives—something she doubted she could ever be.

Before the gloom from that thought could take hold, she laughed at herself. How had her mind flitted from staying over at Tom's while they got Bobby sorted to marriage?

They weren't involved, she and Tom, nothing whatsoever would be going on between them, except the well-being of a lonely little boy.

The house, which had become as much of a home as houses he'd lived in ever could, seemed somehow lonely after Lauren left. Having seen her off, Tom wandered back into the kitchen, telling himself this was a fancy and as he was never fanciful, it had to be tiredness and letdown after the drama of the previous night playing tricks on his mind.

The previous night! Could someone—this Greg fellow Bobby had mentioned?—have loosened the scaffolding some way? Could anyone hate another person so much they would risk killing many people just to get the one they hated?

He opened the refrigerator door, pleased he'd shopped the previous day, so he *did* have bacon and eggs, and in the freezer some potato cakes that fried up like the hash browns served at fast-food outlets. Bobby would probably enjoy them, although when Tom had bought them, he'd been indulging his own weakness for the fried-up slabs of grated potato.

But the idea of hatred had taken root in his head.

Did he not understand hatred because he'd never felt it—not even for his cold, disdainful, uncaring grandmother? Did one need to know how to love in order to learn how to hate? He'd accepted long ago he didn't understand love and was reasonably sure he'd never feel it. Not again! Not after losing his sister, his protector, the laughing, loving Jane. Much reading on the subject had confirmed his gut feeling that many children who grow up without being loved can't learn to love in their adult lives.

Not that he wanted love in his life—the screams of abuse his parents had been yelling at each other when the car had crashed thirty years ago still echoed in his head whenever the word was mentioned.

He shook off the strange mood of introspection and pulled the makings of breakfast from the fridge, but once they were set out on the table, the memories sent him back along the passage, to look in on the little boy asleep on the bed, tear stains on his cheeks.

'I'll fight for you,' he promised the sleeping child. 'I'll check out every damn relative the Children's Services people produce and if you don't like them, you'll stay with me. We'll cope, the two of us…'

But even as he whispered his promise to the sleeping boy, he wondered if he could do it. If Bobby stayed with him then he, Dr Tom Fletcher, would finally *have* to learn to love, because he couldn't let Bobby grow up as he'd grown up—fearing love, repelling any tentative advance of it, denying love, denigrating it…

He rested his head on the doorjamb and sighed.

'I can't smell bacon.'

He looked up to see Lauren at his front door. She had changed into a calf-length skirt, blue-green in colour, made of some light material that swirled around her legs. On top she wore a white tank top that showed off her tan, and framed there in his doorway she looked so lovely that for a moment he wished he *had* learned how to love.

'Come on through. I was just checking on Bobby. Have you got bags to carry in?'

'Bags?' she teased. 'I'm not coming to stay for ever. I've got enough in my tote to see me through a few days. Once Bobby's sorted…'

She'd reached him now and studied his face, frowning slightly. 'We *will* get Bobby sorted, won't we?'

She was seeking reassurance, which was so unlike the Lauren he thought he knew that he hurried to give her the same promise he'd given the sleeping child.

'Of course we will—properly sorted—no interim measures or temporary foster-homes or anything else. We've told him we'll take care of him and we will.'

He was pleased to see the tenseness in her shoulders ease, and felt a surge of excitement arc through him when she touched his arm and said quietly, 'You're a good man, Tom Fletcher.'

It was pleasure at her praise, nothing more, but he moved away, aware he'd have to be very careful to avoid opportunities for touches while Lauren was staying in his house. He'd always been attracted to her, and as he'd grown to know her over time, he'd been pleased she'd refused to go out with him, because he knew his attitude to affairs left some women hurt and the one thing he would hate to do was hurt Lauren.

Although with Lauren living in the house, perhaps…

He muttered several swear words under his breath, ashamed where his thoughts had led!

And as it turned out, he didn't have to go out of his way to avoid touches as they'd barely finished a late breakfast when people began arriving. One of the residential workers from the refuge was first, bringing Bobby's and Joan's belongings and some toys for Bobby.

'I'll put Joan's cases on the top of my wardrobe with other stuff,' Tom offered, while Lauren comforted the worker, who'd been friendly with Joan.

Mike came next, looking so worried Tom ushered him into a chair on the veranda so Bobby wouldn't hear the conversation should he wake.

'There's evidence the scaffolding was tampered with on one side. Some of the pieces of the shaped metal, clamps and elbows and such, that hold the bars together had been loosened enough for the joints to give way.' He paused and looked directly at Tom. 'We were lucky the outcome wasn't far worse. If you and Cam hadn't acted so swiftly in getting people off the stands, I hate to think how many might have been killed. But getting back to Joan, a couple of people have mentioned seeing Greg Carter under there, but we can't find him. We've put out an Australia-wide alert for his car, but it hasn't been spotted either.'

'What about relatives for Joan or Bobby? Have you got any further with that?'

Mike's shrug gave the answer. He turned to Lauren, who'd

come out onto the veranda with a tray of cups and the coffee pot—refilled, apparently.

'Do you have any details of family members in the file at the refuge?' Mike asked her.

Lauren shook her head.

'Joan never mentioned anyone, but she wasn't from the Cove. The refuge did have her aunt as a contact person, but I remember minding Bobby for her some time last year while she went to Sydney for the aunt's funeral. We'd have a lot of Joan's details—Medicare number, driver's licence and maybe even her birth certificate. Do you want me to check what they have?' Lauren told him.

'No, I'll call over there,' Mike told her, 'but getting someone to put a trace on her details on a weekend might be difficult. Are you two happy to keep the boy here today?'

Tom saw the look in Mike's eyes as he asked the question, sending it into the air between the two of them. It was a look that suggested another question was hovering in Mike's mind—a question about whether the two of them were linked in some way.

Seeing each other and keeping it quiet—at least until now!

Small-town gossip was likely to link them anyway, if Lauren stayed on. Would it hurt her? Upset her?

Lauren didn't want to answer Mike's question. After all it was Tom's house, and he had promised earlier he'd make sure Bobby was okay, but as the silence lengthened she thought she'd better reply.

'We're happy to keep Bobby and we'll take good care of him,' she said, then felt her third blush in two days rising into her cheeks, because *she'd* linked herself and Tom together with that 'we', linked them as publicly as her staying on in Tom's house would in the minds of the townsfolk.

Red on the outside and cringing on the inside but it was too late to retrieve the words!

'Good,' Mike said, nodding, then adding, 'Well, that's settled,' as if something more than Bobby's immediate future had been decided.

He'd no sooner departed than Jo arrived, announcing that she and Cam had called in at the hospital and she'd left Cam there talking to one of his patients who'd been admitted with severe lacerations to his legs.

'And what's this I hear about you two?' she demanded, turning to smile at Lauren before she added, 'Not content with borrowing the encyclopaedia, you've moved into the library?'

'We're minding a child, in case you hadn't heard that part,' Lauren told her, hoping she'd put enough ice into the words to prevent Jo taking her joke any further.

'Bobby Sims, of course, and he's definitely a two-man job—or a man and woman job.'

The grin that accompanied the words told Lauren her ice had done no good at all. Jo was revelling in the fact that she and Tom had been thrust together.

'Mind yourself,' Lauren warned her friend. 'One day you'll take that step too far.'

Jo chuckled, totally unabashed by Lauren's scold, and turned her attention to Tom.

'You look after this woman or you'll have me to answer to,' she told him.

Tom knew it was nothing more than light-hearted chatter so why did the words resonate within him?

Because he'd seen vulnerability in Lauren the previous evening, and it had disturbed him?

Vulnerability in a woman he'd always considered totally together?

Lauren, meanwhile, showing her more usual strength and determination and not waiting for Tom to reply, was telling her friend just where she could go and what she could do with her smart remarks.

'And since when did I need looking after?' she finished, but Jo just grinned a totally unrepentant grin and departed, heading for the hospital, although as she crossed the yard she turned back to Lauren.

'I'll do any shifts you were taking at the refuge while you've got Bobby. I'll phone you later.'

Jo was telling Lauren, not asking—evidence of their close friendship—but though Tom was pleased Jo would pick up any slack at the refuge for Lauren, it was the other phrase—to look after Lauren—that still lingered in his head.

It meant nothing, he told himself. In fact, having Lauren in the house was going to interfere with his life no end—he could hardly bring women here while she was here.

Not that his love life was important right now—definitely not with, well, not only Lauren but with Bobby in the house.

He'd promised Bobby.

Could a man have any kind of social life with a kid around?

Was he really so shallow that he was thinking this way?

And had he been wrong about Lauren all these years?

Did she need looking after?

He leant forward and rested his head in his hands and heard himself groan.

'Migraine?' Lauren teased.

He looked up and glowered at her.

'I don't know what's come over me. Here I am, a normal, easygoing male, doing my job, minding my own business, generally enjoying life and suddenly I'm making promises to a kid I barely know, and obviously losing my marbles altogether.'

'You're worried about Bobby,' Lauren told him. 'And worrying about him has not only brought back a lot of unwanted memories of your own but it's got you thinking far too far ahead. You're probably already worrying about how you can entertain your women friends when you've got a houseful of unwanted guests.'

He gaped at her. Was his head made of glass that she'd read through the knotted thoughts inside it so easily?

Then he glowered, because it was very uncomfortable having someone around who *could* do that, especially the bit about the women.

Although she'd missed the bit where he was worried about her as well.

She ignored the glower, held up the coffee pot and he nodded, and to top off the wild emotional swings he was experiencing, he found himself smiling because suddenly it was very pleasant to be sitting on his veranda with Lauren pouring coffee for him.

CHAPTER FOUR

TAKING care of Bobby consumed the rest of the day. He woke hungry and belligerent, and nothing changed throughout the programme Lauren and Tom devised to keep him busy.

They started with a surf, choosing the long southern beach so he wouldn't have to see the scene of the previous night's disaster, but the boogie board Tom lent him was too old, the surf too rough, the sand too sandy, and when, in desperation to find something to give him pleasure, Lauren suggested they go to a fast-food outlet for dinner, of course the one she suggested was the wrong one.

Back at Tom's house, an exhausted Lauren supervised a reluctant Bobby's bath, got him into pyjamas and was intending to send him to bed when she realised he'd slept until early afternoon and while she and Tom might be exhausted after a drama-packed night and long, exhausting day, Bobby was still running on a full tank.

'Can I watch some of the DVDs from over at the hospital?' he asked, and Lauren glanced at Tom who mimed a despairing 'Anything!' at her, so she took Bobby's hand and led him across to the hospital to choose a DVD he'd enjoy.

She'd been relatively surprised when he'd let her hold his hand, so it wasn't totally unexpected that he shook her off before they walked up onto the veranda where there might be people who would see them. But the fact that he'd let her hold it even for a short time heartened her, as he'd avoided physical approaches all afternoon.

'It isn't us he hates, just his situation,' Lauren said to Tom a little later. They were sitting on the veranda just outside the French doors from the living room, so Bobby could see them if he looked out.

'I wish he'd talk about it, even ask something,' Tom replied, speaking quietly, although the sound was so loud on the DVD Lauren doubted Bobby could hear them.

'He's blocking it from his mind. If he doesn't talk about it he doesn't have to think about it and he's very aware that thinking about it causes pain and grief.' Lauren sighed, then added, 'He'll work his way up to it. Well, I hope he will.'

She was expecting an objection when the DVD finished and she told Bobby it was bedtime, but he went willingly enough, cleaning his teeth first, then leading the way into 'his' room.

His little face was set, his lips tight, the tension in his body so obvious Lauren wondered how she might help him release some of it.

Giving him a hug and a goodnight kiss would probably result in another punch.

'You don't have to go to school this week if you don't want to,' she said, desperate for an opening that might encourage him to talk—*if*, of course, he wanted to. 'It's the last three days of term and nothing's happening so you can miss them.'

'Why wouldn't I go to school? It's the only time school's fun, this last week. We muck around, throw water bombs, so course I'll go.'

Oh, dear, the belligerence was still there—in force! Could she mention what had happened?

Gently?

'You do know the other kids will talk about the accident and it might upset you?'

His face tightened and for a moment she thought he might cry. At least that would give her a chance to comfort him.

'It wasn't an accident.' The words burst from his lips. 'Greg *did* something. Have the police got him? Do they know he did it? Do they know he killed my mum?'

Tom had moved into the doorway of the room, no doubt intending to say goodnight to Bobby. Lauren glanced at him, aware the despair she was feeling would be written on her face.

To her relief Tom came closer, sitting down on the other side of Bobby's bed.

'The police know Greg was there and they are looking for him,' he said to Bobby. 'They'll find him.'

'Will they bang him up?' The little boy—and he appeared *very* little and *very* alone right now—looked from Tom to Lauren then back to Tom. ''Cos if they don't I won't go and live with him. He's *not* my dad, and if anyone makes me I'll run away and keep on running away.'

It wasn't that Tom was closer, he just moved faster, reaching out to take Bobby in his arms.

'We've promised you we'll look after you,' he reminded Bobby, 'and we will. We will *not* let you go anywhere you don't want to go, or anywhere you might be unhappy.'

The terrible tension was released. Bobby's tears this time were quiet and when they'd ended, Lauren and Tom shared the task of tucking him into bed, assuring him again and again he was safe with them. Then they kissed him, one on each cheek, Lauren telling him she'd be beside him if he woke up in the night.

'You want a story?' Tom asked, surprising Lauren, who'd

brought in a book from the refuge but had forgotten about it in the emotional conversations.

'You'll read it?' Bobby asked, and Tom agreed he was up to the task.

Lauren left them to it, the little boy lying on his side, his hands clasped under his head, listening to Tom read a story about a boy who sucked his pet bird into the vacuum cleaner by accident.

Apparently it was weird enough for Bobby to enjoy it, although when she peeked in a little later, the child was asleep, Tom pulling the sheet up over him in case the night grew cool.

'Can we make promises like that to him—telling him we won't let him go anywhere he doesn't want to go?' Lauren asked Tom when he joined her in the living room where she was tidying up the mess Bobby had created while watching the DVD.

One crisp packet, one empty milk glass, one plate with one chocolate biscuit—melted and sticky—still on it, and various bits of torn-up paper he'd got from somewhere.

Tom watched in silence as she tried to piece the paper together, and when he didn't answer, she pushed a little further.

'Being Bobby, any relative they find could be the kindest, most loving and generous person in the world and he'd find fault with him or her.'

'I know.'

Okay, so Tom had finally replied, but 'I know' wasn't much help.

'And?' Lauren prompted.

Tom sighed and came into the room, slumping down in what Lauren thought of now as *his* chair. And that's what the torn paper was—the newspaper folded at the crossword that had been on the arm of that chair earlier in this tumultuous day.

'I think what he needs right now is reassurance,' Tom said, weighing each word as he tried to speak the random thoughts that fluttered like the bird in the vacuum cleaner through his head. 'If we can give him that now, while he comes to terms to some extent with his mother's death, then we'll deal with the next stage when it happens. Eventually, if a relative is found who is willing to take care of him, we will have to not only suss that person out but persuade Bobby to at least give him or her a go, but until Mike finds a relative, let's not worry.'

'That's easier said than done,' Lauren muttered, standing in the middle of the room with the tray of dirty dishes and debris in her hands.

Tom looked up at her and smiled.

'Isn't it always? We, doctors in particular, say don't worry to people knowing full well they're going to go on worrying. "Don't worry" must be the most ineffectual phrase in the English language. Now, do you want some real food? My stomach doesn't seem to think that a chicken burger and chips, most of which Bobby pinched from my packet, will get me through the night.'

'You can't go on feeding me,' Lauren protested. 'If I'm staying here a while, I should throw in for food.'

'We don't know how long you're staying,' Tom pointed out, getting out of his chair and coming across to take the tray she was still holding in her hands—close, so close she realised there were dark rims around the grey of his irises, not to mention dark shadows of tiredness beneath his eyes.

'Let's get a pizza delivered, my shout, or Chinese or whatever,' she suggested. 'What would you like?'

Had she rushed into food conversation because a sudden sense of intimacy had crept over her as they'd stood—so close…

'Pizza for me, from the wood-fired oven place. You like

pepperoni?' Had Tom felt the same intimacy that he'd backed up a pace before he'd answered?

'Love it, and plenty of olives and feta cheese and prosciutto as well, please, but I'm paying.'

'You're a guest,' he repeated. 'Guests don't pay.'

He moved away now, taking the tray through to the kitchen. Should she follow—wash and dry the plate and glass? This was the problem with staying in someone else's house—you never knew just what you should or shouldn't be doing. And standing with him in the kitchen—washing up or drying—they'd be close again. That probably wasn't such a good idea when an image of his eyes lingered in her head, and an uneasy reaction to his closeness rippled in her body.

She was still dithering when she heard him on the side veranda, phoning the pizza place, and then, from the snippets of conversation she could hear, calling the hospital as well. She knew he'd been over there for a while before they'd gone to the beach, and all but three of the patients admitted the previous night had been discharged. As far as she knew, none of the remaining accident victims were in a bad way, but checking again and again, she knew, was part of Tom's make-up. He was thorough in all he did, probably the most effective member of the co-ordinating team for the refuge, always coming up with suggestions and ideas.

The refuge! She hadn't given the problems there a thought—and what had happened to the cheque she'd been supposed to accept last night?

Better to think about the refuge than to think about Tom.

It was only the enforced cohabitation—what a word!—that was stirring up the attraction she'd always felt for the man, attraction she'd been able to hide behind what she considered a relaxed but true friendship, only too aware it couldn't be anything else.

'Pizza on the way. Would you like a cold drink?' She was still dithering outside the living room, lost in tangled strands of thought, so when he suggested they sit outside again and offered a selection of cold drinks, she allowed herself to be guided to a chair and said yes to a glass of the new low-alcohol wine a local vineyard was producing.

It would be interesting to try the wine but, more importantly, it was unlikely the low percentage of alcohol would weaken her determination that Tom should stay a friend and nothing more.

Unfortunately, it wasn't the low-alcohol wine that weakened her, it was the sense of well-being that crept over her as she sat on the shadowed veranda, looking out over the town towards the ocean, hearing the soft splash of the surf on the beach, seeing the lights on the Christmas tree, secured, fully upright, without fanfare some time during the day.

Not only well-being but belonging, which was stupid as Crystal Cove was where she *did* belong, having grown up in the hills behind the town. But this belonging was something different—an ease within herself, even though she wasn't alone.

And, no, it couldn't *possibly* have anything to do with Tom…

'What would make a man do what Greg Carter apparently did?'

So Tom wasn't thinking of well-being or ease—of course he wasn't.

Glad to have a new focus for her thoughts, Lauren considered the question.

'Perhaps Joan had told him she wasn't going back to him, no matter what he promised,' she said quietly. 'Joan's been a regular at the refuge since it opened and every time she's gone back to whoever was abusing her. Greg is the second man she's been with since I met her. It's a cyclical thing, abuse, but with Greg the intervals between incidents have been becoming shorter, which has pushed her to think more clearly about the future. She'd taken a part-time job at the local supermarket, and was determined to learn to stand on her own two feet.'

A sudden wave of grief for the woman washed through Lauren and she added, 'Sad, isn't it, that we've talked of Bobby and the future but not of Joan herself—not of a young woman killed when her life had barely begun and when a new and hopefully better future seemed to be beckoning.'

Tom shifted his chair a little closer, and reached out to take Lauren's hand, offering comfort as she mourned a woman she'd been supporting for years.

'I think that's something Bobby will be pleased to know later on—to know his mother was trying to make a new life for herself—although if it triggered the action that led to her death it probably isn't something we need to talk to him about right now.'

Tom heard Lauren sigh and wished he could do more, wished he could take her in his arms and promise her everything would be all right, but that was another of those empty promises—nothing more than words like 'don't worry', because who could guarantee 'forever' happiness? Life didn't work that way.

Fortunately the pizzas arrived before he could get too lost in the kind of introspection he usually avoided, finding his life was simpler and easier if he lived it on the surface and didn't delve too deep. That was how he'd survived as a child in care, never asking why him, or trying to work out how he felt about things, simply plunging into whatever life happened to have on offer at the time.

'Shallow, I suppose.'

He was pulling slices of pizzas, fighting with the cheese on top, onto his plate as he spoke.

'Do you prefer thick crust?' Lauren's question jerked him out of the rarely explored region of his mind.

'Prefer thick crust? Why would you think that?'

'You muttered something about it being shallow—I thought you meant thin.'

She was peering at him, a slight frown on her face, worry in her lovely eyes.

'No, you're hearing things, why on earth would I call a pizza shallow?'

At least the silly conversation made her smile.

'Okay, I'm hearing things,' she said, still smiling, and Tom decided that having Lauren on his veranda, smiling and eating pizza with strings of cheese hanging from it, was even better than having Lauren on his veranda pouring coffee for him.

Which, all things considered, was a very unsettling idea, given that even in his student days he'd hated having to share his living space with anyone. He'd worked all the hours he'd had available from lectures or study to pay rent on a tiny bedsitter so he *didn't* have to share.

Another legacy of a childhood in care when he'd rarely had his own room, and had been made to share his few possessions?

He didn't know, and wasn't going to think about it, in case thinking about it confused him more than he already was confused. He'd just accept it, and it was only a temporary situation anyway, although…

'What if Mike can't find a relative who would be kind to Bobby?'

Lauren looked up so suddenly a string of cheese got stuck to her chin.

'I honestly don't know, Tom,' she said, frowning again, but maybe because she was having trouble unsticking the cheese. 'I realise your own experiences make you dubious about him being placed in foster-care, but we keep reading stories in the paper about really wonderful foster-parents, who've had dozens of kids through their doors, all of them turning out happy and well adjusted.'

Tom found himself sighing.

'I know,' he said, gloom descending to cloud out the happiness he'd felt earlier. 'Probably most of the foster-parents who cared for me were wonderful as well, but maybe I see myself in Bobby—the perennial misfit, resentful of kindness, suspicious of it, not understanding simple fun and laughter, always seeming to be on the outside, looking in.'

'Do you still feel that way?'

The question startled him.

'Me?'

Lauren smiled as she said, 'Yes, you. I think you do—I think you stay detached. We've been friends for, what, eighteen months? We've been on committees together, shared concerns over patients, been to parties at the homes of mutual acquaintances, yet I don't really know you at all.'

She paused, then added, a little sadly, 'Or you me, I suppose. Maybe we're both the kind of closed-off people who don't...well, not don't make friends because we both have friends and good friends, but maybe we're both people who don't share their lives easily.'

The conversation was, fortunately, interrupted at that stage, Mike pulling up on the drive beyond the front veranda steps, then striding towards them, the grim set of his face telling them it was bad news.

'The initial opinion of the experts looking at the scaffolding is that someone tampered with it, so we're looking for Greg Carter as a murder suspect now. As far as Bobby is concerned, we've not found any relatives as yet and with Christmas fast approaching I doubt we will. Children's Services have suggested he go to one of their emergency foster-families'

'No!'

'No!'

Tom beat her denial but not by much.

'We'll keep him here. We'll manage,' Tom added, and he sounded so positive Lauren knew they would. Somehow they would cope with suddenly having shared parenting—however temporary—of a bewildered, orphaned child.

'My workload is down to practically nil, and now Jo has Cam working at the clinic she'll help out as well,' Lauren added, wanting to reassure Mike that she'd be available for Bobby.

'And Christmas?' Mike asked. 'If we don't find relations or a placement for him, what about over Christmas?'

'I hate the word placement,' Tom muttered, and Lauren understood it brought back too many bad memories for him, but she'd already been planning Bobby's Christmas so rushed in to explain.

'I was going to be in town for Christmas anyway, keeping an eye on things at the refuge then going out to my parents' farm after New Year. I'll keep Bobby with me then take him to the farm later in the holidays Tom'll be welcome there whenever he has time off—it's only three-quarters of an hour's drive so shouldn't be too difficult. If Bobby likes it there, I know the family will be happy for him to stay on when Tom and I have to work. I'll stay up there and commute, we both could, although if Tom has late nights—well, he always has the house and—'

She stopped abruptly, aware she'd been doing exactly what

Tom had accused her of yesterday—rushing into words, saying things that had probably embarrassed Tom who undoubtedly had his own plans for Christmas. And now she thought of it, just where did Tom's latest lady-love fit into all of this? How come she hadn't given that poor woman a thought when she'd not only begged Tom to be her date for the tree raising, but had now shifted into his house?

She tried to think if she'd heard of Tom seeing anyone recently. Maybe a woman up the highway at Belrose? Or had that been last year?

Totally mortified now, she stared out towards the ocean, wondering why the human form couldn't vaporise itself and disappear…

Tom and Mike were talking so perhaps they hadn't heard her or if they had, had simply ignored her. And hopefully their conversation had been relevant enough for them not to have noticed her embarrassment.

Noises of departure brought her back to the here and now and she managed to say goodbye to Mike, but as he drove away she turned to Tom.

'I'm sorry, talking about arrangements without discussing them with you, including you in my plans when for sure you have your own plans for how you want to spend any time you get off, and another thing—I can't believe I didn't think of it earlier, but is my staying here going to get you into trouble with your girlfriend or girlfriends?'

Tom waited patiently until she reached the end of her apology—at least, she thought it was an apology although maybe that had got lost somewhere along the way—then he smiled.

In fact, now she considered it, he'd been smiling all along. She'd noticed his lips twitching while she'd stumbled over her words in her haste to get them out.

'Quite finished?' he asked, and she sighed, then shrugged and shook her head.

'I'm sorry,' she said, in case she hadn't said it earlier.

'No, and no, and no,' Tom said in a deep but gentle voice that coiled into her chest and seemed to clutch at her heart. 'No apologies are needed. How can you apologise when all you were doing was showing kindness and friendship? And, no, though I'm working over Christmas, I have no plans for my time off after it and would be delighted to spend it with you and Bobby and even go to the farm if your family don't mind, and finally, my sweet Lauren, there's no girlfriend in my life at present and even if there was, how could any worthwhile person be upset by you and I getting together to care for a lost and lonely little boy?'

Utterly relieved by his understanding, and perhaps a little excited by the 'no girlfriend' bit, although that was stupid, Lauren raised her head and looked at him, wanting one more assurance.

'That's all we're doing, isn't it?' she whispered.

Was it doubt that flickered in his eyes?

The same doubt she'd felt when he'd said it?

Was that all they were doing?

He leant forward and kissed her, a barest brush of lips on lips, yet her lips foolishly responded, clinging for a moment, wanting more.

Was she mad?

Fortunately, before she could decide, Tom straightened up and smiled.

'What else could it possibly be?' he teased, which wasn't reassuring at all, particularly as the coil around her heart tightened while her breath caught in her lungs and panic swept like jagged lightning through her mind.

She'd *wanted* the kiss to continue?

She sought refuge in her bedroom, where she dug her nightshirt out of her tote. What had possessed her to bring the one that had fat cherubs with bows and arrows—a gift from a grateful patient—all over it? She'd never really looked at the pattern before but peering at it now, yes, they were definitely Cupids. Not that nightwear Cupids could actually *do* anything…

Cupid was a myth.

But on consideration the Cupids were better than the hospital creation *and* the hot peppers on her other nightgown—the one her young nephew had given her for Christmas last year. Young nephew, Jake—Jake would be at the farm when she went up after Christmas. He was ten, a nice kid—nice enough to put up with Bobby's insecurities? She hoped so because that's all his bad behaviour was, an outlet for uncertainty…

And what was *her* outlet for the uncertainty besieging her right now?

Not thinking about it!

Ignoring it!

No other way to go…

She grabbed the Cupid nightshirt and her toilet bag and headed for the bathroom. Shower, clean teeth, bed, sleep—simple.

Simple, right up to the sleep part. She lay on the quite comfortable folded duvet on the floor and tried not to think about the man who owned the duvet. Tried to rationalise her thoughts—hadn't she known Tom for nearly two years, so why now start going gooey over him? Coils around her heart indeed! Although—

The although shocked her so much she sat upright on her makeshift bed and stared into the darkness.

No, of course she wasn't going to consider the although!

As if the fact that he wasn't seeing anyone at the moment meant he might want a brief affair with her!

But everyone in town would assume it's happening…

So?

So why not?

Heat coiled now, low and swift, reminding her that her body was meant for more than simply existing—it was meant for pleasure…

She sighed into the darkness—physical pleasure was something she'd read about often enough but never experienced, not with a lover.

A lover—that's all Tom would be.

An experienced lover capable of showing her physical pleasure.

A *very* experienced lover.

Could she do it?

She'd lost count of her blushes over this particular weekend but felt the heat rise again in her cheeks that she could be thinking such a thing.

As if Tom would be interested in *her*! Not after all the times she turned him down.

Not after he'd stopped asking…

And as if she could let it happen!

Lead him on then let him down as her stupid fears conquered her before they could even get close to physical pleasure?

No, she couldn't humiliate herself like that in front of Tom…

Tom lay in bed, missing his duvet, although it was hot enough not to need any covering. In actual fact, he suspected he was missing the woman who was sleeping on his duvet, although he could hardly be missing her in bed when she'd never shared his bed, and she was still in his house, so he couldn't really be missing her.

These musings having reached a dead end, he sent a silent apology to Emily up in Belrose whom he had been seeing in a casual, no-strings kind of way for the past few months. He mentally apologised for denying her existence earlier, though he knew full well Emily wouldn't be upset if their casual arrangement ended. In fact, he suspected she was ready to end it herself, or perhaps had ended it, refusing the last few times he'd invited her to come down or suggested he drive up for a visit.

It was a pity in a way about Emily because it was exactly the kind of affair he enjoyed—the woman far enough away to not expect him to be constantly dancing attendance on her, an out-of-town arrangement so no one was hurt by gossip, and a woman who had a healthy enjoyment of sex for its own sake, not wanting things he couldn't offer, like love or commitment.

He didn't have to consider love where Lauren was concerned, but he certainly had committed himself to her and Bobby for the foreseeable future. And apparently Lauren had committed herself to him and Bobby because she was including him in family post-Christmas plans.

She'd explain the situation to her parents, he was sure of that, so they'd have no expectations of him as a possible partner for their daughter—a future son-in-law.

Son-in-law? The thought of him being such a person was so totally out of whack he smiled into the darkness, then felt a little sad that it should be so foolish an idea…

But he drifted into sleep with the position on his mind, wondering just what was involved in being a son-in-law—something he was never likely to be…

CHAPTER FIVE

THE next morning, as Lauren came into the kitchen, desperate for a cup of tea and a little peace and quiet before Bobby awoke, Tom looked up from where he was reading the paper at the table and said, 'Do you think we could give Bobby one really good day doing something special—just being a boy and enjoying things?'

Lauren considered it for a moment, then grinned at her host.

'Let's go for a picnic in the mountains. Up to Streatham. There's a Sunday morning market there with buskers and other entertainers—men and women on stilts, clowns, face-painting. We can go on from there to the national park and barbeque some sausages, have a swim in the pool below the waterfall, take a walk through the rain-forest—just have a complete nothing day.'

She looked to see how Tom was reacting, then remembered he had a job—responsibilities!

'Oh! Sorry! I should have asked. Are you even off duty?'

'You're doing it again,' he said, smiling at her in such a way the coils tightened once again—this time around her heart. 'Rushing into words. I've already been to work, beside which, I'm the boss, I can take a day off. Streatham's only a twenty-minute drive. If an emergency crops up, I can get back in no time at all. And if I'm not mistaken, we can get breakfast at the markets. Little *profferties* and German sausages and waffles and ice cream—'

'And cups of fruit salad and home-made yoghurt should we just happen to think the child needs a healthy breakfast,' Lauren put in, but Tom just grinned unrepentantly and reminded her that it was a day off so they should be able to eat what they liked.

When Bobby awoke he was wholeheartedly in agreement with the plan, even to the breakfast of the little Dutch pastries with icing sugar and honey and cream.

'And I can ride a camel,' he added, excitement sparkling in his blue eyes. 'Mum took me once and they had camel rides. Have you ever ridden a camel, Tom?'

Tom smiled at Bobby's excitement and admitted camel riding wasn't among his experiences, and then caught Lauren laughing at him when Bobby offered to let Tom ride with him.

''Cos you can ride with two people. Me and Mum did it!'

'It's good he's talking about his mother and things they did together, isn't it?' Tom asked Lauren, while Bobby was off getting his swimmers.

'Very good,' she replied, still smiling, presumably over the prospective camel ride.

But whatever it was over, that smile melted something inside Tom's body, softening his bones in some way—weakening his resolution to stand alone in life.

He had no idea why he should feel this way—no explanation for it, not even an understanding of exactly what had shifted—but he took it as a warning and knew he had to stand back a little, armour himself against thinking this temporary togetherness with Lauren—and Bobby—was anything other than a convenient arrangement for the sake of an orphaned child.

The Streatham Markets were alive with colour and music and people. Flags tossed in the wind, acrobats tumbled across a grassy area, avoiding the camels in their bright saddle-cloths and fancy, plaited reins. Stilt-walkers towered above the crowds while stall-holders extolled the excellence of their produce.

'Can I have waffles *and profferties*?' Bobby asked, when the decision had been made to eat first and explore later.

'You can have waffles or *profferties* and yoghurt or fruit salad with whichever one you choose,' Lauren told him. 'You know all about good eating, and having fruit or veggies with your meals.'

'Yoghurt's not fruit,' the smart eight-year-old reminded her.

'There's fruit in this yoghurt and it's delicious. It's what I'm having.'

'Tom's having *profferties*.'

Lauren knew she'd lost but far more disturbing—after all, they could do good food later in the day—was the strange feeling of not exactly family but togetherness she was beginning to feel. She, who'd always been so self-sufficient in her personal life, accepting that a husband and children weren't in her future, was finding this simple outing with a man and a boy extremely unsettling—emotionally so…

It could be tiredness or stress, of course.

Yes, she'd put it down to that!

But she didn't feel tired *or* stressed. In fact, she felt more alive than she had for a very long time—alive to the sounds and scents of the market, alive to the vibrancy in the air around her, alive, too, to the two males, one big one small, who walked with her through the narrow lanes between the stalls towards the *profferties* stall.

'Fancy coffee or plain?'

Tom's question broke into her musings. Just as well, for who knew where they might have led? She turned to look at him, intending to reply, and caught something in his expression—an unguarded moment perhaps—that seemed to reflect the pure pleasure she was feeling.

Weird!

'French vanilla if they have it,' she said, in reply to his raised eyebrow, but when he smiled she knew she'd been right. He, too, had been enjoying their stroll through the markets even if he probably hadn't been considering the family vibe she'd felt.

They settled at a table beneath a canvas market umbrella, Bobby excitedly pointing out all the things he could see, telling Tom the camels were over that way.

'Sure you're not coming on a camel ride?'

For the second time on the outing, Tom's question brought Lauren out of a muddle of thoughts she knew she shouldn't be having. Mike would find Bobby's family. He'd be moving on.

'Sure of it,' she told Tom. 'I'll check out the fresh fruit and vegetables to stock up for the week. Anything you don't eat?'

He smiled at her and she found she had to concentrate on not panting, so tight had her chest become.

'Turnips,' he said.

'They're not in season anyway,' she told him, pleased she'd been able to answer calmly—pleased she'd been able to speak at all!

If Mike didn't come up with family for Bobby soon, Lauren was going to be in trouble. It had been okay fighting the silly attraction she'd always felt towards Tom when they met at work or with mutual friends, but living with him, being with him when he was relaxed and smiling and raising that darned eyebrow at her—well, how could her body *not* react?

She mused on it as she trailed through the fruit and vegetable stalls, then down the craft aisles picking up little odds and ends to put in a stocking for Bobby for Christmas—even if Mike found family, she could give him a stocking. But she was choosing articles almost at random because her mind was back at the idea of a possible affair. Dependent, of course, on Tom being interested, and then there was the thought that, although she was certain he was probably the best man in the world—he had experience on his side—to help her past her stupid fear of intimacy, might she be using him to get over this fear?

Loud yells brought people running through the stalls and though Lauren didn't want to add to the chaos, she had a sinking feeling in her stomach that whatever upheaval was in progress, there was a chance Bobby would be at the centre of it.

'It wasn't my fault. The stupid camel stood up too soon!'

Tom, seated high above Lauren on the camel Bobby had fallen off, confirmed that the animal *had* lurched into a standing position, back legs first, and it had been almost inevitable that Bobby should fall off. The unfortunate part was that he'd fallen onto the camel's handler who had let go of the reins as the pair tumbled to the ground, and the camel had gone loping off with Tom on board.

Someone had caught the camel, but with Bobby and the handler still untangling themselves and arguing over whose fault it was, no one knew how to make the creature kneel so Tom could clamber off.

Lauren couldn't help it. She began to laugh and soon all

those who'd seen the fun were laughing with her, even Tom and the handler. Everyone but Bobby, who came and put his arms around Lauren's waist, whispering desperately, 'It really wasn't my fault!'

She hugged him hard—he was so good to hug.

'Of course it wasn't,' she assured him.

'Tom won't be angry?'

'Tom? No, he's laughing too.'

The second reassurance worked, for now Bobby smiled.

'It *was* funny seeing Tom bouncing up and down on the camel as it ran across the paddock,' the child admitted, making Lauren eye him just a little suspiciously. But even a little devil like Bobby couldn't have engineered the bolting camel.

Could he?

'Of course not, it was a pure accident,' Tom told her when he'd been rescued from the camel and Bobby was enjoying a ride on a small Ferris wheel.

'I thought so,' Lauren responded, then she turned to Tom. 'He's so insecure,' she said, 'so in need or reassurance, especially when things go wrong. It's as if everything that's ever gone wrong in his life, maybe in his family's life, has been his fault.'

Tom touched her shoulder, frowning slightly as he asked, 'Aren't all kids like that? I know I was.'

Lauren considered it.

'No,' she said eventually. 'As a child I never felt that way, and as far as my family went, no, I didn't ever think it was my fault things went wrong, unless, of course it was like the time I let the calves in with the cows and there was no milk the next morning.'

She thought for a moment, before adding, 'Later, maybe, teenage guilt stuff—I felt to blame for that,' then was sorry her thoughts had turned that way as it swept a cloud over the bright day they'd been having.

Though only for her because here was Bobby back from his ride and who could have clouds hovering over them when they had a child as full of life as Bobby was to entertain?

Laden with good, and a few not so good things to eat—every boy deserved a chocolate cake made in the shape of a spaceship—they left the markets, driving further up the foothills of the mountains, stopping at the national park and walking along the track to the bottom of the falls that splashed down in a thin silver stream from high above them.

As Lauren had been cramming towels and bathing suits for Bobby and herself into her tote she hadn't actually considered how she'd feel wearing her rather skimpy bikini in front of Tom. Yesterday at the beach, she'd worn her other bathers—a decorous blue swimsuit that she wore for exercise swims—but it had still been wet this morning hence the bikini.

What she also hadn't considered was the effect seeing Tom in his swimming trunks would have on her body. Yesterday he'd been in the water with Bobby so she hadn't had a lot of time to take in broad shoulders that sloped to a narrow waist and hips, pecs a weightlifter would be proud of, a six-pack—yes, definitely defined—and a flat stomach she could only envy.

He had the most beautiful male body she had ever seen, and she was positively gawping at it.

Gawping at it and thinking things she shouldn't think about it—about how it would feel to touch the skin that slid tightly over those muscles—and how touching it would make *her* feel…

Fortunately Tom was busy explaining to Bobby that the he couldn't climb the rock beside the waterfall and jump in because you never knew what was under the water in creeks and waterholes and you could be badly injured, so she could afford a little gawp.

'Or dead?' Bobby asked Tom, reminding Lauren she had too many responsibilities right now to be considering chest appeal.

She studied the child, wondering if the question was prompted by thoughts of his mother, but as he didn't elaborate, she decided it must have been nothing more than a casual remark.

The boy and the man with the chest she wasn't going to look at any more slid carefully into the water, shrieking at the icy coldness of it, splashing and shouting so the rainforest all around came alive with the joyous noise.

And once again a strange feeling stole over Lauren—a feeling of family—of belonging—of wanting something she'd always told herself she didn't want—convincing herself she didn't want it because she knew she couldn't have it…

Icy water should have the same effect as cold showers, Tom told himself, as he shivered in the green depths of the mountain pool. One look at Lauren in the silky scarlet bikini that hinted at more than it covered and his body had forgotten she was just a friend, and also that, at the moment anyway, he was in a position where he couldn't do anything about any lust or attraction he might feel.

She was a guest in his house and therefore off limits.

'I can dive!'

Bobby's declaration brought his mind back onto his responsibilities. The kid hadn't climbed the high rock, but he was out of the pool, standing on the bank, arms raised for a dive.

'Let me check first,' Tom told him, and he swam beneath

the cool green water, checking there were no hidden obstacles that could injure Bobby as he entered the water.

'Okay, it's all clear, but always check. Will you remember that?'

Bobby grinned at him.

'Always check! I'll remember!'

Then he belly-flopped into the water, sinking under the surface then emerging in a mass of bubbles, arms and legs, shrieking his delight so loudly Tom heard the beat of wings as birds in surrounding trees took flight.

But the sheer joy of the child tugged at something deep inside Tom's heart, and whatever the something was, it niggled around and disturbed all the comfortable decisions he'd made about what he wanted out of life. No hassles, no complications—he'd never added no children because he'd never considered marriage, but…

'Can you dive?' Bobby asked, his face shiny with water and his eyes gleaming with excitement.

'I can but I'm not going to dive into the pool even though I've checked the bottom because it's a bit shallow for me. If I hit my head I could break my neck and be paralysed for life—that's the kind of terrible accident you can have from something as simple as diving into a pool.'

He was talking to air by the time he'd finished his instructive mini-lecture, Bobby now swimming underwater, bubbles rising to the surface to show his progress.

Still bubbles rising, but hadn't he been down there too long?

How long was too long?

How did parents know these things?

Bobby burst to the surface with a loud 'Did you see that?' and relief washed through Tom's body. He was assuring Bobby that he *had* seen it and had been very impressed when out of the corner of his eye he saw a blonde sylph in a scarlet bikini sliding into the water. Were sylphs water beings or did he mean sprites? Naiads? Nymphs? Whatever! The name no longer mattered as Lauren slipped into the water and swam towards him, starting all the unacceptable reactions again.

Sleek as a seal, she swam his way then, thank you, Lord, turned to grab Bobby's legs and tumble him over in the water. Tom eased back onto the bank of the creek and watched the pair play, Bobby's joy so palpable Tom felt a rush of pleasure that he'd had a part in providing it.

But there'd be other days when joy was absent, Tom reminded himself. Not all day perhaps, but at least for part of them. No one could promise unending joy. Was that where parents came in? Could they act as buffers in the bad times? He realised they couldn't protect their child or children from every hurt or worry but they could help them cope with things that happened to them?

He slid into the water again, reminding himself Bobby wasn't going to be his long-term responsibility so he didn't have to consider things like this. To his surprise, he found *that* thought profoundly depressing and it was only Bobby leaping onto his back and trying to duck him that brought him back to laughter.

Sensing the swim was nearly over—Bobby was getting cold—Lauren slipped from the water and pulled on her long shift, too embarrassed to have her body on view to Tom for longer than was absolutely necessary. She carried the picnic basket over to a table near a gas-fired barbecue, and began to unpack it.

'Did you bring drinks?' Bobby demanded, arriving, towel-wrapped, beside her.

'Juice or water, both in the cool box,' Lauren told him, and ignored his grumbles, knowing he was used to drinking fruit juice because it was all they had at the refuge, although fizzy soft drinks were allowed on treat nights.

Bobby chose water then he sidled up to Lauren.

'Can I help?'

She was so surprised she had to repeat the request in her head in order to process it. This was Bobby, the child who refused to help in any household chores.

'You can set the table for me,' she told him. 'There's a cloth in the picnic basket, and some plastic plates, and the sauce and bread.'

And to her further surprise Bobby set the table beautifully, spreading out the cloth, laying out the plates, shifting things here and there until satisfied with his arrangement.

'Where's Tom, did you drown him?' she asked, then immediately regretted the joke as Bobby's face quivered with alarm.

'Here's Tom!' The missing man emerged from the trees near the waterfall.

'I thought I saw something there and wanted to check. Have you ever seen a tawny frogmouth owl, Bobby?'

'An owl? A bird owl?' Bobby asked, so much disbelief in his voice Lauren had to smile.

'An owl,' Tom confirmed. 'Well, we call them owls although they are really a bird like a nightjar. Come and look while the barbecue is heating up! There are three of them, the parents and a youngster, in a tree near the waterfall. They must have a nest there. Tawny frogmouths use the same nest for their eggs every year.'

Tom led them along a track through trees, eventually stopping in a clearing and pointing up at the three birds sitting on the branch of a tree. The two adults had their beaks pointed upwards so they looked like two small branches, but the little fledgling was still practising this manoeuvre and kept moving.

'Are those two big ones really birds?' Bobby asked, and just then one of them moved, peering down at the onlookers before taking up his statue pose again.

They stood quietly, watching the birds, Bobby obviously intrigued, asking questions about nests and eggs and how Tom had spotted them.

'I was lying on my back in the pool and one of them must have moved and caught my eye so I had a closer look,' Tom explained.

'I'm glad you found them,' Bobby said. 'I've never seen birds before—well, I've seen birds but not owls or whatever they are, not sitting like that so near and all.'

He turned and grinned at his two adult companions.

'If they live there all the time, we could see them every time we come here, and maybe they'll get to know us and we could give them mice or something good for them to eat,' Bobby said.

Lauren knew she'd stiffened, and felt Tom's shock as well—a realisation that things were getting more complicated than they'd intended.

'I think they eat insects or maybe mice,' Tom said, and Lauren took his hand and squeezed it gratefully.

'Good recovery,' she whispered, as Bobby darted back towards the barbecue. 'But we probably need to think about how he's seeing this temporary care arrangement. We don't want him hurt again, losing us as carers...'

Her voice trailed off because she knew that wasn't exactly what she'd meant. What had shocked her was how much *she'd* felt the family vibe, as the three of them had delighted in something as simple as a family of birds sitting in a tree.

The situation was rife with danger, and not just the danger of more damage to Bobby's security. Danger that became instantly apparent when, perhaps in response to the family vibe, Tom brushed his hand across her shoulder, somehow turning her, so once again, as if some unseen puppeteer was manoeuvring both their bodies, their lips met. The coil around Lauren's heart tightened, but it was the heat that flared within her that shocked her most, making her press herself against Tom to ease the pain of it. His arms held her close, and as their lips parted and the taste of Tom turned heat to scorching need, she lost herself in feeling, freezing only when his hand touched the outside of her shift above her breast—

'The sausages are cooked!'

Bobby's voice brought her back to her senses, although she couldn't look at Tom, aware she'd backed away far too quickly, breaking from his arms with a forceful, panicked push.

Aware he must be wondering what on earth was going on…

But danger was forgotten as they ate sausages in bread with lashings of tomato sauce, and followed up with chocolate rocket cake. They walked off this repast by climbing to the top of the waterfall, up a slippery slope with spray cooling the climb.

'Home time,' Tom said eventually, and after visiting the owls once more, they drove back to town as the sun was setting behind the mountains.

Tom offered to supervise Bobby's bath '—I don't need one, I've been swimming!—' while Lauren unpacked the picnic basket and fixed toasted sandwiches for tea. The message light was flashing on Tom's phone but she ignored it, having phoned the refuge from her mobile earlier to assure herself all was well there.

It wasn't until Bobby was asleep in bed that Tom checked

his messages. Lauren was cleaning up their supper things so heard Mike's voice on the answering-machine.

'Still no joy in finding any of Bobby's relations,' he said. 'Are you two okay to keep him a little longer?'

More than happy as far as he was concerned, Tom answered silently, but the disturbing part of the message was the way Mike had linked them. 'Are you two okay to keep him?' Mike had said it as if they were a couple, and not only that but Tom had quite liked the way it had sounded.

Given the fact that all he'd wanted, all his life, had been to live alone, that reaction was disturbing. Oh, as he'd grown older he'd realised the value of friendship and had some good, even close friends, and naturally as he'd matured he'd learnt the pleasures of female company and again had made arrangements that fitted in with the life he'd planned all those years ago.

And he'd been happy—he knew he had been—so why were silly incidents like looking at a family of tawny frogmouth birds, not to mention a casual kiss, disturbing him?

'*Are* we okay keeping him?'

At least she had emphasised the 'are', not the 'we', although the 'we' disturbed him in the same way the moments near the tawny frogmouths had.

'Of course,' Tom told her, ignoring concerns multiplying in his head. 'Well, I am, anyway, for as long as possible. He needs a bit of stability right now.'

Lauren smiled at him and whether it was the relaxing day, or the memory of what had happened *after* they'd been watching the owls, the smile started a different warmth from the one he was becoming used to feeling in Lauren's presence.

It was a pleasant, gentle warmth, spreading easily through his body, not zeroing like heat downward to his groin.

Not desire at all, just warmth…

Very strange!

'I think I'll turn in now,' Lauren said, hovering in the kitchen.

'No, it's far too early. Join me for a nightcap on the veranda. I've a lovely chocolate liqueur, or a very nice old malt whisky. Just a snifter?'

Another smile and a nod of agreement.

'But no drink,' she said. 'I'm just as happy to sit and look out over the ocean.'

So they sat, and for some reason, before long, they held hands.

It was comfortable, and companionable, and although he knew he must be wrong to be thinking this way, it seemed to Tom, after a while, that it might almost be better than sex…

Then he remembered the kiss they'd shared in the rainforest and knew he was probably wrong…

CHAPTER SIX

TOM'S new, unprecedented reactions to Lauren needed thought, while the effect her presence in his house was having on him required a lot of consideration. He took both the thought and the further consideration with him when he went to bed. They'd sat for an hour, maybe a little more, desultory conversation starting and stopping between them, nothing startling, nothing even important, catching up on each other's recent lives, discussing all the little things about bringing up a child that neither of them had ever considered.

'Not that he's ours,' Lauren had said, and he'd caught a note of not sadness but definitely regret in her voice.

'No, he couldn't be,' Tom had told her, and felt the same regret inside him.

Not that he wanted an eight-year-old boy.

Not that he wanted a child of any kind.

Children needed commitment.

Children needed love…

He stopped thinking about Bobby and children in general and definitely stopped thinking about love, eventually drifting off to sleep, thinking about a woman in a bed two rooms away…

Not that sleep lasted long, the jangling summons of the phone bringing him into a sitting position to answer it—

something he'd trained himself to do after he'd learned that answering the phone lying down meant risking going back to sleep.

Lauren met him in the passage as he pulled on his shirt before hurrying across to the hospital.

'Accident?' she asked.

Tom nodded, then touched her on the shoulder.

'I'm sorry the phone woke you. Go back to bed. I could be a while.'

'Good luck,' she whispered, and now he understood why he'd felt not lonely but a little strange lying in his big bed earlier—he was becoming accustomed to having Lauren in his house, having someone who cared about him enough to pour him coffee, eat meals with, or say good luck when he went out into the night to face the terrible things people could do to themselves or others.

'Thanks,' he said, and bent to kiss her, aiming for her cheek, changing his mind at the last moment because the kiss that had somehow happened near the waterfall had tasted sweet and clean, and he wanted to check the taste again, to feel the softness of those lips, trembling just slightly beneath his.

He left the house with the taste of her on his tongue and an image of her in his head—standing in his house in a very short nightshirt covered with fat angels of some kind. Had she stiffened when he'd kissed her?

Her lips had responded, as they had earlier, but earlier she'd definitely pushed away, and this time…

A paramedic from the ambulance was wheeling a gurney into the ER when Tom reached the hospital. On it, hooked up to monitors and oxygen, was a young woman with dark hair—vaguely familiar, although Tom couldn't say how he knew her.

The marks on her neck were vivid red welts and she lay carefully still, as if other parts of her body were hurting.

'What do we know?' he asked the paramedic.

The man turned to him, shock on his face.

'It's Mrs Williams, Nat Williams's wife. His mother phoned for us.'

'Police?'

'Nat's mother said she wanted to but Mrs Williams said no.'

'It's assault—we have to report it,' Tom said, but he was already bent over the woman, checking the readouts from the monitors, taking in all he could of her outward appearance, lifting her hair and feeling her skull for irregularities, thinking about the damage strangulation could do to the airway, spinal cord and blood vessels within the unprotected structure of the human neck.

'I'm Tom Fletcher, a doctor,' he said, but the woman on the gurney didn't respond, a blank look in her eyes telling Tom she either didn't hear or couldn't comprehend.

Blood vessels could be occluded in strangling, blocked arteries causing lack of oxygen to the brain, blocked veins causing increased pressure—so many dangerous possibilities.

'She spoke to you?' he asked the paramedic.

'Just to whisper no when the older Mrs Williams said she was calling the police.'

Tom signed the transfer papers, then read quickly through his copy, checking all that had been done for the woman so far.

She had an oxygen mask on her face but no intubation. Mrs Williams was breathing so apparently her airway wasn't severely compromised. In such cases, endotracheal intubation wouldn't have been attempted in the field…

His mind raced through what he knew of strangulation injuries—the airway could swell later and intubation become necessary with little warning. She had an oximeter on one finger and her blood oxyhaemoglobin was good—he didn't need an arterial blood gas test right now.

Laryngeal fracture was possible, he'd need to do a CT scan of the neck and probably the head, although the first thing to do was make her comfortable.

He set down the papers and began his own examination, speaking quietly to her as he turned her head to examine the bruising, feeling her skull for any other damage, calling for the portable X-ray machine so they could check her here without moving her again.

'Can you hear me?'

She nodded.

'Can you talk?'

A whispered 'No', so weak and shaky Tom regretted asking her, especially as she was crying now, silent tears sliding down her cheeks.

He touched her shoulder.

'It's okay, we'll look after you. Just nod or shake your head to answer, but don't shake hard, okay?'

He wiped the tears away, patting her cheek gently at the same time.

'Are you hurting anywhere else?'

A nod.

'Your head?'

A shake.

'We'll work our way down,' Tom told her. 'Shoulders?'

A nod and her left hand lifted to point to her right shoulder.

He should have seen it earlier, but she was so thin her

bones stuck out everywhere, the knot where a broken bone had healed masking the dislocation.

'Your shoulder has popped out of its socket,' he told her. 'Easy to fix. I could give you a fast-acting general anaesthetic but don't want too much fluid running into you right now so I'll use a couple of local anaesthetics to numb the area around the joint and pop it back in.'

He was doing his best to sound casual about the situation, not wanting to inflict more fear on her—especially fear of more pain.

'I need to X-ray it but I'll give you the injections first so they can be working while we do the X-rays.'

The machine was wheeled into place as he injected the local anaesthetic, then he helped her into a sitting position, feeling her wince and knowing she was probably hurting all over but being as gentle as he could. One of the nursing staff was an excellent radiography technician and fortunately she was on duty, taking the shots he needed with minimum fuss.

Tom called another nurse in to hold Mrs Williams in a sitting position while he checked the negatives, realising he'd need to do another X-ray once he'd manoeuvred the joint back into position—then later a CT scan for ligament damage—thinking all the time, blocking the thought of how the injuries might have occurred from his mind with what needed doing right now.

Blocking the thought of Lauren from his mind as well, refusing to think about her uncharacteristic reaction to Nat Williams.

The ball slid into place in the socket, and a second series of X-rays confirmed it was in place. He held his patient's arm in position against her chest and helped her to lie down again.

'Later on, I'll put your arm into a sling to keep the shoulder stable and you'll need to keep it as immobile as you can until the swelling and inflammation around the joint subside.'

She nodded, her eyes almost closed. The anaesthetic, pain and shock would be making her feel incredibly weary, but Tom knew he had to complete his examination—already interrupted to ease her pain—although if her airway remained unimpaired he could leave the scans until the next day when there'd be a radiographer on duty and specialists available in Port. He could send the scans over the internet to the experts if there was anything worrying on them.

Still talking to her, he lowered the sheet that covered her, not entirely surprised to see that she was naked beneath it—not entirely surprised to see the yellowish marks of old bruising on her breasts. People used near-strangulation in erotic sex games and if she didn't want the police involved it could be she was a willing participant.

In which case shouldn't her husband have accompanied her to the hospital?

Her husband, Nat Williams, the man Lauren…feared?

No, too big a leap to make, concentrate on the patient. Alyssa Williams. He called her by her name when he spoke to her this time but she was beyond responding, not unconscious but sleeping.

He completed his examination, almost certain she couldn't have been a willing participant in whatever sex she'd endured when he saw the bruising on her inner thighs. Yet another instance of the destructive forces of love, he told himself, sickened by the woman's injuries, angry that a man could get away with such things because his victim refused to seek help…

He left two nurses to carefully collect the evidence needed for a rape kit, explaining that it might not be needed but wanting the evidence kept anyway, reminding them to take photos, apologising to Alyssa for the intrusion. Once that was done, they would clean her carefully and dress her in a hospital gown, women helping another woman in trouble, gentle hands and soft voices.

He cursed softly to himself as he wrote up his notes, aware all the time of tension deep inside him, tension not entirely connected to his patient. Part of it was, of course, the tension he always felt when he saw the damage men could inflict on women.

The other part was personal and the cursing was because he'd never mixed his personal and professional lives, yet now he couldn't help but feel a niggling suspicion, not to mention a deep, fierce anger, that the same man might once have harmed Lauren!

It's all supposition, he reminded himself, dragging his mind firmly back to the patient in question.

'Is there a private room free?' he asked one of the nurses.

'There's that room near the veranda. The woman from the stands' accident went home this afternoon,' the nurse replied.

'Let's take Mrs Williams there,' he said, then, although he knew it was probably useless to remind them of patient confidentiality, he did point out that if word about this got around town her husband might see to it that she suffered even more.

'And none of us would like that on our consciences,' he reminded the two women.

They nodded, both of them, he guessed, as affected by the woman's injuries as he was, and probably more horrified by who had inflicted them—after all the nurses were locals and had probably known Nat Williams in the past.

Like Lauren?

No, the nurses were both older, so hardly likely to have gone out with him, and the patient confidentiality he'd just spoken of applied to him as well so he could hardly question Lauren about her relationship with Nat…

'I'll stay with her,' he said, when they'd settled Alyssa in the bedroom. 'I'm a little worried about her airway and would rather be on hand if anything goes wrong.'

He sat beside the woman and dozed a little in the chair, waking as the sky lightened across the ocean, and the details of the little town started becoming clearer, lights dimming and finally disappearing as the sun rose and proclaimed a fresh, new day.

Fresh? He felt like death warmed up and it wasn't only tiredness dogging him.

'Phone, Tom.'

He took the handpiece and walked out onto the veranda before answering.

'This is Karen Williams, Nat's mother, Alyssa's mother-in-law. How is she?'

'She's resting, Mrs Williams. She'll be all right.'

'She won't be all right,' the forthright woman declared. 'Not if she goes back to him. I can't believe my own son—but, still, he's not your worry. Can you talk her into going to the police? She'll say he was drunk, he didn't mean it, but he's got to be stopped, do you know what I mean?'

'I do, Mrs Williams, and while I agree, I believe it's up to Alyssa to make the complaint. The children, are they all right?'

'I'll make darned sure they are and that they stay all right, you can tell her that, and she can come home here as soon as she's ready, because he won't be staying here, no matter how big a local hero he thinks he is.'

Tom assured her he'd pass the message on, and returned to Alyssa's room to find her awake, staring at the ceiling, the blankness in her eyes disturbing him more than the very visible bruising on her neck.

'That was your mother-in-law on the phone. She said to tell you the kids are fine and that she'd welcome you home any time. She wanted to assure you Nat wouldn't be there.'

Tom sat down by the bed and took Alyssa's hand.

'She also thinks you should report him to the police.'

Alyssa shook her head, so tiredly Tom knew she'd been told this before and had probably argued it out with herself many, many times, for some reason always coming up with an excuse to protect the man who battered her.

Love?

'I know something of domestic violence,' Tom told her, while his head was scoffing at the 'love' question. He might not know much about love but he knew for sure it didn't inflict pain on the loved one. 'I'm on the board of the local refuge. If you want to talk about it to someone who understands…'

He was about to mention Lauren when his own suspicions stopped him, although Lauren was definitely the person he should bring in.

'It's only when he drinks, and maybe does a line of coke,' Alyssa said.

Tom put the two drugs together in his mind. Coaethylene—more toxic than either drug on its own—caused heart problems not to mention liver toxicity, and the combination accentuated the effect of both drugs.

He wondered just how long Alyssa could go on making excuses for her husband, listening to his words of love, empty words, accepting gestures of love, expensive gifts, believing he loved her because she wanted, perhaps needed to believe?

Until he killed her?

Anger at the man pounded through Tom's body.

He wondered, too, about his reaction. He'd seen evidence

of domestic abuse before, too many times, but had never felt the strong surge of impotent rage that he was feeling now…

Yet in spite of the rage and whatever the cause of it—more than Alyssa's injuries?—he had to bring Lauren in on the case.

Time to get his head straight!

He left Alyssa in the care of a nurse, asking that someone stay with her at all times, and walked across to his house, drinking in the quiet of the early morning, allowing it to soothe his warring feelings.

Quiet until he entered the front door and heard the argument going on in the kitchen.

Smelt the smoke.

'Paper doesn't get into a toaster by accident, Bobby, and you know it. Dr Tom's being good enough to let us stay here and you want to thank him by setting fire to his house?'

The strain in Lauren's voice suggested this wasn't the first time she'd remonstrated with the child they'd promised to protect.

'Didn't set it on fire,' came the sullen reply. 'Bit of smoke, that's all.'

'A bit of smoke that ruined the toaster,' Lauren pointed out, at which stage Tom considered his options. One—go quietly back to the hospital and try to find a bed there to snatch a couple of hours' badly needed sleep. Two—see if he could sneak into his bedroom without them hearing, and attempt to sleep there. Or, three, join the pair in the kitchen, perhaps acting as jury to the judge and accused.

At least the prospect of entering the kitchen had diverted his anger!

He called out a slightly forced 'Good morning' and proceeded to the kitchen, where Lauren's pathetically grateful smile more than made up for Bobby's scowling countenance.

'Little mishap?' Tom queried, winking at Lauren to let her know he'd heard the basics.

'It was nothin',' Bobby told him. 'She's fussing 'bout nothin'.'

'I'm not fussing, Bobby,' Lauren said, so gently Tom wondered at her patience. 'I'm just asking you not to do silly things that might injure you or damage Tom's property. Okay?'

Bobby glared at her, and recognising an impasse when he saw one Tom stepped in again.

'Let's all go down the road for breakfast,' he suggested, although he was so tired and mentally confused he wanted nothing more than to escape into his bedroom. 'We can eat, then, if you want to go to school, we can drop you off, or if you don't want to go to school, you and Lauren can make plans for the day. Okay?'

Bobby frowned at him.

'You're not angry?' he finally demanded.

'Angry about what?' Tom asked.

The little boy shuffled awkwardly, then looked up at Tom, his dark eyes holding a plea—for understanding?

Or simple affection?

'I bust your toaster,' he said.

'Oh, that's okay,' Tom told him. 'We can buy another one. Just as long as you don't do it again or set fire to the house, we'll be okay.'

Bobby beamed at him, then shot Lauren a look that said, See, he's not upset, far more clearly than words ever would have.

Lauren accepted it with good grace, smiling at Bobby and ruffling his hair.

'Come on, then, let's go.' She turned to Tom. 'We talked about school and Bobby's decided not to go. We're going to go shopping for some boots he can wear at the farm when we go out after Christmas, and some new jeans in case he wants to go riding—'

'And a checked shirt and a cowboy hat,' Bobby finished for her.

He scooted off to his room and Lauren looked at Tom, reading the exhaustion in his face but so grateful for the way he'd handled the situation she wanted to hug him.

Again!

'Thanks,' she said instead. 'I realise it's the last thing you want to do but we'll eat quickly.'

Tom ignored her gratitude, instead lifting the eyebrow that she so envied as he said, 'Cowboy hat?'

Lauren grimaced.

'I know! I tried to explain it wasn't exactly the wild west, our family farm, but he has this image in his head and I can't get rid of it. Still, he'll need a hat so it might as well be a cowboy hat.'

'And what was he burning in the toaster?' Tom asked, and Lauren had to frown.

'I've no idea. I didn't think of that—I was just so upset to see the flames shooting out of the thing…'

She crossed the room and opened the back door, retrieving the ruined toaster from the veranda railing, fishing inside it with her finger, pulling out a corner of paper that had escaped incineration.

'A photo perhaps?' she said, bringing it across to show to Tom, but as Bobby had reappeared, an ancient wallet clasped in one hand, Tom slipped the scrap into his pocket and the conversation ended there, while the conversation he knew he had to have about Alyssa hadn't even started.

Bobby was their immediate priority, he told himself, and

Alyssa was having further tests and then would need to rest. If Lauren could see her this afternoon…

If…

Their breakfast was surprisingly enjoyable and Lauren realised that it was because Bobby was relating well to Tom, accepting his word that wholegrain bread made men stronger than white bread so the little boy ordered wholegrain toast, and generally following Tom's lead in both ordering his breakfast and then in the order of eating it—finishing eggs before they tackled bacon, finishing that before they ate their beans.

'I can never understand why some people do that,' Lauren finally declared. 'It's the taste of bacon and beans and egg all together that makes breakfast such a good meal.'

Tom smiled at her and although it was a weary effort, it lit the coils of heat again and she had to sternly admonish herself that this was work, not playtime. Well, kind of work!

'I like things to taste of what they are,' Tom told her, then he winked—second time this morning—and she felt a shiver run through her, as if the wink had somehow made the simple statement naughty.

'Me too,' Bobby declared, and Lauren laughed, aware the little boy who needed someone special in his life had found himself a hero.

They left the café, Tom admonishing Bobby to be good for Lauren, Lauren telling Tom to make sure he went home to get some sleep.

'And don't detour via the hospital,' she added, as Bobby wandered off to look in a toyshop window. 'You know they'll call you if they need you.'

Tom hesitated on the footpath, his face serious—frowning, in fact, drawing her slightly away from Bobby.

'I've got to detour via the hospital to check some scans

and, later, I need to talk to you,' he said, very quietly. 'I need you to see someone, if not today then tomorrow.'

Lauren frowned right back at him.

'You sound as if you're forcing those words out against your will. You ask me to see people all the time—well, not *all* the time, but often enough, so what's different?'

Before he could reply, Bobby disappeared into the toyshop and with a hurried 'Sorry! We'll talk later,' Lauren rushed after him.

But the strained uncertainty on Tom's face bothered her.

Perhaps it was just tiredness.

She caught up with Bobby as he began to take a display of plastic animals apart, but it was Jo who stopped the destruction.

'What are you doing here?' Lauren demanded, unable to believe her previously workaholic friend was in a shop on a Monday morning.

'I'm the designated shopper for the refuge, remember,' Jo replied, detaching Bobby from a seriously large rocket ship at the same time. 'And now I've got an employee I can take time off now and then.'

Lauren smiled automatically, how could she not when her best friend was practically glowing with happiness? But then another image, Tom's worried face, the shadows in his eyes, flashed across Lauren's mind.

'Great!' she said to Jo as a solution occurred to her. 'How about you ask Bobby to help you choose the toys? I really need to talk to Tom about something.'

Jo frowned at her—everyone was doing it!

'I won't be long,' Lauren added, all but tripping over the words because suddenly it seemed she *had* to know what was worrying Tom. 'Bobby knows the kids in the refuge at the moment and he'll know what they want. Maybe shop then have an ice cream in the park. He's fine as long as he's eating. Phone me if you have a problem, and I'll be at the hospital or Tom's house when you finish.'

She turned to Bobby, who was only too pleased to be able to spend longer in the toyshop, although he did extract a promise from Lauren that they'd get the cowboy hat later.

Jo raised her eyebrows at the mention of the cowboy hat.

'I'll explain some other time,' Lauren promised, then, because she felt she was somehow letting him down, she gave Bobby a hug and a quick kiss on the cheek, refrained from telling him to be good, and hurried up the hill to the hospital.

Tom was in his office, frowning again, but this time at some X-rays he had up in the light box, but his face lightened as she knocked briefly and walked in, and she felt a rush of pleasure that she could change his mood.

Or maybe it wasn't her—maybe he'd just needed a distraction…

'You've killed our kid?' he joked.

'Jo's got him buying toys,' Lauren explained. 'You looked worried when you said you wanted to see me so I thought I'd come up while I had the chance.'

Where to begin?

And did he really want to discuss this with her?

Tom studied the beautiful face of the woman opposite him. Yes, she was concerned—of course she would be, having picked up on his concern earlier—but the smile she'd flashed as she'd talked of Bobby still lingered on her face and he was ninety-nine per cent certain he was going to wipe that smile away and probably replace the questions in her eyes with dark, unfathomable shadows…

'Jo won't keep him all day!' the beautiful woman prompted, and Tom sighed, then came around from behind his desk, took

Lauren's hand, and led her to the small couch beside a coffee table that he considered the informal section of his office.

He sat down, drawing her down beside him, still unable to find the words he needed, so in the end he blurted out the one question he probably shouldn't have asked.

Blurted it right out!

'Did Nat Williams abuse you?'

Instant regret as she turned pale beneath her golden tan, and her fingers tightened so hard on his he felt a stab of physical pain as well as the internal jolt he'd earned from hurting her.

'Why do you ask?'

He heard the quiver in her usually placid voice, and felt her fingers grip tighter, then, while he watched, she detached herself both mentally and physically, straightening up, breathing deeply, letting go of his hand and moving a little away from him on the couch.

Hazel eyes scanned his face, so intensely focussed he knew she'd see any hint of him dissembling.

'The admission last night—or early this morning—was Alyssa Williams.'

Lauren's reaction was immediate.

'Was she strangled?'

Tom was too shocked to reply but his face must have answered for him.

'Dear Heaven! What have I done?' she cried, springing to her feet and pacing back and forth in front of him, muttering more to herself than to him, wringing her hands in such an agitated manner he wondered if he should attempt to hold her, calm her.

Or would a man's touch be too hateful to her right now as bad memories flooded her head?

Before he could decide, she was speaking again.

'I should have said, should have spoken out, told someone, anyone. Maybe he could have been stopped and who knows how many women he's hurt since then? Women I could have saved if I'd only said something.'

Her voice was becoming strident, regret, fear, guilt and memories melding together to throw the usually controlled woman he knew close to panic. Thrusting aside any doubts, he stood up and caught her as she paced, holding her hard against his body, talking, talking, talking…

'You're a professional,' he reminded her. 'How old were you anyway? Had you even heard of this kind of abuse? Who would you have told?'

He held her close, feeling the emotion that shook her body, while anger grew again inside him.

Anger solved nothing, he reminded himself, but how else to react to Lauren's gut-wrenching sobs as the walls she'd erected around the past shattered into sharp, destructive shards?

He let her cry, talking, reassuring, unaware most of the time of what he was saying, simply letting words fill the air in the hope they might help, and maybe they did for she finally eased away from him, not abruptly, but gently, and this time *he* took his handkerchief from his pocket and handed it to her.

She dried her eyes and slumped back onto the couch, pouring herself a glass of water from the carafe he kept there, sipping at it, eyes downcast, breathing deeply again. He sat beside her, not too close, concerned for her and uncertain how to show it, aching for her but knowing he couldn't show his own emotion.

Earlier he'd known a hug was needed but now?

'I'm sorry,' she said, finally turning to face him and resting her hand on his knee. 'I had no idea all that was going to come boiling out, but I've lived with guilt over what happened for so long…'

'Guilt? Why should *you* feel guilt? Guilt's your emotion talking, not your brain!'

He couldn't help it—the words just bulldozed their way out, tight with suppressed anger at the man who'd hurt her, not at Lauren.

Her touch firmed on his knee and she actually found a smile—a small, feeble effort but still a smile.

Silence rested between them, not entirely easy, but he guessed she was finding the words she wanted, perhaps needed, to say, so he rested his hand on hers and told himself to keep his mouth shut.

And ignore the ache that still filled his chest…

'It wasn't guilt at first,' she finally began, hesitantly producing the words. 'It was shame.'

The memory coloured her cheeks and he had to remind himself he was there to listen, not to take her in his arms again.

'Terrible shame because I thought it was my fault, or that it always happened with sex and I was just too stupid to know.'

She looked up at him then, her eyes enormous in her pale face, the pathetic smile wobbling slightly.

'Stupid, isn't it? All the study I've done since, all the women I've met and talked to and counselled and advised since then, and yet my own past has the power to affect me like this—to turn me back into my sixteen-year-old self who was so overawed that someone like Nat Williams could like me, I'm a quivering mess just thinking about it! Not only that, but I'm still blaming myself for what he did—taking the 'it must have been my fault' line like every abused woman I've ever met, although some of the guilt is probably more to do with not telling, but at the time, well, I had no idea it shouldn't be like that and it was so awful, so truly horrible, I couldn't even talk to Jo, my best friend, about it, let alone my mother, or Jo's dad, who was our doctor. I thought he loved me—thought maybe it was normal. I kept thinking—what if that's what sex is all about? I guess the only thing that I did do right was to stop seeing him, or maybe I wasn't even strong enough to do that—maybe he went off to a competition somewhere and that was that. I can't even remember that part, only the—'

She broke off so abruptly Tom forgot about being there to listen. Anyway, he could listen with her in his arms. He moved so he could hold her once again, wrapping his arms around her, bringing her body against his when she relaxed into his grasp and leant against him, the air and the words that had floated on it going out of her with the suddenness of a pricked balloon.

Tom held her, not talking now, not wanting to talk, but his mind raced along tangled paths that became clearer as all she'd said slotted into what he knew of Lauren. Her empathy with battered women came from deeper down than study, while her detachment—in particular, her avoidance of relationships with men—had grown from an experience of something that should have been passable at least, good, or even wonderful at best, but had been horrifying and painful and—

He couldn't think about it, simply tightening his arms around her and holding her for as long as she needed to be held, comforting her, reassuring her.

Just holding her…

For ever?

Now, where had that thought come from?

Not for ever, just several minutes, then the Lauren he knew returned, smiling at him, a better effort this time, mopping at her face with her handkerchief once again then leaning over to kiss him quickly on the lips.

'Thank you,' she said, simple words but he knew they were heartfelt. 'You need to grab some sleep and I need to rescue Jo from Bobby, but I'm okay now and I'll definitely see Alyssa whenever you think she's ready for a visit.'

She hesitated, cocking her head to one side and studying him before adding, 'I'm okay, Tom, I really am. I guess all that stuff had to come out, but I can be totally professional with Alyssa, please don't doubt that.'

Tom thought his heart might break, so badly did it hurt just listening to Lauren's assurances, which he knew covered the fragility she must be feeling. He cupped her head with the palms of his hands and looked deep into her eyes.

'Of course you'll be professional—I never for a second doubted that!' he managed, but the words were gruff, roughly spoken, blurted out because he wanted to do so much more for her but had no idea how to begin to help her or even if she needed, or would want, his help.

But he had to try.

'And being a professional you must know that regrets are wasted. Do you really think you might have stopped him—Nat Williams, king of the Aussie surfing world, a testosterone-filled young man who thought he was God?'

He pressed his lips to hers, very gently, before adding, firm now, authoritative, 'None of this is your fault, Lauren, none of it, and you'd better believe that!'

And he kissed her again—just a kiss—a friend's kiss with maybe a hint of the would-be lover in it so she'd know the man who'd kissed her by the waterfall—the man she'd definitely kissed back—was still there for her…

And *that* thought hurt his heart again…

CHAPTER SEVEN

I REALLY have to stop crying all over Tom!

Lauren shook her head as the random thought echoed in her brain. Of all the things to be thinking!

It was obviously a symptom of her shattered state and her state *was* shattered, her insides like mush for all she was pretending everything was okay.

Perhaps thinking about crying against Tom's chest was her brain's way of avoiding what she should be thinking about—although thinking about the past and in particular her past with Nat was hardly going to achieve anything right now.

She shivered in the summer sunshine as she hurried down the road, glad she had a job ahead of her—shopping with Bobby—knowing later she'd have to sit down and have a proper think—about the past, about professionalism and Alyssa Williams, and probably about what poor Tom must be thinking of his houseguest right now.

He was right, of course, about her rushing into words when she was anxious or confused, but to have rushed all those words out to him—to Tom of all people.

Her mind balked and she knew it was because of the way she'd been feeling about Tom lately—about the stupid coils of heat—and now he knew about her past, about Nat Williams, well, the heat-coiling stuff should stop right now because Tom was probably…

Probably what?

As if she had a clue how anyone would react to revelations of past abuse, let alone how Tom might react! If anything, given his experience with the refuge, he'd probably be more understanding than most, but when she'd tried, that one time, to explain to a then boyfriend why the idea of sex terrified her—

She blanked that memory out and turned her mind to Bobby. His welfare was far more important than her attraction to her host.

She'd concentrate on Bobby.

'You've been a long time.' Bobby's accusatory glare was rather spoiled by the fact that the words were spoken around a double ice-cream cone. 'We've been waiting for ages!'

'At least three minutes,' Jo added, though Lauren sensed relief in the words.

'Trouble?' she queried quietly, while Bobby chased a pigeon off a park bench.

'Not really,' Jo assured her, 'but he's certainly a full-attention job.'

She paused, peering closely at her friend.

'Bad news? Had Tom heard from Children's Services?'

Lauren shook her head.

'I'm the bad news,' she muttered, shaking her head as she remembered her total meltdown. 'But I'm okay now or I will be soon and one day I promise I'll explain, just not today.'

Jo knew her well enough not to push, contenting herself with a kiss on Lauren's cheek and a quick shoulder squeeze before chasing Bobby around the park bench, threatening to kiss him.

'No sloppy kisses!' he said, standing at bay, then, to

Lauren's delight, he added in a very embarrassed mutter, 'Except for Lauren.'

The past didn't exactly vanish but the day grew brighter and she bent to hug the little boy, thanking Jo for minding him and promising to get together soon.

'Now we can buy the cowboy hat?' Bobby asked, and she had to laugh at his persistence. The past would definitely have to go back into its box for a while. As Jo had said, Bobby was a full-attention job!

'*Now* we'll buy the cowboy hat,' she agreed, and hand in hand they walked down the road to the clothing shop, Lauren hoping that taking Bobby shopping would be challenging enough to blank the past from her mind, for a while, at least.

He soon proved he was up to the challenge. Tact, that's what was needed, tact and patience. But as she discussed his choice of clothing, she couldn't help but remember her own behaviour when she'd shopped as a child with her mother, always wanting something too extreme, too trendy, too poor in quality to last.

Who had shopped with Tom?

The grandmother?

Foster-mother?

Some well-meaning woman from Children's Services?

Tom!

What must he be thinking of her? Dumping all that angst on him like some hysterical teenager…

'This shirt?' Bobby was holding up a shirt with tassels on the pockets, Western style. Lauren brought her attention back to the boy she was with, tucking all thoughts of Tom—boy and man—away in the back of her mind.

'But I'm a growing boy.' This was Bobby's next protest when, having agreed to the tasselled shirt, she stood firm and bought the jeans that fitted him, not the pair with fancy studs and stitching that were two sizes too large.

'We'll buy you new ones when you grow,' Lauren promised him, then heard her own words and hoped that someone, if it wasn't her, would keep her promise to the child.

She paid for their purchases and led him out of the shop, keeping to the shade as they walked up the hill to the hospital and the sheltering house beside it.

Tom managed to grab an hour's sleep, and woke, if not full of energy, at least refreshed. The house was quiet so he assumed his guests were still shopping.

A long, hot shower, shaving under the hot water, refreshed him enough to dress then phone the hospital, pleased to hear that the full-body scan he'd ordered for Alyssa Williams had been carried out and the film sent through to a radiologist in Port Macquarie, the large regional town down the road.

'We're waiting to hear the results but Mrs Williams wants to go home,' Tom's colleague told him. 'What do you think?'

'Definitely not until we hear the radiologist's report. I'm concerned about oedema in her head, damage to her larynx, torn ligaments around her shoulder and other internal soft-tissue damage. She's also pregnant, which complicates things. Keep reassuring her the children are okay—their grandmother is looking after them.'

'Are you reporting it?'

Not until I've discussed it with Lauren, he thought but didn't say, then wondered if his hesitation was because of Lauren or his patient.

'Not yet. I've asked Lauren to talk to Alyssa later today, when she's feeling up to a visit,' he explained, assuring himself it was Alyssa's well-being in the forefront of his mind.

The question of reporting it haunted Tom. Reporting it

would bring in a whole raft of outsiders—Lauren among them—but starting with the police. They would question Alyssa, talk to her about the options she had, advise and consult, and generally attempt to help her out of the situation in which she found herself.

A situation she might not want to escape no matter how sensible escape would be.

His stomach clenched at the thought of what battered women went through both physically and emotionally or maybe clenched at the thought of what the teenage Lauren had suffered, but his stomach would just have to live with it.

'Alyssa's emotionally fragile,' he continued to explain to his colleague. 'And right now she's also a long way from her own family and friends so she's lacking support, although her mother-in-law is behind her and all for reporting it. I'm concerned that pushing her into the system might make things much harder for her. Let's leave it until Lauren's seen her.'

He ended the conversation, promising he'd be over at the hospital before long, then sat down on the veranda to try to sort out the increasingly twisted strands of thought inside his head.

Ignoring the strand that was Lauren, he considered how Alyssa must be feeling. She was American so being out here in Australia might mean she was cut off from her family and friends. But he knew enough about DV situations to know the woman was nearly always isolated from her support very early on in the relationship.

Tom looked hopefully down the drive. Lauren would know what to do.

Was he being fair, asking this of her?

Oh, she'd handle it, for all the emotional storm she'd suffered earlier. The professional Lauren he knew could handle anything, but at what risk to the woman inside her professional armour?

Realising that his thoughts were becoming more tangled than ever, he gave up trying to sort the muddle and returned to the hospital.

Lauren and Bobby walked slowly home. The house was quiet but the door to Tom's room was open, the bed unmade but empty.

'He must have gone back to work,' she said to Bobby, but he was far too excited unpacking his new clothes to worry about his protector, while Lauren was relieved to find she could avoid the man for a little longer, her embarrassment over her meltdown still burning in her, while guilt still nibbled around the edges of her mind.

Fortunately she had Bobby as a diversion—a very good diversion as it happened when he unpacked his new clothes and announced, 'I'll put them on now and ride the bike over to the house to show the other kids.'

Lauren wanted to protest that they needed to be washed first, but his face was shiny with excitement and she couldn't dampen it. Although riding over to the house? It was only a couple of blocks, but how old should kids be before they were allowed to ride bikes around town on their own?

She'd been driving the old ute on the farm when she wasn't much older than Bobby but, never having lived in town, she wasn't certain of the 'rules'!

'I could drive you over,' she suggested, thinking about time and when Alyssa might be well enough for a visit. Her mind was swinging between Bobby and the patient while she resolutely ignored any thoughts of the past. 'I can put the bike in my car and you can ride it around the yard when we get to the house, although most of the kids will still be at school. So what if we do this?'

Bobby offered her a suspicious glare, the shiny excitement gone, and she knew she had to put him first—at least until Tom could take over the child-care or she could get Jo back to babysit.

'What?'

'We wash your new clothes because sometimes new clothes are stiff and prickly and washing will make them soft, and by the time we've put them through the dryer, the kids at the house will be home from school and you can show them then.'

'So what'll I do now?' her small guest demanded.

Watching another of the hospital DVDs would be the ideal solution, but Lauren was sure that too much TV was bad for children.

'How about you help me work out how to use Dr Tom's washing machine? Mine's different but you're a boy so you should be able to work it out for me.'

Blatant sexism in that statement but she knew she had to keep him occupied, though getting the washing machine started wouldn't take for ever…

'Get any other dirty clothes you've got out of your bedroom,' she told him, and though he balked he did go off, muttering to himself, returning with what must be the entire contents of his small duffel bag.

'It's all dirty,' he announced. 'Mum hated washing.'

'I don't think anyone loves it,' Lauren told him. 'But with machines it's a lot easier. My old granny used to boil all the clothes in a copper. It was outside the house, and you had to light a fire under it, and carry the water to it in buckets.'

'Like a witch's cauldron? The thing witches put stuff in to make spells?' Bobby asked, and as Lauren acknowledged the old coppers were very like a witch's cauldron, she wondered if he'd seen such things on television or a DVD or if he was a reader.

She hoped it was the latter and made a mental note to collect some more books that might suit him from the refuge.

The refuge!

She'd had so much on her mind since Friday she hadn't even collected the cheque from the fundraising. Would it be enough to keep the refuge open?

For a short time at least…

Should she be concentrating on that rather than an orphaned little boy?

Of course not! Right now Bobby needed her, and later Alyssa needed her, and later again—well, then she'd think about the refuge…

The boy who needed her most was in the laundry, carefully studying all the knobs on the washing machine, eventually telling Lauren they should look for a book of instructions.

'Not because I can't work it,' he assured her, 'but we don't want to bust Tom's washing machine.'

Tom, not Dr Tom—well that was okay, Lauren decided. Tom had moved from the professional Bobby might have seen at the hospital where he was Dr Tom to everyone, to a protector.

A friend?

Lauren hoped so.

She found the washing machine manual on a shelf above the machine and wondered for a moment where someone coming into her house might find hers—in a box under the bed perhaps?

In with her recipe books in a basket in the kitchen?

Turning her mind back to Bobby, she found him studying the illustrations and comparing them to the machine, taking total responsibility for the operation. He set all the buttons and dials and got it going, Lauren crossing her fingers behind her back that it would work because he was refusing to allow her to look at the book.

'It will take forty-eight minutes,' he announced, closing the book but keeping hold of it. 'What can we do for forty-eight minutes?'

Have a reasonably good panic attack, was Lauren's first thought but she forced the past—and what lay ahead—from her mind again.

'Have lunch? I know it's late but we had a late breakfast and you had ice cream with Jo but we should have something to eat. And we should do some grocery shopping while we're out, so we're not eating all Tom's food. We'll make sandwiches and while we're eating we'll write a shopping list. You can tell me what you like to eat.'

'Sausages,' Bobby announced, 'and Tom's got a barbecue, I saw it outside on the veranda. I like barbecued sausages in bread with tomato sauce, only I like ordinary sausages best, not the fancy ones like we got at the markets yesterday. They were okay but I like shop sausages best.'

Thinking of sausages was a sure cure for panic attacks!

The market sausages were probably healthier, but however much he liked sausages of any kind, Lauren doubted they were nutritious food for a growing boy—not if eaten every day. She thought about this as Bobby opened Tom's pantry and surveyed the spreads available for sandwiches, announcing he'd have peanut butter.

'And he hasn't got any cereal, so you'd better put that on the list,' he added. 'I like Frosty Flakes, the kind with the gorilla on the packet.'

Lauren had never heard of Frosty Flakes let alone seen a gorilla on a packet of cereal but she found a pen and paper and obediently wrote Frosty Flakes on it, adding milk, which would surely be needed to go with the cereal.

And sausages in case he really wouldn't eat anything else.

And bread.

And tomato sauce…

Later she'd have a think about nutrition but right now it seemed a good idea to have food in the house that Bobby would actually eat.

Caring for a growing boy, as Bobby had called himself, was certainly throwing up some challenges…

Bobby was on his fourth peanut-butter sandwich—when to stop, something else she'd have to check—when Tom walked in. Lauren's stomach squelched and embarrassment flooded her body, but Tom's easy grin restored a little of her equilibrium, enough for her to ask, 'Peanut-butter sandwich?' as casually as if she hadn't been weeping all over him only a couple of hours earlier.

'Thanks,' Tom said, his grin turning into an 'everything's okay' kind of smile just for her, the message in his eyes telling her they'd get through this, although what Tom had to get through she didn't know…

He ruffled Bobby's hair as he walked past to subside into a chair beside the young boy, who, Lauren noticed, moved in his chair, just a little closer to Tom.

Fair enough, she could have done with being closer to Tom herself, so confused did she feel.

Not that she could rely on him to sort her out. He was a friend, nothing more.

'Coffee or tea?' she offered, dragging her attention back to her housewifely duties, passing him a sandwich.

'Coffee would be lovely but you don't have to get it.'

She smiled at him, a real smile this time, as Tom's remembered kindness while she'd stuttered out her confession warmed the cold and shaken bits inside her.

'That protest lacks oomph,' she teased him. 'To make it really effective you have to pretend to be getting up from the chair, probably groaning a little with the effort.'

He smiled back at her and for a moment she felt a stillness in the air, the room disappearing from in front of her eyes—as if some cataclysmic change was occurring.

Surely not from a smile.

It was a hangover reaction from earlier.

Although…

Steadying herself, she boiled the electric kettle and poured the water over coffee grounds in Tom's plunger, mentally adding coffee beans and a new toaster to the shopping list.

Waiting for the grounds to settle before pushing the plunger, she sniffed the delicious aroma and thought how a smile couldn't stop the world from turning.

Something had, she reminded herself.

She pushed the plunger down slowly, forcing the grounds to the bottom of the jug, then poured two cups, one for Tom, one for herself, hesitating at the kitchen bench, surely not afraid to turn around?

Surely not worried he'd smile again?

'Was it my fault?'

Lauren had, very carefully—wary of smiles—put Tom's cup of coffee on the table in front of him when, right out of the blue, Bobby asked the question.

Startled, she turned to look at the little boy. The usual scowl was gone from his face, but he was frowning, clearly worrying about something.

'The toaster?' she asked, then before he could reply, she added, 'Don't worry, we'll get a new one when we do our grocery shop.'

Bobby shot her a look that clearly said, Stupid woman.

'Greg hitting Mum—was it my fault?' he demanded, his voice cracking slightly so Lauren understood this had been bubbling away inside him for some time.

She knelt beside him but Tom was quicker, lifting Bobby onto his lap and giving him a tight hug before tilting the boy's face up to his.

'Now, you listen to me, young man,' Tom said, gently but firmly. 'There is no way any of what happened between your mum and Greg was anything to do with you.'

Bobby buried his head in Tom's shirt so his next words were muffled, but no less devastating for not being clear.

'He'd say I was a brat and swear about me when he was yelling at her or hitting her so it had to be my fault.'

She saw Tom's arms tighten around the distraught child, and heard him murmuring soothing words, assuring and reassuring Bobby that grown-up people might behave very badly from time to time but it was never the fault of the child or children in their lives.

Echoes in his words resonated deep inside Lauren and she felt she, too, was getting absolution for the guilt and shame she'd carried for so long.

Something worked for Bobby, too. After rubbing his head against Tom's shirt one last time, probably wiping his nose on it, the little boy clambered off Tom's knee, announcing he had to check the washing, and disappeared into the laundry.

Lauren shook her head, her own problems forgotten as she considered what Bobby had been carting around in his young conscience.

'You wouldn't believe we have a child health worker talking all the time to these kids about them not being responsible for adult behaviour. That's the one essential employee at the refuge because we're aware of the damage DV does to the kids who are exposed to it, but we mustn't be using the right approach that Bobby was still worried he was to blame. Are we doing it wrong, Tom?'

He reached out and took her hand, and once again it seemed as if the world had disappeared, leaving only the two of them on the planet, but now wasn't the time for be worrying about whatever was happening in her head—or heart maybe?—she had to work out how to do things better for the children at the refuge.

'I doubt any amount of counselling, or play-acting, or support can take away a child's memories of violence. My parents didn't hit each other but they yelled and no amount of psychology study or analysis or counselling—and, yes, I've had it—has eradicated from my head the sound of their voices screaming abuse at each other as the car crashed and killed them.'

He paused, and Lauren, so shocked to hear what had happened to her friend, turned her hand over so she could squeeze his fingers in silent support.

'You'd think I'd hear the crash, the noise of shrieking metal, maybe even my sister crying out before she died, but, no, I hear their voices…'

'Your sister died as well?'

The words were out before she could stop them, although now they *were* out she had a vague memory of him mentioning the sister being killed.

Tom didn't pause to answer. He was already on his feet, dropping a light kiss on the top of her head, telling her he had to get back to work, and that Alyssa was sleeping but if Lauren could call in later…

He'd had a sister?

Of course there was no reason why she should have known.

Sure, they were friends, but friends didn't tell each other everything.

His sister had also died.

The little boy he'd once been—the one in the strange bed—had lost his whole family?

Water sloshing around her feet brought her back to the present.

'Bobby?'

'It's not my fault!'

And it wasn't. Something had clogged the drain in the tub beside the washing machine—the tub into which the waste-water from the machine ran. By the time they'd cleaned up the mess and hung out the washing—she'd opted not to use the dryer, fearful of what else might go wrong—there was only an hour before the shops shut and they had to put off the visit to the house to get their groceries.

And some time this afternoon or evening she had to visit Alyssa!

Mopping up after Bobby seemed a far easier task…

CHAPTER EIGHT

TOM returned to an empty house but a suspiciously clean kitchen and laundry floor. Having experienced similar problems with his washing machine, he didn't need to see the clothes hanging on the line to understand what had happened.

Small-boy clothes! Surely the sight of a child's clothes hanging on a clothesline couldn't give him a swirling feeling in his stomach. Hunger, that's what it would be. One peanut-butter sandwich did not a lunch make! Although hadn't he had the same feeling when they'd looked at the owls?

Owls—kisses—Lauren…

To distract himself from thoughts he couldn't handle, he looked out at the clothesline again, then frowned. Not all the clothes were new! What looked like the contents of Bobby's entire wardrobe were strung up on the lines. Had some of the clothes been in Joan's case—the case he'd tucked up on a high cupboard—also dirty? He should check.

Or get Lauren to check.

But thinking of Lauren and what she'd been through in her sensitive adolescent years made his stomach swirl again so he turned back to the pantry and refrigerator and made himself another peanut-butter sandwich, just in case it was hunger.

But the peanut-butter sandwich did nothing to chase away

the images of Alyssa's battered body, and now his mind kept imposing Lauren's face on the images.

He had to *do* something! Something practical. Joan Sims's suitcases!

He opened the first one, and stared at the contents, completely bewildered by what looked like an open-weave canvas and lots of bits of wool—little bits of wool. Nothing else as far as he could see so he closed the case again, feeling slightly embarrassed to have opened it.

But he desperately needed a diversion and if clothes needed washing…

He opened the second case—normal stuff—toiletries and, yes, clothes, some clean, but a big plastic bag full of garments obviously intended for the laundry.

Tom took the bag through to the laundry, dumped the lot in the machine and got it going, checking first that the outlet wasn't clogged. He considered putting in some of his own clothes—Joan's didn't nearly fill the machine—and put his hand into his pocket, thinking the trousers he had on could go in.

At first he couldn't work out what the piece of paper was, or why he had it, but one glance at the charred edges and he knew. It was whatever Bobby had been burning in the toaster, a picture of something.

This morning seemed a very long time ago, but at least this was another diversion.

Forgetting about adding more clothes to the wash, Tom started the wash then carried the scrap of singed paper into the kitchen and put it down on the table, smoothing the edges carefully so the charred bits didn't break away. He turned it around, studying it from different angles, finally seeing in the darkened paper what looked like the image of a witch—someone with a tall hat anyway.

A magician?

Merlin?

The name floated up from some distant well in his brain. Had he had a book with Merlin the Magician in it?

A favourite book?

Another memory rose from the sludge—Jane reading to him, reading loudly so her voice almost drowned out their parents' shouting.

Someone else was shouting. His visitors! Bobby's voice shrill with what Tom guessed might become a familiar plaint, 'It wasn't my fault.'

Lauren's voice was more controlled. 'Tom, if you're home, could you give us a hand?'

He headed for the front door, pleased to be dragged away from what were becoming very disturbing memories, while the question of why Bobby would be burning a picture of Merlin—or any wizard or witch—still hovered in his mind.

'We shopped,' Lauren explained as he relieved her of a couple of green reusable shopping bags so she could attend to whatever disaster seemed to have befallen Bobby.

'I can see that,' Tom told her, smiling because for all the anguish and emotion of the morning there was something very special in seeing Lauren walking into his house with shopping bags—and *that* thought he'd set aside for further consideration later.

'Bobby's bag had the eggs,' Lauren added quietly, kneeling on the ground beside the boy, who was trying to separate a bottle of tomato sauce from runny, gooey, well-smashed eggs.

'Let's take the whole bag over to the tap and wash things there,' she suggested, and although Bobby's face turned mutinous he did pick up the bag and head towards the outside tap. Lauren detached the hose, but wasn't fast enough to move back as Bobby turned the tap on—hard—so water sprayed all over her and the shopping bag and a large part of the veranda.

To Tom's surprise Lauren didn't protest, simply waiting until Bobby had readjusted the pressure then thanking him for doing it, as if being soaked to the skin was an everyday occurrence. A very damp Lauren pulled the contents of the bag out one by one, and together the pair washed egg off everything, including the bag itself.

'There are more bags in the car if you can drag yourself away from your role as onlooker and carry them in,' Lauren said, and Tom realised he'd stopped at the top of the steps and was still holding the bags he'd taken from her, riveted by the sight of the body the wet clothes revealed.

'I should go over to the hospital,' Lauren said when, clad in clean, dry clothes, she joined him in the kitchen where he was unpacking groceries, supervising Bobby's bringing in of the laundry through the window.

'And I should go with you, at least to introduce you,' Tom told her, thinking more of being there to support Lauren through what would have to be an ordeal than the need for a formal introduction. 'Is Jo still available for babysitting duties?'

Lauren studied the man who'd asked the question. Had there been something more in his voice than the casual words suggested?

'Are you worried I'll fall apart again?' she asked—well, all but demanded as the mess of emotion inside her came back to churning life.

'I'm her doctor,' Tom said gently, and Lauren cringed with shame at her reaction.

Obviously?

She didn't know, but for some reason Tom was holding her

again, tucking her body against his chest, brushing his lips in her hair as he murmured assurances at her.

'I would never doubt your professionalism, you must know that,' he was saying, but although the words were calming the churning going on inside her, the warmth of his body against hers was doing other things to other parts of her, sending shivers of excitement along her nerves, down passageways to the apex of her belly, starting up a longing she barely understood in a body that had never felt satisfaction.

This was ridiculous!

Impossible!

What had happened to the professionalism Tom had just assured her she had?

A patient needed her.

That was urgent.

Less urgent but of equal importance was the problem with the refuge.

So why was she wasting precious time clinging to Tom Fletcher like misplaced barnacle?

'Bleagh!'

Bobby had returned and Lauren sprang away from Tom, then, with cheeks she knew must be aflame, she mumbled and bumbled her way back to the conversation.

'Jo—I don't—perhaps working—not good—could you—?'

'That was just a hug, Bobby,' she heard Tom say through the fog in her brain, 'but now I'm going to give Lauren a good kiss so if you don't want to watch and maybe get some pointers, you can turn your back.'

And with that Tom kissed her firmly on the lips, not solving anything because she ended up more confused than ever, the kiss having electrified the shivers into arcs of lightning.

She did manage, eventually, to push away, and find enough words to make a proper sentence.

Several proper, albeit short sentences!

'Jo's working this afternoon. I can introduce myself to Alyssa. Maybe you and Bobby can fix dinner.'

And on that note she fled, although Bobby's strident protest about women's work followed her out the door—heaven only knew what Tom's protest might have been…

Lauren headed through the hospital, checking with a nurse on the way where she might find Alyssa.

The woman lay very still in the bed, curled into a ball but facing towards the door. Facing potential danger? Her dark hair spread across the pillow, knotted and tangled in places where no doubt she'd twisted and turned, and the brown eyes that opened at Lauren's entrance were dark pools of misery.

'I'm Lauren Cooper, and I'm not here for any particular reason except to see if there's anything I can do for you. Brush your hair? I'm a dab hand with waterless shampoo. I could get you sorted in no time.'

She edged closer as she spoke and was relieved to see a slight smile lighten the woman's beautiful if haggard face.

'I'm a friend of Tom's, the doctor, and I'm also the hospital psychologist if you want to talk to a professional at any time, but for now I thought you might just like someone to talk to as a friend, or just be here with you for a while.'

Alyssa nodded to the chair set against the wall of the small room.

Lauren pulled it closer to the bed, and sat down in it.

'Do you need a hug?' she asked gently, and Alyssa's tiny smile grew a little broader.

'I'm too sore for hugs—bad shoulder,' she whispered, 'but a hand squeeze perhaps?'

Lauren swallowed hard and took the woman's hand, gently squeezing the fingers then clasping the hand in both of hers, sitting quietly while Alyssa became used to her presence in the room.

Eventually Lauren spoke—quietly and carefully.

'I know you wouldn't want your children to see you like this, but would you like me to bring in some photos of them? I know Karen Williams. I could drive over to her place and get some snaps or take some new ones of the kids and print them out on my computer if you'd like recent ones.'

Alyssa's dark eyes studied her in silence then, in a trembling whisper, she asked, 'Not right now but later, would you go and see them? Make sure they're okay. Karen keeps phoning to tell me they are but I need someone to see them.'

The desperation in that husky voice meant Lauren had to swallow again before she could reply.

'I can only imagine how you must feel,' she murmured. 'Of course I'll go but even before I see them I can assure you that if Karen Williams says they're okay, they will be. She's one tough woman!'

There was a brief silence then Alyssa spoke again.

'I suspect she might have had to be,' she whispered.

'What makes you think that?' Lauren asked, although she already suspected the answer. Domestic abuse wasn't genetic, but sons often learnt from their fathers.

'Why else would she be so supportive? Why else would she be backing me against her own son?' Alyssa whispered, tears trickling down her cheeks.

'At least you have her in your corner, and me, and all the hospital staff. You do know that, don't you? No matter who the perpetrator is, domestic violence isn't tolerated in this town. That's one reason we encourage women to report it.'

Alyssa shook her head, not violently but tiredly.

'I just couldn't do it—couldn't go through the court process. I thought I could once before but pulled out and so I know I won't this time. At least, not yet.'

She moved on the bed, shifting with discomfort, then her dark eyes fixed on Lauren's face.

'I remember you from the tree raising. Before the accident. You knew him, didn't you?'

Lauren nodded, understanding exactly what Alyssa had meant by 'knew'.

'Did he hurt you?'

Lauren nodded again, and Alyssa turned her hand so now she was holding Lauren's, two women united in pain, one present, one past…

'It's finished,' Alyssa finally said. 'I kept trying for the girls' sakes. He's a good father, he really is, but not any more. Karen's phoned my father and he'll be here in a day or two. He'll take us home—back to Wisconsin, where we belong.'

Her voice broke on the last words, and she cried again, heartbroken sobs, streaming hot tears, and Lauren understood that they were tears of grief—grief for lost dreams and for the love that couldn't be…

When the storm of emotions ended, Alyssa slipped into a deep and hopefully more restful sleep. Remembering her promise to get photos, Lauren phoned Tom to check Bobby hadn't burnt down the house, then drove out to the Williams place, about twenty acres nestled in the foothills of the mountains, a sparkling creek running through it, small cabins dotted here and there among the trees.

Dogs barked as she pulled up to open the gate into the house yard of the property and ahead of her she could see two little girls chasing chickens around a shady tree. A photo like that should reassure their mother!

Karen was waiting on the veranda at the top of the steps

when Lauren pulled up on the drive. The little girls had scuttled back to the house and now peeped out from behind their grandmother's skirts.

'Lauren Cooper!' Karen said as Lauren emerged from the car. 'You don't know how often I've been thinking about you. About that refuge you run and how I might help, but I guess you've come about Alyssa, not to chat.'

The opening conversation was surprising—even startling—but the light was fading fast and if Lauren wanted outside photos she'd better get going. She dug her camera out of the car.

'I popped in to see Alyssa at the hospital,' she said as she climbed the steps towards the reception party at the top. 'I thought some pictures of the kids might cheer her up so I wondered if you'd mind if I took some. I can print them off at the office and take them in to her.'

Lauren smiled at the two little girls.

'I'm Lauren,' she said.

The elder girl just stared at her, but the younger, about three, Lauren guessed, was more friendly.

'I'm Eve and that's my sister Zoe,' she said, and gravely put out her hand to shake Lauren's.

Zoe then yielded and put out her hand too, and Lauren shook them both.

'Go and see if you can get the hens back into the pen,' Mrs Williams told the girls, shooing them away with her hands.

It must have been a task the girls were delighted to do, for they went whooping and cheering on their way, leaving Karen and Lauren on the veranda.

'They won't come to any harm out there—the dogs will watch over them. I want to talk to you for a moment.'

Lauren heard the strain in Karen's voice and saw the woman's face was full of pain.

'I'm so ashamed of what he did—a son of mine—but you need to know, everyone needs to know, I'm on Alyssa's side in this and I've got her father coming over to take her home so she'll be safe. But there's something else—the something I should have done earlier. Nat's father was the same and I didn't tell and now I know I should have.'

She paused, looking directly at Lauren.

'I've been thinking of the past and the future for the last three years, since you started the refuge. I want to help there—volunteer—to talk to the women about getting out from under men like that and taking control of their lives. I did it in the end—too late now I know Nat's followed in his father's footsteps—but I made something of myself and I want those women to know they can as well.'

Lauren moved towards her automatically, and took the older woman in a tight, warm hug.

'That would be wonderful,' she said. 'Just wonderful! Everyone in town knows how well you've done with your farm-stay business so it would certainly give the women hope.'

'I'd like to give them more than hope,' Karen continued. 'I'm giving up the farm stay as a business for myself and I want to offer this place to the organisation. The women could use it for weekends and holidays, or they could run it themselves as a farm-stay place. I'd like any women in the house right now to come for Christmas if they'd like that. If Alyssa's still here, it would be good for her too. There are heaps of animals for the kids to play with and plenty for the women to do. What do you think?'

Lauren's mind had, at first, had trouble keeping up, but now it leapt ahead as she envisaged what having a business like this would mean to the refuge. She could keep the safe house open, and find employment for at least some of her charges. There was heaps to work out of course, but…

She gave Karen another huge hug, muttered a thank you, promised to talk soon, then dashed back down the stairs to take photos before the light faded.

'Look!' she said to Alyssa a little later. 'Kids with hens, kids with eggs, kids with the calf, Zoe hugging the big dog, Eve trying to pick up the little dog. They are lovely girls, a real credit to you, and I can assure you they're as happy as they can possibly be with no Mom around right now.'

Alyssa took the photos and leafed through them, smiling and crying at the same time. Finally she propped them up everywhere she could, on the little table, on the stand beside the bed, even handing some back to Lauren and pointing to the window, so Lauren could stick them in the frame.

'Thank you,' she whispered, and held out her hand. Lauren took it and squeezed it again—a hand hug.

'Hair now?' she suggested, and to her surprise Alyssa nodded, so Lauren hurried off to get the things she kept in the bottom of her filing cabinet in the office. She was walking down the passage with her basket of special treats when she ran into Tom.

'Have you persuaded Mike to put Bobby in the lock-up?' she demanded.

Tom grinned at her.

'Close! Very close! Mike did call by just as we'd put the roast in the oven and as he was going over to the refuge and Bobby wanted to look for something over there—some mysterious something that wasn't packed in his luggage—he offered to take him and return him in…'

Tom glanced at his watch.

'Another three-quarters of an hour.'

He peered at the basket she held in her hands. 'Red Riding Hood on her way to Grandma's house?'

Lauren grinned at him and lifted the pink towel that hid the basket's contents.

'Dry shampoo, clean brushes and combs, body moisturiser, hand cream, foot rubs—very refreshing with a touch of mint—revitalising face masks for the serious long-stay patient, in fact, everything that might be needed to pamper someone who's not feeling crash hot.'

He looked up from the basket, right into her eyes, and something in his sent a shiver down her spine, but all he said was, 'You are a good woman, Lauren Cooper.'

He continued on his way, Lauren on hers, although she was distracted from the task in hand as she spread a towel on Alyssa's pillow then sprayed the dry shampoo onto the woman's long dark hair. She chatted away to Alyssa as she brushed and combed, then, finally satisfied, began to massage lotion into Alyssa's hands, but while she was explaining that she'd discovered how much better it made hospitalised women feel if they were pampered a little, her mind was on Tom, and the look she'd seen in his beautiful grey eyes…

Not that a relationship between them could go anywhere, she reminded herself. Relationships meant sex.

At least Tom wouldn't think she was nothing more than a tease.

At least Tom would understand…

The squelch of disappointment in her stomach told her she didn't want Tom understanding. If anything, she wanted him as a lover, but could she handle the physical side of being a lover herself?

Too many question marks hovering in her head. She'd think about the refuge and how they could make, with Karen's help, a home-stay business work. Or think about Bobby.

But thinking about Bobby brought a new squelchy feeling in her stomach. If ever a little boy needed love and stability in his life, it was Bobby.

Could she give him that?

She was sure she could.

But didn't he also need a father?

'Was that good psychology or instinct this afternoon, that you didn't yell at him but let him sort out the tap pressure himself?' the man who wasn't Bobby's father asked Lauren later. They were sitting on the veranda, the roast dinner finished, although a full moon together with streetlights had meant Bobby could still show off his bike skills.

Clad in his new jeans, boots, shirt and cowboy hat, he was doing wheelies on his bike on the front drive, while they acted as audience.

Lauren looked at the man who'd asked the question, a man she knew but, she was realising, didn't really know.

She wondered if he really wanted to know, or if it was her way of avoiding talk of Alyssa and how she, Lauren, had handled the visit.

'I think he's been yelled at enough in his life, or heard enough yelling, and although there are times when I could scream at him, I really, really don't want to do it. Do you know what he was doing when he broke the eggs?'

Tom smiled, and something shifted in her chest, but she couldn't fall in love with Tom—that was a given—so stuff happening in her chest had to be ignored. And who said anything about love?

'Tell me,' the man she wasn't going to love asked quietly, and now it was Lauren's turn to smile.

'He was showing me how you could swing a bucket or a

bag around in big circles in the air and stuff didn't fall out of it.'

'Ah, I've done that trick with a bucket of water,' Tom replied, smiling even more broadly so the something in Lauren's chest got worse. 'I got very wet if I remember.'

Picturing the scene, Lauren had to chuckle.

'Well, Bobby was obviously much better at it than you, because nothing fell out but the dozen eggs got jostled by the cans of baked beans and sweet corn and the bottle of tomato sauce, hence the mess.'

'We can buy more eggs,' Tom said, and the 'we' in the sentence told Lauren that she should move out as soon as possible—before this 'we' business went any further—before she started to think that maybe, somewhere along the track, they might actually make a 'we'.

Which she knew full well they wouldn't.

Couldn't.

'Did you see that?'

Bobby's cry brought her attention back to the reason she was here with Tom, living in his house, and feeling all kinds of emotional turmoil because of it.

Bobby was twirling around on the bike, the front wheel off the ground.

'Fantastic!' Tom said, just as Lauren was about to tell the child to stop doing something so dangerous.

'Fantastic?' she echoed, but quietly, as Bobby rode off to try another trick.

'He's trying things, pushing limits,' Tom told her. 'That *is* fantastic! It also shows he's feeling okay—kind of settled with us for all that's happened to him over the weekend.'

Trying things—pushing limits—wasn't that what she had done? Oh, she'd been older than Bobby was—a teenager—

but going out with Nat when he'd been known to be wild had maybe pushed the limits too far.

Was that why she'd never told anyone about the abuse?

'I can understand kids wondering if it's their fault their parents are making a mess of life.'

The words came out of her thoughts—unconsidered—and the smile Tom turned on her this time made her wonder if he'd guessed that.

'You should be over feeling shame or blame,' he reminded her, picking up on her thoughts—taking her hand to hold it in his.

'Look at this one!'

Bobby's call distracted them both and they watched him run the bike up a ramp he'd constructed from a brick and a bit of ply he'd found somewhere, then flip it in the air before landing on two wheels, wobbling slightly but carrying on, one arm raised in triumph as he yelled his success to the heavens.

They clapped and shouted praise, but as he spun away, Tom squeezed Lauren's hand and they sat and watched the boy until the wind blowing in from the ocean turned cold and Lauren called him Bobby to bed.

But when the bathed, pyjama-clad child came into the kitchen to say goodnight, Tom remembered the scrap of paper Lauren had rescued from the toaster.

He pulled it out of his pocket and laid it on the table.

'Why did you want to burn it, Bobby?' he asked gently, then felt like a monster when tears welled in Bobby's eyes.

''S nothing!' Bobby growled, pushing away from the table. He slammed his chair back with such force it toppled over, and once on his feet he snatched at the singed and blackened scrap, clutching it to his chest as he dashed from the room, heading for his bedroom.

'At least he didn't run away,' Lauren said quietly.

'Unless he's in there packing,' Tom muttered, wondering why on earth he'd spoiled a pleasant evening by bringing up something Bobby obviously wanted forgotten.

'What was on it?' Lauren asked.

Tom saw the anxiety in her voice mirrored in her eyes, and *had* to touch her again, reaching across the table to rest his hand on hers.

'I don't know—it was too badly burned to tell, although it *seemed* to be a picture of a witch or a wizard perhaps, but I couldn't really tell.'

'Merlin!' Lauren breathed, her face lightening with the word as though the magic of the legendary man was working within her. 'Of course! I wonder where it is?'

'Where Merlin is?' Tom looked around. 'Wasn't he a shape-shifter? Could he be my oven, or perhaps my washing machine? It's definitely possessed!

Lauren laughed and Tom found the rage he'd been holding at bay was gone, replaced, yet again, by the strange contentment he kept finding in the simple presence of this woman in his house.

'It's a rug Joan was making for Bobby. He loves all things Merlin. I imagine he saw a movie at some time that had Merlin in it and now he knows things I didn't know. For instance, in my mind Merlin was always connected with King Arthur, but Bobby informed me he was around long before that.'

She grinned at Tom across the table before adding, 'I must admit I was so suspicious that he'd know such a thing that I looked it up and he was right. If there was a real Merlin—or a person Merlin might have been based on—then he was around way before the legends of King Arthur began.'

Unfortunately—or perhaps fortunately for Tom's peace of

mind—the smile gave way to a frown as Lauren continued, 'Maybe it's at the refuge. That's what he went to look for earlier with Mike.'

Tom met her frown with one of his own. He was totally bamboozled now.

'What's at the refuge?' he demanded.

'The rug, of course. I'll go over there later but right now I'd better reassure Bobby.'

She left the room while Tom's mind replayed the conversation, finally settling on 'a rug Joan was making' as the most salient part of it. Canvas and bits of wool? A rug in progress?

He didn't want to get Bobby's hopes up by mentioning it right now, but as soon as he was through the goodnight session with the little boy, now soothed by reassurances from Lauren, he'd check that suitcase again.

In the bedroom Lauren was reading the bedtime story, and standing in the doorway, looking at the fondness—no, love—in her face as she looked down at Bobby, he felt a surge of—it had to be protectiveness—so strong he had to lean against the doorjamb for a moment.

It was the family thing again.

CHAPTER NINE

'It *is* the rug,' Lauren said a little later, lifting the mess of canvas and wool out of the suitcase and spreading it on the table. 'And, see, it's nearly finished.'

She looked up at Tom, eyes gleaming with excitement.

'I know there are two rug hooks because sometimes one of the helpers worked with Joan. There's not so much to do—let's get it done tonight.'

She was practically shimmering with expectation—and no way could he pour water on *that* shimmer!

But…

'Hook a rug? You're talking to a man who has to get the dry cleaners to sew his buttons on!'

'It's easy. I'll show you!' Lauren declared, which was how Dr Tom Fletcher, who normally on a Monday night might be enjoying a little female company, found himself sitting at his kitchen table, pushing bits of wool through holes and knotting them to make sure they stayed in place.

Which was fine as far as it went, but working on a small rug—Merlin the magician or not—meant sitting in very close proximity to Lauren, feeling her warmth, her softness when she moved, breathing in the clean, fresh scent of her, blowing fine fair hair out of his face when she spun to fix something for him.

He hooked and tied and hooked and tied and all the while the urge to take this woman in his arms grew stronger and stronger.

'Concentrate!' Lauren chided at one stage, but her voice seemed a little shaky, the rebuke far from firm.

Was she feeling it as well?

Could something as simple as hooking a rug have brought another dimension into their relationship?

His body certainly seemed to think so! Yes, they touched from time to time, skin meeting skin, thigh meeting thigh, hard to avoid it, but even when they weren't touching he could feel her presence, feel it tantalising his body in a way he couldn't remember feeling before.

Was it because she was off limits? Not only because she'd already rejected him or because of what had happened in the past, but because she was a guest in his house—definitely off limits! So could the heat building in his body be put down to the lure of forbidden fruit?

He hoped so.

He really did!

'Okay, we're done!' she declared, some hours later.

'Just as well, given it's after midnight,' Tom grouched, although his chest filled with pride and he all but forgot the heat as Lauren lifted the finished product, holding up the picture of the bearded old man in his tall, pointed hat.

'It's fantastic!' he said, and he leapt to his feet, knocking over his chair as Bobby had earlier. But who cared about the chair? He grabbed Lauren and the rug in a tight clasp and swung her around in the air. 'We did it!' he crowed. 'We did it!'

After which it was only natural that he should kiss her, and although there was two inches of tightly knotted wool between her body and his, his heart surged with a wild emotion when her lips fluttered uncertainly for a moment before opening beneath his kiss and, suddenly, there was Lauren kissing him back…

They had two inches of wool and carpet between their bodies so it couldn't be the siren song of lust that had her returning Tom's kiss. But returning it she was, drawn into it by some emotion too powerful to resist.

It was just a kiss—a celebratory kiss—nothing more, she kept telling herself, yet her lips clung to his, opening to his invading tongue, revelling in the moist warmth, the sharing, the sheer physical delight that kissing Tom was spreading through her body.

She tingled in places she hadn't known existed, heated in places she knew shouldn't be so hot, her nerve endings quivered and her hands began to tremble so she let go of the rug, which remained firmly stuck between them, and clasped her hands around Tom's neck, sliding her fingers into his hair—silky hair that stirred her quivering nerves even more.

Maybe it was because the whole time they'd been working on the rug, sitting so close to each other, her body had been feeling things it shouldn't, alive with an excitement she didn't understand—well, she did understand it, she just didn't want to think about why she'd been feeling it!

The kiss deepened and she clung to him more tightly, all questions forgotten.

Tom had shifted too. His arms had been clasped around her, but now *his* hands were in *her* hair, and it seemed, although she was probably imagining it, that his fingers were trembling too…

He whispered her name, the all-but-soundless 'Lauren' seeming to float from his lips, wrapping her in a bubble of new sensation.

A tiny mew of protest fell from hers when his mouth lifted for that fraction of a second, and though it was a wordless noise he seemed to understand for the kiss resumed and she allowed herself to stop thinking altogether, to stop analysing and categorising her sensory reactions and just enjoy them as tendrils of physical delight bound them together.

Could a kiss last for ever?

So it seemed to Lauren, although eventually they drew apart, as if by some mutual but unspoken agreement, the rug falling to the floor between them, Merlin the magician a crumpled bundle on the floor.

It was a moment in time, Lauren realised, when they—or maybe she—could move forward, and though she was confused about where such a choice might lead—confused about the whole situation—she knew the decision was up to her.

Excitement urged her forward, while fear held her back—no, not fear, for she knew Tom would never hurt her, but trepidation…

'I think I have to trim the top of it,' Lauren whispered, bending to pick it up, knowing there was fierce colour in her face and hoping Tom might assume it was because she'd bent over.

He looked at her, saying nothing, studying her as if she were a new acquaintance, or perhaps a chance-met old one, until, when the silence had stretched, it seemed, for even longer than the kiss, and the rug was grasped in front of her in a white-knuckled grip, he asked, 'That's it?'

She tried for calm, control and composure.

'What's it?' she asked, and he turned and walked away, along the hall, down the steps, heading who knew where.

Lauren sat down at the table, picked up Joan's sharp scissors, and began to trim the uneven ends of wool until the rug was smooth and thick and a perfect representation of the wizard Bobby so admired.

Tom checked his patients in the hospital, looking in on Alyssa who was sleeping, a nurse never far away, keeping watch over the fragile and vulnerable woman. He couldn't help but picture Lauren lying there and the cold anger filled him again, although this time the heat that lingered in his body from the kiss had diluted it, allowing him to consider the things he'd learned.

Lauren's disjointed confession of her abuse bothered him in many ways. Was she still suffering the after-effects? *Was* that why she hadn't dated since he'd known her?

He wasn't vain enough to think it was why she hadn't dated him, but if she *was* still avoiding intimacy…

As if he could help her! he scoffed to himself.

Oh, he knew physical intimacy extremely well, but helping someone over any other kind of problem with intimacy—well, hardly! Not when he'd avoided it all his life!

Yet deep inside he felt a need to do something for the woman who was living in his house—for the friend he'd found in Lauren.

For the woman he'd kissed?

Well…

The only thing he did know was that it wasn't his old friend Lauren whom he'd kissed, or she who'd kissed him back. Something had shifted in their relationship, and as they were bound together by their responsibility to a lost and lonely little boy, he'd darned well better get it shifted back.

He returned to the house, making a noise as he came up the steps, hoping she'd hear him and come out so they could talk.

At two in the morning?

She didn't, but when he found his duvet back on his bed, he looked into Bobby's room, seeing, on the floor beside the bed, the finished rug—carefully placed there as a surprise for Bobby when he woke up.

That was so typical of Lauren—the Lauren who sought to make people's lives easier and happier, their paths smoother—that he smiled and for a moment forgot the Lauren that he'd kissed…

Had there been a promise implicit in that kiss?

This was the question running through Lauren's head as she tossed and turned on the very comfortable bed in the second spare bedroom of Tom's house.

On her part, not his, she meant.

Tiredness made her thoughts swirl uselessly around in her head, while her body continued to whisper traitorous messages.

But Tom deserved better than to be led on by promises, then rejected when she turned frigid at the first really intimate touch.

On top of which would be her humiliation when that happened—the numbing despair and overwhelming embarrassment.

In front of Tom?

She couldn't contemplate such a thing so, no, there had been no promise implicit in the kiss, and if, by chance he'd read one, she'd surely made things clear when she'd grabbed the rug as if it were a lifeline, chattering on about trimming it.

She must have slept, although as she leapt out of bed in response to Bobby's yell, she knew it hadn't been for nearly long enough. Near numb with fatigue, she rushed to Bobby's room, to find him dancing up and down on the little rug.

'Look, it's here!' he cried. 'It's finished. My Merlin rug. Mum made it—she must have finished it without telling me. Look!'

He grabbed it off the floor and held it up for inspection, and Tom, who'd joined Lauren in the entrance to the room, put his arm around her waist and gave her a gentle squeeze, sharing the pleasure of their achievement and the joy of the little boy.

'It was in a suitcase at the house,' Tom told Bobby, while Lauren pleased the boy by examining the rug more closely, exclaiming over it while hoping he wouldn't notice a couple of blisters from the rug hook on her hands.

'It's beautiful,' Lauren told Bobby as he took his treasure back and held it crumpled tightly in his arms. Tears shone in his eyes and she drew him close, so once again she was hugging someone with the rug between them.

If she hadn't raised her eyes to Tom it would have been much easier to go with the pretence of no invitation in a kiss, but the flare of complicity in Tom's eyes, and the slight smile on his lips, told her it wouldn't be that easy.

Fortunately, because she was feeling totally lost—way out of her depth in a sea of emotion she didn't understand—Tom took control of the morning routine.

'Breakfast?' he suggested, and Bobby pulled away from Lauren.

'We've got Frosty Flakes!' he told Tom, darting out of the room, the rug dropped to the floor.

'Clothes and bathroom first,' Tom said, as Lauren bent to straighten the rug. 'Wash face and hands, clean teeth, get dressed. We'll all have breakfast together.'

To Lauren's surprise, Bobby trotted obediently towards the

bathroom, then she looked down at the Cupids on her nightgown and wished she'd beaten him to it.

But she *could* get changed.

'Lauren!'

Too late! Tom's had rested his hand on her shoulder, catching her as she turned away from him, and though her nerves jangled at his touch, and fear he'd bring up the promise in the kiss stiffened all her muscles, he simply smiled and said, 'We did good, huh?'

The slang expression made her smile and she raised her hand to exchange a high five with him, then darted to her room, reminding herself that touching any part of Tom, even the palm of his hand in a high five, was fraught with danger and would only make her decision to deny her reactions to the kiss even harder.

As it turned out, Tom was called to the hospital before the first Frosty Flake was poured then after breakfast Bobby was whipped away by the mother of a friend of his from school, who'd phoned first to ask if he would like to go down to Port Macquarie with her and her son. Her older boy would be with them, she'd explained, and the three lads could go to a movie while she did some last-minute Christmas shopping.

Which left Lauren on her own and with plenty of time to visit Alyssa once again. She went into the office first to check for messages and mail and was about to leave when Tom walked in.

'Did you come over to see Alyssa?' he asked, and something in his voice made her look more closely at him, although looking too closely at Tom was something she'd been avoiding this morning.

His face was drawn, and he paused before adding, 'She was pregnant, Lauren. She's lost the baby. I did a D and C this morning so she'll still be a bit woozy.'

Her mission forgotten—for the moment—Lauren slumped down into her chair.

'Hell and damnation,' she muttered. 'The poor woman!'

Tom shrugged and shook his head, looking not defeated exactly but so down, it took iron control on Lauren's part to prevent herself standing up, crossing to him, and giving him a hug. She knew how much he loved obstetric work and how hard he took such occurrences, and a comforting hug would have been natural.

It's what she would have done before all this began, she reminded herself.

Even yesterday she would have hugged him, before she'd cut the tendrils of desire that had wrapped around the two of them with that stupid rug remark…

He hesitated in the doorway. Was he waiting for the hug?

She *wasn't* going to hug him!

And eventually he walked away, leaving Lauren feeling guilty that she hadn't offered *some* kind of comfort.

Except it would have had to be a hug.

It's what she did.

To her, gathering someone in a strong embrace often did more good than a thousand words. As well as offering comfort, hugs could transfer energy. They could invigorate and rejuvenate, and unlike drugs they had no unpleasant side effects. She knew enough of her own psychology to know she'd taken to hugs as a way of initiating physical contact with people back at a time when it had been very difficult for her to be touched. Back then she'd realised that the hugger could break away any time—the one who hugged was in control and control had been very important to her.

Hugging Tom, however, was a very different matter. Hugging Tom would have side effects for her—not unpleasant but unsettling, tempting—*stupid*!

She'd go and see Alyssa—give her a hand hug and sit with her a while—then go over to the refuge and work out the Christmas plans for the families in the house. Tell them about Karen Williams's offer and see what they thought…

Bobby returned mid-afternoon, full of talk about his day's adventure, the movie—not that good—and the treat they'd had, eating at a fast-food outlet. Lauren had slipped a casserole into the oven, thinking the vegetables in with the cubes of lamb might be well enough disguised for Bobby to eat them without complaint.

'Can we go over to the house and show the kids there my new clothes?' he asked, when he'd finished describing his day.

'I thought you might be tired,' Lauren said, while wondering if his ability to latch onto something and not let go was a normal 'kid' thing, or a 'Bobby' thing. She'd been certain he'd have forgotten about showing off his new clothes by now.

'I suppose we can,' she said, 'but we can only stay an hour or so because dinner's in the oven.'

'What is it?' her new protégé demanded, suspicion flashing in his eyes.

'A casserole.'

'Yuck—sloppy stew! Why can't we have sausages?'

'Because you need a balanced diet, we all do, and there is no way I'm cooking one thing for you and something else for me and Tom. You'll just have to handle the sloppy stew tonight. Tomorrow we might have chicken.'

She expected to see the scowl he brought out when things didn't go his way, but to her surprise he grinned then dashed off, presumably to get dressed in his new clothes.

They stayed longer than they'd intended at the refuge. The women were so excited at the prospect of taking their children to a farm for Christmas they wanted every detail, and Bobby was having a good time with the children he knew so he'd been happy to stay. As a result the sun was sinking towards the horizon when they drove home, and even the usually indefatigable Bobby was showing signs of tiredness.

'There's Tom!' Bobby shouted as they pulled up in the drive. Lauren turned her head and saw the man she was avoiding thinking about walking towards the house. Hard not to think about him when just seeing him made her heart jolt in her chest.

They got out of the car and waited until he joined them, Lauren sniffing the air, sure she'd smell the delicious aroma of a simmering casserole as she walked through the door.

Perhaps the breeze was blowing it the other way.

They all headed for the kitchen, which had fast become the hub of their little household, Bobby yammering away at Tom, Lauren growing more anxious about the casserole.

She crossed to the oven and felt the outside.

Cold!

'Problem?' Tom asked, and she turned to see him smiling, but with that one eyebrow raised.

Big problem, her mind replied as she battled her reaction to that smile, so by the time she was ready to reply he, too, was feeling the oven.

'It helps to turn it on,' he said, standing so close she could feel the warmth of his body, while the smile that accompanied the words exacerbated all the tremors and tingling and heat rioting within her body.

'I *did* turn it on, look!'

Indignation helped and she stepped back to point at the dials, but for some reason a nothing exchange of words about an oven was proving as seductive as that darned kiss had been and she was losing strength in her knees and willpower in her mind.

Could he be feeling it?

She had no idea!

Her experience was limited, and in retrospect mostly embarrassing, so she had no idea if the man peering into the depths of his oven, poking at things with his fingers—he *had* turned it off first—was feeling anything other than aggravation that his oven was broken.

'It worked okay last night when we cooked the lamb,' Tom said, turning a mystified face towards Lauren as she stood there beside him, contrarily revelling in all the sensations his closeness was causing when she should have been moving to Antarctica.

A snigger from somewhere behind them gave the game away, Lauren catching on first and turning on the eight-year-old demon who had come into their lives.

'What did you do?' she demanded.

'Nothin'!'

The predictable response was accompanied by a hurt look but Tom had sussed Bobby out, turning on the switch for the kitchen light and finding it, too, wasn't working.

'Power board,' he said to Lauren. He grasped Bobby gently by the shoulder and steered him towards the back door. 'Now you'll turn it back on, young man, and any more of those tricks and the bike goes into storage for a week, understand?'

An outwardly contrite Bobby turned the power back on, explaining to Tom as he did so that one of the big kids from school had once turned off the power to all the houses in their street.

'Inwardly the little devil's gloating,' Lauren said to Tom, as Bobby went into the living room to watch a TV show while she found something else to have for dinner. 'He wanted sausages, not sloppy stew for dinner.'

'So we can't let him win, can we?' Tom told her, enfolding her in a smile that made her heart melt. 'What else do we have?'

'Look for yourself. There's cold meat, salad, cheese—things I bought for sandwiches for lunches.'

Tom poked his head into the refrigerator, then started to haul stuff out.

'When I was a kid I hated salads, so maybe a salad will be a just punishment.'

The smile this time was more of a grin but it had the same effect. She had to get out of there and, speaking of that—thinking of it—why hadn't they heard from Mike, or someone from Children's Services?

And why hadn't *she* phoned around to find out what was happening in the search for Bobby's relatives?

Surely not because she was enjoying living here?

'I'll just check he hasn't found the water main,' she said, and fled the kitchen, needing to get away from Tom while she worked out just what was happening in her head.

Was she escaping him? Tom wondered as he watched Lauren whisk from the room.

And if so, why?

Surely she hadn't been feeling the tug of attraction he'd felt as they'd stood at the oven! It was an *oven*, for heaven's sake, and a none-too-clean one at that! Yet he'd lingered there, mind blank for all he'd been poking things, his body revelling in being close to Lauren's, drinking in the hint of the dusky perfume she used, the softness of the hair that brushed his face as she moved.

He had to do something about this—maybe go visit Emily at Belrose, although that would be the act of a cad, using one woman to forget another, and he'd never done caddish things…

He made a salad instead—the old-fashioned kind of salad his foster-mothers had always made. Trendy, tossed in a bowl then dumped on a plate salads were all very well, but for someone like him—and Bobby—who liked individual tastes, a pile of grated cheese next to the mound of grated carrot beside the slices of tinned beetroot and the slices of ham and tomato was how a salad should be. He put the three plates in the refrigerator and went to find his 'family'.

They were on the front veranda, Lauren gently questioning Bobby about relatives.

'I haven't *got* any grandparents,' Bobby protested. 'There used to be an old lady Mum called Aunty but she died. We never saw her anyway 'cos she lived in Sydney.'

Not wanting to interrupt, Tom watched from the doorway, studying Bobby carefully and deciding the child wasn't upset by this lack of relations. If anything, he seemed to accept it as the natural way of things.

'I don't need any old relations,' Bobby continued. 'I can just stay here with you and Tom.'

Tom's attention switched to Lauren. How would she handle this?

'For the moment, definitely,' she said, reaching out and rubbing Bobby's thatch of hair. 'The problem is that there are rules about who children live with, and there are people whose job it is to find the best places for kids to live and it might be they find a nice aunt or uncle you didn't know you had and it might be that aunt or uncle would *like* you to live with them.'

'Would not!'

Bobby's denial was so swift Tom moved, thinking he might strike out again, but he remained sitting in the chair, staring out at the darkening sea, his jaw set in a way Tom now recognised as a fight against tears.

'Who's for some dinner?' he called from the doorway, then he stepped onto the veranda where he, too, ruffled Bobby's hair. 'Cold salad, thanks to you, champ,' he said. 'And don't bother telling me you don't like salad. You're a growing boy, you need your vegetables.'

Bobby rose without a murmur and to Tom's surprise the child put his arms around Tom's waist and gave him a hug. He quite possibly wiped his wet eyes and dribbly nose against Tom's shirt at the same time, but what did that matter, compared to a hug from a lonely, confused, bereaved little boy?

They sat at the table in the kitchen, and as Tom put the plates on the table he couldn't help but feel a sense of…not pride exactly but deep satisfaction, as if somehow he'd made a family.

'I like salads like this.' Bobby's appreciative comment broke into Tom's slightly shocked consideration of how the words 'family' and 'satisfaction' had wormed their way into the same sentence in his mind. He, who was happy as a loner…

'And I'm sorry, Lauren, about the 'lectric switch.'

Lauren smiled at the miscreant.

'Not to worry,' she said easily, then turned the smile a little brighter. 'Just think, you can have the casserole tomorrow.'

Bobby grimaced but didn't object, apparently accepting defeat in the matter of sloppy stews!

'No relations?' Tom asked. It was some hours later. Bobby was asleep in bed, barely lasting out his second bedtime story, his face angelic in the glow of the small night-light Lauren had found for him.

Now his temporary parents were sitting on the veranda,

enjoying an after-dinner coffee and the peaceful sound of the waves washing on the beach below the town.

Lauren turned towards him, the light behind her so her face was shadowed, but he could hear real concern in her voice when she answered.

'Would you believe I didn't even try to find any relations today? I saw him off with his friends, then went across to the hospital, got involved with Alyssa and had a talk to Karen Williams, came back and prepared dinner, and didn't at any stage give a thought to Bobby's future.'

She sighed so deeply he wanted to touch her—to comfort her—but touching Lauren was habit-forming, and possibly addictive, and definitely not a good idea given even standing near her had fired his body to an aching desire.

'Not only did I not do anything about the poor kid, but I don't want to think about *why* I didn't contact anyone,' she finished.

'You're not in charge of finding relations,' he reminded her, surprised to find himself in sympathy with her over not wanting to contact people. 'Mike's handling that with Children's Services and it's up to them, not us. All we're doing is looking after him for now, making sure he feels secure, and knows he's safe with us.'

I think, he added to himself…

'Except if we don't find some relation soon, I'll have to talk to him about Joan's funeral. He's a little boy, Tom, he shouldn't have to be involved in things like that, yet what happens if I don't talk about it and later find he wanted input? Maybe there's a song Joan liked that he'd like to hear played. I don't know!'

Forget the aching desire—this was a woman who needed a hug!

Tom stood up, hauled her out of her chair and put his arms around her.

'*We'll* talk to him,' he told her firmly. '*We'll* help him decide what he wants—together! And if he doesn't want to know—or if he doesn't want anything to do with any of it—then we'll back him up on that, but you're right, we do have to talk to him.'

He felt her body relax against his, her curves fitting into him as if they'd been fashioned to match his shape, and the desire he'd been trying to forget burned through him, so his muscles tensed and his arms drew her closer, closer, closer, until he was pressing kisses on the top of her head, on her forehead, on her eyelids, working slowly downwards until she lifted her head to him and pressed a kiss onto his lips.

Lauren kissing *him*?

He needed no second invitation, his mouth opening over hers, devouring her lips, seeking entry to her sweet, moist warmth, coffee flavoured but Lauren flavoured as well. Soft breasts pressed against his chest, moving now and then when she dragged in a deep, replenishing breath before returning all her attention to the kiss.

The Kiss—it was assuming capital letters in his head, for never had kissing someone been so satisfying. Generally seeing it as little more than a prelude to making love, he usually got the kissing part over and done with quite quickly, but right now he didn't want this kiss to stop.

Her arms had crept around his waist, her hands sliding up, then down, cupping his butt, squeezing it, holding him tightly to her, evidence of his arousal pressed into the softness of her belly.

She moved against him, moved enough to make him groan.

Stupid!

Why make a sound?

Now she was gone, slamming away from him so suddenly she nearly fell.

He caught her—saved her from falling—held her steady, watching her chest rise and fall as she sucked in air—saw the tears in her eyes and the quiver on her lips as she tried to speak and failed.

And when finally a word did emerge, it was hardly what he'd expected. It was a trembling and shame-faced 'Sorry', stricken eyes raised to his, panic as well as embarrassment written on her face.

He drew her close again, and held her, just held her.

'Sorry for kissing me?' he asked gently, when her trembling had eased and she'd once again relaxed against him.

Well, almost relaxed against him…

She shook her head, then lifted it—no coward, his friend Lauren.

'Sorry for—for leading you on—for encouraging you—for kissing you like that. Sorry I'm so damn inept at this stuff. Sorry I'm not what you need, Tom. Believe me.'

She paused, as if waiting for him to say something, but what could he say? Besides, silence often worked because the person who found the silence most awkward would fill it…

And finally she did!

'You know my history—you've seen Alyssa in hospital. I know as a psychologist I should have sorted myself out by now, but…'

Even in the shadowy light of the veranda he could see the colour in the cheeks and pain for her—for her embarrassment and for the things she'd suffered in the past—shafted through Tom's body.

'I'm no good with intimacy.'

She didn't mumble the words, or try to hide her face against his chest, although it was there, readily available to her. She looked up into his eyes as she said it, defying the flaming cheeks and quivering voice that evidenced her embarrassment.

'I have had boyfriends since Nat, Tom. Heaven knows, it's been a long time, and I've tried. I've truly tried, but comes the time—well, the important time—and I can't do it. I go rigid. I'm no good to you for all I'd like to be…'

Tears slid down her scarlet cheeks and Tom folded his arms around her and wondered how she'd take it she knew he'd like to mingle his tears with hers, as his pain for her took on another dimension—sinking to a depth he hadn't known he could feel.

He held her and he rubbed his hands across her back, offering comfort, nothing more. She snuggled into him, accepting comfort.

When it changed he had no idea, but change it did, with Lauren raising her face again, kissing him, cautiously at first, eyes wary, questioning, yet her body responding to his touch.

He eased himself away, and looked into those changeable eyes.

'Are you doing this for me? Do you feel obliged in any way?'

She flushed, the colour so delicate he had to touch her cheek to feel the warmth.

She shook her head, her gaze roaming his face as if some answer to an unasked question might be loitering there.

She opened her mouth to speak, closed it again, shrugged, then finally said, 'It's probably the opposite. I think *I* might be using *you*.'

It nearly broke his heart.

The heart he hadn't thought he had.

The kind of heart you had to have to experience love…

He wanted to say please use him all she liked, but knew

that would be crass. He wanted to say he'd do anything for her, whatever she wanted, but couldn't have explained why. He wanted, more than anything, to make love to her and that thought shocked him so much he couldn't speak at all.

He didn't make love. Making love wasn't in his repertoire, he practised mutually enjoyable sex.

'You'd rather not?' she asked.

He looked at the woman he hadn't answered while all these confusing thoughts had been racing through his head.

'I don't know what I'd rather,' he admitted. 'Going further—and, yes, I'm so attracted to you I'd like nothing more, and forget the using-me part, that's nonsense—but going further could complicate our lives. Do you realise that?'

She studied him again.

'You mean if it didn't work? If we weren't suited? When we part but have to work together? Is that what you're thinking?'

'All of those,' he told her, but he kissed her anyway. 'But aren't we getting ahead of ourselves here?'

Lauren didn't know.

In point of fact, she knew nothing—absolutely nothing. Her brain had ceased to work while her body ached with a raw need that the kissing had generated, and which now pulsed through her body like a high-voltage charge.

She'd warned Tom what might happen if they went further.

He couldn't say he didn't know.

And he'd warned her of future consequences.

'I don't care,' she whispered to him, and kissed him again, giving in to the sensations his firm but gentle touch was sending into all parts of her body, the brush of his fingers across her breasts spearing more need down between her thighs. She squirmed against him, mindless, barely registering his suggestion they move into the bedroom, barely aware of Tom closing the door behind them, leading her to that great raft of a bed, talking, touching, soothing, exciting, then soothing again, damping down fires before recharging them, her limbs now boneless, her nerves quivering, the charged wanting something she had never felt before.

'Just touch my face at any time you want to stop. Or say the word,' Tom whispered, his voice muffled as he spoke against a wet patch on her neck, a patch he'd licked and kissed and teased until she turned and twisted with desire, not knowing how to do the same to him, to excite him as much as he was exciting her.

Her first touch was so tentative he may not have felt it, but the warmth of his skin sent a tingle through her nerve endings so she splayed her hands across his chest, pushing his shirt to one side, relishing her own responses, learning the hardness of his muscles, the shape of his chest, a light line of hair arrowing downwards.

Follow it?

Did she dare?

Lost in the haze of sensations that were her body's response to Tom's ministrations, she felt her body relax, giving in to the jolt of pleasure his touch on her nipple produced, giving in to the quiver of anticipation as his questing hands slid lower. But she wanted to be more than a passive recipient of these delicious sensations, she wanted to explore, be part of the game, to learn what gave him pleasure while still discovering it herself. She let her fingers slide lower, and lower, Tom's hand now joining hers, helping her cup him, *his* hand moving to brush across her mound, shooting new darts of excitement through her body.

The silky skin firmed beneath her touch, Tom's finger

probed gently into her, while excitement skittered now, her breathing slowed…

'Are you okay?'

Tom's husky words drifted through the air around them, but Lauren could barely discern their meaning. She knew she'd passed the bounds of other experiences—knew too that they'd *never* been like this—and most of all she knew she didn't want to stop.

'I'm pretty sure I am,' she managed to reply, but now his fingers were working some magic on her body so it came out as a strangled squeak.

Was it Tom's experience or because it *was* Tom, a man she was fairly sure she loved, that had released her from the memories of the past, the fear of pain that had probably built up in her mind to a level beyond any she had felt?

Her woozy mind lost the thread about then, and her body didn't care about the answer. All it wanted was more of the same. Perhaps some release somewhere along the line, from the tension—exquisite tension—that was building and building in her body…

Then it came, the release, lifting her high into the air, the world in limbo as all thoughts and memories disappeared and she was lost to sheer sensation.

She shattered, pressed against Tom, came apart again, then, knowing she needed more—*he* needed more—she drew him into her body, clasping him inside her, moving again until she heard him gasp and felt his long-withheld release. She held him to her, relishing the weight of him on her body, wondering if his weight would help her put herself together again…

'I never knew!'

She wasn't certain how much later this was, if they'd slept or just lain together, but finally she'd found the words. Not the 'Thank you' she probably should have said, but the words to reveal her wonder—the miracle of it all…

He was gone when she woke in the morning, leaving her alone in the enormous bed, and inevitably all the things they'd considered the previous night about complicating things came rushing back to her. Questions she'd never considered hammered in her head.

How did she face a man when she'd done things like she'd done to him during the long night? How to face him without blushing? How to look at him without thinking of him naked? Without remembering how he'd felt inside her?

Fortunately, the sound of Bobby stirring—yawning loudly was Bobby's way of announcing he was awake—in the next room reminded her of her responsibilities and while a rush of shame—how could they have done *that* with Bobby in the house?—swept through her, she got out of bed, clutched her discarded clothes to her, and bolted to her bedroom, where she hurriedly dressed and raced to the kitchen so she could pretend she'd been there all along when Bobby did appear.

Except Tom was there before her, making coffee, smiling at her. And forget blushing, she was certain her whole body had turned scarlet. Was that how scarlet women got their name? She'd lost her mind, obviously, and was now standing in the kitchen door, staring at Tom, thinking totally irrational thoughts and with no idea how to retrieve a little sanity.

'Coffee?' Tom asked, as if it was just an ordinary morning, although maybe his smile was just a little softer—teasing almost?

'In a cup? With milk and sugar how you like it?' he persisted.

Apparently she hadn't answered him, but how could she when her mind was replaying every instant of last night and her eyes couldn't take in enough of his strong-boned face, a shadow of black stubble on his chin, his lips curled into the very slightest of smiles, and his broad, muscled chest, tanned skin spread like satin over it, the little pathway of hair—

Heat flooded her again but now at least she'd found some words.

'You could at least have pulled on a shirt!' she muttered at him, and he laughed, then set down the coffee pot and came towards her, sliding his arm around her shoulders and giving her a hug, and then a swift kiss.

It was interrupted before it could be anything but swift by Bobby's 'Bleagh!'

Somehow they got through breakfast—Lauren recovering slightly once Tom *did* pull on a shirt—but although she'd expected him to head off to the hospital as soon as the meal was finished, he lingered, helping with the dishes, hanging around, finally suggesting they all sit on the veranda for a while.

Something in the way he spoke brought Lauren out of her confusion over the night's events and a cold shiver of presentiment rushed through her. Had Mike been in touch—had he found Bobby's family? Or maybe 'things being different' meant Tom had had enough of them staying with him…

Lauren made more coffee—she'd need something to keep her going!—and joined Tom and Bobby on the veranda.

'We need to talk, Bobby,' Tom began. 'I know you're only a kid, but because it's about your mother we do need to talk to you about what happens next.'

'I ain't got no relations!' Bobby said, and stood up, ready to flee if there was any suggestion of him going to someone he didn't know.

'It's not about relations, it's about business,' Tom said, and with a wave of relief she shouldn't have felt, Lauren caught on. She reached out and took Bobby's hand, pulling him onto her knee.

'Remember,' she said gently, 'when Carrots the red guinea pig at the refuge died—what did we do?'

Bobby squirmed on her knee then turned and faced her. 'We buried it. We had a—whatya call it—funeral.'

'We did,' Lauren said. 'And we sang some songs and some of the kids talked and then we had a little party because Carrots had been a really good guinea pig and we were saying thank you to him for making us happy.'

'So?'

Tom watched Lauren's face. In fact, though he hoped he wasn't being obvious, he'd been watching Lauren's face since he'd woken up—at first watching her sleep beside him, her serene beauty catching at his heart, and then when she'd come into the kitchen, doubt and wonder mingling in her eyes, embarrassment colouring her cheeks. He'd read no regret, which had relieved him enormously, and now he was just watching—waiting—wondering just how she was going to get from the guinea pig to Joan…

When he'd started the conversation he hadn't known how he'd get there either, so had been relieved when Lauren had caught on, but now?

'With people, Bobby,' Lauren was saying quietly, holding Bobby against her in the chair, 'we do the same thing. We have a funeral and we celebrate the human spirit—like with your mum, we'd talk about the things she did to make you happy, and the good times you had together, and the Merlin rug she made for you, and everything happy and fun we can remember.'

'Then we'd bury her?'

No fool, this kid, Tom thought, and felt a twinge of pride in his protégé.

'It's only her body we bury, because when you die your spirit leaves your body so all the fun parts and memories stay on with all the people who knew your mum, and with you especially. And we have a choice of how we want our bodies to be treated when we die—if we want them buried or cremated, which is burnt. They're only like the shells we used to live in, like houses for our spirits, so it's not as if it's the person who's being buried or cremated, but we have to decide what we think your mum would have preferred to have happen to her body.'

Okay, so she'd taken a while to get there, but she'd made it, and this time Tom felt pride in Lauren for handling it so well.

So far so well!

At least Bobby hadn't belted her one!

'Do we have to watch?'

Tom wasn't sure how to take that question, Bobby's tone giving no indication of his preference.

'Only if you want to,' Lauren told him. 'If you want to go to the funeral then that's fine, we'll all go, but you don't actually see the fire with a cremation.'

'That's good because she wouldn't like to be buried, I know,' Bobby declared, 'but I want to go and I want to sing her song.'

'What song is that?' asked Tom.

'It's about a rainbow and a fat man from that place where the surfers all go sings it, and it's Mum's favourite.'

Tom looked blankly at Lauren, who smiled—an ordinary, everyday Lauren smile that for some reason made his heart clench and his stomach knot and a kind of panic start inside him.

'"Somewhere over the Rainbow",' she was saying while his panic attack continued. 'A Hawaiian man sings it with

"What a Wonderful World" like a medley. Joan used to bring the CD to the refuge. It could be in with her things.'

She gave Bobby a hug and promised him they'd sort it out, while Tom wondered if he could sort out what was happening to him.

Perhaps if he went to work…

Was it because he'd expected Lauren to feel a little awkward this morning but hadn't considered how he, himself, might feel that seeing an ordinary Lauren smile had sent him into a spin?

It couldn't be love.

He didn't do love.

Love was destructive.

Love had killed his parents and his sister, the sister he'd loved.

And evidence of love's destructive force was right here in front of him—in an orphaned child, although maybe Greg's feelings for Joan had been more about control than love.

But evidence of love was definitely there in Bobby, the child talking of the song his mother had loved—a little boy wanting to show his love by singing it for her…

'I'm going to work!'

It was an abrupt departure—too abrupt—but he couldn't be worried about that. He had to get off the veranda before the tears pricking at his eyes at the image of the eight-year-old singing about rainbows—singing about hope——came streaming down his cheeks…

CHAPTER TEN

TOM must be regretting it, thought Lauren. How could he not be? A man like Tom, used to experienced, sophisticated women who could probably offer him all kinds of sensual pleasure, having to concentrate solely on her!

'School today!'

Lauren stopped staring after Tom's departing figure and concentrated on Bobby.

'You *want* to go to school?'

Bobby nodded, then added, 'But I have to take something to share to eat, like cake. It's last day so we play games and have a party and watermelon then we have watermelon fights.'

Lauren forgot her own problems and smiled, remembering the last day of summer term when she'd been at school. Definitely watermelon fights but there was no time to bake a cake.

'Come on, then,' she said to Bobby, 'Get ready and we'll call at the bakery on the way and get a cake.'

Bobby sped away, appearing minutes later in his new jeans and tasselled shirt and cowboy hat and, no, she didn't have the heart to object for all she knew he'd get cake and watermelon over all of it.

'Can I tell them about the funeral?' he asked, as they drove down to the town.

Was this normal?

How did one know?

'Of course,' she told him, 'but as we haven't made all the arrangements, you can't tell people a date. Just say we'll put a notice in the paper.'

Silence, then one small hand crept onto her lap.

'You and Tom'll do that? You'll do the notice and…?'

She stopped the car for his voice had thickened, and she put her arms around him, assuring him they'd do the lot, he had no need to worry.

'And you'll take me?'

'Of course we will,' she said, hugging him to her and sniffing madly. 'We'll be right there beside you all the time.'

Choosing a cake soon took precedence over gloomy thoughts of funerals, so the little boy who marched proudly through the school gates in his new gear, Lauren by his side with the chocolate cake, had all of Bobby's old swagger, something his teacher noticed right away, greeting him warmly then sending him off to find his friends.

He raced away, then came bounding back.

'You know we get out early on last day,' he said to Lauren, and although they'd never got around to discussing her collecting him from school, she felt a thrill of pleasure that he'd assumed it would happen.

'What time?' Lauren asked his teacher, who was obviously dying to ask questions about Bobby's future but didn't want to intrude.

'Any time after one,' the teacher said, then she touched Lauren on the arm. 'He needs normality, that little boy.'

Lauren nodded, but as she walked back to the car, doubts descended.

She and Tom were hardly normality.

And this temporary situation wasn't normal.

Stability was normal—that's what Bobby needed.

Could she adopt him on her own?

Fired with determination to sort things out, she drove directly to the hospital where she settled at her desk and phoned Mike.

'What's happening? Who's in charge of finding a relative for Bobby? Who do I need to speak to, to regularise his temporary care with me?'

Mike provided phone numbers but offered no joy as far as relatives were concerned. As far as anyone could discover, Bobby *had* no relatives.

The woman at Children's Services was harassed.

'You've no idea how many families break up over Christmas,' she muttered at Lauren. 'He's fine to stay with you for the moment but his name must be somewhere in the system so someone will eventually be in touch with you. There's all kinds of official stuff to go through to make him a ward of the state, which he'll have to be.'

'Over my dead body!' Lauren said, slamming down the phone and startling the occupational therapist who was walking past the door, and making Tom, who'd come through the door, raise an eyebrow.

'Over your dead body?'

'Some stupid woman talking about making Bobby a ward of the state,' Lauren told him, so angry she was surprised she couldn't see wisps of steam rising in the air around her head.

Tom came further into the room and pulled up a chair to sit across the desk from her.

'He probably will have to be made a ward of the state before we can officially adopt him, and if you think about it, you'll know that's right,' he said, as calmly as if they were carrying on some conversation they'd begun earlier, 'but it doesn't have to happen right now and, anyway, it's only paperwork.'

'What did you say?'

Lauren spaced out the words so he'd have no trouble hearing them.

The eyebrow lifted.

'About him being made a ward of the state? It's only paperwork?' Tom asked.

More wisps of steam!

'You know I don't mean that!' she growled. 'I mean the bit about our adopting him. *Our* adopting him!'

He grinned at her and although her anger was still simmering nicely, the grin did distract her, sending tremors of a desire she'd never felt before—strong physical desire—through her body.

'I thought about it as I walked over to the hospital earlier. Bobby's happy with us, and he's a kid who deserves a break. I think between the two of us, we could do a good job with him. We'd probably have to get married to make the officials feel more comfortable, but I can't see that being too big a problem—'

He broke off so the grin could come back—widening into a teasing smile that sent molten spears of longing sizzling down her nerves.

She had to forget last night and spears of longing and concentrate on practical matters—except she couldn't find what practical matter she wanted to concentrate on.

Marriage?

'You don't want to get married!' she reminded him. 'You've held forth often enough on your single-and-loving-it philosophy. You've never pushed your ideas on other people, but you've made it very plain that marriage and children weren't in your long-term plan for a happy life, while as for love—a destructive force, I think you called it.'

He was silent for so long she wondered if she should have kept her mouth shut, but the marrying idea had come so out of the blue she could barely think, let alone express her disbelief more rationally.

And there was another problem with the whole situation—the problem of a little bit of her skittering around in an excited tizzy and bouncing up and down in delight, twittering 'marriage' into her befuddled brain.

'I did love someone once,' Tom finally said, jolting Lauren back to earth, the excited twitter firmly squelched. 'My sister Jane. And she loved me! It didn't matter how our parents fought, Jane was there to shield me, and to hug me and tell me things would be all right.'

He paused, and Lauren waited.

'Bobby hasn't got a Jane, but he has got us. I know we can't wipe away what he's suffered emotionally and possibly physically over the years, but by giving him the best possible life we can offer, surely we can help him forget a lot of it.'

So the excited bit had got it wrong, Lauren realised, but she also realised that if she hadn't known she loved this man before this moment, she knew she loved him now. Sitting there, offering his future to a little boy, committing himself to love the child, how could she not love Tom?

But wouldn't loving him make what he was asking harder?

Loving him, could she marry him, knowing he didn't love her?

He'd loved his sister once, and Lauren was reasonably sure he was growing fonder and fonder of Bobby—heading towards love—but he didn't love her.

And why should he?

But marriage without love?

For the sake of a child?

How confused could one woman get?

'A relative might turn up,' she said, desperate to shift the conversation to somewhere she might be able to get a grasp on it.

Tom frowned at her.

'You don't *want* to keep him?'

Lauren thought of the way the little boy's hand would creep into hers, and the warmth she felt in her body when he did that.

'Of course I want to keep him,' she muttered at Tom. 'It's all this marriage stuff that's got me stymied.'

Then a thought occurred to her, and although she knew she'd flush scarlet as she asked, she knew she had to raise the subject.

'This isn't some noble gesture on your part after our—we—after we—after last night?' she finally managed, and he laughed.

'Darling Lauren, if I proposed to every woman I'd slept with I'd have been incarcerated for polygamy long ago.' He paused then his face grew serious. 'Though speaking of last night, you're okay?'

He reached across the desk and took her hand, which she'd stupidly left lying on some papers in the middle of it.

'No regrets?' he pressed, squeezing her fingers and looking into her eyes as heat swept through her.

She shook her head and tried to mumble something about last night not being anything to do with anything, but he laughed again.

'You don't think so?' he teased. 'Don't you think it's quite important that a married couple enjoy each other in bed?'

He'd turned her hand and was tickling her palm with his thumb and she could barely sit still in her chair, so erotic was this simple touch, but the 'married' thing was still haunting her. There had to be another way. Tom didn't really want to be tied down in marriage and she wasn't going to—couldn't, she rather thought—marry someone who didn't love her…

Could she?

'I'd better get back to work before we do something we shouldn't do right here on your desk,' he said, giving her fingers a final squeeze and walking briskly from the room, stopping in the door to add, 'See you tonight,' in a voice that sent further shivers down her spine.

Lauren, deciding it was impossible to even attempt to sort out her feelings about whatever was going on between her and Tom, went off to visit Alyssa, who was feeling much more comfortable and talking about taking Karen back to the US with her and the children.

'My dad's coming over, you see,' she explained to Lauren. 'I'd lost touch with him—well, it was hard because he hated Nat right from the start—but now we can begin again, Dad and me, and Karen's never travelled and if she's not at home, Nat can't take out his anger on her. She was telling me she wants to give her place to the refuge and the woman who's always worked for her will stay on so someone knows the feeding routine and how the farm-stay business runs.'

Lauren smiled.

'I see you've got it all worked out,' she said.

'Thanks to you,' Alyssa told her. 'You've no idea what having clean hair and some moisturiser did for my confidence. I'm sad about the baby but maybe that's for the best, too. I've known for ages I should leave Nat but I didn't dare. Known I should report him, too, but he kept promising… Anyway, now, with Dad and Karen by my side, I know I can do both and I can make a new life for me and the girls.'

Lauren bent and kissed Alyssa's cheek.

'I'm sure you can,' she whispered. 'You deserve happiness in life, everyone does, so go after it.'

Go after it?

The words echoed in her head as she drove to collect Bobby from school.

But would marrying Tom be going after happiness, or going after pain?

Didn't love need to be returned?

Bobby was waiting at the school gate, a cardboard box at his feet.

'I got this from my teacher. She was going to throw them out and I know where Mum kept the decorations at home so can we go and get them 'cos Tom's got none at his place and next week's Christmas.'

Bobby's rush of words left Lauren nearly as confused as Tom's marriage conversation had earlier, only less inwardly distracted.

'Decorations, for Christmas,' Bobby repeated, and Lauren caught on.

'We'll have to see Mike at the police station. He's got your mother's house keys,' she said.

'I know where the spare one is,' Bobby offered. 'Mum left one out for me in case she mightn't be at home.'

So! No reprieve of driving to the station and talking to Mike.

Lauren studied the excited child.

'You're sure about this?' she asked, taking a rather grubby hand in both of hers. 'Sure you'll be okay going into the house with your mum not there?'

Bobby looked at her, his blue eyes filling with tears.

'I gotta do stuff like that!' he muttered angrily. 'Like the funeral too!'

'Oh, Bobby!' Lauren whispered, and she pulled him into her arms and cried with him.

But as it turned out they didn't have to do 'stuff like that' for two of the women who knew Joan from the refuge were at the house, and all Joan's belongings were already packed.

'The landlord wanted the place emptied,' one of the women explained to Lauren, 'so we thought we'd pack it all up and keep it for whenever Bobby might want it. These boxes here are his toys and books.'

'And decorations?' Bobby demanded, and one of the women produced another box, probably labelled by Joan herself.

They helped Lauren load Bobby's boxes and the decorations into the car, promising to find room to store the rest, and Lauren drove home, insisting Bobby keep his seat belt on as he rummaged through the boxes in search of forgotten treasures.

The house was empty and although Lauren had grave doubts about decorating Tom's house without his permission, nothing was going to stop Bobby. First he opened the box he'd brought from school, digging through the contents.

'We had a real tree at school. A tree in a pot, but Mrs Stoddart must'a taken it home. We need a tree.'

'Can't we just put up decorations?' Lauren asked.

Bobby sent her a pitying look.

'Where will Santa put the presents if there isn't a tree?' he demanded, and a new worry surfaced in Lauren's head.

Presents!

They'd have to get presents for Bobby.

More than a stocking filled with oddments, for sure!

What's more, they'd have to figure out what he might have asked Santa to give him.

Lauren's mind was jerking around like a chicken in search of seed, until Bobby's voice brought her to the present.

''Cos we don't have chimneys for Santa to come down here at the Cove, we have to have trees,' the boy causing most of her confusion—though not all—informed her.

'Right, a tree,' Lauren said. 'Does it have to be live or can we go and get one of those green ones from one of the shops in the mall?'

Bobby considered this for a while.

'I s'pose one of them would do, but it should be real,' he told her.

What had he said earlier?

Mrs Stoddart had a tree in a pot.

'Okay,' Lauren told him. 'Let's go to the nursery and see what we can find. Once we get the tree we'll know how many decorations we need for it.'

'Could we get some lights for outside while we're out?'

Images of tremendously decorated houses—houses that won prizes for their Christmas light displays—flashed through Lauren's mind.

'Maybe just a few lights,' she agreed.

Perhaps because he was used to not getting everything he wanted, Bobby didn't argue and they set off to buy a tree, Bobby choosing a four-foot-high Norfolk pine, then to the mall where, to Bobby's credit, it was Lauren who went mad.

Why *not* get two small light-outlined reindeer to put out the front? And as for the blow-up Santa, well, he could sit on the veranda, while the strings of lights with smaller strings dripping off them would look fantastic stretched along the eaves.

They staggered home to find Tom staring at the contents of the boxes they'd half-unpacked.

'Christmas decorations?' he said, his voice so carefully neutral Lauren had a moment's panic.

'You don't like them?'

Had he heard that panic in her voice that he smiled and touched her gently on the arm?

'How would I know whether I like them or not when I've never had them in my own home?'

Lauren blew out the breath she'd been holding and smiled back at him.

'That's good because there's a few more bits and pieces in the car.'

Four hours later, having stopped only briefly to consume the casserole that had finally been cooked, they finished the decorating.

'Turn the lights on, turn them on!'

Bobby was bouncing up and down with excitement, but Tom refused to press the switch connected to the various power-boards spread around the house.

'I think you should do it,' he said, and the blatant adoration in the little boy's face as he looked at Tom caught at Lauren's heart.

He pressed the switch and the lights came on slowly. The strings of blue and red and green changing colour all the time so they looked like water dancing in a coloured fountain. The two little reindeer nodded at each other on the front lawn, one dropping his head lower, perhaps pretending to eat moss. Santa, to everyone's surprise, not only lit up from inside, but began to 'Ho, ho, ho' in fine spirit and the star Tom had somehow affixed above the front entrance flashed its brightness to the town below.

'It's beautiful!'

Awe filled Bobby's voice, and Lauren, slipping her arm around his shoulder, had to agree.

'Tomorrow we'll do inside,' Bobby announced, and now Lauren glanced at Tom.

'Okay with you?' she asked.

He nodded.

'As long as there aren't too many lights,' he told them. 'This is an old house and the power supply's already under strain.'

'Just on the tree—one string. Mum's had them for ages,' Bobby declared, and Tom agreed one more string of lights wouldn't hurt.

He'd moved, so he, too, had his arm around Bobby, his hand touching Lauren's arm, the three of them linked.

A family?

That's what Bobby needed.

And continuity. His mother's string of Christmas lights on the tree each year, the new decorations going up. It was about continuity and knowing now what she did about Tom she could understand why he'd felt their marriage would be the answer for Bobby. The little boy would have a real family—one for life—not a series of so-called 'families'—being moved on for whatever reason.

But marriage?

She could see Tom's point of view that only with their marriage could Bobby have the security he needed, so why was she hesitating?

Surely not because she, who'd never considered marriage as an option in her future, was suddenly quibbling over a marriage without love?

They turned out the lights and went inside, falling easily into Bobby's bedtime routine, Lauren's turn to read the story.

Tom was gone when she came out of Bobby's bedroom,

presumably called back to the hospital, and instead of worrying over love and marriage she turned her attention to practical matters, putting Bobby's dirty clothes into the laundry, emptying his school-bag of books and notes and clutter, wondering how on earth they could find out what he wanted for Christmas, wondering if he'd object if she suggested he take a turn on Santa's knee at the local mall—surely Santa had some way of passing on requests.

She was smoothing out the papers from his school-bag, checking each before she tossed them, in case there might be something important there.

And there was!

An envelope addressed in an adult hand to Tom and Lauren, and inside another envelope with 'Santa' scrawled across it in red felt pen.

Lauren slit the second envelope open, unfolding the piece of paper inside.

> 'Dear Santa,
> For Christmas I would like a bike with red weels and red handl bars and red pedls and a nice dress for Mum and for her and Greg to stop yelling.
> Yor frend
> Bobby'

Lauren smoothed her fingers over the paper again and again, barely aware of the mess her splotches of tears were making on the words. She was still sitting there, still weeping, when Tom came in.

'I'll marry you,' she said, sniffing loudly then dashing her wrist across her eyes in the hope of stopping the tears.

'Well, I'm glad I've made you so happy,' Tom teased, but

his grey eyes were full of concern as he came towards her, squatting by her side and taking her restless hands in his.

'We must promise never to yell,' Lauren added, looking at the face of the man she loved. 'No matter what, no yelling.'

'I can handle that,' Tom said gently, then he leaned forward and kissed her on the lips.

'And we've got to find a red bike for him,' she added, and Tom, deciding that the only way he'd make sense of what was going on was to read whatever had upset Lauren in the first place, removed the piece of paper she held in trembling fingers and read the letter. Then he stood up, hauled Lauren from the chair, and hugged her tightly.

'You're a good woman, Lauren Cooper,' he whispered in her ear. 'A special woman.'

He'd have liked to add how special he found her, to have talked of love, but his realisation of love—his about-face acceptance of it as anything other than a destructive force—was too new, too fragile, to be brought out into the open. Besides which, talk of love might totally freak Lauren out, just when she seemed to be agreeing to his marriage idea.

So he held her, hoping he might be able to tell her without words, wondering if his adoration of her body, something he intended showing her very soon, would make her realise how he felt.

'We need to find a red bike. I can hardly take Bobby shopping with me to look for one. What should we do?'

Tom eased away and put his hand beneath her chin to tilt her face up towards his.

'You're thinking bikes and I'm thinking love!'

Whoops!

He had no idea how the word had slipped out, but now it hung, like the fat blow-up Santa, in the air between them.

'Love?' Lauren echoed, so uncertainly Tom *had* to hug her again.

'Yes, love,' he whispered. 'A four-letter word I'd never thought I'd find a use for, but having found you and Bobby there's no other word to cover it.'

He eased away again and once more tilted up her face to he could look into those clear hazel eyes.

'Do you mind very much?' he asked, and saw her frown.

'Mind what?'

Nerves churned in his stomach. In fact, he was reasonably certain that if he raced off and threw up he'd feel a darned sight better, but now he'd started with this love thing he'd better keep at it.

'Mind my loving you?'

Could she hear the uncertainty in his voice—the fear?

She looked more puzzled than she had earlier, clear eyes clouding over as she kind of squinted at him.

'You love me?' she queried, definitely disbelieving.

Tom straightened up—it was time to show some spine.

'I do,' he said firmly, and just to prove it, he kissed her.

Hard!

Then hot!

Then heavy as his body took control and claimed her mouth, consuming it as if he could take her into his skin and be one with her.

Her response didn't exactly say she loved him, but it certainly indicated she didn't mind his kisses. Right now there was the question of love…

One-sided love?

Surely she could have said 'I love you', or even 'Me too' when he'd said he loved her, but no, when she did speak it was to ask if he knew of any bicycle shops in Port that might stay open late at Christmas time, adding, 'Because we could get Cam and Jo to babysit and drive down to get the bike, but we should phone first to make sure they've got a red one of the kind an eight-year-old would want.'

'You want to drive to Port to buy a bike?'

He'd eased away from her, needing distance so his brain would work.

'Not necessarily tonight,' she said in a kindly voice. 'But we need to know what evenings they'll be open and we need to find out if we can get one already put together. My brother bought one for his son and it took until dawn on Christmas morning to put it together and even then it went backwards because he'd done something wrong with the chain.'

Tom slumped into a chair.

'Did you miss the bit of conversation earlier when I said I loved you?' he demanded.

Her face went still, then she shook her head.

'No, I heard it,' she said, 'but I thought it might be best not to talk about it in case it was an aberration.'

For a man who'd never done the love declaration before, the conversation was becoming unnecessarily convoluted.

'Me loving you an aberration or me saying it an aberration?'

Lauren shrugged.

'Either, I suppose, or maybe both. I just thought if I didn't mention it then it could just go away, and anyway the bike *is* important, you know. It's in Bobby's letter to Santa.'

She passed him a scrappy piece of paper she must have had crumpled in one hand all this time and he smoothed it out and read it, swallowing hard when he'd finished.

'We won't yell,' he promised Lauren, who nodded back at him.

'And we'll find a bike.'

She nodded again, and Tom knew it was now or never.

'So,' he said, 'with that sorted, let's get back to love.'

Did she cringe?

Was she afraid to tell him she didn't love him?

The thought brought a wave of panic through his body and all but melted his brain, but he stiffened, told himself to be a man, and waited.

And waited…

'You want me to start?' he finally asked, although he felt that was wrong because he'd already said it, but what the hell, here it went.

'I love you, Lauren,' he said, loud and clear, adding a kind of addendum to the original idea by saying, 'I think maybe I have for a while—kind of loved you anyway, but wary of seeing more of you, seeing you romantically, in case it *was* love, and I was so convinced I couldn't do love I steered clear.'

She smiled and stepped a little closer. Close enough to touch but not touching.

'Do you know when you get excited about something you trip over your words?' she teased, using words he'd said to her some days ago. 'But I love you too. And like you, I think it was probably there for a while, but feeling how I did about intimacy, I didn't want to let you down.'

'As if you could ever let me down,' Tom told her, gathering her into his arms and holding her carefully, as if she was a precious object that might shatter with too much pressure. 'As if you could ever let anyone down! You're kind and good and thoughtful and loving and probably far too good for me, but you and me, we're all Bobby's got so maybe we're stuck with each other.'

And with that he kissed her, gently at first, letting the embers of their physical love flare gradually back to life, igniting them both so they were sliding fingers onto skin beneath frustrating clothes when a 'Bleagh!' from the doorway had them springing apart.

Tom recovered first, holding out his arm to bring Bobby into the circle of their love.

'Get used to the sloppy stuff, kid,' he said, 'there's going to be a lot of it around.'

And Lauren proved it, by hugging Bobby hard and kissing his unruly hair and then his ear and then his cheek until he squirmed and shrieked in protest and Tom knew he'd found a family…

CHAPTER ELEVEN

LOOKING back, Lauren realised that the big mistake they made was leaving Bobby with Jo and Cam while they drove to Port to buy a red bike. Two nights before Christmas and the shops were open until midnight. Not only that, but all the Christmas decorations were reduced in price and she discovered for the first time how much the man she loved loved a bargain.

'What on earth...?' Jo demanded, as they began staggering into the house laden with boxes and bags of decorations.

'He likes a sale,' Lauren explained, looking helplessly at the pile of new acquisitions. 'We're never going to get them all up.'

Tom came in, Cam following with the last of the purchases.

'I've put the bike over in my office at the hospital,' he told Lauren, then he looked at the two women. 'Well, what are you waiting for? Do you think these decorations are going to hang themselves?'

'You want to do them tonight? It's nearly midnight,' Lauren protested.

Tom shot her a quick grin.

'This from a woman who had me knotting a rug at two in the morning!'

'Knotting a rug?' Jo echoed feebly, looking from one to the other then shaking her head, while Cam was already digging decorations out of boxes, demanding scissors and insisting they all get busy.

'Think how Bobby will love it when he wakes up,' Tom whispered to Lauren, standing so close she could feel the tendrils of warmth and love wrapping around them once again.

'Fair enough,' she said, and she joined the others, until the whole house was hung with decorations, a giant paper bell over the dining table, mistletoe over every doorway—Jo and Cam taking far too much advantage of that—the tree alight, in spite of Tom's misgivings, with bright balls of glistening colour. Every window had its own frame of tinsel, the veranda railings were wound with greenery, and up on the roof—though what two respected medicos were doing on a roof in the middle of the night!—was a full team of reindeer and a sleigh big enough to hold the blow-up Santa Lauren and Bobby had bought earlier.

Once it was done, they sat down to enjoy a cold drink, the pleasure they would give the little boy warming all of them.

'So much has happened,' Jo mused, 'since the stands went down. What could have been a terrible accident minimised by Tom and Cam's fast action.'

'We were lucky,' Tom said. 'All but one of the patients have been discharged and he'll be home for Christmas.'

'Bobby wasn't so lucky,' Lauren reminded them.

'Not in losing his mother,' Jo said, 'that was terrible, but then look where he ended up—with two of the most loving people in the whole Cove. Yes, he'll grieve and you'll both help him keep his mother's memory alive, but for the rest of his life you'll be the only parents he knows.'

'Which is a very scary thought,' Tom said, but he reached out and took Lauren's hand, adding, with a smile, 'Although it's kind of exciting, too, isn't it?'

She leant across and kissed him on the lips.

'Very exciting,' she said.

'Well, there's a nice surprise,' Jo said, standing up and tugging Cam to his feet. 'Methinks it's time we left these two to talk about parenthood.'

'Should we?' Tom asked when they'd departed.

'Should we what? Talk about parenthood? Or maybe go to bed?' Lauren teased.

'Minx!' Tom said, taking her in his arms, his heart—his entire body—so full of pleasure or gratitude or maybe love that she could tease him like that it was a wonder he could speak at all.

She nestled closer.

'We've the rest of our lives to talk about parenthood,' she whispered.

'And to go to bed,' he answered, adding even more quietly, 'Together!'

Bobby's delight the next morning made all the work they'd done the night before worthwhile, and that evening, Christmas Eve, as they stood by the tree on the foreshore, singing carols, they could look up and see their Santa in his sleigh, and the star shining right on the apex of the roof, guiding them home.

The damaged stands had been cleared away earlier in the week, but they stood on the other side of the tree, Bobby between them, his high, sweet voice rising to the heavens, his electric candle held steady in his hands.

Tom looked down at him, then at Lauren, with her arm around the child's shoulders, then he turned to look out at the ocean and knew he'd come home. After all his wanderings, he'd finally come home, and not only had he found a home, he'd found a family to live in it, his family—his loves!

Had Lauren caught his thoughts that she turned towards

him and the hand that had been resting on Bobby's shoulder reached out to touch grasp his fingers?

'I love you.'

She mouthed the words above Bobby's head and squeezed his fingers.

'And me you,' he said, but he spoke aloud, making Bobby turn towards him.

'What?' the child demanded, and Tom knelt in front of him.

'I was just saying "I love you",' he told the little boy, then before Bobby could protest he kissed him quickly on the cheek.

The carols ended, and with arms wrapped around each other they walked home up the hill. Home to the Christmas lights and the star of hope—home to the future.

Together!

* * * * *

Special Offers

Every month we put together collections and longer reads written by your favourite authors.

Here are some of next month's highlights—and don't miss our fabulous discount online!

On sale 16th December

On sale 16th December

On sale 6th January

Find out more at
www.millsandboon.co.uk/specialreleases

Visit us Online

0112/ST/MB353